P9-BZC-896

RED HOOK ROAD

ALSO BY AYELET WALDMAN

FICTION

Love and Other Impossible Pursuits
Daughter's Keeper

NONFICTION

Bad Mother: A Chronicle of Maternal Crimes, Minor Calamities, and Occasional Moments of Grace

RED HOOK ROAD

a novel

AYELET WALDMAN

DOUBLEDAY
NEW YORK LONDON TORONTO
SYDNEY AUCKLAND

DD
DOUBLEDAY

This book is a work of fiction. Names, characters, businesses, organizations, places, events, and incidents either are the product of the author's imagination or are used fictitiously. Any resemblance to actual persons, living or dead, events, or locales is entirely coincidental.

www.doubleday.com

Library of Congress Cataloging-in-Publication Data
Waldman, Ayelet.
Red Hook Road / by Ayelet Waldman. — 1st ed.
p. cm.
1. Domestic fiction. I. Title.
PS3573.A42124R43 2010
813'.54—dc22
2009020023

ISBN 978-0-385-51786-7

PRINTED IN THE UNITED STATES OF AMERICA

3 5 7 9 10 8 6 4 2

To Michael, as ever

RED HOOK ROAD

PRELUDE

The flower girl had lost her basket of rose petals and could not bear to have the photograph taken without it. Altogether she had been something of a disappointment in her role. She had forgotten to sprinkle the petals as she walked down the aisle of the church, remembering only once she reached the front pew. Perhaps she had been distracted by the transformation of the nave, the oiled and gleaming oak pews, the glass wall sconces sparkling, their long tapered candles lit for the first time in years, all the shutters on the windows flung open, letting in the light of the golden afternoon. And, everywhere, flowers. Purple and blue hydrangea woven into vines, long swags draped between the rows of pews and across the back of the altar. Shiny brass buckets of lupines and greenery on either side of the twin curved staircases leading up to the pulpit.

The flower girl had been adopted as a toddler from Cambodia and, despite the good intentions of her adoptive mother, had never before been included in this kind of family event. When she finally remembered her assignment, she widened her dark eyes, scooped up a handful of the white petals from her basket, and threw them back up the aisle as hard as she could. They made it no farther than the second row, where they flurried down onto the messy gray topknot of the vice president of the Red Hook Library Ladies' Auxiliary. There was a burst of laughter, and the bride, measuring her way down the aisle, paused in midstride. The laughter abated. Would the bride be upset at the disturbance of her stately procession, so perfectly executed in last night's rehearsal? Or would she exhibit the sense of humor reported by the groom to have been what first attracted him to her when they met ten years before?

The bride, honey-haired, with a high, smooth forehead and wide-set eyes the color of agate, hesitated only a moment before she grinned. Anxiously held breaths were exhaled and everyone took up his or her prior occupation. The weepers dug through their purses for bits of crumpled tissue. The pinchpennies resumed their calculations of the bills for flowers and candles. The gossips craned their necks to take careful note of who had and who had not been invited. The young women committed to memory every bead, pearl, strap, button, and length of silk of the bridal gown so they could later describe it in sufficient detail to those who had not been fortunate enough to garner an invitation of their own. The young men toyed with the keys in their pockets and longed for the ceremony to end so they could get to the music and the bar. The children fidgeted. And the older men glanced surreptitiously at their watches, trying to figure out if the ceremony would outlast the rubber game of the White Sox series at Fenway.

Now, after the service, standing on the top step of the pretty white clapboard church, the flower girl wept over the loss of her ribbon-and-rose-bedecked basket, and the bride promised her that the photograph would not be taken until it was found. Two of the groomsmen were dispatched to search inside the church. The lilac-clad bridesmaids went off to hunt among the rose arbors and white stone paths of the church's garden, where the wedding guests waited in the shade cast by the church's tall steeple, enjoying the view of sailboats cutting white grooves across the small cove, and ignoring the pastor's warnings not to crush his carefully tended flower beds. To his wife's annoyance, the father of the bride insisted on looking for the basket in the bridal couple's waiting limousine. "But the flower girl was never *in* the limo," the mother of the bride said. The father of the bride could not deny this, but nonetheless went to have a look. This was the way of their marriage. Although they were in staunch agreement that she knew best, he would generally ignore her advice.

As for the father of the groom, he had slipped around the back of the church for a much-needed cigarette. When the photographer tried to reassemble the party on the front steps of the church, he appeared to have joined the flower basket in its nuptial limbo. There was some alarm when his absence was noted, primarily on the part of his current girlfriend, who had insinuated herself, some thought brazenly, into the photograph. His ex-wife, the mother of the groom, turned to her younger son, the best man, and said, "Get your father. He's around back having a cigarette." To the photographer she said, "We'll start without him if we have to. Won't be the first time."

The photographer busied himself with the bridal couple, adjusting the straps of the bride's beaded bodice to cover the tan lines from her bathing suit, swirling her long silk train around her feet, and arranging her pearl-edged, tulle veil fetchingly over her right shoulder. He pulled loose a single curl of her blond hair and twisted it around his finger so that it sprang into place, framing and softening the broad planes of her cheek. He spent some time on her lush bouquet, shifting around the purple irises, lobelia, and periwinkle to disclose the lupines, the very last of the season and, he'd been told, the bride's favorite flower. A few minutes before, he had gotten a fine shot as the couple ran out of the church into a shower of silver and gold Mylar confetti. The confetti caught the late afternoon sun and he'd captured the bride and groom laughing and ducking beneath a winking archway of light. Now, tiny flecks of fire were nestled in the whorls of the bride's intricately arranged hair and in the tulle netting of her veil. Bright shards of light starred the groom's shoulders.

Perfect, the photographer thought. The beautiful bride and handsome groom, the family in their finery arrayed against the crisp lines of the white clapboard church, the sapphire sea just visible at the edges of the frame. If only he could get them all to keep still.

"Do we want to take those off?" the photographer said, pointing to the groom's steel-framed glasses.

The groom glanced at the bride, who nodded. He tried to slip the glasses into his jacket pocket but it was a brand-new pocket, still sewn shut. "Give them to me," his mother said. He handed over the glasses and blinked his pale blue eyes. Without his glasses on his features looked softer, more boyish, his face gentle beneath his mariner's tan and peeling nose—even vulnerable—as though his outmoded aviator frames had afforded him a kind of armor, a protective visor. The bride smiled sweetly at his defenseless expression and he gave her a quick peck on the cheek. "Watch her makeup," the photographer said.

"It's all right," the bride said.

The father of the bride returned from his pointless search of the limousine, and the photographer found a place for him on the steps, taking care to hide the man's feet. Early this afternoon, when the father of the bride went to put on his black dress shoes, he had sat on the edge of the old iron bedstead in the bedroom of the family's summer home, holding them in his hands, and said, "Fuck."

His wife turned from the mirror, where she was attempting to rub away some of the foundation she'd inexpertly applied to her face. "What's wrong?"

Wordlessly he held up two black oxfords, almost but not quite identical, the toes of both shoes curving in the same direction.

"For heaven's sake," his wife said. There was an obvious observation to be made about his having two left feet, but she forbore.

There had been no time to drive the thirty miles to the closest shoe store, and anyone who might have lent him a pair of dress shoes was coming to the wedding. His wife having vetoed the only other choices in his summer closet (Birkenstock sandals and taxicab-yellow gardening clogs), he wore his tennis shoes with his suit. He would wear the same outfit two days later, but by then his inappropriate footwear would be the least of anyone's concerns.

The photographer placed the mother of the bride next to her husband. "Smile," he said, his tone hovering somewhere between affection and reproach. "You're happy!"

And she *was* happy, and proud, too. But she was also fretting about getting over to the Grange Hall for the reception before the guests started to show up. Earlier she'd had no choice but to leave the caterer struggling on his own to light the Grange Hall's balky old stove. He had shooed her away, promising he would either get it working or use the stove in her own kitchen next door. But she was still worried that the passed hors d'oeuvres would not be ready in time for the arrival of the guests.

"Come stand next to me, Dad," the mother of the bride called to her father, who sat perched on a low stone wall that separated the plain-faced church from the wild summer profusion of the garden.

The bride's grandfather rose in painful increments and, leaning heavily on his cane, made his way to the bottom of the church steps. The photographer helped him up the steps, and the mother of the bride slipped her arm through his, stilling his tremor with the gentle pressure of her hand. She shifted her hip, as if urging him to lean against her, but he stiffened, uncomfortable as always with any reminder of his infirmity. He was eighty-eight years old, a violinist, once a prodigy of the Prague Conservatory, who had made his debut at age twelve on the stage of Smetana Hall to jubilant, almost fawning reviews. He had performed regularly for more than seventy years, until just a few years ago, when the first symptoms of his Parkinson's appeared.

A lifetime of performing had given him a considerable formal wardrobe and he owned a second pair of patent leather dress shoes, nestled in a felt shoe bag on the back of his closet door. They were no help to his son-in-law, however, since the old man's dainty foot barely filled a size 6.

The bridesmaids returned from the garden. "No luck," said the bride's younger sister. She winked her left eye, not out of amusement but because there was a speck of pollen or dust caught behind her contact lens. Her unruly dark curls had been woven into a simplified version of the bride's elaborate hairdo, but tendrils had escaped around her face and neck.

The bride bent over and cupped the flower girl's chin in her hand. "Baby, we don't really need it, do we? You'll still be beautiful, even without your flowers."

The nine-year-old flower girl, from whom more competence, perhaps, might have been expected, looked wan, her leaf-gold skin sallow against her gown of lavender tulle. Even her thick black hair, cut in the China-chop her adoptive mother insisted upon, looked flat and dry, wisps of it sticking up at odd angles around her head. She was humiliated at having failed so miserably at a task that she had been determined to execute without flaw. "I'm sorry," she whispered.

"Okay, then," the photographer said. He turned to the bridesmaids. "Let's have you three lovely girls stand here." He motioned them to the second step. Only someone who knew that none of the bridesmaids liked her dress would have noticed the faint reluctance with which they took their places, first the bride's younger sister, then the bride's roommate from college, and then her closest friend. The bride had done her best to choose a style flattering to all three girls, one that could, she hoped, be easily worn again, but her sister resented the childish empire waist of the simple dress, purple turned the friend's handsome face to an active shade of green, and the former roommate was in the seventh week of an unexpected pregnancy and hunched her shoulders to hide the lascivious swell of her breasts.

The groom's brother returned with his father and a reek of tobacco smoke in tow just as the other two groomsmen sheepishly exited the church and announced their failure to locate the missing basket, whose absence was rapidly taking on, in the photographer's experienced view, unfortunate symbolic implications for the company. Only the groom's mother noticed the skunky odor trailing the young men, but in the interest of not slowing down the process any further, she refrained from berating them for smoking a joint in the church.

The flower girl finally collapsed under the weight of her embarrassment and burst into tears. The mother of the groom, who would discover the basket two days later when she went to purge the church of all evidence of celebration, pulled a handkerchief out of her sleeve and wordlessly handed it to the girl.

"Oh, dear," the bride said. Once again she crouched down next to the flower girl and cupped her cheek with her hand. "It really doesn't matter, honey," she said sweetly. "The picture will look fine without the basket."

From down the row the bride's grandfather said, "Some people might consider a basket of petals to be a bit de trop."

The bride glanced at him and laughed appreciatively.

"Here," said the bride's sister to the young girl, handing over her maid of honor bouquet. "Hold my flowers."

When the photographer developed the film—a week later than he originally intended because, after all, there was no rush—he would be troubled by the lack of balance in his composition: the puffy-faced flower girl clutching a long, trailing bouquet, the maid of honor holding nothing. He had missed this disturbing lack of symmetry because he was eager to take the photo, not to mention busy trying to keep as many people as he could between the groom's mother, in her paisley, and his sister, in a frighteningly clashing pattern of shimmering metallic green. The groom's mother had worn this red paisley eleven years before, to her daughter's wedding, and although she had known even then that neither the cut nor the color did her any favors, it would never have occurred to her to waste money on another new dress.

So the photographer steered the groom's sister to the very end of the row, where she stood, glowering, her yellowed fingers twitching for their accustomed cigarette. She did not bother to conceal her resentment about being shunted aside. She was already furious about what she considered the unacceptable exclusion of her daughters, the groom's only nieces, from the wedding party. Not trusting her future sister-in-law to choose a dress that would minimize her corpulence, she had declined the bride's invitation to serve as a bridesmaid, but she was angry that her girls had not been given a role. She didn't think much of the bride's excuse—that they were too old to be flower girls but not old enough to be bridesmaids. The groom's sister had never thought much of the bride, or of her family, and she was only too happy to have had her opinion of them confirmed. However they pretended otherwise, she thought, the bride and her family were nothing more than typical "from-aways," with their fancy summer cottage and their sailboat that probably cost more than what she earned in a year of honest work. In making this unfavorable judgment she was untroubled by the fact that a year of honest work was considerably more than what she had ever found herself moved to undertake.

Between this unhappy woman and her mother the photographer inserted the father of the groom and his girlfriend. The girlfriend, whom the father of the groom would leave not a month after the shutter snapped, hooked one arm around her man's waist and slipped her other hand between the buttons of his stained white shirt, pulling the fabric out of shape. He stared impassively ahead of him, ignoring both her hand on his chest and what he was sure was his ex-wife's disgusted gaze. In fact, the mother of the groom was not even looking at her ex-husband, distracted instead by the three groomsmen horsing around on the step below her. The young men had started partying last night at the rehearsal dinner; they'd been almost too drunk to set off the fireworks that the groom and his younger brother had driven all the way over to New Hampshire to buy. On the way to the church this morning they had nicked three bottles of champagne from the cases stacked up in the Grange Hall, taken the groom down to the beach, and toasted him over and over, until he'd accused them of trying to get him too drunk to walk down the aisle. And then there was the joint they had just smoked when they were supposed to be searching the church for the flower girl's lost basket.

"Stand straight and shut up so we can get this damn picture taken," the mother of the groom said, poking her younger son in the back.

"Ow, Mum. Jeez," he said. "You got me right in the kidney."

"Now, if you'll all just look at me," the photographer said from behind the lens of his Hasselblad. "And smile!"

In the shot that the bride's mother selected from among the proofs that showed up at her house a long five weeks after the wedding, most of the subjects were smiling, but none of them with the radiant exuberance of the bride and groom. With their blond hair, their suntans, and their nearly identical wide smiles, the bridal couple looked almost like brother and sister. They had fallen in love at sixteen and over the next ten years had, despite distance and difference, never swerved in their determination to reach this day. Their faces in the photograph were alight with joy, and for a long time the bride's mother would not be able to pass the picture hanging in the front parlor of her summer house without feeling a knot in her stomach and a rush of tears. In time the photograph would recede into the general oblivion of furnishings and knickknacks. But even years later the bride's mother would sometimes think of that afternoon in early summer, of the rustle of the fir trees that separated the country church from the winding main road, of the lavender lupines in the bridal bouquet, of the waves lapping the rocks of the tattered shore, and of the kiss her daughter's new husband placed on his new wife's cheek at the very moment the photographer clicked the shutter.

THE FIRST SUMMER

1

The house in East Red Hook, a village a few miles outside the town of Red Hook proper, was a flight of Queen Anne fancy, with a witch-hat turret, obsessive gingerbread, multihued brickwork and tile, and a secret room hidden behind a bookcase. It was built in 1879 by a gentleman named Elias Hewins, to the precise specifications of his much younger bride. Elias had purchased the acres of rolling oceanfront meadow for a song from a farmer who'd finally given up on coaxing anything edible from the obdurate Maine soil. Elias had sited his new house to make the most of its view across East Red Hook's small cove, out to the tiny islands scattered along the Eggemoggin Reach like crumbs on a wide blue tablecloth. Elias's son Nathaniel was born, lived, and died in the house, then passed it on to his six adult children, all of whom had long since abandoned the Maine coast. Only Nathaniel's youngest child, his only daughter, possessed the resources and the inclination to return to East Red Hook from New York City, where her husband had moved her. She transformed the house where she was born into her summer home, and for decades thereafter she and her daughter Alice passed their summers in the village, with Alice's father visiting as often as his business interests would allow. In the summer of 1940, when Alice was twenty-six years old, already in the eyes of her parents an old maid, she met a young violinist, a Jewish refugee from Prague, whose exile had landed him in, of all places, Red Hook, where he was performing with the town's renowned summer chamber music program, at the Usherman Center. After a brief courtship, Alice married Emil Kimmelbrod, and the couple bought their own summer house, down the road in Red Hook. Their high-spirited little daughter, Iris, spent the better part of every summer at her grandmother's, where she was free to run and play without concern for the silence demanded by her father's rigorous practice schedule.

If they thought of it at all, Iris and her parents assumed that Iris's grandmother had either bought out her siblings, the five sons of Nathaniel Hewins, or had inherited their shares in the house as in turn they died, but upon the old woman's death it was revealed that no such formal transfers of ownership had ever taken place. Iris's grandmother left her not the ramshackle old summer house but rather only the one-sixth share that was hers to bequeath. It took Iris nearly seven years to track down every last one of the twenty-nine heirs, some of whom had no idea that their origins lay in a harborside village of white clapboard, blueberry bogs, and lobster boats on the Down East coast of Maine. Most of the heirs were willing to sign away their claim to the rotting and sagging old house in return for their small fraction of its fair market value. But one cantankerous second cousin twice removed, a Texan, refused to sign a quit claim until Iris offered him significantly more than the $443 that was his share. Over the objections of her husband, Daniel, who, while he enjoyed Maine well enough, felt no ties to the land or the house that would justify such an expense, Iris wrote her distant cousin a check for $3,000. As soon as the deed was clear, she began the renovations, which were to consume her time and energy for years of summers to come. Her projects were so numerous and her plans so intricate that until the last moment there had been some concern that the latest work—adding a shower to the downstairs powder room—would not be finished in time for the wedding of Iris's daughter Becca to John Tetherly, the son of the woman who had been coming to clean the house since before the death of Iris's grandmother.

Elias Hewins had nurtured pretensions of being a gentleman farmer, and not long after he built the house, he deeded a small strip of adjoining land to the local chapter of the National Grange of the Order of Patrons of Husbandry. The Grange had constructed on the land a simple structure, with long, narrow, shutterless windows, a front room large enough for a town meeting, a tiny branch of the large library in Red Hook in back, and a kitchen. For generations the Grange Hall was a center of village life, but by the time Iris took possession of her house it was little more than a hollow shell forgotten by the village that owned but neglected it. The hall's fixtures, including its cast-iron woodstove, were long since lost to vandals and unscrupulous antique hunters, and the library was in use for only the three months of summer.

To Iris the Grange Hall was as much a part of her family's legacy as was her own house. More, perhaps, because while the house where she had spent her childhood making noise away from the hush that obtained at her parents' cottage was her home, the Grange Hall was her connection to the village itself, a symbol of the integral part her ancestors had played in the communal life of this sliver of Maine coast. Although for the past few generations they had been coming only as summer visitors, the existence of the Grange Hall proved that before that they had been *Mainers*. Their mortal remains populated an entire neighborhood in the town cemetery. There was a Hewins Pond, and a Hewins Road, and one found the name written not only on headstones in the cemetery but under portraits of long-dead deacons in church halls, in birth and marriage rolls, over the doorway of one of the oldest commercial buildings in town, and on the pedestals of monuments to the dead of Bull Run, Ypres, and Iwo Jima.

She knew there was probably something absurd about it, but this record in stone and paper of her belonging to Red Hook was critical to Iris's sense of herself, of her place in the world. Half of her history derived from a part of Europe that no longer existed, a vanished land of thirteenth-century synagogues, of cemeteries with thousand-year-old graves carved with Hebrew lettering. This side of her heritage was as lost to her as were her father's parents and siblings, killed at Terezin, and thus the Maine side, the Red Hook history, took on greater importance. Red Hook might only have been her summer residence—the rest of her life had been passed on the Upper West Side of the island of Manhattan—but her roots went deep into this rock. She had planted her daughters here, like perennials that bloomed every summer. Even her husband, a transplant less suited, perhaps, to the climate and the land, had, she thought, laid down his own, albeit shallow, roots.

After she took title to her ancestral home, Iris, with her customary energy and passion, took on the project of restoring the Grange Hall, applying to the state for grants, organizing rummage and bake sales, hosting bean suppers, and petitioning her neighbors, summer visitors and local people, to donate toward the hall's renovation. In the end, she'd dipped deep into her and Daniel's savings, one of the reasons that they were still making do with an ancient, unreliable furnace long after the Grange Hall had resumed its service to the village as an all-purpose gathering space.

Today all her hopes for the Grange Hall and for the place that she had made for herself in the village had reached their apotheosis. In this beautiful building first imagined and financed by her great-great-grandfather, her daughter would celebrate her marriage to a man whose roots in the town went deeper even than her own.

Last week, John, Becca, and a gang of their friends had repainted the Grange Hall, and the brilliant white paint shone fresh and promising of all the renewal that summers in Maine had always meant to Iris and her daughters. Yesterday the bridesmaids had picked hundreds of flowers and woven fragrant garlands to festoon the wood banisters leading up the porch steps and around the front door. The hall was a riot of purple, violet, lavender—shades of Becca's favorite color. How the girls had managed to gather so many lupines this late in the season, Iris couldn't imagine. Early this morning, Iris had filled the room with votive candles, setting them in circles on every table and in long glimmering rows on the windowsills.

The feeling she and Becca had been going for in decorating both the Grange Hall and the Unitarian church was a kind of rustic opulence, at once simple and glorious. Profusions of fresh flowers in hand-tied bouquets tucked into mismatched china vases, white wooden folding chairs looped with garlands, place cards written not by a calligrapher but in their own hands. She and Becca had scoured the thrift shops and rummage sales for the white lace tablecloths that were draped over the twenty round tables. The caterer, a summer visitor who served with Iris on the library board, had designed a simple but elegant meal. Organic produce from nearby farms, beef and pork from a local man who did his own slaughtering, bread and rolls baked by the local food co-op, lettuces from Iris's own vegetable garden, and a wedding cake made by a friend of the groom's who had recently received his certificate in culinary arts from Central Maine Community College.

The caterer had obviously managed to get the range lit, because the waiters were making the rounds with the miniature crab cakes, sliders, and lobster puffs. The guitarist of the band due to play later in the evening began warming up the crowd with a prelude by Robert de Visée. Trust Becca to find a blues band fronted by a classical guitarist, Iris thought.

Iris glanced up at the ceiling and frowned. One of the strings of white Christmas lights draped over and through the rafters had come loose; if it dropped any lower it was liable to get tangled in someone's hair. Iris's eyes skated over the crowd, searching out her husband. Daniel Copaken was standing on the other side of the room, his hands shoved deep in his pockets, rocking back and forth on his heels. She caught his eye and beckoned him over with a raised eyebrow. He picked his way through the crowd, stopping to shake a few proffered hands and bending over to receive a kiss on the cheek from one of their elderly neighbors.

"It looks great in here," he said, when he finally reached her.

"It does, if I may say so myself," Iris said. "But look up there." She pointed at the strand of wire hanging from the rafter. "The lights are falling down."

Daniel patted his pockets for the glasses he had forgotten on his nightstand. He squinted up at the misbehaving lights. "No problem," he said, climbing up on a chair. Daniel was a boxer when he and Iris met—a Golden Gloves middleweight with more than a few wins under his belt—and though he had grown thick around the middle, the muscles beneath his skin more like mere flesh and less like chunks of Red Hook granite, his broad shoulders still strained the fabric of his jacket, and after thirty years he was still in possession of the grace that had made him a formidable opponent in the ring. He sprang up from the chair and caught hold of the rafter, then chinned himself high enough to hook his left arm over the top of it while he grabbed hold of the wayward string of lights with his right. Then he paused, momentarily flummoxed.

"Hey, Iris," he said. "You wouldn't happen to have a tack on you?"

"A tack? No."

"Shit." He hung there in the middle of the air a moment, studying the problem of the string of lights with total absorption, seemingly unaware of the spectacle he was making. As ridiculous as it was for a man in a wedding suit to be swinging through the air like a middle-aged Spiderman impersonator, Iris couldn't help but admire the shape of his body, the line of his trapezius muscles beneath his smooth cotton shirt. In the end Daniel looped the string a few times over the rafter, and then tied the end to it as well as he could with one hand.

"Move that chair, would you?" he said.

Iris returned the chair to the table from which it had come, and Daniel swung a moment longer, then dropped to the ground with a lightness that was surprising in a such a solidly built man. The guests who were near enough to have observed his gymnastic demonstration called out their appreciation. Mary Lou Curran, an older woman, a summer visitor who had chosen to retire in the cottage she, like Iris, had inherited from her grandparents, applauded. Daniel took a slight bow.

"I guess I wore the right shoes after all," Daniel said, holding up one bright white-sneakered foot.

"Yes, I guess you did," Iris said, trying with all her heart to mean it.

Daniel never took himself too seriously, which for much of their life together had made him a good counterpoint to Iris, who, as she was painfully aware, took everything too seriously, including herself. When things were working well between them, he was an easygoing, at times lackadaisical yin to her fiery, at times domineering yang. Her intensity was strong but could be scattershot, all over the place; she needed the deliberate, phlegmatic cool that Daniel brought to bear. The touch of his big hand on her arm was a reminder to slow down, take a breath. But at the same time she felt that he needed her, too, to help him keep his low-key, unruffled manner from turning into detachment or outright indifference. When it looked as though he might fail to reach a goal that he had set for himself, whether through lack of focus or lack of fire, she was there to keep him on course, to help him bear down. When things were not running smoothly, however, when they found themselves at odds, as they had so often lately, this disparity of temperament served only to heighten the fissures and fractures in their relationship: she was a nag, and he was a slacker, and everything they said and did seemed calculated to offend, provoke, or drive the other insane.

For the first twenty years, their relationship of mutual contradiction and complement had worked well. They had been content, despite an inequality in their marriage that would have challenged other couples.

After Daniel failed to make partner at his law firm and ended up scratching out a meager living as a clinical instructor at a mediocre law school, her income had far exceeded his, not an easy feat when you considered that he was an attorney and she a professor of comparative literature. But she was an unusually successful professor. Her specialty was Holocaust studies, and her book on the role of dark humor in the survivor memoir had been a startling commercial success. It was still a standard college text even now, twenty years after its publication, and brought in a steady stream of royalty checks. Daniel's income from his current position as a clinical instructor at Brooklyn Law School was barely more than half of hers. But this disparity did not bother either of them. Iris enjoyed the authority her status as provider gave her and Daniel always said it was a relief to him that she earned enough to allow him to have a job with low stress and the summers off.

Increasingly, however, and to her shame, Iris had found herself wondering what it might have been like to have married a more successful man. It had nothing to do with money. They were comfortable enough and had never longed for wealth. But she wondered what it would have been like if she had married someone who loved his job, and was good at it, like she was. Someone who possessed a basic professional and personal competence. Someone who could be trusted not just to do what he was told, and do it with grace, but to recognize what needed to be done and take the initiative to do it. Someone who could be trusted to pack both his right and his left shoes.

Mary Lou Curran patted Iris's arm with a gnarled hand decorated with a large blue moonstone ring, the precise shade of her ropy veins. "Congratulations to you both," she said. "You must be very proud."

"We are," Daniel said.

"I've always liked that John Tetherly," Mary Lou said. "He's a fine young man."

True enough, Iris thought. Her new son-in-law was above all else a decent man, warm, affectionate, with a gentle deadpan manner that cloaked a streak of sharp Down East wit. Iris had liked him from the first time Becca brought him home, when they were teenagers. That first evening he entertained them at dinner with stories about the trials of running the yacht club rowing camp, how the little ankle biters would invariably need to go to the bathroom just after he'd gotten them all buckled into their life jackets and set out on the water, how they'd hurl their oars over the side whenever they got bored or angry. John was a talented storyteller who could contort his handsome face into dead-on impressions. He was also preternaturally gifted with his hands, a master carpenter and boatbuilder. Even when he was just a teenager, Iris had relied on him to take on tasks beyond Daniel's limited do-it-yourself skills. John had cheerfully unplugged drains, replaced rusted pipes, and repaired broken window sashes. Just last summer he had helped Iris replace the rotting bead board paneling in the upstairs bathroom.

"He works at the yard, doesn't he?" Mary Lou continued.

"He's a yacht designer," Iris said.

Whatever concerns Iris might have had about her daughter marrying a local man without a college education had been assuaged when John had, with her encouragement, not to mention financial assistance, enrolled in a yacht design course at the internationally renowned Landing School in Kennebunkport. John was an artist and a craftsman, and, Iris thought, a fine and suitable partner for her daughter, who was herself no intellectual. Like John, Becca's gifts lay in her hands, and in her musical heart.

"He's a builder," Daniel said. "Everyone down the yard works with their hands."

True, Iris thought. But why was it so important to Daniel to assert John's tradesman's credentials? It was almost as though her husband resented the young man's efforts to better himself. Or, more accurately, her efforts to encourage him.

"What are the young couple's plans?" Mary Lou asked. "Will they stay in Red Hook?"

"Yes," Iris said. "John's got a good job at the boatyard and they live in our house in the winter, so their expenses are very low."

Daniel said, "But they're hoping to sail down to the Caribbean. To run a charter business down there."

"Well, we'll see what happens with that," Iris said. "His boat's a long way from being finished."

For the past few years John had been working nonstop on restoring a 1938 Alden schooner that he'd found in a boatyard in Machias, where the cruiser had been rotting for as long as anyone could remember. He'd been sent up for a load of rare hardwood—the owner of the Machias yard had some padauk, a termite-resistant and rose-scented wood that he wanted to get rid of. But when John arrived at the yard he was sidetracked by the derelict schooner in dry dock in the farthest corner of the yard.

The way John told the story, it was love at first sight. He was boatstruck, he said, even before he saw the name looped in fading white cursive across the stern. And then? Well, how could he *not* buy a boat named *Rebecca*?

The Alden, however, had already been a source of conflict between Iris and Becca. Becca, who now earned a simulacrum of a living teaching sailing and working odd jobs in the winter, was a violinist who, even if she didn't share her grandfather's prodigious gifts, certainly possessed talent sufficient for a career as an orchestral musician. She had begun playing as a toddler, on a one-sixteenth-sized violin, and all of them, including the girl herself, had expected her to have a musical career. And then, at age twenty, she abruptly quit, dropped out of the New England Conservatory of Music, and moved in with John. Iris had hoped that after a little while Becca would come to her senses and return to her music. She had told her daughter that even if she wanted to remain in Red Hook with John, she could still continue her career. Bangor, with its more than adequate symphony, was ninety minutes away, and during the summers the Usherman Center brought dozens of the country's best musicians to the area. But her older daughter was the one person in Iris's life who was unresponsive, even insensible, to the force of her arguments. Once the girl made a decision, she could not be swayed, and she had decided that, as she would never be the kind of musician she'd dreamed of being, she no longer wanted to play. The final blow had come last year, when John had run out of money for the restoration of the boat. Becca had rebuffed her parents' offer of a loan and sold her violin, cashing in her past, she said, for an investment in her and John's future. Iris had been furious, and the two had a series of bitter arguments that resulted in their not speaking for nearly a month.

Eventually, they made up, or rather chose not to revisit the subject of their disagreement, until today, when Becca, while waiting for the limousine to drive her to the church, had announced that she and John were planning on using the money they received as wedding presents to finish the restoration of the boat. Iris did her best not to lose her temper, but her disgust at the foolishness of such an investment when the money could be spent on, for example, the down payment on a house, had been all too clear. Their argument would have escalated but for Daniel's insistence that they not allow any unpleasantness to disturb the joy of the wedding day.

"The Caribbean?" Mary Lou said now. "Can one really make a living sailing the Caribbean?"

"If anyone can, John will," Daniel said. Then, seeming finally to notice that he was in danger of renewing the argument he himself had previously squelched, he said, "Can I get you ladies a drink? Mary Lou, some champagne?"

"I'll take a G&T," Mary Lou said.

"I'll get it," Iris said.

She arrived at the bar to find that the young members of the bridal party had made a disturbing rush for the alcohol, and had by now completely crowded out the other guests. Iris put a restraining hand on one of the groomsmen's sleeves, and tried gently to steer him out of the way. At the same time, Jane Tetherly, John's mother, swam into the fray.

"Enough of that now," Jane said, pushing the young people aside. "You need to wait your turn. You're not the only folks who need a drink." Barking at the bartender to move over, she rolled up her sleeves and began pouring drinks. "Take this," Jane said, handing a tumbler of vodka and cranberry juice to one of the girls. "And I don't want to see you back here until everyone else in this room's got a drink in their hands."

Iris watched Jane thrust drinks at the kids and shoo them away from the bar. Jane knew how to take charge, you had to give her that. Jane popped the top off a bottle of beer and took a long gulp before wiping the mouth of the bottle with her sleeve and passing it to one of the boys.

Within a few minutes Jane, with the assistance of the much slower bartender, managed to fill the groping hands of the young people and send them on their way. She looked up and caught Iris's eye.

"What can I get you?" she asked.

"Leave that and go enjoy yourself, Jane," Iris said. "You're going to get us in trouble with the bartenders' union." For some reason Iris always found herself assuming a false jocularity with Jane. She made bad jokes, and Jane never laughed, or even smiled. And still, Iris would do it again the next time they met.

Jane pursed her lips and then shrugged. "Fine," she said. Briskly, she wiped her hands on a napkin. She had splashed tonic across the front of her dress, and when she stepped out from behind the bar you could see the wet fabric clinging to her heavy thighs.

As with so many awkward, painful, or hopeless situations, there was a Yiddish word for the relationship that as of this afternoon obtained between Iris and her cleaning woman. Her father had reminded her of it before they left for the church, as she was rushing around straightening up the house.

"You'll have to fire Jane," he'd said. "It will be awkward to have her cleaning your house now that the two of you are . . ." What was the word he'd used? Iris had motioned him out of the way with her broom, refusing to concede that there was any need to let Jane go. The woman owned and managed a service, Iris argued; it had been years since she had actually cleaned houses. In truth, Iris knew that Jane had cleaned the Copaken house just last summer, when one of her "girls" (who ranged in age from sixteen to seventy-six) had gone into preterm labor.

If Iris and Jane were not on close, or even truly amiable, terms, at least, Iris thought, they could take comfort in the weekly smoothness of their transactions. Iris had once supposed that, with the kids dating each other, she and Jane might gradually achieve a more familial, or at least a simply friendly, relationship. After all, but for the lucky accident of Iris's grandmother having married a banker from New York rather than a local fisherman, and her father being a concert violinist rather than a boat-builder, they might have had similar lives. But Jane had no interest in any relationship with Iris other than the most formal, her manner making Iris so uncomfortable that she inevitably found herself fulfilling what she imagined to be Jane's worst expectations of the fancy-pants New York from-away: frivolous, silly, and, above all, condescending. When Iris spoke to Jane, her voice crept into a high, shrill register and she said the most absurd things, like commiserating over the high cost of heating oil, as if the Copakens had anything like the financial concerns of the Tetherlys. It maddened Iris to find herself forced to act out the position of lady of the manor. In New York she knew and socialized with people whose financial straits were far more dire than Jane's without ever confronting this attitude of resentful deference.

Iris had little hope that they'd be like family, but she was determined not to allow this distance to evolve into dislike. She reminded herself that she admired Jane—here was a woman with no education and a miserable freeloader of an ex-husband, a woman who had started and succeeded at her own business. She was a veritable feminist role model.

Iris sighed. There was a reason, she thought, that the English language contained no word for the relationship created when one's children marry.

Machetunim, that was it. Iris and Jane were now *machetunim*. As, Iris supposed with a barely repressed shudder, were she and Frank, a legendarily mean drunk who in the winter drove snow plows and in the summer worked the roads, and who seemed no more capable of having fathered sweet, talented, open-hearted John than Jane did of having mothered him.

When Iris returned to Mary Lou's side she found that someone else had already provided the old woman with the desired drink.

"Just put it down on the table," Mary Lou said to Iris. "I'll get to it soon enough."

Mary Lou was now surrounded by a group of Red Hook Library Board ladies, or perhaps they were garden club ladies, or Red Hook Women's Club ladies, or VFW Ladies' Auxiliary ladies, and they quickly turned their attention to Iris, their voices blending into a bubbling murmur of good wishes.

So interesting with that canopy, what was it called? And the glass. They'd heard about that before, of course, but never seen it. A lightbulb? Not a glass at all? My, how clever, because a glass might not break, and then where would you be? The minister seemed not to mind having the rabbi there. But then the Unitarians wouldn't, would they? Just try that at St. Paul's. Can you imagine Pastor Osgood tolerating all that Hebrew?

And Becca's dress! So lovely, with the tulle and the beading. We heard she bought it in New York. Little Annie Field, from over by Dorchester way, she had her dress made in Boston, but New York, my goodness. What a distance. But, then, you live in New York, don't you? Though your grandmother and my mother were in grade school together. And then your mother met your father in town, didn't she? Of course he was from away. Just up for the summer, at Usherman Center. European, isn't he? Oh my, Prague. A refugee, wasn't he? Well he was certainly lucky. To have gotten out in time.

The ladies' attendance at the wedding was, Iris thought, an acknowledgment of her status as *almost* if not quite *of* this place. A few years before, an eager new librarian had inspired a mania for genealogy in the ladies and their retired husbands. The children who showed up at the library after school to pretend to do their homework found all the computer terminals and the long wooden tables full of grandparents peering through their cataracts at volumes of census records and church baptismal certificates. The luckiest of the amateur genealogists proudly created six- or seven-generation family trees filled out in spidery handwriting and complemented by gravestone rubbings on large sheets of delicate tracing paper. The ones whose great-great-great-great-grandparents were part of the original sixty Protestant families whose settlement of the township was a condition of the General Court of Massachusetts's land grant began treating the scions of later-comers with a gracious condescension. Those whose family trees were sprinkled with names like Chenard, Benoit, and Giroux developed what the Roundys, Woods, and Hinckleys considered something of a perverse pride in their Acadian roots. Still, everyone agreed that if you couldn't trace at least a few relatives to the period prior to the late-nineteenth-century invasion of the summer boarders, then you had, in all honesty, to consider yourself from away. Iris's family name, Hewins, popped up on the township rolls far earlier than that. In fact, the largest porgy oil business on the Red Hook Peninsula had been owned by one Benjamin Hewins, whose father, Nehemiah Hewins, uncle of Iris's great-great-grandfather Elias, took a musket ball to the fleshy pad of his thumb while serving in the 3rd New Hampshire Regiment at the Battle of Bunker Hill. These impeccable credentials somewhat made up for the fact that there was another branch of Iris's family that came to Red Hook in the late 1880s, only because they could not afford summer cottages in Bar Harbor.

From across the room, Ruthie Copaken watched as her mother attentively and gracefully chatted up the Red Hook ladies. It never ceased to amaze Ruthie how Iris, who was notorious for not suffering fools gladly, seemed to have an infinite amount of patience for these women. She attended every last bean supper and blueberry breakfast of the season, and never missed a library board meeting, even if its sole purpose was to debate, for the umpteenth time, whether it was appropriate to have a hermit crab tank in the children's section. (*It's a library, after all,* some of the ladies argued, *not a zoo.*) Iris, whose intellect was so firm and frightening that Ruthie's New York school friends, themselves the daughters of bankers, doctors, and professors, tended to panic at the prospect of a conversation with her, spent her summers trying to befriend the wives of lobstermen, few if any of whom had even gone to college, and none of whom she would have bothered to exchange more than pleasantries with if they lived in New York. That was what was different about Maine, especially Red Hook, Ruthie thought. When she visited friends in their summer homes out in the Hamptons or upstate, they never bothered to socialize with the locals, even going so far as to avoid the bands of local kids who hung out on the beach or in the parking lot of the Dairy Queen. In Maine the division between local people and summer people was as stark, but much more complicated. The locals were the ones who viewed the from-aways with a certain amount of disdain, and it was the from-aways who, in some sense, scrambled for approval. It always made Ruthie a little uncomfortable to watch her mother go so far out of her way to be friendly.

To her sister, Becca, on the other hand, it all came so effortlessly. Unlike her mother, Becca did not actively seek out friendships with local people. She just happened into them naturally. Becca genuinely neither noticed nor cared where someone was from. If they were cheerful and amusing, if they tempered their comic sarcasm with kindness, if they could be trusted to douse a foresail and tack a jib, if they could make a decent pie—Becca was an avid baker whose blueberry peach crumb crust pie had won a blue ribbon in the county fair two years running—she was happy to be their friend. Perhaps it was because Becca had been with John for so long that she was free of snobbery. She clearly didn't view the local people as her social inferiors, which Ruthie always thought her mother sort of did, no matter how hard she tried to pretend otherwise.

When Ruthie could no longer stand to watch her mother feigning enthusiasm (or, worse, perhaps, actually being enthusiastic) about the upcoming rummage sale on behalf of the Methodist church's new roof, she crossed the room and slipped through the bevy of ladies to her mother's side.

"Hey, Mom," she said.

"Hi, honey," Iris said. She slipped her arm around Ruthie's waist. "Are you enjoying yourself?"

"Yes," Ruthie said. This was not entirely true. She never knew what to do with herself at big parties like this one. She always felt like her conversations were the wrong length. Either she flitted aimlessly among people, or she clung to someone long after, she was certain, they'd lost interest in anything she might have to say. At school she never went to big parties, not even the ones held regularly in her own dorm. Still, this was her sister's wedding. She should be having more fun.

With a final "Thank you so much" to the ladies, Iris steered Ruthie away.

Once they found a spot with a good aspect over the room, Iris said, "You look beautiful, darling."

Ruthie sighed. "Oh, please."

"Ruthie! You look lovely."

"I look like a twelve-year-old in this dress."

"You don't like it?"

"No."

"Well, why didn't you say something? Why didn't you tell Becca you didn't like it?"

"Because she was all about the purple." Ruthie gave her skirt a shake. "What was I going to say? Your favorite color makes me look like a grape?"

"The purple looks wonderful on you. It makes you look rosy and beautiful."

"The color's not even the worst part. The cut is so infantile."

"I don't understand you, Ruthie. You had all the opportunity in the world to make your opposition known. Becca would have let you wear anything you wanted."

"You're right. I probably should have said something." Iris was just never going to understand that this was not the kind of battle Ruthie could ever have won. Once Becca got an idea in her head, good luck fighting it. "Anyway, what time is it?" Ruthie said.

"I don't know," Iris said. "Getting close to seven, I imagine."

"How much longer are Becca and John going to be? They're so busy memorializing their wedding, they're going to end up missing half of it."

"It shouldn't be much longer," Iris said. "The photographer said he just wanted a few shots of them down by the water."

The beach below the church was almost ridiculously picturesque, with the lobster boats, some white, some painted in bright colors—red, mint green, sky blue—to match their buoys, bobbing in the harbor. The beach was known for its sea glass, and the gray-brown sand twinkled with amber and green pebbles, even, occasionally, light blue, yellow, and pink, and every so often a magical bit of red. The grassy slope down to the beach was sprinkled with wildflowers, still in full bloom. If you looked up from the beach you could see the town laid out like a miniature village through which a model train would make its way, all white clapboard and shiny black shutters. It was no wonder that every bride and groom married in the town ended up with a photograph silhouetted against the scenic backdrop of sea, hill, and town. Iris and Daniel had their own version of that wedding picture, Iris in her turquoise minidress decorated with tiny mirrors, Daniel dressed up in a mod, double-breasted, peacock-blue suit, standing on the edge of the dock, the sea sparkling behind them. Maybe on her parents' next anniversary, Ruthie thought, she would reprint their wedding picture and put it in one of those double frames alongside Becca and John's.

"I bet that ridiculous limousine broke down," Ruthie said. None of them had approved of the limousine Becca's foolish girlfriends from the yacht club had insisted on paying for as a wedding gift. Ruthie had been surprised that Becca had agreed to it, especially because she rarely hung out with those girls anymore. Other than Jasmine, Becca's oldest summer friend, she mostly spent time with the girlfriends and wives of the men John worked with at the boatyard, some of whom were local girls, some of whom came from other oceanfront towns where their husbands had learned the craft of wooden boatbuilding. Ruthie supposed that Becca had accepted the gift of the limousine because she hadn't wanted to hurt anyone's feelings.

"I'm sure they'll be here in a few minutes," Iris said.

Ruthie said, "Hey, Mom, do you think Becca's expecting us to decorate their car? With, like, shaving cream and cans?"

"Oh, lord. I hope not."

"Well, I hope that the best man has it under control, because it was *not* on my list."

Iris had prepared a flowchart of all the wedding tasks and provided each member of the family with a personalized to-do list, updated weekly, and then, as the day got closer, daily. Trashing the bride and groom's getaway car had not been on anyone's list.

"Don't worry about it, honey," Iris said. "I'll take the fall if someone needs to."

Ruthie watched her mother scan the crowd, her eyes finally alighting on Mr. Kimmelbrod, sitting at a table on the far side of the room, alone but for Samantha Phelps, the flower girl, who was perched on a chair on the opposite side of the same table.

"Honey, will you go make sure your grandfather's okay? He's sitting over there with just Samantha for company."

"She's so cute," Ruthie said. Samantha was tall for her age, with a perfect bee sting of a mouth, and shiny dark eyes. Who could resist a lavender-taffeta-clad little girl, no matter how ineptly she'd strewn her petals?

Becca had invited Samantha to be her flower girl only a week ago, and they'd had to pay the dressmaker twice the cost of the dress because of the late notice. Ruthie was surprised that Iris had never objected to the added expense, but perhaps it was because Samantha's story played on her heartstrings. She had been adopted six years ago by Jane's niece, Connie, whose husband had promptly run off with the NCO of his army reserve unit and not been heard from again. Over the years Connie had been in and out of the psychiatric hospital outside of Augusta, leaving Samantha to the less than tender ministrations of her aunt Jane, the only one of Connie's relatives who'd been willing to take the girl.

Iris and Ruthie watched Samantha sway in time to the music. "She likes the band," Ruthie said.

"She's adorable," Iris said. "But I can't imagine that she and your grandfather have much to talk about. Go over and sit with him, why don't you, Ruthie."

Sending her daughter away made Iris feel vaguely guilty, as usual. Ruthie could be so needy, so desperate to know what Iris was thinking, so afraid that something might be going on from which she was excluded. When she was small and someone would tell a family story or simply share a recollection, Ruthie would always ask, in a tone of great desolation, "Was I *born* yet?" She clung close, Ruthie did, both to her older sister and to Iris. It used to drive Becca out of her mind, the way Ruthie would follow her around, asking to be included in every game, especially when Becca had a friend over. The girls were five years apart and not particularly well matched as companions. Becca's patience, though long for a child—she loved her sister—was not infinite. Sometimes she would set on Ruthie, pushing her out of the room or shrieking at her just to go away.

Iris would scold Becca for these outbursts, even punish her, but in truth she'd sympathized with her. Ruthie's neediness could be exhausting. Even as a baby all she'd wanted to do was sit on her mother's lap, one pudgy hand slipped into the top of Iris's shirt. Iris would be twitching in her seat, thinking of all the things she had to get done, the articles that needed writing, the house that needed cleaning, the bills that needed paying. There was dinner to make and there were papers to grade, but Ruthie would nestle her head firmly under Iris's chin, content just to sit and breathe in her mother's scent. When Iris finally succumbed to her urges and lifted Ruthie off her lap, the baby would weep in deep despair, as if her mother had left her on an orphanage doorstep, an anonymous note pinned to her little terry-cloth romper, instead of having merely set her down on the kitchen floor while she unloaded the dishwasher.

Iris knew most mothers would have killed for a placid baby like Ruthie, but Iris had preferred her older daughter's energy. Becca had been an active and animated child. She'd slept little and was quiet in Iris's arms only when she was nursing. She walked at nine months, so early that she looked like an animatronic baby barreling through the house on too-small legs. As a baby, Becca bored easily, so Iris scheduled music, gym, and art classes, outings to the park, visits to the museum in the winter and the beach in the summer. Their days began at dawn and ran at full speed until dark, when Iris collapsed into a deep and dreamless sleep until Becca woke her up with an excited cry and an effervescent smile, ready for more. She twitched, wiggled, and moved so much that Iris once insisted on an appointment with a pediatric neurologist. There was, of course, nothing wrong with the girl.

Becca's hectic motion ceased only when she heard music. Then she would pause, wrinkle her brow, and concentrate with a furious focus, her hands held out, fingertips extended, as though they were antennae through which the sound entered her body.

Iris had gone back to work when Becca was six months old, and the baby had adapted easily to day care. She liked the stimulus, the constantly changing cast of characters. When Iris tried to take Ruthie to day care, on the other hand, the poor thing had cried so hard that she made herself vomit day after day, until the day care center finally told Iris she'd have to find alternative arrangements. Iris and Daniel hired a nanny they couldn't really afford, but at the time Iris was closing in on tenure and there had been no way for her to take another semester off.

It seemed obvious to Iris that some parents were better suited to certain kinds of children, and vice versa. Some children's personalities mesh with their mothers, and others do not. Loving Becca was as simple as breathing, like a reflex—a knee jumping when hit by a doctor's hammer. But loving Ruthie took concentration. It was not that Iris loved her second daughter any less. It was more like there was a nearly imperceptible hitch, a millisecond's pause, before she was reminded of the ferocity of her maternal devotion. It was ironic, really, because Iris had far more in common with Ruthie than with her eldest. Ruthie was an intellectual, for whom academic work was a pleasure rather than a chore. When she was younger, Daniel used to joke that the words *extra credit* gave Ruthie the same thrill that the words *snow day* gave to other children. Like Iris, she was rarely found without her nose in a book; she had read through the entire contents of the Red Hook

Library children's collection by the time she was in middle school and had taken on the role of unofficial children's librarian, priding herself on being able to find a book to suit the tastes of the most discerning—or least bookish—patron. But despite these similarities, and despite the fact that Becca had not once in her life read a book that was not assigned for school, it was Becca whom Iris found easier to love.

"Hey, Grandpa," Ruthie said when she arrived at his side. "What happened to Samantha?"

"The flower girl? She informed me that she needed to use the restroom, so I assume that's where you'll find her."

Mr. Kimmelbrod had set his place card neatly on top of his plate and hung his cane from the back of his chair. His trembling hands were folded in his lap.

"I wasn't actually looking for her. I was looking for you. How are you?"

"I'm well, thank you," he said, in his customary formal tone. Although technically Czech, Emil Kimmelbrod's family had always considered themselves German Jews, hyperrational, self-controlled, disciplined—altogether similar in temperament to the people who would soon begin to slaughter them so efficiently. Even after sixty years in the United States, Mr. Kimmelbrod comported himself with a Teutonic decorum. He wore a necktie at all times, kept a handkerchief in his pocket, and disliked familiar terms of address. This formality was born of his reserve, and his reserve reflected his control. Mr. Kimmelbrod was as devoted to structure—musical, personal, ethical—as other men were to the idea of the divine. He was not a *controlling* man—he did not care to dominate anyone other than himself—but his veneration of discipline and technical perfection was legendary.

From the moment she could toddle over and climb up into his lap, Ruthie had resisted—if not, in her loving way, scorned—this terrible formality. Without having words to express what she felt, she recognized and embraced the emotional ferment behind her grandfather's precise reserve, the passion that others saw expressed only in his music. She pressed secret kisses to his sober cheeks and clutched his diffident fingers. She insisted on calling him Grandpa, a usage he would have tolerated from no one else. Even Becca, with whom he had spent so much time—although he had not since she was a young child been her teacher, he had directed her musical education—did not see, or break, through him so effortlessly. Certainly Becca never adopted this casual tone of address. When she was with other musicians she called him Mr. Kimmelbrod; at home she called him Grandfather.

"Are you getting tired?" Ruthie said, sitting down next to him. He patted her small hand with his, all blue veins and swollen knuckles. A single lock of his wiry white hair had sprung loose from the grip of the violet-scented pomade he applied every morning. It dangled by the long, fleshy lobe of his ear. Ruthie gently smoothed the hair back into place. She knew how much he loathed being even a little unkempt.

"I'm not tired," Mr. Kimmelbrod said, although of course they both knew this was untrue. Ruthie could always tell when his strength was failing, but, more important, she always knew when it wasn't, when he felt fine—unlike his daughter, who insisted on viewing him as perpetually infirm. Mr. Kimmelbrod's first noticeable symptom of Parkinson's disease was the one that had caused him to stop performing: the thumb and forefinger of his right hand had begun a rhythmic motion as if they were trying at furious speed to roll a pill. There followed an infuriating cascade of symptoms: periodic rigidity and inflexibility of his muscles; a lack of balance that sometimes caused him to freeze, worried that another step would send him crashing to the ground; and the shrinking of his handwriting to a crabbed and wavering cryptogram.

Mr. Kimmelbrod abandoned his career abruptly. He refused the farewell gala his supporters had sought to put on at Town Hall, the scene of his American debut, where he had brought a jaded audience to its feet with heartrending performances of Bach's Partita in D Minor and Ernst Bloch's 1920 Sonata no. 1. With a certain grim resolve he had sold all his instruments, except for the Dembovski, his beloved 1742 Guarneri del Gesù, which had been purchased on his behalf by a group of wealthy benefactors a few years after his arrival in the United States. Thereafter he redoubled his attention on his teaching, which until that time had been secondary in his mind to his concert career. He had come to realize that his legacy would be in the musicians he trained, not in the musician he had been himself, and his expectations of his students had risen, even as his own abilities diminished. Meanwhile, the Dembovski lay in its case in a drawer, dreaming its simple fiddle dreams. The Dembovski wanted to sing, but there was no hand in which it could come alive.

"What are you thinking about, Grandpa?"

This was a favorite question of his granddaughter's, one that, despite its intrusiveness, he usually tried his best to answer. He said, "I was thinking about my violin, and whether I owe it the right to be played."

"You can still play it," Ruthie said.

"Not well enough."

"Can you ask someone to play it for you? Becca would play it, I'm sure."

"I could give it away to someone who could play it."

Ruthie raised her eyebrows, aghast. "You couldn't give the Dembovski away, Grandpa. It's a part of you."

Could he really give the violin away? Mr. Kimmelbrod wondered. As much as the Dembovski felt like a piece of his body, so, too, had it always been, in many ways, his adversary, not unlike his body in recent years. The violins of Giuseppe Guarneri del Gesù were like that. Unlike their more famous cousins, the Stradivariuses, they did not make life easy for those who played them. They were demanding mistresses, willing to give up their beauty only when approached with the proper rigor and respect. That was why he loved the Dembovski, why he'd refused to accept any other instrument. The glory was in the challenge. Although of course now there was no battle, no struggle. The war that had borne such remarkable spoils was over.

Mr. Kimmelbrod said, "Unless it is played, a violin is nothing more than a beautiful piece of wood."

"Don't give it away, Grandpa."

"No, I won't. Idle thoughts, no more than that."

Ruthie scooted her chair closer to her grandfather's and laid her head on his shoulder. "Just let me know if you want to go home. Mom has people assigned to be designated drivers."

He raised an aristocratic eyebrow. "She is so thorough that she has both assigned *and* designated them?"

Ruthie smiled. "Would you like a refill of your drink?"

He glanced at his half-full glass of wine and shook his head. She sipped her own drink. "I think the rest of the bridal party plans to get completely wasted," she said.

"Is this your plan, as well?" he mocked her gently. "To get 'completely wasted'?"

"That, or blotto. I haven't decided. I'm such a party animal."

He squeezed her hand. He knew that Iris worried about Ruthie being "unsociable," but he admired her for it. Becca, ebullient and lively, enjoyed parties, gatherings, celebrations of all kinds. As committed as she had once been to her music, she had never quite been *serious*. In this way she was different from most violinists he had known, both his contemporaries and his students, who generally held themselves at a remove even from other musicians. His own temperament was more typical of the violin virtuoso: confident, yet introverted. Self-sufficient and a bit obsessive. He sometimes wondered if Becca's gregariousness and sociability had not been the cause, or at least the harbinger, of her failure to fulfill her early promise.

And then here was Ruthie, standing in a corner of the room at a party, smiling if someone happened to glance her way, watching, observing, virtually guaranteeing that no one would get close enough to appreciate the sharp wit beneath her shy exterior.

"So, Becca and John aren't here yet," Ruthie said. "Weirdly."

"They are having their photographs taken back at the church, no?"

"I suppose so. But it's taking so *long*. How many pictures do they need?"

"Several thousand, it would seem."

Ruthie sighed and then leaned over and pressed her cheek to her grandfather's, rubbing her soft skin against his scratchy chin. She inhaled deeply. She loved the way he smelled, like polished wood, rosin, violets, and 4711 Kölnisch Wasser. "Should I get you some of the hors d'oeuvres?" she asked. "Mom and Becca spent months on the menu. I'm sure they're delicious."

He was about to demur but then realized that indeed he *was* hungry. How like Ruthie to notice that even before he did. "Yes, please. That would be very nice."

As Ruthie picked her way through the crowd she looked up at the strands of fairy lights looped among the rafters. They were so pretty, she thought. It was amazing, really, the transformation of the Grange Hall. Looking around at the white lace-draped tables, the lush flower arrangements, the flickering candles, it was hard to imagine the room's other incarnations, certainly not its regular Wednesday morning setting for a low-impact aerobics class. Most of the Wednesday regulars were here today, and Ruthie had never seen them so dressed up. Heels were high, dresses occasionally sparkled, and there were even one or two broad-brimmed and feather-trimmed hats.

By the kitchen Ruthie came upon the other two bridesmaids, Jasmine and Lauren, positioned next to the swinging door where Lauren could catch the waiters as they exited the kitchen with their full serving trays.

"I am so hungry, I think I'm going to die," Lauren said, snatching two miniature hamburgers as they passed by. Ruthie took a couple and put them on a napkin. Jasmine shook her head at the waiter's proffered tray; Ruthie couldn't remember ever seeing Jasmine eat. Last night at the rehearsal dinner Ruthie had watched in fascination as Jasmine ransacked a lobster, extracting every last flake of meat, then rotated her plate so that her boyfriend could avail himself of the results of her industry. Lauren, on the other hand, seemed to be eating for two.

"I wish I knew what was keeping Becca and John," Ruthie said as she accepted a few lobster puffs from a passing waiter. Her voice trailed away as out of the corner of her eye she saw the front door of the Grange Hall fly open, pushed so hard that it banged against the wall, the noise of heavy oak against plaster like the crack of a gunshot. On the rebound it swung back onto John's brother, Matt, as he stumbled into the room. He was ashen, his bow tie askew, his dark hair standing up on his head. Ruthie stared at him, her stomach dropping and then seizing, like an elevator brought up short in the middle of a free fall. His eyes communicated his panic like an electric pulse over a wire.

Ruthie stood frozen in place, as if nailed to the ground. Matt lingered in the doorway, his shoulders shaking in his ill-fitting suit jacket.

Suddenly, and with another bulletlike crack, the door swung open again. Two large men in uniform—crisp black slacks, blue shirts, police badges, a loop of leather strap across the chest—walked in. Sheriff's deputies. One of them bumped into Matt and for a moment they clutched each other for balance, like fighters in a clinch. The deputy regained his footing and gently, almost tenderly, pushed Matt out of the doorway. The deputy took off his wide-brimmed hat. He and his partner wore identical expressions, mouths turned down, eyes narrowed. They scanned the crowd until they located Ruthie's father standing on the far side of the room.

Ruthie felt a band growing tight across her chest, crushing the air from her lungs. She opened her mouth and gasped, the sound of her breath at once hollow and rasping. The deputies shouldered their way across the room, leaving behind them a broken parting in the crowd. Highball glasses hovered halfway to the mouths of guests whose small talk caught in their throats. Ruthie dropped the napkin she was holding, and a lobster puff rolled away across the gently sloping, wide oak planks, stopping only once it reached the barrier of a beige stacked heel. The foot in the shoe kicked the mushroom away.

"Ruthie?" Jasmine said. "Ruthie, what's wrong?"

Ruthie, freed at last from the electric grip of Matt's gaze, lurched away, elbowing people aside as she rushed toward her father. She stared at the older deputy's bent head, his murmuring lips, too far away to hear what he was saying. Her father grabbed the back of one of the pretty white slatted chairs, crushing beneath his thick fingers its ornamental corsage of purple flowers. He staggered. One of the deputies caught him around the waist, and eased him into the seat.

"Dad!" Ruthie said. As she skidded to a stop in front of the chair, she tumbled from her left high heel, her ankle buckling painfully to the side. "What happened?"

Her father shuddered, and upset a water glass as he groped for it, soaking the white tablecloth and the mauve wrappings of the little party favors Iris had arranged at every place.

"What happened?" Ruthie said again, and then, as her father broke down, "Daddy?"

Ruthie had never seen her father cry. At his parents' funerals there had been a dampness in the corners of his eyes, but wild, hoarse weeping was impossible, a dark miracle, no less wondrous and terrible than if her father had suddenly burst into flames.

"Stop it," Ruthie whispered. "Stop it!" She clutched at his sleeve, shaking his limp arm. "Please, stop."

Daniel gulped and then pulled Ruthie onto his lap. He buried his face in the nape of her soft neck and held her tightly.

Across the room Iris stood, her blood rushing hollow in her ears. She had seen Daniel and Ruthie crying, knew that they were hanging on to each other as if the seas were rising around them. But the only person in the narrow focus of her horror was the sheriff's deputy, illuminated as though trapped in a blazing spotlight. He held his hat over his heart, the chin strap caught on the shiny metal of his badge. The noises of the crowd faded to silence, and somehow Iris heard the deputy's words from across the distance of the hall as though he were whispering them into her ear.

11

Someone had switched on the two racks of fluorescent tubes slung from the Grange Hall's rafters, and the gaily decorated tables and flower arrangements looked tawdry in the harsh light, like crumpled and torn Christmas wrappings after the gifts had all been opened. The fairy lights twined through the wires shone wanly, like headlights in the daytime. The candles had guttered and gone out, the place settings stood stacked and pushed aside, and a skyline of dirty tumblers and wineglasses was crowded at the far end of the empty buffet table. All joy and expectation had been drained from the room, and in their absence what had seemed whimsical and elegant was now gaudiness, pretense. For a while the guests stayed, clumped into small groups. Whether up from New York for the weekend or summer people who'd known Becca since she was a sag-diapered baby digging in the rocky sand on Red Hook beach, the Copakens' friends stood together, gripping one another's hands and shoulders in a sudden camaraderie of disaster.

On the other side of the room stood the locals, the families of Jane and Frank and the few people not related to her whom Jane had invited. Unlike the from-aways, they were largely silent, each standing at a slight remove from the others, as though encapsulated in an invisible bubble of shock.

Everyone drank. Whether they were lobstermen or investment bankers, they placed their orders and drained their glasses in one or two gulps. The bartender was kept busy, although his work was simpler now. No one was ordering G&Ts or sea breezes. It was all scotch or bourbon, neat.

Then, as if by some inaudible signal, all together, the locals started to gather their things and head for the door. The summer people and out-of-town guests hesitated only a moment before following, a few stopping on their way out to lay a useless hand on Daniel's shoulder or offer Iris a hug she could not bear to accept.

The Copakens and the Tetherlys sat at separate tables, each family in its own stunned huddle. Someone, perhaps it was the caterer, had stripped these tables of place settings and flowers and set down pitchers of water and a few glasses, though a bottle of rye, Jane thought, might have been more welcome. Frank was not among them. He needed a smoke, he had said, and to Jane's relief, after fifteen minutes he was still not back. His slatternly girlfriend had gone after him. Now Jane didn't need to worry about what her son-of-a-bitch ex-husband might do or say. Infuriating, how even ten years after their divorce, he managed to embarrass her, as if his disgraceful behavior were still a reflection on her. She had been young and stupid enough to marry him, and she was paying for it still. And now the best of the three good things to result from her stupidity was gone.

John was dead. Even as she thought the words to herself, Jane felt a strange distance from them and her surroundings. She was proud that she had not broken down, that she hadn't made an exhibition of herself. She was strong, like her mother, who had never cried, not even on the night her husband had been lost at sea. Jane was not the victim of her emotions. In fact, she was under such firm control that she was able to watch, dispassionately, as the old Wylie sisters, Jane's clients for many years, sidled up to the long table on which were heaped dozens of gaily wrapped presents, some impressively huge and showy with ribbons, others tiny, no larger than a single silver spoon. Euphenia and Eudoxia Wylie conferred like a team of lawyers in front of the gift table, whispering behind their hands. Jane was not too overcome by sorrow to fail to observe as Eudoxia reached with a furtive hand for a shapeless package wrapped in silvery, well-creased snowflake-patterned paper; and plucked it off the large pile.

Jane smiled grimly. Her world might have been stood on its ear, but at least the fundamental tenet of her philosophy—that no matter what they pretended, people looked out only for themselves—remained reliably in place. Look at the Wylie girls (as they were known, though both were well beyond girlhood or even middle age). Pillars of society, sat on the vestry of St. Paul's Episcopal Church, ran the charity jams-and-jellies booth at the

Blueberry Festival. Proud descendants of one of Red Hook's founding families. Yet they still paid Jane to clean their drafty old barn of a house what they'd paid her mother twenty years before—$10, an extra $2.50 if she did the windows. The really shocking thing was that Jane, a woman who never hesitated to speak her mind and get what she was owed, let the old birds get away with it. Jane had stopped being a woman who let others take advantage of her a dozen years ago, the first time that John calmly put himself between her and Frank Tetherly's right hand. John was strong without violence, masculine without rage. He had shown her that she did not have to take for granted the history of men and women in her family. She could be different, too. She had borrowed money from her mother, hired a lawyer, and threw Frank out of the house. And from then on if someone tried to take advantage of her or failed to treat her with respect, she showed them the door. But she had never shown Euphenia and Eudoxia Wylie the door, even though after she paid her girls their $7 an hour each, it ended up costing Jane to clean their house. The Wylie sisters had been the first to hire Jane's mother after Jane's father died, and more than once their paltry $10 a week had been all that stood between Jane's family and empty bellies. Even after her situation had improved, Jane's mother had retained a soft spot all her life for the Wylie sisters. When she was a little girl, Jane had spent many an afternoon playing checkers with Miss Doxie, the more easygoing of the two, while her mother scrubbed out their icebox and swabbed Lysol around their kitchen floor.

Jane watched the two old women shuffle with their reclaimed booty out of the propped-open door, the floral fabric of their good Sunday dresses stretched across their flat rumps in a crosshatch of creases.

Maureen, Jane's daughter, followed her gaze. Maureen's face was puffed up even more than usual, her eyelids and the end of her nose as pink as a rabbit's.

"Cheap old bitches," Maureen said.

Jane shrugged.

Matt put his head down on the table.

"You need to throw up again?" Jane asked. The boy, like his father, had a weak stomach. Matt shook his head, his cheek still pressed to the table. "Good," she said.

Matt had been following the limousine in John's car—it had been his job to drive it to the reception—and had barely escaped getting into the collision. When the first sheriff's car pulled up to the scene, they found him on the roof of the crushed limousine, trying to pound his way through the sunroof to get to his brother and Becca.

At the next table Iris sat, her face gray and crumpled, like a used tissue. Her mouth hung open, sagging at the corners, a thin string of saliva wavering between her lower lip and the bodice of her silk gown. Jane felt an unkind relief at seeing Iris's face made ugly by grief. Usually the woman looked perfect, even when she wore her gardening clothes—a beat-up old straw hat, khaki shorts, and an old white shirt of her husband's, tails hanging down her thighs. Jane would rush in, sweaty and dirty from a day driving the girls from one house to another, picking up a bottle of Windex if they were low, swapping vacuums when one blew out, getting down on her hands and knees to help scrub a floor if they were running behind, and there Iris would be, cool and elegant, sipping a cup of tea on her screen porch, a pile of papers on her lap, a pencil holding her mess of curly black hair in a knot on top of her head. She always offered Jane a cup and Jane always refused it. No need to sit through ten minutes of awkward chitchat with someone with whom you had nothing in common.

Now, though, with her makeup smeared, blurring her features, for once the woman looked worse than Jane. How could she allow herself to break down like that, in front of everybody? Jane had never understood this willingness on the part of these from-aways to peel up the scabs of their emotions and let everyone see their festering sores. They were like children that way. They had no shame and even less self-control.

Look at the girl, Ruthie, lying across her mother's lap, her whole body shaking. Maureen indulged in no such melodrama; she had two daughters to stay strong for. Although Jane could not deny that Maureen and John had never got on. Maureen had picked and prodded at the boy his whole life, and yet John had never laid a hand on her. He gave as good as he got, but never physically, teasing her instead about everything from her weight to her cooking. Even as adults, when all this nonsense should have been behind them, they never managed to heal the rift; Maureen never tired of saying that John had his nose in the air ever since he got back from the yacht design course and started as an assistant designer at the yard instead of paying his dues at the bottom, like everyone else had to.

Jane had kept Matt out of the troubles among his siblings by taking him with her to work, just like her mother had done with her. After school and during the summers when he was a small boy she used to fill a basket with his G.I. Joes and Tonka trucks and deposit him at the kitchen table of whatever house she was cleaning. Before he was old enough to resent having to tag along with her, Maureen was out of the house and Jane could safely leave him alone with John. She'd felt bad about that, both for John, who spent most of his free time keeping an eye on his little brother, even dragging the boy along to his job at the yacht club in the summer, and for Matt, who got thrown out of his mother's orbit so early. But there was no point in feeling guilty. She did what she had to do to survive. Her kids knew that and understood. Once her business had begun to see a decent if sporadic profit, they'd come to appreciate that the sacrifice was worth it. Jane had regularly bailed Maureen out; the girl never kept a job for longer than a couple of months, and the welfare check stretched only so far. Jane had helped pay for John's design course, and she had made up the shortfall between Matt's scholarship and the costs of his college tuition and expenses. Her kids had been appropriately grateful. They were well-mannered people. They knew how to behave.

Jane glanced over at the Copakens, still crying, the lot of them. Only the old man managed to keep himself under control. A proper gentleman, he'd always been.

Jane swallowed, her throat suddenly dry. She poured herself a glass of water, scowling at the way the pitcher shook in her hand. She gulped down the water and wiped away the sweat that dappled her forehead. When she turned her head it felt like her brain kept moving, bumping into the side of her skull with a thud. Suddenly she could feel the heat emanating from Maureen's and Matt's bodies, warming the air. She couldn't breathe. She put a hand to her cheek. It was at once clammy and hot.

"I have to get out of here," Jane said, struggling to her feet.

Maureen said, "You want to go home?"

"No," Jane said, collapsing back in her chair. Then, suddenly, she knew where she needed to be.

"I have to see it."

"You don't want to do that," Matt said, not looking at her.

Maureen said, "The deputies'll tell us as soon as we can go see him. They said we should wait."

"I have to see him now," Jane said, forcing herself to stand up. "I'm going down to Jacob's Cove."

"They won't let you down there. They blocked the road on either side of the cove," Matt said. He put his head back down on the table.

"Like hell they won't." She tried to remember where she'd left her car keys. In the ignition, she thought. Unless she'd slipped them into her purse to make sure none of the kids tried to drive off after having a few too many. Or that Frank didn't do the same. It would not be the first time the idiot drank so much he forgot that the van wasn't his anymore.

She had left her purse under a chair at the head table. She stood up and set off toward it on unsteady legs.

"Miz Tetherly?" said the younger deputy. He'd been left to babysit them while the older one returned to the scene of the accident. "Miz Tetherly? You need something?"

"Nope," she said.

"Miz Tetherly? You want me to drive you somewhere?"

"I can drive myself. I'm going to see my son."

The deputy grimaced. "Oh no, ma'am. That's not a good idea. When they've got everything . . . you know . . . when they get them over to the hospital the sheriff'll call over here and I'll take you. You know. To identify the . . . your son."

Jane glared at him. "I'm not going all the way to Newmarket to see my son." She had her purse looped over her arm now.

"Jane?" Iris said, struggling to lift her daughter up off her lap; the girl was sprawled across her like a giant baby, her arms wrapped around her neck and her head drooping over her shoulder. Ruthie clung to her mother, ignoring Iris's effort to free herself. With a final heave Iris pushed the girl over to Daniel. "Jane? Are you going? Are you going over there?"

Jane sighed and looked away.

"Jane?" Iris said.

"Yeah," Jane said finally. "I'm going over there."

Iris pushed her hands roughly across her cheeks, rubbing away her tears. Ruthie tried to grab her hand but she shook her off. "I'm going with you," Iris said.

"Iris," Daniel said. "Sit down."

She ignored him, setting off toward the front door of the hall.

"Mommy!" Ruthie called.

Jane's jaw twitched. The last thing she wanted was Iris's company.

"Let's go," Iris said.

Jane narrowed her eyes, sizing Iris up.

"Let's go," Iris said again.

Jane set her shoulders. "Fine," she said, walking out the door, knowing, without looking, that Iris was following close behind.

III

Jacob's Cove lay on Red Hook Road about halfway between town and the little village of East Red Hook. From the Unitarian church in Red Hook to Jacob's Cove was about four miles, and the village of East Red Hook was another three and a half miles farther along. Unlike the town of Red Hook, which had grown larger and more prosperous in the period between its founding in 1778 through the mid-nineteenth century, when the wooden shipbuilding industry reached its zenith, and on into the 1880s, when it began its current incarnation as a summer destination for people from away, the village of East Red Hook at the beginning of the twenty-first century was no larger than it had been at the end of the eighteenth. It was composed entirely of a dozen houses, the Copakens' among them, a post office open or closed at the postmistress's whim, the Grange Hall, and an empty storefront that had been home to Witham's Country Store until the last Witham daughter closed up shop and moved down to Florida.

A tidal cove, Jacob's was deep and swimmable when the tide was in, nothing more than a broad, shining mudflat when it was out. At high tide in the summertime, the narrow arc of rocky beach at Jacob's Cove filled up with beach chairs and blankets. Young mothers liked the cove because the water was shallow and a little warmer than at other beaches. Teenagers liked it because no one bothered them about smoking, or hollered at them if they threw their beer bottles up the rocky creek that fed the cove, where they shattered among the bottles that their parents and grandparents had thrown there before them.

There was little traffic along Red Hook Road, and thus people tended to take its curves faster than they should have. The blacktop was scrawled with a wild alphabet of wobbly skid marks written by kids showing off, boys trying to frighten their girlfriends. The stretch running alongside Jacob's Cove was not the most dangerous, but there was a sharp bend just before the cove. In the late afternoon, the sun hung low in the sky and dazzled the eyes of drivers coming around the bend.

Jane and Iris were coming from the direction of East Red Hook, however, and so the setting sun lay behind them, casting long shadows into the deepening blue shade of the evening. Iris had never ridden in Jane's van before. It was cleaner than she would have expected, cleaner than her own car, which was full of crumpled chewing gum wrappers, half-finished bottles of water, and used tissues. Iris often thought of her car as a kind of automotive portrait of Dorian Gray, betraying in its disorder and dirt a side of her personality that in all other areas was ruthlessly and efficiently tamped down to nonexistence.

The ride, as brief as it was, seemed to Iris to last forever. Jane drove slowly, staring through the windshield, her eyes fixed to the road, her brights on, as though her excess of caution would erase other drivers' prior failures. Iris had to grit her teeth to keep from shouting at Jane to step on it, although she knew that there was no point in hurrying.

About fifty yards before the cove a sheriff's cruiser was parked athwart the road, blocking traffic. A deputy stood next to the cruiser, waving his arms at them to stop. Jane braked, and cranked her window down. At once the acrid smell of burning rubber filled the car. Iris coughed, her eyes watering, but Jane didn't even wrinkle her nose.

"Let me through," Jane said.

The deputy recognized her. He hesitated for only a moment before shrugging and going to move the cruiser.

Jane kept the window down and drove slowly. The urgency drained from Iris; she now wished for the ride to last as long as possible. To last forever. At first, before they rounded the final curve that gave onto the cove, they could see nothing of the accident. Looking out the window, Iris marveled at how normal, how beautiful, everything looked. At one end of the cove a patchwork of farmland led down to the rocky coast, brown where the fields lay fallow, pale green where the hay waited to be mowed, mossy green where the fruit in the blueberry bogs had yet to ripen. In a small pasture above the water a dappled gray pony stood, one of its rear legs tucked up to its belly, its tail flicking across its back. So perfect and perfectly normal, yet the air was thick with the sulfurous stench of burning metal and rubber, raw and harsh as it passed into Iris's lungs, and where normally there would be only the whispering of the wind in the pines or the hollow cry of a loon, there was a strange and frightening grinding sound. A faint roar.

When the women rounded the corner, flurries of ash streamed into Jane's open window, dusting her left arm, leaving flakes of gray across the red paisley. There was an SUV lying on its back in the middle of the road, flames flickering from the crushed and charred front, spewing a boil of smoke. A crew of volunteer fireman struggled to control the blaze.

Jane slammed on the brakes, and Iris jerked forward against the seat belt's restraining shoulder strap. They stared at the crash. Two sheriff's cruisers and the Red Hook volunteer fire department's hook and ladder straddled the road on the far side of the wreck. Blue and white lights flashed from the racks on the roofs of the cruisers. Roping off the area directly around the accident scene were swags of yellow police tape mocking the swags of flower garlands that still decorated the church a few miles up the road. The limo lay with its back end in the brackish water of the cove, submerged halfway up the passenger doors. The front end clung to the asphalt, its hood buckled and ripped open on one side. The driver's door had been forced open and now hung from a single hinge. Because the tide was still in, the fire crew—most of whom Iris recognized—wore waders, bright yellow, hip-high. They worked in water up to their knees, trying to tear through the crushed metal of the right rear passenger door with the Jaws of Life.

Iris stared through the windshield of the van, unable to move, but the slam of Jane's door jarred her out of her paralysis. She followed Jane up the road. Just as they reached the police tape, two banks of lights mounted on tall tripods snapped on, flooding the scene with a harsh and truthful radiance. Now Jane and Iris could see well what had been invisible in the twilight: the angry black skid marks looping across the road; the blue tarps spread out and covered with bits of charred metal in orderly rows; the burned-out cab of the SUV; the three long, lumpy black bags laid out on the gravel shoulder at the side of the road.

Another observer might have failed to notice the fine strands of blond hair caught in the zipper teeth of the centermost bag. An observer who had not spent the past twenty-six years watching that hair grow from a patch of soft fuzz over a baby's ears to a thick cascade of honey curls. Someone who had not washed it, combed out its tangles, braided it, tied it with ribbons on school picture days, who had not affected unconcern when, one Thanksgiving, the yellow hair was suddenly purple, shaved to the skin on one side. Someone who did not know that hair better than her own would not have noticed it wafting in the light breeze blowing in over Jacob's Cove. For the rest of her life Iris would be haunted by occasional dreams of Becca's long blond hairs snared in the zipper of the black body bag.

Iris clamped down on the scream that rose inside her, swallowing as hard as she was able to. She turned from the body bag and watched as one of the firemen climbed up onto the top of the limousine, reaching out a hand to steady himself on the roof like a surfer on his board. With three precise blows of his ax he hacked at the sunroof, and it gave way, the sheet of glass collapsing in on itself.

Sheriff William Paige, who had been standing on the shore watching the crew do their grim work, looked over his shoulder and saw the two women coming toward the crash, five feet of sunset between them. They were dressed for a party, and even if he hadn't been warned by a radio call from his deputy, he would have known who they were: two mothers, come looking for their children.

He jogged up to the barrier, his holster bouncing against his hip. With one leather-gloved hand, he held the police tape down so that they could step over it. The slender, wan-looking one allowed him to take her hand and help her over, but the other, the one with the fierce, plain Down East face, refused with a single shake of her head any help he was fool enough to think he could provide. Sheriff Paige had learned over his many years in the department that the best—the only—way to express condolences in such situations was briefly, almost blandly.

"I am so sorry for your loss," he began. Then he explained to the women what, as far as he could tell, had happened.

Until this evening, the Newmarket-based limousine driver would never have had any cause to drive this stretch of Red Hook Road. He would not have been familiar with it, and thus would not have anticipated the problem of the sun. If he took the turn too fast and too wide, and then was blinded as he came around the bend, he would have hit the car coming the other way.

The women stared at the sheriff intently as he talked, watching closely as he drew a picture in the air with his pointed finger.

When he finished his explanation he paused for a moment. Then he said, "I don't think any of them knew what hit them. They didn't suffer." For a moment he felt embarrassed at what was not, he knew, an entirely honest attempt at solace. He had no idea whether or not they had suffered. How could he?

Normally the sheriff would not have bothered to come down from Newmarket for a traffic accident. Accidents happened all the time on these winding country roads, people died, especially in the winter, with ice and bad wipers and nothing to do to pass the long dark nights but stay warm over a bottle. Yet there was something about this particular accident; the bride and groom dead at the scene. It was like an old English folk song, he thought, or a tragic poem. He had found himself unable to stay at his desk when the 10–50 came in, and had driven all the way down here, lights flashing and siren wailing, to see it for himself. It was as bad as he had expected, as bad as any accident he had ever seen. The fire in the SUV had burned hot, transforming the body of the driver into a scoriated husk that barely resembled a man. But the two bodies they'd already pulled out of the limousine were worse. Crushed skulls, skin punctured by jags of broken bone, blood everywhere.

"Is that John?" Jane said gruffly.

"Ma'am?" the sheriff said.

"Is that John or Becca they're trying to get out of the car?"

"That's John, ma'am. The boys are working on extracting him. You can see that side's crushed pretty bad. But they'll get him out."

"If they haven't extracted him yet," Jane said, "then how do you know he's dead?"

Sheriff Paige frowned and then, uncharacteristically, turned away from her gaze. For a moment he looked down at his shiny black boots. Then he forced himself to wipe his expression clean and meet her eyes.

"He might be alive in there," Jane said, her voice harsh and loud.

"No, ma'am."

"How do you know? You haven't gotten to him yet. You don't know."

"I'm sorry, ma'am. He's gone."

"You don't know that," Jane said, her voice rising. "They haven't even gotten to him yet."

"When they moved the . . . bride, the men made sure."

By now Jane's face was bright red, and beads of sweat gathered at her hairline. She wiped the back of her hand roughly across her forehead. "He might be alive in there. He might be breathing."

"I'm sorry, ma'am. He's not. We're certain of that."

"You don't know. He might be all right in there. He might be alive." She inched closer to the wreck.

The sheriff said, "Please, Mrs. Tetherly, if you'll just calm down, the firefighters will do their jobs and we'll have his body out in a minute or two."

"Calm down?" Jane shouted. "Calm down? You've got some nerve, you son of a bitch."

He placed a restraining hand on her shoulder. "Let's just move back behind the police tape. Give the men room to work."

"Get your hands off me." Jane jerked her shoulder, flinging his hand away. Then, suddenly, she lunged for the sheriff, grabbing the front of his shirt with both her hands. She was a big woman, strong from years spent clomping up and down stairs, hauling heavy vacuum cleaners and baskets of laundry, and she had a good grip on his shirt. She shook him, yelling, "Get him out!" One of his buttons popped off and stung her on the chest. The round red mark that the button made on her thin, freckled skin would, over the next week, slowly fade to a yellow bruise and then disappear, but for the rest of her life, whenever she thought of her dead son, she would rub the spot, sure she could feel a small, dimpled button of sorrow.

Sheriff Paige gently but firmly removed Jane's hands from his shirt and held her wrists for a long moment. When he let her go, she collapsed. He caught her in his arms and eased her to the ground.

Iris knelt down by Jane's side. The sheriff backed away, motioning to his deputies and to the fire chief to give the women some space, a little air, as if inches and oxygen would make it easier for them to assimilate the horror of their children's deaths.

Jane sat in the dirt, thick legs splayed, head hanging, elbows resting on her thighs, hands limp between her knees. Iris hovered next to her, watching as tears rolled from Jane's closed eyes, down the length of her nose, hung there for a moment, and then dropped onto the pebbly soil. Iris put her hand up to her own face. Her eyes felt dry, gritty, like she'd opened them into a sandstorm.

The tide was going out and the firemen rolled down the tops of their tall, rubber waders. With a screech of metal against metal, they finally managed to pry the car door off its hinges. Someone turned off the motor of the Jaws of Life and its grinding roar gave way to a sudden silence. Iris could hear the creaking of the trees, the hiss of the wind in the leaves, a single, mournful loon calling across the water, the sound of tires on the sandy grass at the edge of the road. Then doors opening and slamming, one by one. She didn't turn around to see who it was.

Two of the volunteer firemen stood in front of the car, a shield, Iris thought, to block her and Jane's view as they pulled John's body out of the car. Only once it was hidden from sight in the black body bag did they step aside. Iris watched them carry the bag, two men on either side, to the pointless ambulance. The four of them then picked up the second bag, and methodically loaded it into the ambulance, too. Then the third. Then the fourth. Then, quietly, without slamming them, one of the firefighters closed the rear doors of the ambulance. The engine started and the ambulance rolled slowly away, skirting the cruisers that partially blocked the road.

Iris stood up. She hesitated for a moment and then offered her hand to Jane. The other woman shook her head and hoisted herself to her feet. They stood side by side, staring at the twisted wreckage, then, wordlessly, they turned and walked to their families, who stood beyond the police tape. Maureen and Daniel stood together, Daniel squinting against the smoke from Maureen's cigarette. Matt hung back, close to Daniel's car, which he had pulled up next to Jane's.

Daniel opened his arms and Iris came over and leaned into them, closing her eyes. She felt his heart beating beneath the firm muscles of his broad chest, and for some reason the steady thump allowed her to resume her tears.

"Let's go home," Daniel said. "Matt, Maureen, do you two want to go with your mother?"

"I'm staying," Jane said flatly. "I'm staying until they tow it away."

The sheriff, who stood at a small remove from them, said, "We've got a flatbed coming in from Newmarket to haul the cars up to the Department of Transportation yard."

"Why do you want to do that, Mum?" Maureen said. "It's just a damn car."

"Still."

Maureen sighed, dropped her cigarette to the dirt, and ground it out with the pointed toe of her shoe. "I got to get my girls home," she said. "So I'm going to go with them"—she stuck a thumb in Iris and Daniel's direction—"if that's all right with you."

"No matter," Jane said.

"You want me to take Samantha home with me, or are you going to pick her up on your way?"

"You take her. Matt, you go, too."

"That's all right, Mum. I'll stay with you." It was obvious from everything about him—his tone of voice, the expression on his face, his slumped shoulders and back—that staying at the scene of the accident was the last thing he wanted to do.

"I don't want you here. Go."

"Mum."

"Go!" she shouted.

Matt looked at Daniel, his eyebrows raised, his shoulders shrugged as if to say, What am I supposed to do now? When no reply was forthcoming, he said, "All right, Mum. I'll be waiting for you at home. Don't stay too long." Then he called out to the sheriff, "You won't let her stay too long, will you?"

"Don't worry, son," the sheriff said. "The truck will be here soon."

Matt crammed his hands into his pockets and followed Maureen, who was trudging back to the car. Daniel, his arm around Iris's shoulders, tried to lead her away.

"Wait," Iris said. Her voice was calm despite her tears. "Officer?"

"Yes, ma'am?"

"Who was riding in the other car?" Iris said.

"Excuse me, ma'am?"

"The other car. The SUV." She pointed at the wreckage. It was just possible to see beneath the charring that the truck had once been white. "Who was driving it?"

"Man from Bucksport way. I've got a couple of deputies heading out to tell his family."

"Was he drunk?"

"We won't know until the autopsy. But if I had to guess, I'd say probably not."

"And the limo driver? Was he drunk?"

Daniel said, "You know he wasn't."

"So what happened? Why did they crash?" Iris said.

Sheriff Paige said, "The limo driver probably had the sun in his eyes, maybe took the turn too wide. The way I read it, the Explorer swerved out of the way and got its wheels up on those rocks and that's what flipped it. Unstable as hell, those trucks. Doesn't take much for them to turn turtle." He looked at Matt. "That about what you saw, son?"

"Yeah," Matt said. "It just flipped and rolled right over the top of the limo."

Daniel pulled Iris close. "Let's go," he said.

When they reached the car she paused and looked back. The fire in the SUV was finally out and only a small plume of black smoke still rose from the car's broken carcass. There was no moon, and so the cove and the trees had faded into the darkness. The two banks of spotlights each sent out a sharply delineated bend of bright white light. One strip of light illuminated the SUV, the other the limousine, which was no longer in water but lodged in mud, the ebbing tide having begun to recede from the shore. The two zones of light overlapped in the middle of the road. In that small, brilliantly lit space, Jane stood facing the wrecks, her broad back to Iris. Her arms and hands hung limply by her sides. A gust of breeze sent the hem of her dress swirling around her legs.

Jane stood in that little island of light like a sentinel, a lighthouse on an uninhabited, forbidding coast. Iris gripped the car door with her hands and stared at Jane. She had never seen anyone look so completely alone. How could they drive away and leave her there, enclosed in the husk of her grief? Iris started to call to her, but just then Jane bent down and picked something up off the ground. With a jerk of her strong arm she sent the rock arcing high toward the limousine. It landed with a crack on the shredded roof. Iris jumped at the sound.

"Iris," Daniel said, gently pressing down on her shoulders, maneuvering her into the car. "Let's go home."

Jane bent down for another rock, and Iris quickly ducked into the car, so that she wouldn't have to see or hear it land.

IV

When the call came from Sheriff Paige early the next morning to tell them that Becca's body was waiting for them at a Newmarket funeral home, Daniel assumed he and Iris would make the unhappy trip together. Iris, however, refused. She was sitting on the screen porch, curled up in her wicker armchair, its floral chintz cushion worn white at the seams. She had been sitting there since before dawn, when they both had given up the pretense of sleep. "I already saw what I needed to see," she said.

"But don't you want to make the arrangements?" Daniel asked. It was uncharacteristic of Iris to leave something this important to him, to trust that his decisions would reflect or even begin to approximate her wishes.

"No," she said, simply, and laid her cheek on her bent knees, a fall of curls hiding her face from his view.

The Dunn & Burpee Funeral Home, on Main Street in Newmarket, was a large brick house of approximately the same vintage as his and Iris's home in East Red Hook. It was plainer in design, bereft of gingerbread and scrollwork, with a turret but no widow's walk, yet was somehow more imposing for its simplicity. The last of a block of stately homes constructed in the nineteenth century by the owners of the copper and granite mines that had once brought wealth to this now slightly seedy small city, the funeral home was flanked on one side by an auto parts store and on the other by a boxing gym called the Maine Event. The gym had always caught Daniel's attention when he came to Newmarket, but as he had hung up his gloves thirty years before, he never had cause to walk through the door.

Today, before mounting the broad stairs that led up to the front door of the funeral home, he stood for a moment on the sidewalk and stared at the blank steel door of the gym. The door banged open and a beefy young man stepped out, his head too small for his overdeveloped body. In one hand he carried a plastic milk crate full of iron dumbbells. He dropped the crate on the ground to prop the door open.

"Hey," the young man said, when he noticed Daniel watching him. "What's up?"

"Nothing much," Daniel said.

Inside the funeral home Daniel was greeted by the undertaker, a man of about his own age, in a dark suit, crisp white shirt, and shiny black tie. Daniel looked down at his own faded jeans and frayed polo shirt, embarrassed. The undertaker, not obviously perturbed by Daniel's attire, steered him into a small wood-paneled room and sat him down on a maroon brocade couch.

"Can I offer you something to drink?" he said. "Some coffee or a glass of water?"

"A glass of water would be nice," Daniel said, surprised at how normal he sounded. As if he were shopping for a new pair of jeans rather than a coffin for his daughter.

The undertaker returned with his water and handed him a binder full of pictures of caskets. Daniel leafed through the binder, the sweat from his fingertips leaving smudged whorls on the Mylar-covered pages. With every turn of the page came the thought that every single one of these caskets, the Batesville Imperial Mahogany, the Steel Provincial Gold, the Stainless Tapestry Rose, would one day contain the body of someone's child.

The undertaker, adept at steering the inconsolable through impossible tasks, gently returned to a page at the front of the binder. "Fairfield Poplar is a nice choice for a young woman."

Daniel was suddenly conscious of feeling impatient, bored, even. Not with choosing the casket, or not *only* with that, but as if he were waiting for everything—the accident and his daughter's death—to be over. As if it were a film that was dragging on for too long. The credits would have to roll at some point. If he just held on long enough, the last reel would end and Becca would no longer be dead.

The undertaker quietly cleared his throat and Daniel managed with a great deal of effort to bring his attention back to the specifics of his task. "No, these aren't right," he said. "They're too . . . too much. We're Jewish."

"Ah," said the undertaker, barely concealing his disappointment. "You'll be wanting this, then." He pulled a page from his desk drawer.

Daniel looked at the plain pine box, unfinished, with three velvet looped handles on each side. Was this the casket his daughter would have chosen for herself? Or would she have gone for scrollwork and flounced cerulean satin, regardless of the dictates of the religion that she barely practiced? He shook his head clear of the bizarre image of Becca flipping through this book of coffins as if she were turning the pages of the L.L. Bean spring catalog. He willed himself to recall something, anything, that mattered: the way her hand had trembled in the crook of his elbow as he led her down the aisle.

"Or if you'd prefer something of more lasting quality . . ." the undertaker said, handing Daniel another sheet of paper. This page had a glossy color photograph of a varnished pine casket with long wooden handles on the sides and a wooden Star of David on the gently rounded top.

What would Iris choose? This task felt like a test she had assigned him, an exam for which he hadn't studied, but on which, by some obscure logic, his future depended. Would Iris have tossed the page aside and asked what, exactly, the point was of "lasting quality" in an item whose very purpose was to decompose? Was there some sacred or aesthetic principle he was neglecting? Worried he would dampen the page with his sweating hands, Daniel put it down on the gleaming coffee table.

The undertaker said, "The interior of the Eliazar is crepe, but we can arrange for velvet if you prefer."

Daniel looked from one page to the other. There was no reason to select anything but the most simple box, he told himself, told Iris. The coffin meant nothing. It symbolized nothing. It was only a convenient way of carrying the body of his daughter to the hole in the ground where corruption and biology could take their proper course. But what hole, and where?

Iris would probably want her in the Red Hook graveyard where her own grandmother was buried, despite the fact that it had no Jewish section, something that had bothered Mr. Kimmelbrod enough that he had chosen to bury his wife far from her family, in a nondescript cemetery in

Queens. Daniel was sure, however, that no matter where her own mother lay, Iris would never consider burying Becca anywhere but in Maine.

Daniel felt disconnected from his own past, and thus had difficulty understanding the ferocious pride his wife and daughters took in the Maine part of their heritage. He always felt vaguely embarrassed when one or the other of them told a guest that Ruthie and Becca were the sixth generation to have lived in this house, or when they described a fellow summer resident as a "from-away," or when they painstakingly layered the yearly dump sticker in the corner of the Volvo's windshield in such a manner that you could see all the ones from the years before.

Daniel's family had come to America at the turn of the twentieth century and resided in a series of houses and apartments, first in New York and then in Pittsburgh, the locations of which had long since been forgotten. He felt no great loss at this lack of patrimony, and while Daniel had always enjoyed the summers in Maine—he liked the landscape, the cool air, the way their lives slowed down, all their New York and professional worries forgotten for a few months—he didn't love the place the way his wife did. Daniel could have just as easily summered in the Hudson Valley, Block Island, Oregon—anywhere, as long as they were away from the city. Indeed, he sometimes thought he would have preferred a place where the water wasn't so damn cold and where he didn't spend a good portion of July bundled up in layers of fleece.

"The Eliazar," Daniel said. "Crepe is fine."

As he was signing the myriad documents the undertaker presented to him, Daniel heard a gentle bonging, a muffled doorbell.

"Excuse me," the undertaker said, and left the room.

Daniel completed the paperwork and stepped out into the funeral home's large entryway. There, standing beneath the crystal chandelier, he saw Jane conferring with the undertaker. She had known enough to try to dress for the occasion. She wore a plain blue skirt and a white top that gaped a bit between the buttons, revealing the ribbon at the center of her polyester lace brassiere.

"Hello, Jane," Daniel said, as he handed the undertaker the stack of documents.

"Hello."

They stood awkwardly, Daniel wondering if he should reach out and hug her. If it were anyone else he might have. Or he would have if it were someone not protected by a carapace of New England reserve.

After a few more moments of uncomfortable silence, Daniel said, "How are you?"

"Fine," Jane said. "You?"

"Fine. Well, not fine, really. But, you know. Fine."

Jane pursed her lips in disapproval. Daniel felt an urgent need to leave the room, to leave her and the undertaker behind.

As he was gearing himself up for his good-bye, Jane said, "I just confirmed with Mr. Burpee that we're going to hold John's viewing starting on Tuesday, and then the funeral on Thursday. Unless that conflicts with what you're planning."

"No," Daniel said. "I mean, I'm not sure what we're planning."

"You'll let me know," Jane said. "We'll come, of course."

"Of course."

"You'll let me know," Jane repeated. She gave him the details of John's funeral and then turned her attention back to the undertaker, bidding Daniel good-bye with a curt nod.

Daniel stood in front of the funeral home, blinking in the sunlight. For a moment he could not remember at which end of the block he'd parked his car. He peered up and down the road. He saw the old blue Volvo in front of the auto parts store, but instead of heading in that direction he turned the other way, to the boxing gym.

The Maine Event looked exactly like every other gym in which Daniel had boxed, exactly like he expected it to. A cracked poured-concrete floor on which were spread mats of various colors. A row of heavy bags, another of hooks for speed bags, a wall of mirrors, a corner full of beat-up weights and an ancient Nautilus machine, and, in the center of the room, a ring, roped in red, the padding scuffed and torn in places. The room gave off the familiar stink of sweat and old socks, complicated by the metallic edge of disinfectant.

"Can I help you?" The kid who Daniel had seen out in front of the gym was sitting in a teetering desk chair behind a decrepit desk by the door.

Daniel shoved his hands deep in his pockets and jangled his car keys. He looked at the few men who were working out, one skipping rope on the far side of the ring, another lackadaisically jabbing at one of the heavy bags. Daniel wished, desperately, that he could lace on a pair of gloves and begin wailing on the bag.

Boxing had been Daniel's sport since the summer of 1954 when his father took him on a trip to New York City. It was the first time the two had been alone in each other's company for longer than the length of a ball game.

When their train from Pittsburgh had arrived at Penn Station, the early evening was gray and cold, harbinger of Carol, the hurricane that would soon ride up the eastern seaboard, killing sixty-six people, among them Jane Tetherly's father. Despite the threatening rain, they set out walking uptown, Daniel's father carrying the small cardboard suitcase into which he had packed a single change of clothes for each of them.

Archie Moore was fighting Harold Johnson, and the Copaken men were going there, to Madison Square Garden, to cheer every jab, hook, cross, and uppercut. Archie Moore was one of Saul Copaken's favorites; he felt for him the same devotion that he'd once reserved for Benny "the Ghetto Wizard" Leonard and for Little Joe Choynski, the greatest Jewish heavyweight ever. Daniel had been listening to boxing on the radio with his father for as long as he could remember, but he'd never been to a live fight. In the all too brief period between the entrance of Moore in his black silk Chinese robe and the stumbling final retreat of Johnson to his corner, Daniel experienced an unfamiliar cool blankness that crowded out his thoughts, his anxieties, the expression on his mother's face when she came home from her visits to the D. T. Watson Home for Crippled Children, where Daniel's older sister lived, mutilated by polio, her legs wizened and twisted, her toes curled under like the lotus blossoms of a Mandarin Tai Tai. Watching the fight, all that faded away. His whole world became a twenty-foot square of light, and the thwack of padded cowhide against bone and skin.

By the time Daniel was a student at Harvard, he was winning amateur bouts all over New England. Saul showed up at every one of Daniel's fights, whether they were in Boston or Bangor. He would sit as close to ringside as he could get, wearing the same two-tone zippered cardigan, his gray plaid fedora resting in his lap. When Daniel managed a particularly skilled combination or landed a liver punch that left his opponent gagging, Saul would simply nod his head, nothing more.

After he graduated from Harvard, Daniel took up training and fighting full-time. But within a year or two it became clear that while he had easily beat most of his college opponents, and even held his own in his Golden Glove matches, his professional bouts were less likely to go his way. He was forced to scramble farther and farther afield to get bookings. He fought too hard and had too much of a chin to be hired by managers as a reliable palooka to match up with their up-and-comers, but he didn't win often enough to be considered an up-and-comer himself. More and more he found himself handed the walkout bout, the last fight on the card, which only the diehards bothered to stay and watch. When Daniel met Iris, he'd known for a while that he was through, and he quit without much objection, although with a significant amount of regret.

He had never stopped missing it, and now, more than ever, he ached to be back in the ring.

"Hey, buddy!" called the ham-and-egger behind the desk. "I *said*, can I help you?"

"You got a nice-looking gym here," Daniel said.

"Yeah. So?"

Daniel looked around, wishing that he could once again contract his life to this room, these smells, that he could climb into the ring and shut out the world. "So nothing," he said, and walked out the door.

V

They were gathered on the screen porch, Daniel with his sagging shoulders hunched against the doorpost, Ruthie lying on the couch with her head in Mr. Kimmelbrod's lap, and Iris in the chintz armchair, where she'd been sitting since before Daniel had left for the funeral home. Mr. Kimmelbrod had passed the night at his own house in town and had returned late this morning. Mary Lou Curran and another elderly woman, Vienna Gray, were also sitting with the family, perched on slatted chairs at one end of the long table.

The ample screen porch was a natural place for the family to congregate; it was where they spent most of their time in the summer. One of the first things they had done to the house upon taking it over was to add the porch onto the back, facing the sea. Iris had initially been loath to make such a drastic change to the footprint of the house. Generations of her family had sat outside in the backyard without benefit of screens, listening to the loons and watching the sky change colors, but although she had tried she had been unable to articulate to Daniel and her daughters' satisfaction the inherent moral superiority of stoically enduring the billowing swarms of quarter-sized mosquitoes that whined in their ears and raised welts on their skin.

Iris designed the porch herself. French doors allowed entrance from both the kitchen and the living room. For the floor she'd found wide sugar maple planks, salvaged from a defunct five-and-dime in Bangor, that matched those in the rest of the house. She had the builder trim out the framing around the huge screen windows to echo the house's egg-and-dart moldings. The ceiling was painted in the traditional sky blue, to match the ceiling of the open portico that wrapped around the front and south-facing sides of the house. After completing the porch, Iris had gone on to the rest of the house, painting the walls of the formal living room a mossy green, a lighter version of the deep forest of the banks of built-in bookcases, the long, deep window seats, and the box moldings in the ceiling. She had gone through various shades in the kitchen before settling on butter yellow and white. She had not done much else to the kitchen, and it looked now like an only slightly spruced-up version of her grandmother's, with the original slate sink, the massive O'Keeffe & Merritt enameled stove, and the assortment of hutches and armoires that had always substituted for built-in cabinets. Embroidered samplers dating back generations still decorated the walls, and the rag rug in front of the sink was one of a pile she'd found in a trunk in the attic. Most of the dishes, the silver, the assortment of baking pans and pots, had served generations of Hewins descendants. Iris's only innovation to the kitchen was an island, topped with thick gray granite from the mine on neighboring Okamok Isle, on which she rolled out pie dough.

Every change Iris made was carefully thought out in order to maintain the integrity of her great-great-grandfather's home. Thus, even when they renovated, as when they'd combined two small bedrooms into one large master suite, or added bathrooms, she had insisted that everything be appropriate to the house's history. For the new bathrooms she had found antique claw-foot tubs and pedestal sinks. If she couldn't find original fixtures, she didn't buy reproductions, but instead found modern fittings that were discreet enough not to jar the sensibility that the house maintained.

The house was well loved and well lived in. The sofas were soft and wide, the rugs at once brightly colored and worn with age. The house was full of the detritus of the lives of the Copakens and the generations of Hewinses before them—not just the photographs that crowded the mantelpieces and the tops of the cabinets, but things like a pair of Iris's grandmother's ice skates in the bottom of the hall closet, stacks of sheet music from Becca's childhood in the piano seat, children's artwork hanging on every wall, crinkled and yellowed linen pillowcases from the trousseau of a long-dead relative stuffed into the back of a drawer in the linen cupboard, nautical maps from a hundred years ago lovingly restored and framed, a box of children's costumes containing old prom dresses, a pile of old corsets and stays, dresses and jackets, suspenders and top hats—clothes Iris herself had dressed up in as a girl. The history of Iris's family was encoded and inscribed in every part of the old house, especially on the back of the living room door, which had not been painted for decades in order to preserve the evidence that generation after generation had recorded the growth of its children, from the very smallest, near the threshold, "Eliza, age 9 months," to a red mark six feet two inches from the floor, over which Iris had written Daniel's name. There were thirty-eight different names on the door, most appearing at least a dozen times. As they grew, Iris had marked her daughters' names near her own, so it was possible to see that while Becca at age two had been shorter than her mother at age two and a half, by the time she was thirteen she'd left Iris inches behind.

Now the Copakens gathered on their screen porch with crumpled faces, their red-rimmed eyes a stark contrast to the cheerful decor. People had been in and out all day, bringing food, sitting with them, patting their hands. And crying.

Iris was so tired of other people's tears, of the tears of a friend from the yacht club who'd known Becca since she was little, of a girl who worked in the food co-op, of an old teacher of Becca's from Usherman Center, of one of their New York friends who'd come up for the wedding. These people came ostensibly to offer comfort, but would invariably break down themselves, many as soon as they walked through the door. Iris and Ruthie would cry with them, a fresh bout of tears summoned by every new visitor. The visitors came to provide solace, and so the family's grief must be available for consolation, no matter how exhausted they felt, no matter that all Iris wanted to do was sit alone in a dark room, dry-eyed and sinking into deep shadow. Iris allowed her resentment to build, unaware that in a few months' time she'd be grateful for any sign that people remembered her loss.

Without intending it, the current visitors had caused a flurry of disagreement among the Copakens. Mary Lou and Vienna had come to let the family know that they weren't to worry about the food for after the funeral. A group of volunteers had been formed to take care of everything.

"We just need to know where you plan on doing things," said Vienna, a trim older woman with steel-colored hair chopped off at the chin.

"Doing things?" Daniel asked.

"After the cemetery. Will you come here? Or go to Jane's? Or perhaps somewhere else?"

Mary Lou Curran said, "Some of us thought maybe the Grange Hall, but then there was some question about that. Because of the wedding." Mary Lou and Vienna had been friends of Iris's mother. Like Iris and her mother, they had been spending their summers in Red Hook all their lives. In the few years since Mary Lou had taken up permanent residence, people had come to refer to her, both kindly and unkindly, as the unofficial mayor of the town.

"No, not the Grange Hall," Iris said. "We'll do it here. Unless Jane wants to have it at her house."

"I think Jane's planning something else," Daniel said.

"What do you mean?" Iris said.

"When I saw her at the funeral home she told me they are planning on holding a viewing starting day after tomorrow, and that they're going to bury him at the end of the week."

"At the end of the *week*?" Iris said. "Did you explain to her that we're not allowed to do that? That we've got to have her buried right away? Like, tomorrow?"

"No," Daniel said.

"Oh, for God's sake, Daniel. Why not?"

"I don't know."

Iris glared at him. "Well, did you at least talk about the graves? Where they'll be?"

"John's going to be buried in Frank's family plot in the Red Hook cemetery."

"In *his* family plot? That's crazy. They should be buried in *our* family plot. They should be buried *together*."

"I don't think Jane's thinking that way," Daniel said.

Iris said, "That's ridiculous!"

Vienna and Mary Lou exchanged a glance and then simultaneously got to their feet. "We'll leave you to discuss this on your own," Vienna said. She raised a restraining hand to Daniel, who had risen from his slump against the wall. "We'll see ourselves out."

After they had gone, Daniel turned to his wife. "What do you want to do, Iris? Do you want to bury Becca in your family's plot at the Red Hook cemetery? They don't have a Jewish section. They probably don't even have a Jew."

"They must," Ruthie said, sitting up. "There are plenty of Jews in Red Hook. Right, Grandpa?"

"Summer visitors," Mr. Kimmelbrod said gently. "They aren't buried here. Jewish law requires that a Jew be buried in consecrated land. That is why your grandmother is buried in New York."

Daniel said, "What do you want to do, Iris? There's a synagogue in Bangor, so there must be a Jewish cemetery. We could bury her there. Or we could take her home."

"First of all, when have you ever cared about Jewish law?" Iris said. "And second of all, we *are* home." It didn't matter that her own mother was born in the same hospital on 100th Street and Fifth Avenue where Iris showed up twenty-nine years later. It didn't matter that, except for her four years as an undergraduate at Swarthmore, and the two she spent at Oxford getting her master's degree, Iris had spent her entire life living in the same twenty blocks of Manhattan, first in a modest two-bedroom apartment with an extravagant view of Central Park, then with Daniel on West 78th Street, and finally, for the past twenty years, in a spacious apartment on the Columbia faculty's Gold Coast, Riverside Drive. Iris knew that to most people she seemed like a quintessential New Yorker: a Jew, and a professor of comparative literature with an acerbic wit and a short temper. Not, she knew, the typical biography of the Red Hook native. But Maine was her home, and that of her daughters, too, despite the fact that they'd been raised as city girls, Riverside Park their playground and their backyard, despite the fact that by the time they were in third grade, they knew the phone number for Empire Szechuan by heart.

"There are as many Hewinses in the Red Hook graveyard as there are Tetherlys or Stoddards. Becca belongs here," Iris said. "Dad, don't you think that would be better? We should bury Becca here."

"I can't say," Mr. Kimmelbrod said. "This is for you and Daniel to decide."

The thought, unbidden, came to Iris that her father had not always been so retiring when it came to decisions about Becca. It had been he, after all, who had given her permission to abandon her musical career, he who had said that Becca was correct in her assessment of her own abilities. "We'll bury Becca here," Iris said, firmly. "With my family, and with John. I don't believe in that 'consecrated land' business. I'm sure the rabbi who did the wedding won't mind if we bury her here, with her family."

"Whatever you want," Daniel said.

"That's what I want," Iris said. "We'll have the funerals together. I'll talk to Jane."

Daniel asked, "Do you want me to come?"

This would be, Iris thought, the first time she and Jane would interact not as employer and employee, nor as mothers of the wedding couple, nor in the crazed fog of that first hour after the accident. This was the first moment of their new relationship. Was there a Yiddish word for this new relationship, she wondered bitterly. Did *machetunim* apply when the points of contact were dead?

"I'll take care of it myself," Iris said.

VI

At six o'clock in the morning on the second day after the accident, Jane unlocked the door to the Unitarian church and hesitated on the topmost step, steeling herself against what she knew awaited her inside. The wide oak door seemed heavier than usual as she put her shoulder to it, and for a moment she felt an unfamiliar and intolerable lassitude. Then she shook it off, set her jaw, and shoved the door open. As she had expected, the church had not been cleaned. In the past, at the behest of the sexton, the ladies of the congregation would have assumed that responsibility, but now those willing to carry out the chore were too old, and the younger women, while happy enough to arrange flowers for the pulpit on a Sunday, were less inclined to get on their knees and polish the wooden pews. The small congregation could no longer afford a sexton's salary, and so instead had hired Jane's cleaning service to maintain the church for a nominal fee. It was her job, and she saw nothing undue or surprising in the fact that today, of all days, no one had thought to relieve her of it.

She had forgotten about the church herself until just a few hours ago, when she shot up in bed with a creak of the old oak bedstead, having passed the second night after the accident as she had passed the first: awake, watching the shadows cast by the tangled fringes of her bedside lamp play across the walls, noting the progress of a brownish water stain creeping across the ceiling. Last week she had asked John to take down a bit of the sheetrock to see if he could find the source of the leak, and he had promised to get to it as soon as he and Becca returned from their honeymoon. She was going to have to do the job herself now, and she would need a ladder. It was when she thought of the folding aluminum ladder they had used to light the tapers in the church's sconces that she remembered the mess and the burden that awaited her.

The nave looked forlorn, the candles burned down to stubs, the flowers wilted and brown at the edges. The aisle was littered with shriveled rose petals, and someone had torn loose one of the hydrangea garlands looped between the pews. Beneath the pulpit, a galvanized bucket of flowers had toppled over onto its side, leaving a white-rimmed water stain on the pale blue carpet. The rest of the carpet was spotted with smudged footprints and the tiny pockmarks left by stiletto heels. Jane shook her head. All those ladies from New York teetering around in their impractical shoes.

Armed with a bucket of cleaning supplies, Jane made her way down the aisle, ripping down the loops of garland and bundling them into a black leaf bag that she tied to her belt loop. The physical effort involved in jamming the garlands and the drooping and withered floral arrangements into the bag, of bending over to pick up bits of trash, of leaning into the pews to return the hymnals to their racks, did her good. Since losing her temper with the sheriff at Jacob's Cove, Jane had felt weighted down, numb, and lethargic, as though her blood had stopped flowing in her veins. But now the repetitive motion, the comforting, familiar exertion of cleaning, seemed to unbottle and roil all her stagnated feelings: Jane cleaned the church in a perfect fury. She was furious with Becca's spoiled-brat friends for having hired an out-of-town limousine when a car would have done; furious with the photographer for being so slow, so dawdling and methodical; furious with the Copakens for planning such an elaborate wedding; furious with John for having entangled himself with that useless, pretentious, hapless family in the first place. And, most of all, she was furious with her son, her good, strong, beautiful son, for dying.

She filled bag after bag with dead and dying flowers, and dragged the bulging sacks down the aisle behind her. She jabbed at the sconces with a penknife, prying loose the candle stubs, then scraping out the last bits of wax. She jerked the vacuum along behind her like a foolish, recalcitrant child, banging the brush loudly against the sides of the pews. She took care only when emptying the glass vases of their blown and rotting treasure: she could reuse the vases at the wake.

She had arrived at the church planning only to throw away the trash and vacuum up the rose petals. But by the time Iris showed up, Jane had polished the brass sconces, oiled the leather cushions on the seats behind the altar, and climbed the ladder to take a Q-tip to the seams in the wood of the window casings, scraping out years, generations, of dust. Jane was on the ladder, hands black with grime, strands of limp brown hair pasted to the sweat on her face, stinking of hard work and spray cleaner, when Iris walked in.

Iris hesitated in the doorway of the church, looking around with an expression of dull wonderment at the thoroughness, Jane supposed, with which Jane had erased all evidence of the wedding. The woman seemed to be looking for some trace—a flower arrangement, a candle, a card-stock program—but it was all gone, bagged and stacked and ready for a trip to the county dump.

"Matt said I'd find you here," Iris said.

From her perch Jane could see strands of white in the part of Iris's hair. She wondered for the first time if Iris might not be the older of the two of them. Because of the way she always dressed—like a teenager in jeans cut off at the knee or khakis and a wrinkled man's button-down shirt—Jane had always assumed that Iris was younger. Grief or insomnia had aged her by a dozen years.

"What do you need?" Jane said, and then, less harshly, "I mean, is there something I can do for you?"

Iris blinked, eyes huge and swimming in the thick lenses of her glasses. Jane had never seen her in anything but reading glasses, perched on the tip of her nose.

"It's about the funeral," Iris said. "Daniel and I . . . Jane, we really hope that you'll reconsider and agree that the children should be buried together."

So this was it, then. Iris had come to assert her will over this, as she had over the wedding, as she had even over John's education. Why, Jane wondered, had she imagined she would be free of Iris's intervention in how to bury her son?

Jane lowered herself slowly down the rungs of the ladder and followed Iris to the front pew, where she took a place as far from Becca's mother as civility would allow. As soon as she sat down she was overwhelmed by exhaustion, by a sense that she might never be able to get up again. She loathed the idea of sharing her son's grave with these people. However long John and Becca dated, they'd been married for less than an hour. Less than an hour! Why should they spend eternity side by side? Yesterday she had made it clear to Daniel that she was not interested in a joint funeral or a joint gravesite.

However, yesterday she had also been operating under the assumption that John would be buried in the small Tetherly plot that her ex-husband's grandfather had bought for his descendants. But when she got back from the funeral home and called Frank to tell him to make the arrangements with the undertaker, her ex-husband had informed her, without even a trace of sheepishness, that he had sold his interest in the plot years ago. "Didn't know I'd need it, did I?" he'd mumbled, clearly half in the bag. It was a miracle he could remember that he'd ever had anything to lose.

There was no Stoddard plot; Jane's family lay sown here and there throughout the cemetery. She would have to call Town Hall and inquire about a plot. No doubt she would end up with one of the new ones, across the road, far from the water. And even that would cost a bundle. Her business did well enough in the summer, but she had no cash reserves, and paying for the casket had already depleted the scant savings she possessed. The casket had been far too expensive—she had chosen a more elaborate one than she should have. To buy the casket and pay for the embalming she'd had to dip into the money she set aside every year for property taxes. She had no idea how much the burial plot would cost, but whatever it was, it would certainly be more than she could afford. She'd end up with no money with which to last out the winter.

"My family is all in the Red Hook Cemetery," Jane said now.

"That's fine. Mine is, too," Iris said.

Jane narrowed her eyes slightly. Iris was one of those from-aways who insisted on their Maine roots, as if a lifetime's worth of summers made you of a place. As if who your family was, what your stock was, wasn't what tied you, but rather just the fact of your presence. As if a Jew from New York who had never suffered through a black, bleak March in Red Hook had any idea what it meant to be a Mainer, or had any of the hardy tenacity it took to live here.

Iris continued, "My great-great-grandparents are buried in the Red

Hook cemetery. You know the tall white obelisk down by the water, to the left of the Wescott family crypt? That's my great-great-grandfather Elias Hewins. He bought all the area along the slope leading down to the bay for his family. For us. My grandmother's buried there, too. We could put Becca and John at the far edge, closest to the water."

It figured that Iris would own the nicest part of the whole graveyard, the area with the most magnificent view. The area where John would have most wanted to rest, if he had ever given a moment's thought to the question.

So there it was. Jane could insist on burying her son alone, away from his one-day wife and her summertime family, and go into debt to buy a strip of patchy grass on the far side of the road in a lot crammed between the post office and Granville's building supply. Or she could acquiesce and bury John with the view of the sea that he had loved, the water he had sailed and fished since he was a boy.

Jane said, "Fine."

Iris looked startled, taken aback by having gotten her way so easily. "Really?"

Jane shrugged, not quite believing it herself.

"You'll let us bury them together. In our plot."

"Might as well," Jane said.

"Thank you," Iris said. She extended her hand, as if about to touch Jane, but Jane reared back, and then discovered a sudden and pressing need to scrub a spot off the back of the pew with the rag she still held in her hand.

Iris pulled her hand back into her own lap and said, "Daniel said that you plan on having the viewing tomorrow."

"Yes."

"If you did it in the morning, we could have the funeral later on, in the afternoon."

"That's not the way it's done," Jane said, shaking her head. "People will need time, they'll want to come by after work, some will be coming from far away. We can't just do it all in one day."

"The problem is, as Jews, well, we don't embalm," Iris said, in the patient tone of voice Jane imagined she adopted with her slower students.

"Five days is a long time. Too long. I understand that you've always done things a certain way, but if you would consider a compromise we'd be so grateful."

As far as Jane could tell, when this woman asked for a compromise she was really demanding that things be done her way.

"We might be able to do it the next morning," Jane said.

"We really can't wait."

"Not even a single day?"

Iris bit her lip. Then she said, "Okay. I think we can do that."

"Good," Jane said. "We have our ways of doing things, too."

"No. No, of course. Thank you, Jane. Really." But this time Iris did not sound quite as grateful, and after that she seemed to run short of things to say to the woman alongside of whose son her daughter's body would lie until doomsday.

"I'd better finish up," Jane said.

Iris stood up. "I won't take any more of your time." She looked around the stripped and scrubbed church. "Did you—I'm sorry you had to clean this up on your own."

"No matter," Jane said. "It's done now."

Jane sat in the pew until she heard the church door click shut, leaving her alone once again. She leaned her head back against the pew and closed her eyes. It was a day, she told herself, a single day. A few hours that would be misery to get through, with or without Iris and the rest of the Copaken family. And after it was over she would have nothing more to do with them. After that there would be only a pair of gravestones by the sea.

And really, was that so bad? After so many years Jane had grown fond of Becca. Becca was a good kid. She didn't butt in where she didn't belong—she always waited to be asked, and then when you asked her for help or an opinion she gave it without drama or attitude, often as not with a smile, a cheerful remark. And the girl had loved John. That was obvious. If she had not come from a summer-cottager family, Jane probably wouldn't have had any objection to the marriage at all.

Jane gathered up her cleaning supplies, draining the bucket into the sink in the cleaning cupboard next to the sacristy, rinsing out the sponges, and stowing away the vacuum. On her way to return the ladder to its place, she happened to glance behind the pulpit. There, lying on its side, was Samantha's basket of petals, its lavender bow unknotted. Jane turned from it. She put the ladder away, and then wiped her dusty hands on her jeans.

Only once she'd rubbed away the worst of the dirt on her hands did she pick up the basket. For a moment she ran her fingers along the woven willow branches. She closed her eyes, remembering the frantic search for the basket, Samantha's annoying insistence on finding it before the photographs could be taken, Becca and John's patient indulgence of the girl. John had been such a fond and easygoing man; he had demanded so little. Kind and strong. Generous, perhaps to a fault. A son whom any mother would have been proud to call her own.

With an angry grunt Jane threw the basket to the ground and stamped on it. The sound of the willow splintering, the feel of the sticks breaking beneath her heavy shoe, satisfied her deeply. She brought her foot down again and again, until all that was left was a pile of broken sticks, a grimy twist of purple ribbon, and a smear of crushed petals. She crammed the broken bits of the basket into the last open trash bag, and hauled the bags out to her truck. On the way home she stopped at the county dump and swung the bags up onto a high, stinking mound of garbage, where they belonged.

VII

John Tetherly's relatives and friends were dressed in dark clothes—cheap black suits, navy blue skirts, black blouses, muted ties. Becca Copaken's mourners formed an odder assortment. Most of them had come up from New York for a wedding but stayed on for a funeral, and thus had nothing even remotely appropriate to wear. Even the regular summer people were at a loss. No one packed funeral clothes for a summer in Maine. Had it been a cold day things would have been easier—most people had a sweater or two tucked away in their luggage. But it was a perfect summer day: the sun sparkling off the water, not even a single white cap marring the calm sea. The summer people and the New York people had confronted a choice: to wear their casual Maine summer attire, their Easter-hued golf clothes or tennis whites, or the clothes they had worn to the wedding four days before. All chose the last. Once again they sat in the white clapboard church in their festive seersucker suits, their pastel linen sheath dresses, their silk summer prints, their gay ties, their open-toed sandals and white bucks.

The funeral wasn't as awkward as Iris had feared. Or, rather, it was so awful, painful, and miserable that all logistical difficulties were beside the point. The church, stripped by Jane of its wedding finery, looked bare. Its spartan Unitarian iconoclasm was far easier for a Jew to bear, Iris thought, than Catholic fripperies would have been. It was almost possible to forget that they were holding their daughter's funeral in a church.

The shutters were thrown open, letting in bold shafts of sunshine that tapered and crossed over the coffins. Iris sat in the same pew, in the same place she had occupied at the wedding, watching light fall in a lattice over the wood beneath which her daughter lay. There was no room in front of the pulpit for the caskets to lie side by side, so instead they lay end to end, Becca's simple pine coffin, its only ornament a Jewish star, like a rickety boxcar behind the gleaming locomotive that now held John. His casket was of burnished poplar, its four corners fitted with squat neoclassical columns carved at the tops with a figure of a sloop in full sail. At one end of the casket there extended a half-open drawer lined with powder-blue ruched satin, on which was embroidered the same sloop and the words "Sailing Home." In the drawer were keepsakes and messages from John's family and friends. The casket was grotesque, an unwitting parody of a sailor's casket, and although Iris had nothing to do with its selection, she was embarrassed by it. And yet, at the same time, she found herself wanting to explain to John's people that Becca's coffin was so simple not because she and Daniel were cheap but because Jewish law mandated a modest receptacle. Except that she wondered if the law might not really be about modesty and humility before God but instead might merely encode and validate the inherent miserliness of her people. Within a few days Iris wouldn't remember who spoke or what they said. But the two contrasting caskets, the mismatch between the boxes that Jane and Daniel had each chosen to hold the remains of their children was an image that would stay with her for the rest of her life.

After the service the pallbearers lined up on either side of the caskets. They were strapping men, John's relatives and friends, a few sons of friends of the Copakens, and Matt, poor Matt, the smallest and slightest among them. But after they had each taken hold of a handle, one remained unmanned, and for a moment there was a hint of confusion. Then a large man stepped forward and grabbed hold of the free handle. It took Iris a moment to recognize William Paige, dressed not in his sheriff's uniform but in a plain blue suit.

The pallbearers loaded the coffins into the two hearses, which then set off down Main Street. Most of the funeral guests chose to walk behind the hearses along the quarter mile of road that led from the church to the graveyard. The black hearses rolled slowly in the lead and stretched behind them like the long, multihued tail of a kite came the mourners, half in their somber suits, half in their gay wedding clothes. An older couple, tourists, wearing identical lobster T-shirts and moose-antler ball caps, walked out of Seafarer's Gifts and stopped in the middle of the sidewalk, staring. The husband raised his camera to his eye, but the wife, more sensitive than her attire might suggest, stilled his hand. A green minivan with New Jersey plates pulled up behind the last of the marchers and honked.

Because Mr. Kimmelbrod had needed Daniel to drive him to the gravesite, Iris and Ruthie walked alone at the head of the procession, directly behind the creeping second hearse. Over and over again Iris found herself reading the letters and numbers of its license plate, the word "Vacationland" repeating itself in her head.

As Iris passed a wooden sandwich board by the side of the road inviting her to a bean supper at the VFW, she pried her eyes away from the hearse and looked out over the water. Squinting at the boats in the harbor, she named them silently. *Wind Dancer*, the Fields' sloop. *Cool Change*, the Barretts' gaff-rigged cutter. *Afikomen*, the Ziffs' topsail schooner. Iris remembered how Becca used to call *Afikomen* Red Hook's token Jewish boat. Then, last summer, the new owner of the Red Hook Inn launched a Boston whaler named after his mother: *Mitzie's Mazel Tov*.

Today somebody had anchored a large brigantine in the reach, out beyond the small bay, and for a moment Iris watched the square sails on the first mast billow gently in the wind. Onshore, that wind calmed to a soft breeze that played over her cheeks and cooled the midafternoon air. Iris stopped and lifted her face to the breeze. She closed her eyes and stood, motionless but for the loose tendrils of her hair shifting in the gentle breath of wind.

"Mom?" Ruthie said, cupping her mother's elbow gently in her hand.

Iris startled, realizing suddenly that the hearse had pulled far ahead. Behind her the procession had bunched up and spread out, ground to a halt, no one willing to pass the grieving mother with her face turned to the sky and sea. She took a last look at the faraway boat, and then began to walk again, quickening her step to catch up to the hearses, which had by now turned into the cemetery. The procession followed the hearses as they drove between the two stone pillars and down the dirt road that wound among the gravestones. At the water's edge the hearses stopped opposite a large hole cut in the sod next to which someone had set up two rows of white plastic chairs. Mr. Kimmelbrod and Daniel stood at a slight remove from the grave.

The pallbearers brought the coffins down the slope from the hearses and settled each of them on one of the motorized lowering devices over the graves. Mr. Burpee, the undertaker, owned only one such device; he had recently upgraded to a Master, with a telescoping stainless-steel stand, selling his old Standard to help defray the cost. In thirty-four years of burying the dead, he had never before needed two units at once, and to meet today's needs he had been obliged to borrow a second device from a Bangor colleague, an old Imperial, not as nice or new as his own. He had briefly considered lowering one of the coffins with a simple arrangement of straps and poles, but the idea of one coffin gliding smoothly down into the hole on its cams while the other jerked and lurched in the gravediggers' hands offended him. Especially because it would make the most sense, in that case, to use the motor on the heavy poplar casket and let the boys struggle with the lighter pine box. With the deceased girl being a Jew from away and the boy a local, he feared people would have interpreted the disparity in lowering devices as prejudice. Which it certainly was not. Mr. Burpee had no problem with Jews, in spite of the fact that it cost next to nothing to bury one.

Iris and Ruthie came up to where Daniel and Mr. Kimmelbrod were standing and Iris took her father's arm as they walked across the grass to the plastic chairs set up in front of the double grave. She helped him into his seat and then sat down next to him. Jane, who had walked far behind, at the tail end of the procession, sat at the other end of the row. There were three empty chairs between them.

"Ruthie, come sit down," Iris said.

Ruthie sat next to her mother, and then Maureen, after settling her two daughters and little Samantha in the second row, took the seat next to Jane. Maureen turned to her brother. "Matt," she said, patting the seat between her and Ruthie.

"It's okay," Matt mumbled. Two splotches of dark red stood out on his pale cheeks. "You take it," he said to Daniel.

"That's all right, son," Daniel said. "You go ahead."

The chair remained empty as the silver-haired minister stepped forward and intoned Psalm 23. They were indeed in a green pasture by quiet waters, Iris thought. But she felt no one guiding her on the path to righteousness or anywhere else. Each of them was utterly alone in the valley of the shadow of death. Each grief separate and unique. Iris couldn't imagine goodness, mercy, and love following her now, even on a glittering summer day like today. Not with her daughter lying in the dark in a plain pine box.

After the minister said what he had to say, the rabbi began to pray in Hebrew. He was redheaded and unprepossessing, and so short that the bald spot incompletely covered by a maroon velvet yarmulke on the top of his dead barely grazed the reverend's bony chin. An angry red rash was doing its best to escape the confines of his beard. But his voice as he led them in the Kaddish was deep and sonorous, a nourishing stew served in a battered tin cup. There were few people, even among those who had never before heard the Jewish prayer for the dead, who didn't cry. One of the few to remain stubbornly dry-eyed was Mr. Kimmelbrod, for whom the prayer meant little, so many of his family having been sent to their deaths without even the minimal comfort of its incantation.

As the caskets were lowered into the ground, the whir of the motor reverberated in Iris's head. Suddenly she regretted her decision not to look inside the coffin when the undertaker had offered to open it for her. At the time she had said no at once, but now she felt a desperate urge to yank open the lid before it was too late—for what? To ensure that Becca was really there? To take her dead body out of its box and hold it one last time? Iris clenched her jaw and closed her eyes.

She tried to will herself not to remember the quarrel with Becca over John's boat that had marred the afternoon of the ceremony. Why had Iris not apologized? How could she have let an argument, a stupid disagreement over money, become the last substantive conversation she ever had with her daughter?

She closed her eyes and listened not to the voice berating her inside her head but to the sounds coming from the crowd of mourners. The creak of a chair, the rustle of a skirt in the breeze, a nose being blown. She felt the presence of all these people massed behind as a single entity, breathing, pressing, urging her along on a path she had no desire to follow. She tried to remind herself that she was grateful to have so many people, so many friends and relatives, here. The funeral had drawn a sizable crowd: all the wedding guests, and then many people from town to whom a death offered a kind of hospitality that the wedding had denied them. Whether they were here for Becca or John didn't matter. Only that they'd come.

When Ruthie stood up, Iris opened her eyes. The undertaker's assistant offered Ruthie a miniature shovel. Ruthie scooped up some dirt from the small pile next to the graves and set off across the plank of wood covering the raw earth. She was shaking, and so dirt sprinkled from the shovel, like flour sifted for a cake, until finally the shovel was empty, even before she reached the graves. The undertaker's assistant tried to hand her a long white rose from a basket he had looped over his forearm but she ignored him. She turned back to the pile, dropped the shovel, and scrabbled with her hands in the dirt. She walked quickly along the plank of wood to the open grave and dropped her handful in, carefully sprinkling some over each coffin.

Daniel went next. He, too, stepped past the rose-bearing attendant, took the shovel from the pile, and began to shovel dirt into the grave. The shovel was bright and shiny with a small blade. The muscles of Daniel's back strained against the fabric of his jacket as he dug the toy shovel into the pile of earth. He planted his feet in their bright white running shoes and heaved load after load of earth, as if it were his job to fill the entire grave. The dirt thunked and rattled on the coffin tops. The undertaker, a man whose profession demanded the capacity to be unsurprised by any expression of grief, glided smoothly over to Daniel and put his hand under his elbow.

"How about I take that for you, sir?" he said, indicating the shovel. "You did a good job."

Daniel straightened up and blinked sweat out of his eyes. He looked into the undertaker's blank and comforting face and turned the tiny shovel over, spilling the dirt back on the depleted pile.

The undertaker raised an eyebrow to his young assistant, who lifted an edge of the sod covering the mound next to the double grave and shoveled a little more dirt onto the pile. Then the young man stood the shovel back in the pile and stepped away, his head bowed.

It was her turn now, but Iris found that she could not get up. She tried to stir herself, but she was too heavy, too tired, too sad. She turned a panicked face to her father, who nodded his head once and mouthed the word "Sit." She relaxed against the chair as if she had sought only his permission, and watched as Maureen grabbed a rose and, her bulk precariously balanced at the lip of the graves, tossed it into the hole. Her two daughters followed their mother's example, but when Samantha's turn came the girl hesitated, glancing from Jane to Iris. She took two roses, but also scooped up some dirt in the small shovel, which was for her the perfect size. She tipped the dirt into the grave and then carefully dropped the flowers into the grave, one on Becca's coffin, the other on John's, as if trying by her meticulousness to make up for her failure with the bridal flowers.

Slowly people began stepping forward to make the choice between flowers and dirt that their heart or heritage demanded. Some followed Samantha's lead and took both. Iris hated the white roses, waxy and coarse. Yet if they had been beautiful, it would have been worse. A crime, a kind of vandalism, to crush the loveliness of flowers beneath shovelfuls of earth. She closed her eyes and listened as handfuls of dirt whispered onto the caskets.

It was only after everyone else had finished filing past the open grave and moved on that Iris realized Jane had also stayed in her chair. For a moment the mothers of the dead remained in their places. Then, as if resolved to do what must be done, Jane rose. She stared at the grave, at the mound of earth, at the shovel and the nearly empty basket of flowers. Then, with a shake of her head, she grabbed her folding chair and collapsed it with a loud snap. She handed it to the disconcerted undertaker's assistant and marched away, without a glance at her family, leaving them to follow after.

Mr. Kimmelbrod planted his cane into the ground and rose unsteadily to his feet. "Iris?" he said.

She closed her eyes again. For the past four days the funeral had loomed, an end in itself. As if *this* was what she had to get through; *this* was the miserable task she needed to accomplish. Every action she had taken—confronting Jane at the church, approving Mary Lou and Vienna's menu, ironing her skirt—had been geared toward this moment. Now the funeral was over. Now there was nothing but the hollow expanse of a life without her daughter.

"Iris," Mr. Kimmelbrod repeated. "It's time now." He took one hand off his cane and held it out to her. "I need your help to walk across the grass."

Iris looked from her husband to the child that was left her. They waited on the other side of the grave. Then she turned to her father, standing beside her. Finally she rose. Mr. Kimmelbrod put his hand in the crook of her elbow and together they turned away from the graves.

"Wait a minute, Dad," Iris said. Stepping carefully on the plank, she knelt down, and smoothed out the wet, wadded tissue she held in her hand. She took a handful of dirt. It was dry and pebbly, and some leaked through her fingers. She poured the dirt into the tissue and then folded it into a tiny bundle. She hesitated for a moment, wondering where to put it. She had neither purse nor pockets.

"Give it to me," Daniel said.

She handed him the soggy tissue and rubbed her gritty palm on her hip, leaving a smear of dirt on the khaki fabric of her skirt. She clasped her daughter's hand, gave her father her other arm, and led them across the grass to where the cars were parked, Daniel trailing a few steps behind.

VIII

A dozen books piled in her arms, Ruthie bumped her hip against the handicapped-accessible button and stepped back to allow the library doors to swing slowly open. She strode through the door, eyes down to elude any random sympathetic glances that might be cast in her direction. She made it to the circulation desk just as she began to lose her grip on the books.

It was Mary Lou Curran's day volunteering behind the desk, a task that members of the library board shared during August when, with the influx of late-summer visitors, the circulation of books doubled. Normally, Iris would have been obliged to take a shift or two, but after the accident the board had met in special session and voted to absolve her of the responsibility for the rest of the summer. Mary Lou's hand had been the single one raised in opposition to the motion. Without knowing it, she and Ruthie shared similar notions about the burdens of sympathy. Mary Lou was convinced that it would have done Iris more good to stick to her usual routines than to hole up in the house.

"My goodness," Mary Lou said, stacking Ruthie's books neatly on top of one another. She flipped open a book, and glanced at the due date. "Overdue," she said. "That's not like you. And since when do you read John Grisham?"

A few days ago, Ruthie had received an e-mail from the head librarian gently informing her that a number of books checked out by Rebecca Copaken were now long overdue. "I don't want to trouble your mother at such a time," the librarian wrote. "But there are nearly twenty people on the waiting list for *Harry Potter and the Order of the Phoenix*, and almost as many for *The Last Juror*." Ruthie had not been willing to trouble Iris, either—about the books or anything else. In the six weeks since the funeral her mother had burrowed deep. She spent hours in her saggy armchair on the screen porch, sometimes not even bothering to change out of the old plaid pajama bottoms and white T-shirt of Daniel's that she slept in during the summer. For hours she intently perused back issues of Oxford University's *Holocaust and Genocide Studies*, which was not that different from the way she'd passed all the previous summers of Ruthie's life, Ruthie supposed, except that now Iris no longer punctuated her days of grim research with jaunts on the whaler, sailing with friends, or picnic excursions to Red Hook Hill. Ruthie was not surprised that her mother had become more remote and inaccessible in her grief, nor did she begrudge her for needing to do it; but understanding and accepting her mother's reaction did little to alleviate her own loneliness.

Like her mother, books had offered Ruthie refuge since the accident. Ruthie had retreated to the familiar, rereading all of George Eliot from *Adam Bede* to *Daniel Deronda*. In her return stack was a copy of *Middlemarch*, which was one of her favorite novels. This time her melancholy had infected her appreciation of Eliot's wit.

Ruthie had taken upon herself the task of tracking down and rounding up Becca's library books. This was, in truth, not much different than what Ruthie had always done for her sister. Even as little girls, Ruthie had been neat and orderly, Becca sloppy. When Iris would demand that Becca clean her room, as often as not Ruthie would do it for her. Ruthie had always organized Becca's closet, added her name to cards on presents to make up for her forgetfulness, and returned her library books.

The legal thrillers and murder mysteries that were all that Becca ever read had been scattered and secreted all over the house. Some had even migrated onto the bookcases, where they hid next to generations of summer reading, her great-grandmother's bloated paperbacks, her mother's various literary volumes, her father's biographies and histories. Armed with the e-mailed list, Ruthie found books that Becca had borrowed months before, and one, a water-bloated copy of a Stephen King novel, another edition of which Ruthie knew resided on the bookshelf in Daniel's office, that had been due in June. Of last year. Ruthie arrived at the library this morning with eight of the eleven overdue titles. She had a good idea where the other three were, but she had not been able to bring herself to enter Becca's room to search for them.

Mary Lou took her hand-held scanner and began scanning the bar codes. "Ah," she said. She gave Ruthie a small but understanding smile.

Ruthie said, "They're all really late. Some of them . . ." She fumbled for her purse.

"Oh, don't worry about the fines," Mary Lou said. She tapped a few keys on the computer. "All gone."

"It's all right," Ruthie said. "I brought money."

"Absolutely not," Mary Lou said, pushing away the wad of bills Ruthie pressed on her.

"Please," Ruthie said. "I insist."

Mary Lou considered the matter. "If your money's really burning a hole in your pocket, you might want to bail your young friend here out of trouble. She's a notorious deadbeat."

Ruthie turned and found little Samantha Phelps standing behind her, clutching a substantial pile of books in her skinny arms. Her hair was done up in two painfully tight pigtails and she wore a pair of cutoff shorts and a T-shirt that was at least two sizes too big.

"They're *not* late!" Samantha said. "I know they're not late." She dropped to the ground and began flipping through the books. She seemed to be both outraged and terrified by the idea of having incurred overdue fines. "See!" she said. "August fifth! That's tomorrow. They're not late."

Mary Lou smiled. "Of course they're not, honey. I was just teasing."

Ruthie helped Samantha get to her feet and gather up her things from the carpet, where, in her haste to defend herself, she had dropped them.

"You like audiobooks," said Ruthie, handing Samantha a plastic box containing cassette tapes of Kipling's *Just So Stories*.

"I like the ones with music," Samantha said.

"*Classical Literature with Classical Music*," Ruthie read. "That sounds fun. Did you like the Kipling?"

"It's okay." Samantha shuffled her feet, clearly eager to slip away. "I like the Bach." She pronounced it to rhyme with catch.

Ruthie wrinkled her brow, unable to understand the mispronounced reference. "When I was little *Rikki-Tikki-Tavi* was my absolute favorite story. Do you know that one?" Introducing someone to a book she might love had always been one of Ruthie's greatest pleasures.

Samantha said, "It's on the tape."

"Oh, good. Well, did you like it?"

"Yes," Samantha said. "Especially the music." She looked down at her feet, her long bangs falling across her eyes. Ruthie felt the urge to smooth them away, but instead she crouched down next to the girl and said, "How's your aunt?"

"Okay."

"And Matt?"

"Okay."

"Everyone's pretty much okay, huh?" Ruthie said, gently teasing.

Samantha flushed and glanced down at her feet. She was wearing sandals a size too big for her, her toes hidden beneath the Velcro strap. Ruthie gave into her urge and reached out and tugged gently on one of Samantha's pigtails. The girl stilled beneath her hand. Ruthie could not tell if she found the touch pleasant or disturbing.

"You remember me, right?" Ruthie said.

"You're Becca's sister. Ruthie."

"Yes," Ruthie said. She wanted to say something more, to continue the conversation, maintain the connection, but couldn't think of anything. "Well, you tell everyone I say hi."

"Okay."

Samantha slipped out from beneath the unbearable burden of Ruthie's palm and ran down the hall in the direction of the children's room.

"She's an odd little duck," Mary Lou said. "She's had a hard life, though, hasn't she? That poor mother of hers. It was sweet of Becca to include her in the wedding. I'm sure it meant the world to her."

Ruthie flinched at the casual use of Becca's name. She could not get used to hearing it spoken aloud.

Mary Lou, seeing Ruthie's discomfort, patted her hand and said, "You'll be all right, dear. You know that, don't you? It just takes time."

Ruthie felt tears gathering on her lashes. She blinked them back.

Mary Lou asked, "How is your mother holding up?" Before Ruthie could even begin to fabricate a plausible reply, Mary Lou added, "No, of course. I know. You just give her my regards, won't you?"

Ruthie nodded. She had planned to choose a few books for herself, but suddenly the task seemed insurmountable.

She turned to leave and found herself face-to-face with Matt Tetherly.

"Oh!" she said.

"Hey, Ruthie," he said.

He looked terrible, black smudges not just under his eyes but around them. His lips were so chapped they were peeling. He licked them now, nervously.

"Hey," Ruthie said.

"I was just looking for Samantha." He glanced beyond Ruthie to Mary Lou. "Has she been by to check out her books?"

"She dropped some off," Mary Lou said. "I imagine she went off to choose some more. If I know that girl it's going to take her some time. You'd best find a seat. Or, better yet, go on over to the New Releases table. The new Tracy Kidder just came back, and I know how much you loved *The Soul of a New Machine*."

"I read that!" Ruthie said. "For a psych class on obsession and compulsion."

"Really?" Matt said. "I mean, I guess I can see that. The guys it profiles are complete workaholics."

"Have you read *House*?" Ruthie asked. "That's the book of Kidder's that I really love."

"I didn't read that one. I'm not really interested in architecture or construction."

"I'm not either, but I thought it was really compelling."

Mary Lou, tapping away on her computer, announced, "*House* is in. For some ludicrous reason it's in home improvement. Which probably explains why no one has checked it out in four years. Ruthie, why don't you take Matt upstairs and find it for him."

Ruthie and Matt blushed and looked away from each other self-consciously.

"Go on," Mary Lou said, brooking no disobedience.

As they made their way up the stairs Ruthie said, "You don't have to check it out if you don't want to."

Matt shook his head. "Oh, you bet I do. And I've got to read it, too. She'll be quizzing me on it next time I come in."

Ruthie giggled, and then stopped in her tracks, aghast. She could not believe that she had laughed. Actually laughed. As if anything could be funny now.

Matt glanced back and saw her frozen two steps below. He came back down and stood next to her, not touching her. "It's okay," he said.

His voice was impossibly soft and gentle, and although such sympathy from anyone else would have immediately caused her to break down yet again, this time she felt something ease inside of her. "Let's go get you that book," she said.

She found it for him quickly. He followed her back downstairs and stopped at the circulation desk to check it out. She stood next to him for a moment and then murmured, "I'd better go." Before he could answer she turned on her heel and, with a hasty good-bye to Mary Lou, left the library.

After a quick stop at the market to buy milk, eggs, and a tub of the Moose Tracks ice cream her father was so fond of, Ruthie headed for home. To get from the center of town to East Red Hook without traveling on Red Hook Road past Jacob's Cove was an exercise in complicated navigation that involved nearly fifteen miles of driving, much of it on dirt roads in various states of ill repair. Still, despite the fact that it turned a twelve-minute drive into one that could last as long as forty-five minutes, depending on whether you had the bad luck to get stuck behind a tractor, this was the route that Ruthie had been taking since the accident.

Today, however, during the few minutes she'd spent in the library, a pickup pulling a six-horse trailer had managed to jam itself across the width of the road, its front end hovering over the ditch on one side of it, the rear of the trailer pressed firmly up against a wide tree stump on the other. The driver, a string bean of a man with the long, cadaverous face and the deep-set, dark-rimmed eyes of an Edward Gorey character, leaned against the side of the trailer smoking a cigarette.

Ruthie rolled down her window, "Excuse me," she said. "Are you stuck?"

The driver raised an eyebrow and took a long drag on his cigarette, the ash drawing down nearly to his fingers.

"Are you waiting for a tow truck?" she said.

"Yeah," he replied, drawing out the word in a Maine accent so thick it sounded put on.

"Do you know how long it'll be?"

The man shrugged. "He'll get here when he gets here, won't he?"

Ruthie rolled her window back up and rested her forehead on the steering wheel, imagining the ice cream turning to soup in her reusable canvas shopping bag. After a few moments she put the car into reverse and headed back through town, turning sharply onto Red Hook Road.

She drove quickly at first, taking the turns too fast, allowing her car to drift perilously close to the opposing lane. But as she approached Jacob's Cove, she slowed to the speed limit, checked her mirrors, and began to pay close attention to oncoming traffic. When she rounded the final curve she slowed down even further, fixing her eyes on the asphalt immediately in front of her car, willing herself not to look to her right. She made it nearly all the way past the beach when finally, unable to resist it any longer, she glanced into her rearview mirror.

The strip of beach was full of people lying on gaily striped towels, sitting in beach chairs, making their painstaking way down across the pebbles to the water. An inflatable boat bobbed in the shallow water near the shore, and as she watched, two small boys wearing bright orange life vests grabbed each other's hands and tumbled together over the side and into the water. They bobbed immediately to the surface. Ruthie's eyes filled, but the blare of a car horn snapped her to attention. Her car had begun to drift to the center of the road, too close to an oncoming car. She jerked the steering wheel, overcorrecting, and for a moment her tires bumped along the shoulder. By the time she reached the village and pulled into her driveway, she had stopped crying.

IX

In the meadow behind Jane's house stood a ramshackle barn, long ago painted red but now faded to a murky, peeling brown. John had laid claim to the barn the moment they had moved into the house soon after Jane and Frank's divorce, and it had always been his exclusive domain. Matt was never excluded, but to enter he had always to request permission, a ritual he continued to observe, under his breath, whenever he crossed the threshold, despite the fact that John was no longer there to grant or deny it. It was years now since Matt and John had hauled eleven truckloads of trash out of the barn: generations' worth of broken furniture, empty crates, rotted sails, car batteries spiderwebbed with acid dust, reeking buoys. It had taken them more than a week to empty the barn enough to make room for John's derelict schooner, *Rebecca*. They set up the barn as a makeshift dry dock, and John proceeded over the next few years to renovate the boat, with Matt as his eager assistant and dogsbody.

Coming home from Jacob's Cove on the night of the accident, Matt had crawled up into the half-finished old Alden and stretched out along the inside of the hull, resting his cheek on the smooth planks. He had lain there all night and into the morning, until Maureen had barged into the barn and hollered at him to stop crying like a baby and get his ass inside with the rest of the family where he belonged.

For weeks afterward, Matt had lain around the house playing video games, watching TV, and reading. He'd never returned to work at the yacht club after John's funeral, and after a couple of weeks his mother had given up bothering him about it. His only excursions had been to the library, where he would spend an hour or two surfing the Internet before checking out a pile of books to bring home.

But today, after seeing Ruthie in the library, he found his usual distractions unsatisfying. He tried reading the book she'd recommended, which he had to admit was compelling enough, despite its subject matter, but he couldn't concentrate. There was nothing on TV, and playing video games had come to make him miss John too much. John had given him a PlayStation 2 for Christmas last year, a gift as much for himself as for Matt. It wasn't the same playing Dragon Ball Z or Final Fantasy X on his own.

Finally, he wandered over to the barn and stood in the shadow of the Alden's bereft carcass, staring up at it. He had loved working on the boat with his brother, listening to music, shooting the shit. Just like when they were kids and their aunt used to send them out on their uncle's lobster boat to pull his traps when he was too drunk to do it himself. Their father, as big a drunk as their uncle, hadn't been around much, and even when he was there he would never have dreamed of patiently teaching Matt the right way to handle a router or a caulking gun, or even how to hammer a nail.

John had planned to finish the boat by the next summer, then sail it down to the Caribbean, where he and Becca would get into the luxury charter business. The Alden, though measuring only a bit over forty-eight feet, was roomier than she looked. She'd been designed with full, deep ends, a high freeboard, and a generous beam that allowed for two staterooms—one large and elegant, the other small but fitted neatly—a good-sized galley, and an enclosed head with a comfortable shower. The amidships saloon was well proportioned, with a transom, two berths, and a large drop-leaf table. The idea was that Becca would cook gourmet meals for the rich people, and John would show them a good time: pick pretty coves to drop anchor in, take them out snorkeling. John would always include Matt in this grand scheme, saying that his brother could come down and crew for them after he graduated from Amherst, and Matt would always reply that he had plans of his own: graduate school in oceanography, hopefully at Scripps out in San Diego, where he could study the effects of climate change on the oceans, a field that had obsessed him from the first time he read about what rising sea levels would do to coastal regions like Down East Maine. John would remind Matt that he would still have vacations, and Matt would agree to help him finish the boat, then join him and Becca in the Caribbean for a week every Easter, because their mom would expect him home at Christmastime.

Matt looked around at the tools John had left neatly in their places, at the stacks of hardwood, the cans of varnish. On a makeshift drawing table—just a wooden door propped on two sawhorses—there was a small stack of drawings and blueprints, held down by a well-thumbed copy of Skene's *Elements of Yacht Design*. John's years' worth of *WoodenBoat* magazines filled a small, rough-hewn bookshelf. There was a layer of dust over everything, and when Matt moved the Skene to look at the drawings beneath it, it left behind a clean, square ghost. The topmost drawing was a photocopy of a detailed blueprint of the Alden that John had found in a volume of Alden plans and drawings. Beneath it were drawings he'd made himself, labeled in the precise, confident architect's handwriting that Matt had always envied and admired. Matt's own scribble was illegible even to himself.

Matt gazed from the drawings to the boat and back again, wondering how much work there really was left to do. He flipped through Skene, tried to understand the full-page complicated renderings and schematics. None of it meant anything to him, but he was a quick study, and had been working all this time by his brother's side. Surely there were simpler books than this one, ones that laid out the process of restoration in a way even he could understand. And there were the guys at the boatyard. John's friends. They'd help him.

Inspired, he decided to head on over to the Neptune and see if he could find someone who might be willing to talk to him about the project. But for some reason, when he got to town, he turned right onto Red Hook Road and drove to Jacob's Cove. He slowed down as he drove up to the cove. He pulled off the road onto the broad shoulder. The tide was low, and he could pull the car out onto the rocky strip of beach, facing the water. He turned off the engine, stared out over the water, and let himself remember. WKIT had been playing "Little Wing" by Jimi Hendrix. One minute he was rocking out to the music, and then the next, framed in the windshield of his car was a Ford Explorer sailing through the air in awful slow motion toward the limousine ahead of him. As Hendrix's weary, spacey, soulful voice sang in his head, Matt watched the Explorer drift down on top of the limousine, crumpling it like tinfoil. The noise of the accident still echoed in his brain: an impossibly loud boom, followed by the grinding screech of metal on metal. The limo spun around and careened across the beach, its back end plowing into the bay, sending up arcs of water that shimmered in the orange-red light.

Now hearing the song in his head, things played out differently. "*Riding with the wind*": the Explorer climbs up the shoulder. "*When I'm sad, she comes to me*": the limo swerves away from the truck. "*With a thousand smiles, she gives to me free*": the Explorer plows into the trunk of a white pine, splintering the wood but grinding to a halt. "*It's all right she says it's all right*": the limo driver slams on his brakes and stops short just before hitting the water. "*Take anything you want from me, anything*": the passenger door opens and John steps out. "*Anything*": he lifts his hand and waves to Matt, his back to the sun, his body lit from behind, his face in shadow, but his broad grin still, somehow, visible. "*Anything. Anything.*" Safe and sound.

Matt left the cove and, instead of turning around and heading back into town, drove the rest of the way to East Red Hook. He pulled off the road again, at the lookout next to the little bridge over the reversing falls on the outskirts of the village. At low tide the streambed was a bog of brackish mud, puddles teeming with minnows, and boulders drying white in the sun. At high tide the flow of the stream reversed, the sea rushed in, and the water soon grew deep enough to jump into. From the moment the bridge was built by the WPA in 1935, village kids had entertained themselves at high tide by standing on its rail, waiting until a likely car approached, and then pinwheeling their arms in mock panic and flinging themselves into the water below. Reliably, at least a few times every summer a car full of panicked tourists would screech to a halt.

Whenever he drove this way Matt always tried to watch for the exact moment of the tide's reversal. Would the water foam and swirl, like a huge Jacuzzi tub? Would it slow to a stop and then gradually creep out to sea, like a locomotive grinding into reverse? Would it arc around, like a sailboat coming about to catch the wind? He had never in his life managed to appear at the right time, however; had never been able to catch the exact moment when everything changed.

From the lookout Matt could see the back of the Copakens' house and of the Grange Hall. The Copakens' house shone, its shutters liquid black against the bright white clapboard. Most people Matt knew didn't even bother to paint the rear of their houses. The backsides were often the same dull, peeling red of their barns, or sometimes just bare, weathered planking. Every summer the Copakens' house looked as if it had just received a fresh coat of shiny paint.

A lush, verdant lawn led from the house down to the water and the long white dock, where two dinghies were tied up. The Copakens' beat-up 150 Montauk was moored a few dozen yards out, next to the little sailboat that had belonged, John had once told him, to Becca's grandmother. Suddenly, Matt saw a spiraling white flash take off from the end of the dock. Around and around it spun, higher and higher into the sky, until, with a crack, it became a starburst of light and, fizzling quickly, plummeted to the water. He got out of the car.

It took a little while for the girl standing on the end of the dock in the gloaming to notice him. When she did, she lifted her arm and waved. Matt hesitated only for a moment before taking off at a loping jog across the bridge and down the rocky slope to the beach. He ran up the beach toward her, stumbling once over a piece of dark-gray driftwood.

"It's you," Ruthie said, when, out of breath, he pounded out onto the dock. She had changed her clothes. Her long, bare thighs disappeared beneath the hem of her navy hooded sweatshirt, and he couldn't tell if she was wearing shorts underneath or just a bathing suit. Or less. The collar of the sweatshirt was torn, and above the gaping neckline he could see her bony clavicle beneath her pale skin. She was barefoot, with long, skinny toes and delicate, narrow feet. Heaped next to her was a small cardboard Sam Adams case filled with fireworks.

Once or twice when they were growing up, John and Becca had joked about fixing him up with her sister, but it was only teasing, and Matt always understood that to Ruthie, two years older, he was just a kid. Until now he had never really considered her a peer, a woman, anything but Becca's sister.

"Hi," he said.

"Pretty sweet, huh?" Ruthie said, nudging the box of fireworks with her toe. Her toenails were unpainted, and her foot looked soft, delicate.

"Yup," he said.

"Only I don't think it's really dark enough yet."

"No, not quite."

"I found these in the barn," she said. "They're left over from . . ." Her voice trailed away. He saw now that her nose and the rims of her eyes were pink and faintly swollen.

On the Fourth of July—the night before the wedding—they had held the rehearsal dinner in the Copakens' backyard, a more festive version of the yearly Fourth of July picnic that was the family's tradition. John had been in regular attendance at the yearly picnic, but this was the first time Matt and the rest of his family had been invited. The Tetherlys came—all but Frank, to everyone's relief. The members of the bridal party were there, as well as a number of relatives of the Copakens. There were a dozen or so out-of-town guests and a good many of Iris's and Daniel's friends. Iris served boiled lobster, big bowls of coleslaw and potato salad, and a pot of homemade bean-hole beans baked from a recipe that supposedly came down to her from her grandmother. Iris and Becca had made half a dozen pies, and Matt's mom had contributed John's favorite dessert, a Nilla wafer banana pudding. And at the end of the evening John had given them a fireworks show.

That dinner was the last meal Matt ever shared with his brother. John had been too hungover and nervous to eat much of anything on his wedding day. While Matt's memories of the wedding itself were now completely overshadowed by the tragedy, he could recall with perfect accuracy how happy they had all been at the rehearsal dinner, making toasts, pouring wine, talking about how full they all were before ladling themselves another helping of beans.

"That was a nice party," Matt said. "I mean, John and Becca seemed so happy and all."

At the sound of their names, Ruthie twitched. For the first couple of weeks Matt had felt the same way. Every mention of the names of the dead seemed to light a small hot fire inside him. Then one day a few weeks back he woke up and found that, suddenly, the opposite was true: it was the minutes, the hours, the entire days that went by without someone mentioning John that hurt Matt the most. He had tried to talk about John to his mother, but that went nowhere. So he had started hanging out with John's friends. Every evening he would head over to the Neptune, and stake out a stool in the middle of the bar. As people trickled in they would stop and pass a few minutes with him. Some offered no more than their condolences, some tried to buy him a beer. And that was okay. But what Matt was waiting for were the stories. About the birch bark canoe with swept-up gunwales and a squared bow that John and a friend had built for a middle school project on the Passamaquoddy tribe. About how one hunting season, when another buddy was laid up with a broken leg, John had filled his freezer with venison steaks, because he knew the guy relied on his yearly buck to feed his family. They'd retell John's jokes—Matt must have heard the one about the robber in the sperm bank a dozen times. They'd remind one another about practical jokes John had played on them. The guys, as sad as they were, as much as they missed their friend, always ended up laughing, especially once they'd had a few. And if Matt rarely laughed out loud with them, as long as he was sitting on that barstool he felt okay. He felt like he was close to his brother. He was dreading the end of the summer, dreading the prospect of going back to college and being surrounded by people who had never known John, who had never laughed at his jokes or been the beneficiaries of his unsolicited largesse, who didn't know or care that he was dead.

"I guess we bought too many fireworks," Matt said now.

The weekend before the wedding Matt and John had driven over to New Hampshire. For some crazy reason, John had decided that they'd do the whole drive on back roads, and they'd ended up switchbacking their way through the miles. Half the time it seemed like they were heading east to go west or north to go south.

"I told him to ease up a little, but John just couldn't resist those Catherine wheels and mortar shells."

"It was like, what, a couple of hundred dollars' worth of fireworks?" Ruthie said.

"At least. This stoner kid running the stand sold us a bunch of stuff he shouldn't have. Stuff you're supposed to be licensed for. Sky rockets. Mortar shells. And that awesome Angel Cake stuffed full of Roman candles and aerial shells. That was the one that kind of fanned out when it went off."

"That one was awesome," Ruthie said.

John and Matt had set off the fireworks from the end of the Copakens' dock, aiming them out to sea. There had been one scary moment when a Golden Dragon went astray, spiraling back in the direction of the harbor, but it had exploded high enough in the sky to keep from setting anything alight on its way down.

Now, as they stood on the dock, it was hard for Matt not to remember that night: John kissing Becca on the back of the neck, then pushing her behind him, telling her to watch out or she'd get her fingers blown off; Becca hovering behind John, her long sun-lightened hair tied up in a swinging ponytail. Matt remembered how when the huge Angel Cake was lit, John had grabbed Becca, swung her around, and wrapped his arms around her from behind. Matt remembered Becca leaning against his brother's chest and smiling at the lights exploding in the dark night sky.

"I'm going to wait until it gets dark for the rest of them," Ruthie said now.

"I'll do them for you. You could blow your fingers off," he said. To cover his sudden discomfort at unconsciously echoing his brother, he said, "I saw your grandfather at the Red Hook post office the other day."

"You did?"

"I guess he was maybe with some students from Usherman Center? They had violin cases."

"Yeah, probably students."

"I never heard Becca play," Matt said, anticipating Ruthie's small tremble at Becca's name.

"She sold her violin a couple of years ago."

"Yeah, to help pay for the Alden, John's boat."

"That's right. God, that made my mom so mad."

John had told him that, too. Iris was a tough nut, John used to say, but once you cracked her, she was sweet inside.

Ruthie glanced at him, her mouth registering the barest hint of what looked like a smile. He smiled back and she caught her lower lip between her small white teeth and looked away. He caught himself taking the opportunity of her averted gaze to let his own eyes travel up the length of her body, stopping where her legs disappeared from view. He flushed.

"Do you think it's dark enough yet?" she said.

"Not yet."

After a long, quiet moment during which Matt tried to keep himself from looking anywhere but at her face, Ruthie pointed to a sloop tacking awkwardly back and forth across the inlet. "That's Jeremy Weiss."

Matt dragged his eyes unwillingly away from her and out over the water. He snorted once, derisively. "Dude can't sail for shit."

Ruthie said, "I guess he's about as bad as I am."

"Is that the Sparkman & Stephens? The one John restored?"

"I guess so. I don't really know."

"The guys down the yard knew the kid was going to fuck up that boat. And wouldn't you know it, three weeks after they delivered her, she was right back at the yard. Dumb ass got a net fouled in the propeller. John was ready to kill him."

"Well, I guess that could happen to anyone," Ruthie said.

"Guy's a dumb ass." Matt had no idea why he was making such a big deal out of this. He didn't care about Jeremy Weiss or his boat.

"He's all right," Ruthie said.

The truth was Matt didn't know Jeremy Weiss even to say hello to. Ruthie clearly did, though. For no reason at all he wondered if Jeremy Weiss wasn't Ruthie's boyfriend. If he was, then why wasn't he out here with her? Why'd he leave her to cry over John and Becca's fireworks all by herself?

Ruthie said, "I don't really know him too well. I mean, for all I know he *is* a dumb ass."

A slight breeze brought with it the briny smell of the sea. Matt inhaled deeply. He listened to the sound of the waves splashing gently against the beach. The tide was coming in.

"Is it dark enough yet?" she said.

"Soon," Matt said.

Ruthie said, "When are you going back to school?"

"Next week," he said. "What about you?"

"Tomorrow. I have to get to work on my thesis before classes start and everything gets crazy."

"You're a senior?" Matt said.

"Yes. You're a sophomore, right?"

"Yeah."

"Do you like Amherst?" she asked.

"It's all right."

"You're the first person in your family to go to college, aren't you?"

"John went to college," Matt said. "Or as good as. He did the design course at the Landing School. It's a really hard program to get into."

"Oh, I know," Ruthie said. "Just, you know. A four-year college. Someone said you were the first."

That had to have been John. John had told anyone who would listen when Matt had gotten his scholarship. But Ruthie couldn't seem to bring herself to say John's name.

Matt shrugged. "It's no big deal."

"Sure it is. Amherst's a great school."

Everyone reacted that way when they learned that Matt went to Amherst. Surprised and then overly impressed, as if it were impossible to imagine a kid like him getting into a school like that. As if being from Red Hook necessarily meant you couldn't hack it at a college like that, couldn't be an intellectual. But it wasn't about intelligence, it was about cash. At least half of his high school graduating class had gone to college, although most were at the University of Maine. The only reason he was going to Amherst was because they'd offered him a scholarship. Ruthie hadn't meant anything by it, he knew. She was sweet. She wasn't a snob like most of the summer visitors; after all, she was Becca's sister.

"Yeah, Amherst's all right," he said. "How's Harvard?"

"It's all right," she said.

Matt shoved his hands into his pockets and rocked back and forth on his heels. He tried to think of something to say to fill the expanding quiet between them, but before he could come up with anything she said, "Do you think it's dark enough yet?"

Relieved, he nodded. "I think so. Let's light one and see."

She handed him a yellow plastic lighter. There were two fireworks left: a Roman candle and a small cake, less than a quarter the size of the one that John had used as his finale. Matt chose the Roman candle, set it up, and, after checking that Ruthie was standing far enough away, lit the fuse at the bottom of the paper tube and backed up a step. The fuse burned to the end and the stars began shooting from the Roman candle one at a time.

"So beautiful," Ruthie breathed as the last star dissipated into the navy-blue sky. "Can I light the last one?"

"Okay. Just be careful."

Tentatively, she knelt down next to the cake. The first few times the lighter sputtered and sparked but did not catch. Matt was about to take it back from her when she finally managed to light it. She touched the small flame to the fuse. Instead of rising and stepping immediately back she stayed where she was, bent over the cake, until he grabbed her arm. She allowed him to lead her away, all the while craning her neck to follow the stars and spirals as they took off from the dock and flew high into the sky. Lifting her head to watch the bursts of light, Ruthie lost her balance and stumbled backward. Matt caught her as she fell, steadied her, but did not let her go. Her shoulders were pressed against his chest and her head was tucked beneath his chin. He felt her ribs with his long fingers, his thumbs on either side of her spine. He slipped his arms around her waist and held her, her hair soft against his skin, her weight heavy against him.

He inhaled deeply, smelling the musk of her hair, the faint fruity scent of her skin. He squeezed his arms more tightly around her and matched his inhalations and exhalations to hers as they watched the last of the fireworks flicker and fade away.

THE SECOND SUMMER

1

A typical June day in Maine: rain all morning, then a partial clearing that left the air damp and chilly and the sky tinged with just enough blue to give a tantalizing hint of a summer afternoon. Periodically a gust of wind would shake the tree branches and water would pour down on the small group in the cemetery, dampening their hair and trickling into the gaps between their necks and collars.

Iris, Daniel, Ruthie, Mr. Kimmelbrod, and the rabbi from Bangor made their way slowly on foot down the dirt road to Becca's and John's graves, having left the car parked by the stone gates so that it would not get stuck in the mud. Over the winter Mr. Kimmelbrod had been obliged to take up the use of a walker. Iris held her breath as she watched the pains he took to find purchase in the muddy grass, as if struggling with the fingering of a difficult sequence of notes. When they were about halfway to the waterside, Mr. Kimmelbrod stumbled and seemed about to lose his footing. Iris gasped and lunged toward him, but Daniel reached him first, steadying the walker and making sure he was secure on his feet. As Daniel turned back to the road he tripped over a root, and in the end it was he who fell, landing on his hands and knees in the muddy grass.

"Daniel!" Iris said. She'd meant to sound sympathetic, and yet even to her own ears it came out as a reproach. To compensate, she extended her hand to help him up.

He shrugged it away, got to his feet, and assessed the damage. His knees were filthy and one pant leg was torn.

"Shit," he said, and then, "Sorry, Rabbi."

"No offense taken," the rabbi said.

Daniel swiped ineffectually at the stains.

"Here," Iris said.

"I'm fine," he said, ignoring the tissue she offered him, and instead wiped his grubby hands on the front of his pants.

At the far end of the graveyard Becca's stone lay beneath a white sheet, awaiting its traditional unveiling on the lunar anniversary of her death. Iris had found herself anticipating this day with an unexpected eagerness, not because the ceremony marked the traditional end of the period of mourning but rather because she longed for some fixed point on the calendar of sorrow to give focus to their diffuse and measureless misery. Their grief was so intense and yet so lonely; each of them drifted in his or her private bubble of mourning, sealed off not only from the rest of the world but from one another. Iris felt, or hoped, that what they needed was a kind of official sanction of their mourning—that this ceremony might unite them in recognizing it, naming it, making it holy.

"You have got to be kidding," Iris said, when she saw the marker Jane and the Tetherlys had erected over John's grave.

The stone was dark-gray granite, bearing his name and the dates of his birth and death in large roman capitals. A carving of a schooner in full sail ornamented the bottom, beneath the text, a bud vase was attached to the side, and preserved under shatter-proof glass in the top right-hand corner of the stone was a five-by-seven color photograph of John. The picture had been taken on the porch of his mother's house. He was sitting on the top step, his long legs extending halfway down to the bottom and crossed at the ankle. Something about the photograph's angle or perspective made his bare feet look larger even than they were. His face was partly shaded by his beat-up old Red Sox hat, but you could still see his wide, loopy grin.

Ruthie said, "You didn't put a picture on Becca's, did you?"

"God, no," Iris said. "Sorry, Rabbi."

"No offense taken."

The rabbi pulled from his pocket a small prayer book with a faded leather cover and a handful of smaller booklets, which he handed out to them. He cleared his throat and began reading in Hebrew. His voice was mellifluous and Iris was reminded of how beautifully he had sung the Mourner's Kaddish last year.

" 'A thousand years,' " the rabbi continued, in English, " 'in the sight of our eternal and merciful Father, are but a day; the years of our life but a passing hour. He grants us life and life he has taken away; praised be his name.' "

He paused and glanced at them.

Mr. Kimmelbrod recited, "Amen."

Daniel and Ruthie quickly followed suit, but the word stuck in Iris's mouth. If the years of a normal life were but a passing hour, then the years of Becca's life were no more than fifteen or twenty minutes. Not enough.

The rabbi continued, "Rebecca has been taken from our midst. We are pained by the gap in our lives. Yet love is as strong as death; the bonds love creates are eternal. And ours is the blessing of memory, through which the lives of our departed continue to be with us."

He paused again. Ruthie opened her mouth to repeat, "Amen," but the rabbi shook his head.

Was love as strong as death, Iris wondered. What lasted longer? What took a greater toll?

The rabbi leaned down and peeled the sheet away from the gravestone.

Iris had chosen a marker carved from the same stone as John's—she hadn't really liked the glossy granite, but she had wanted them to match. Instead of calling Jane for the information, she had asked the stone cutter—the only memorial maker in Newmarket—to check his records and use John's gravestone as a template for Becca's. The shape of the stone and the lettering were the same as John's, but Iris had forgone the optional photograph holder and bud vase, and, of course, there was no sailboat carving. She had wondered what kind of symbol she might have chosen for Becca—a violin case, abandoned in a corner? The stone was engraved with the dates of Becca's birth and death, and her name in English and Hebrew.

REBECCA FELICE COPAKEN

Iris had ordered the marker, had in effect designed it—its appearance ought not to have surprised her. But somehow she had managed through the process never truly to visualize it. Now the mass of it, the shining granite fact of it, made her feel light in the head.

"They wrote the wrong name!" Ruthie said, in a tone of dull surprise, squatting down in the wet grass and pointing at the marker without touching it. "It says Copaken. It should be Tetherly."

The rabbi turned to Iris and Daniel and raised his eyebrows. "There's a mistake?"

"No," Iris said. "It's right." She wished she could sit down, but other than the gravestone itself there was nothing but dirt and wet grass.

Not long before the wedding, Becca had announced her intention to take John's name. Iris could recall every word of this argument, as indeed she found now that she could recall every disagreement she had ever had with her elder daughter. It was as if her memory consisted of a series of blurry photographs. The only ones that were focused and sharp showed Becca and Iris arguing. This selective amnesia was hardly a shock; it was in Iris's nature to confront, if not to revel in, the awful truth. And yet her memories of her disagreements with Becca were no more fundamentally true or honest than her fuzzy memories of their other, positive interactions. Why, then, she wondered, did her mind persist in playing and replaying only scenes of unpleasantness?

On that afternoon two days before the wedding, Becca had been making a list of the guests' names, checking them against the names that Iris read aloud from the RSVP cards.

"Is that all?" Becca had asked, once they'd double-checked the spelling of Zaidenshnur.

"Yes, except John's parents. And us, of course."

Becca wrote John's mother's name, his father's, and his father's girlfriend's. Then she wrote her parents' names, her sister's, and her grandfather's. Finally, smiling, she wrote her own.

Iris glanced down at the page. In neat letters Becca had written, "John and Rebecca Tetherly."

"Blech," Iris said.

Becca smiled—pleasant yet firm. She had obviously decided to refuse to allow herself to be goaded into an argument. "Whatever do you mean? It's lovely, don't you think? Rebecca Tetherly. It's musical."

"Oh, it is *not* musical," Iris snapped. "Becca. You're not changing your name."

Becca capped the pen with a firm snap. "Yes, Mom, I am. And it *is* musical. It scans well. Far better than Rebecca Copaken." She said the name flatly, drawing out the A. "Now, that's blech."

"Copaken is a good, solid name. I find it much more musical than Tetherly. And at any rate, that's not the point."

"Exactly," Becca said breezily. "The point is that my husband's name is Tetherly, and my name will be, too."

Iris tried to work some cool into her voice, hoping that it did not come out sounding, as it usually did when she tried to hold back, too Clint Eastwood. "Nowadays," she said, "most women don't change their names."

"You live in such a rarefied world, Mom," Becca said, laughing. "Maybe most *feminist scholars* keep their names, but every woman I know in Red Hook took her husband's name when she got married."

Because she so regretted having changed her own name when she married Daniel, Iris had assumed that her daughters would keep the name Copaken. She had married before women began keeping their own names, and as soon as younger women began doing it, Iris considered reverting to her maiden name. It seemed foolish to have taken Daniel's name when her ancestral connections mattered far more to her than his did to him. The name Kimmelbrod dated at least as far back as the seventeenth century, and she and her father were the last of their particular branch. On the other hand, the family to which Iris felt most connected was her mother's, and so by that logic she ought to take her *mother's* maiden name, or, better still, her grandmother's. Yet if she were to choose a last name based on affinity alone, were she to adopt Godwin, her mother's maiden name, or Hewins, that might have seemed as if she were rejecting the Jewish half of her heritage, rejecting her father, rejecting the family stolen by the Nazis. Moreover, she was a scholar of the Holocaust: it would have been harder for someone named Iris Hewins to be taken seriously in that particular field. In the end she'd decided that she was too well-established to change her name. It was as Iris Copaken that she'd earned her graduate degrees, as Iris Copaken that she'd published her first articles and books. Still, she had assumed that her daughters would never make the same mistake. She should have realized that this, like so many of the assumptions she made about how her oldest daughter would live her life in the wake of feminism and its battles, was doomed to be contradicted. The women of Becca's generation accepted that their lives were without limits and promptly figured out ways to constrict them.

"What women do in Red Hook," Iris had told Becca that day, "is hardly a reflection of the world."

"It's no less the world than New York is. And anyway, I bet if you checked you'd see that most women in New York take their husbands' names, too."

Iris said, "I think you should take some time to think about this. You don't want to do something you'll regret."

"I *have* thought about it," Becca said. Reaching over her shoulder she grabbed her ponytail and twisted it into a firm knot at the base of her skull. She never stopped sounding pleasant, but her will, like her mother's, was iron. "I've thought about it a lot. It's important to me that I have the same name as my husband and my children. I know your argument: my name is my own, I belong to myself, not my husband. I *know* all that, Mom. And I know you're disappointed, but I've made up my mind."

"You have spent twenty-six years as Rebecca Copaken. Both personally and professionally. No conductor or musician is going to know who Rebecca Tetherly is."

Becca laughed. "No musician knows who Rebecca *Copaken* is."

"And what if you get divorced? What then? You'll either end up saddled with a name you don't want or you'll have to go through all the rigmarole of getting your own back."

"Nice, Mom," Becca had said, not without affection. "Two days until my wedding, and you already have me getting divorced."

Iris had not resigned herself to Becca's decision. She kept hoping right up to the day of the wedding—the day Becca died—that when Becca was finally confronted with the reality of the words *Rebecca Tetherly* on a check or a loan application, she would reconsider, back down, see the light. And then, for a time, death had seemed to put an end to all such questions of Becca and the choices she was going to make. But when the time had come to choose the wording for the grave marker, Iris was torn.

On the one hand, there was her argument with Becca—there was always, it seemed, an argument with Becca. But even assuming Becca's intransigence (which was not, Iris thought, a given), the girl had only been a Tetherly, if at all, for one hour. And legally she had never been anyone but Rebecca Copaken; that was the name on her driver's license, on her lapsed passport, on her bank account and Social Security card. That was the name on her death certificate. Furthermore, Iris had argued to herself, or to the memory of Becca, cemeteries and monuments exist to comfort the living, to consecrate a place dedicated not so much to the mourned but to the act of mourning itself. The dead never saw the memorials erected in their honor. Iris and her family were the only people likely to visit Becca's grave. The marker was there for *them*. If it had John's name on it, it would always feel wrong to them. It would seem like someone else was lying beneath the stone.

In making the case to her dead daughter for the decision that she had already made, Iris had allowed herself to imagine—contradicting her last point—that no one would notice, and that anyway, if they did, they would understand that she had made the right choice.

"We have to change it," Ruthie said. Her nose was pink, either with cold or with tears, and her chin trembled.

"It doesn't matter," Iris said.

"It does matter!" Ruthie snapped. "It's the *wrong* name."

Daniel pulled Ruthie close and stroked her hair. "It's done, Ruthie," he murmured.

The rabbi cleared his throat. "There is no rule that prevents you from changing it. But there's no need to decide now. Or even a year from now. This marker is for you. For your family. You can do anything with it that you like." He looked over at John's gravestone. "Although I would counsel against schooners in full sail."

Iris, initially annoyed that he had seemed to give credence to Ruthie's objection, now gave him a grateful smile.

"Perhaps we'll continue now with the Eil Malei Rachamim?" he said.

The prayer was a dirge, slow and mournful, and Iris felt the music reverberate in her chest.

The rabbi closed his book, slipped it back into his capacious pocket, and said, "Now I would like to suggest that in conclusion we take a few moments of silence."

"Wait!" Ruthie said, springing out of her father's embrace. "Is that all?"

"Yes," the rabbi said.

"What about the Mourner's Kaddish?"

The rabbi shook his head. "We cannot say Kaddish."

"Why not?" Ruthie asked, her voice shrill. "It's the prayer for the dead! It's the most important part."

"We have no minyan," the rabbi said. "We are only five people. And we are not permitted to recite the Kaddish without ten."

Ruthie turned to her mother and said angrily, "Why didn't you make sure we had enough people?"

"I didn't know," Iris said.

The rabbi said, "There is no requirement that the Kaddish be said at the unveiling. In fact, the ceremony itself is tradition, not biblically prescribed. You can recite the Kaddish at any synagogue."

"We did this all wrong," Ruthie cried. "Everything about this is all wrong."

"It's all right, sweetie," Iris said, trying to take Ruthie's arm. "It doesn't matter that there's no Kaddish. This isn't even a Jewish cemetery."

Ruthie flung her mother's hand away. "And that was your decision, too, wasn't it!"

Iris caught Daniel's eye and raised her eyebrows, but Daniel shrugged and turned away.

Ruthie hunched her shoulders against the drizzle that had begun to fall. Raindrops merged her tears. "We should have had a real unveiling, with enough people to do it the way it's supposed to be done."

"I'm sorry, Ruthie," Iris said. "I tried to make this special. It means as much to me as it does to you, and a private ceremony seemed like the right way to do it."

"It seemed right to *you*."

"Excuse me," Mr. Kimmelbrod said, his tone so polite and neutral it could not help sounding like a dry commentary on the women's behavior. "I am afraid I will not be able to stand for very much longer. Come, Ruthie. Help me back to the car."

With a last reproachful glance at her mother, Ruthie rushed to Mr. Kimmelbrod's side, and Iris watched them walk slowly back up the path to the cemetery gates.

Daniel massaged his forehead with both hands as though trying to rub away a headache.

Iris said, "Do you think we should have had a larger ceremony? Should we have invited more people?"

"More Jews, you mean? I don't know," Daniel said.

"It just seemed like this was the right way to do it," she said. "Just us."

Daniel gazed at the headstone, reading the inscription over and over again, as if he might have missed something.

"Do you think I made a mistake with her name?" she said.

He didn't answer.

"Daniel? Do you think I made a mistake?"

"I don't know," he said. "I'm going back." He turned away and headed back up the path.

Standing alone with the rabbi, Iris read the name on the headstone again. Then she looked at John's. They were so separate. Clearly intended for such different people. But for their proximity, one coming here would never know that they had loved each other, that for an hour they had been husband and wife. For a moment Iris felt a stab of regret so sharp she winced. She had made a mistake. But how was she to have known? She had no map, no chart, no carefully laid-out instructions on how to memorialize her daughter. How was she supposed to know what to do?

11

How was it, Mr. Kimmelbrod wondered, sitting alone at his daughter's kitchen table a few hours after the unveiling, that a man who had experienced so much death, who was so rapidly approaching death himself, could muster so little in the way of comfort for the bereaved? Shouldn't the magnitude of his losses have provided him with some insight into or ready familiarity with the things, the words and actions, that gave a person solace? And yet he found that, as ever, he had nothing to say to Iris, Daniel, and Ruthie: not at the grave site, not in the car, not on the screen porch where they had sat for an hour, uncomforted, watching the dismal rain. The pall that had been cast over the family for the past year remained in place, unlifted with the unveiling of the stone.

Daniel was gone now, out for a run, and Ruthie and Iris were napping. Mr. Kimmelbrod sat alone at the table, his fingers tented before him, the pressure of tip against tip keeping them from trembling as he contemplated his inadequacy, his ignorance in the face of grief.

What had he learned from the deaths of so many of those he loved? Only that there was no apparent limit to the amount of grief a man could endure if he allowed inertia and the passage of time to push him through his days. What wisdom could he give his children? Only that after a while it became possible to ignore the ache, as one grew used to even the foulest of one's own bodily emanations until some shift of breeze, some change in position, carried the smell again to one's nostrils, and the stomach rebelled.

Alone in the kitchen with the humming of the refrigerator, the ticking of the clock, a man with nothing to offer, Mr. Kimmelbrod's only conscious certitude was of his longing to go back to the place on Peter's Point

Road, to the rooms in which he and his wife had spent all but the first summer of their lives together, to the house that had been his and Alice's first major purchase as a married couple. For eleven thousand dollars he and Alice had bought the little farmhouse on four oceanfront acres because, while he had been more than willing to pass his summers in Red Hook teaching at Usherman Center, there was less appeal in the prospect of living with his mother-in-law. And then, because he and Alice had ensconced themselves so thoroughly on Peter's Point Road, his mother-in-law decided to leave her rambling Queen Anne to Iris.

Lately, however, Iris had begun a campaign to convince Mr. Kimmelbrod that he was too infirm to continue to spend the summers alone in the farmhouse. In New York, she argued, he was surrounded by neighbors, and only a panic button away from the doorman, but in Red Hook the house of his nearest neighbor was nearly a quarter of a mile away, and it might take as long as half an hour or more for an ambulance to respond to a 911 call. He recognized a legitimacy in her argument. Indeed, he understood its validity even better than Iris did, for he had concealed from her, with the rigid discipline he brought to everything he did, the true extent of his debility. Yet he was not ready to relinquish his independence. To allay her concern, he had agreed to make a few small concessions to his age, including a solemn promise to drive only when necessary and otherwise to call upon his family or colleagues for rides. However, he had not counted on the impingement, even the sense of emasculation, this promise would impose on him. To have to rely on another if he wanted to go to the grocery store, or out for coffee, or to work. To wait for a ride for just long enough that he lost interest in the activity that had inspired him to ask for it in the first place. His independence was being taken away, and he was coming to the conclusion that what remained of his life was no more than a short slide to incapacitation and oblivion.

The thought that Becca should have died while he—doddering and shaking, periodically frozen into hideous and panicked immobility, on the precipice of losing control even of his ability to urinate—continued to clutch tenaciously to life, inspired him with an anger so profound that at times he had felt the urge to abandon his customary reserve. This shook him to the core, because his veneration of control, both personal and musical, defined him. It made him who he was as a man, and also as a musician. The music of Johann Sebastian Bach exemplified Mr. Kimmelbrod's devotion to the idea that beauty could be created only through disciplined adherence to pattern. In Bach's dense contrapuntal textures Mr. Kimmelbrod found his ideal: emotional exuberance firmly restrained by discipline, symmetry, and order. He received much the same satisfaction from Bartók and from Schoenberg's twelve-tone logic.

The irony of Mr. Kimmelbrod's career was that despite his commitment to restraint and structure, it was only when he played the Romantic composers, whom he considered emotionally obvious and even florid, that his music rose above mere technical perfection. His Bach Chaconne was lovely and precise, his performance of the Berg Violin Concerto uncontrovertibly flawless, but it was when he played Tchaikovsky's Concerto in D Major, a piece of music he considered overplayed and banal, that he brought even the most jaded of concert audiences to tears. It was only in the expression of conventionalized sentimentality, which he loathed both on principle and by temperament, that his playing truly rose to the level of greatness.

When he played the Romantic pieces for which he was best known, nothing could be more different from the sound of his music than the cool and distant appearance of the musician. Onstage or off, with a violin in his hands or without, Mr. Kimmelbrod had always been tranquil and still. Even before the Parkinson's had frozen his face into an expressionless mask, he maintained an impassive expression, one that revealed almost nothing. Mr. Kimmelbrod had always and thoroughly kept all emotion tamped down, so deeply hidden that it raised a near existential question. Could something be so thoroughly suppressed that it might as well not even exist?

He heard a creaking on the staircase and Ruthie came into the kitchen. Her cheek was seamed in pink from her pillow, and strands of her hair flew around her head, pulled loose by sleep from her ponytail.

"Hey, Grandpa," she said, standing behind his chair and putting her hands on his shoulders and pressing her cheek into the top of his head. "Sorry I was such a baby today, carrying on and making an ass of myself at the cemetery."

Ruthie was the baby, had always been treated that way. With the back of his head he felt her chest expand with her sigh. "Tears are not inappropriate under such circumstances," he said.

"I guess. I think Mom's pretty mad, though."

"Rather sad than angry, I think."

Ruthie lifted her cheek from his head and, after squeezing his shoulders, came around and sat in the ladder-back chair opposite his. "I just wish we'd had enough people there to say Kaddish."

"Kaddish. Tell me, granddaughter, what is all this about saying Kaddish? Suddenly you have found religion?"

"No, it's just—I mean, we're *supposed* to."

"I believe, in fact, that at this point only your parents are required to say Kaddish. Our obligation to do so ended after the first thirty days of mourning."

Ruthie looked aghast. "Is that really true?"

"I am no expert in the Talmud, but I believe yes. Only the parents and the spouse are meant to continue their mourning for the full year. After that they are to stop saying Kaddish, except on the *yahrzeit*, the anniversary of the death."

She gave her head a furious shake. "Well, that's ridiculous. It doesn't make any sense. Grief doesn't just *end* because a group of ancient rabbis said it was supposed to." She frowned. "Did you say Kaddish for Granny?"

No, he thought, he had not. Not after the funeral. Instead he had played for his wife. Music was Mr. Kimmelbrod's only meaningful means of expression. Until he lost his ability to play, Mr. Kimmelbrod had both contained and expressed his emotions only through his music. His violin wrung the emotions from him, translating the unspeakable and wailing it to the world. The Dembovski laughed for him. It flirted and giggled and snickered and howled with glee. But mostly it cried. The Dembovski wept *for* him, because he would not shed his own tears. Because he could not bear to remember the dead.

The Dembovski remembered them—his parents, his brother, his sister. The myriad uncles, aunts, and cousins whose bodies and faces, ideas and loves, memories and bones, were nothing, not even smoke or ash. Because he could not mourn them, the Dembovski del Gesù, carved from a piece of maple by a luthier from Cremona, keened its lamentation, *his* lamentation, for all that had been lost. The Dembovski said his Kaddish for him.

His violin had grieved for his wife, his beloved Alice, with her crooked smile and sly wit. With her knobby knees and sensible shoes. He shed no tears as he kept vigil beside the bed where she lay, the pauses between crepitations growing longer and longer until they stopped. No tears, even on that night when he stepped onto the small stone terrace outside their living room, closed his eyes against the cool night air, took up the Dembovski, and let it weep for the woman whom he loved more than he had ever been able to show.

His disease had progressed so far that by the time Becca died, he could no longer play. He had no way to lament her loss. And without lament, was there grief? If one neither expressed a feeling nor allowed oneself to experience its sensation, then could one be said to feel at all?

He had loved Becca. He missed her. But he felt like he stood at one end of a long, narrow hallway at the far end of which was a lantern in which a small flame flickered. If he squinted his eyes and stared very hard he could just barely make out the shadows behind the light, but the distance was too great for him to see what cast the shadows. Had he been able to play, the Dembovski would have transported him the length of the long, long hallway and brought him into the lantern's glow. Without his violin he was trapped, immobile, much too far away to see or feel. He was wracked with fury and despair at his infirmity, but aware at the same time of being able to feel *that* grief—his grief for his lost talent—wholeheartedly, when it was this very infirmity that distanced him from all his other emotions.

"Yes," he said. "I said Kaddish for your grandmother. At the beginning."

"And for your family? Your parents and brother and sister? Did you say Kaddish for them?"

"Also. A long time ago."

"Do you light one of those little candles for your parents? Like Mom does for Granny?"

"No."

"Why not?"

Mr. Kimmelbrod shrugged. "I do not know what day they died."

Ruthie's face crumpled, and he regretted immediately what he'd said. True as this was, it was an incomplete explanation. He might have lit a *yahrzeit* candle for his parents on the anniversary of their deportation, or even on their birthdays, or on the first of January, or on Groundhog Day, for that matter, but he had never been able to bring himself to bother. What use would it be? What comfort could be found in a feeble flame burning in a jelly jar?

"I'm so sorry, Grandpa."

"Yes," he said. "I know you are."

"But I still think we should do something for Becca and John," Ruthie said.

"*Do* something?"

"You know, like a memorial or something. Or even just a . . . I don't know what you would call it, not a *party*, but, like, a gathering. A celebration."

"A celebration?"

"Yes! A celebration of Becca and John. We'd all be together, everyone. Our family, John's, our friends. We'd all gather together and celebrate their lives."

How to explain to this sweet and naïve child that there was nothing she could do, nothing that any of them could do, that would take away her pain? Just as the unveiling hadn't been enough, so would a "celebration" fail to fill the void. There was only time to rely on, and even time would never quite suffice.

Ruthie leaned toward him eagerly. "We could do it on the anniversary. Or would that be too awful, somehow? Like we were celebrating the day they died?" She wrinkled her brow, the same expression he had seen on her face from the time she was a little baby trying to puzzle out a problem.

"You don't *like* parties, Ruthie," he pointed out, but she didn't seem to hear him.

"We could do it on the Fourth. I mean, Mom and Dad are probably not going to want to have just their *regular* Fourth of July picnic now, and that's the anniversary of the rehearsal dinner. It was a beautiful night. We were all so happy. It's a date that has meaning, but that isn't under a, you know, a pall of tragedy, like July fifth would be."

He felt so tired, drained by the day, by his daughter's pain, by her husband's wordless grief, by his granddaughter's neediness. And yet he was conscious, lacking the Dembovski's voice, of sharing her desire to do something, say something, not to let the moment pass in silence. "I don't know, granddaughter. I don't know that anyone is ready for a party."

Ruthie narrowed her eyes. "Are you feeling okay, Grandpa? Are you tired? Do you want to take a nap in the guest room?"

How was it, Mr. Kimmelbrod wondered, that a child so blissfully ignorant in so many respects always knew how he felt, always read the hints of exhaustion that he managed to disguise from everyone else? He was desperate for the comfort of his own house. "I think perhaps I should be on my way home."

"I'll take you right away," Ruthie said. She helped him to his feet without waiting for him to ask for her arm and helped him to the car. As they started for home he was nearly overpowered by an almost annihilating desire to get into his own cool bed and close his eyes, but his granddaughter seemed so sad, so bereft, so deflated by his lack of enthusiasm for her idea of throwing a party for the dead, that as they were driving along Main Street he found himself, rather to his surprise, saying, "The rain has stopped. Let's go to the Bait Bag. I'll buy you an ice cream cone."

The Bait Bag—most people just called it the Bag—occupied some vague category of structure between trailer and shack, with a few huge lobster pots bubbling on propane burners out back and a deep-fat fryer the size of a kitchen sink. It was located in the middle of town, across the street from the Red Hook Public Library, kitty-corner to the Citgo station. Behind the Bait Bag stretched a small square of grassy yard with a few picnic tables, but nobody ever sat out there. Not because the view of the rear yard of the gas station was ugly, though it was. In addition to the vacant picnic tables, the yard featured a couple of rusted old beaters on blocks and, oddly, a pale pink antique refrigerator missing its door. But these were not necessarily detractions from the ambience. The Bag's customers were accustomed to, if not indeed the proud custodians of, yards full of refuse and junk. It was the bugs that kept people away. For reasons little understood, that patch of grass behind the Bag was home to the cruelest, most vigorous horde of mosquitoes in Red Hook—though there were other contenders. Every once in a while a couple of tourists would wander back there with their red plastic trays and lobster rolls. A moment later they would come running back, swearing and slapping at the red welts rising all over their faces and arms, even the lobes of their ears and the tops of their sandaled feet.

Patrons of the Bag tended to eat either in their cars or sitting on the grass by the side of the road. There was a single rickety old picnic table on the edge of the parking lot, and Ruthie and Mr. Kimmelbrod managed to nab it. They pulled the car into the neighboring parking spot and turned on the radio so they could listen to music while they ate. WBQI was playing the Trout Quintet, and Ruthie attempted to console herself by dipping an order of onion rings one by one into a black-and-white.

Smiling fondly, her grandfather shook his head as, neck tilted back, she dangled the string of greasy onion dripping thick, creamy milkshake over her open mouth.

"It's bad enough you eat those," he said. "But to *dip* them?"

"Before you condemn me, you really ought to try it," she said with her mouth full. "It's the perfect combination of savory and sweet."

"God forbid."

"Tell me you've never had an onion ring. I don't believe you. Granny loved onion rings."

"She did, and I am sure I ate them once or twice with her. Sitting perhaps at this very table. But I promise you that despite having spent all the summers of her life in this hyperborean backwater, your grandmother's manners and taste were too refined ever to permit her to indulge in the abomination you are so enjoying."

Ruthie smiled, but then her eyes grew sad. "I miss Granny."

Alice Marie Kimmelbrod, née Godwin, great-granddaughter of Elias and Alice Hewins of Red Hook, Maine, had died of breast cancer when her youngest granddaughter was eleven years old, in the forty-fifth year of her marriage to Emil Kimmelbrod.

Over the dozen years since she died, Mr. Kimmelbrod's memories of his wife had calcified into a series of images and vignettes. Alice at her dressing table, a row of bobby pins in her lips, rolling her hair—honey blond when they met, then faded to a soft downy white—into a chignon. Alice bent over the old slate sink in the kitchen of the house on Peter's Point Road, the gentle roll of her waist straining against her dress. Alice stretched out on the dock, a filterless Pall Mall dangling from her lips, a fishing rod propped beside her, cracking her long toes. Alice with her eyes closed, listening to him play.

He remembered the way Alice would hold court from a small tufted armchair tucked beneath an east-facing window in the corner of the Usherman Center recital room on warm August Wednesday afternoons, when the students performed. Often she would bring Becca and Ruthie with her. When Becca listened to music she sat perfectly still, her eyes narrowed, her expression rapt. The look of surprised horror on the girl's face when a musician struck a false note always put Mr. Kimmelbrod in secret danger of cracking a smile. Ruthie had sat quietly, too, a good girl, but as she leaned against her grandmother's knee it had often seemed that she was entranced less by the music and more by her grandmother's palm smoothing her hair.

Another memory. Of Alice lying in bed, fishbelly white skin pulled taut over sharpened cheekbones, teeth clamped together to keep from moaning in pain.

Ruthie dunked another onion ring in her milkshake and chewed it slowly. Mr. Kimmelbrod licked his cone, allowing the ice cream to melt on his tongue. She stretched her legs out along the sun-warmed bench and sighed.

They had almost finished eating when a maroon minivan nosed sharply into the parking space next to theirs, scraping the bottom edge of its front bumper against the low cement barrier. Through the open window they heard a woman's gruff voice say, "You want ice cream or not?"

The rear door slid open on its roller, and a small, dark-haired figure stepped out.

"Hey!" Ruthie called. "Hi, Samantha!"

The girl frowned, as if trying to place Ruthie. She waved tentatively. Then she cocked her head to one side and listened. A flurry of piano notes came out of the open windows of the Copakens' car.

Samantha stood there with her eyes closed, her head rocking from side to side.

The driver's side door opened and Jane stepped out, slamming it hard behind her. As she came around the side of the car toward the picnic table she said, "You're being spoken to, miss." To Ruthie, Jane said, "Sorry."

"That's all right," Ruthie said. "How are you, Jane?"

"Fine. We're fine. And you?"

"We're all right."

Mr. Kimmelbrod watched the small, dark-eyed girl. She had long arms, and she stood with her hands held a little in front of her body, her fingertips faintly trembling. Her small, round chin darted in time with the music.

"Do you like the music?" he said.

She opened her eyes and smiled hesitantly, her face suddenly crowded with large white teeth.

"Do you know this piece?"

She shook her head.

"It's Schubert. The Trout Quintet. You've heard it before?"

Again she shook her head mutely.

"Come," Mr. Kimmelbrod said, ignoring Jane's and Ruthie's questioning looks. He patted the seat beside him. "Sit." The girl hesitated and he cleared a small space of paper plates, napkins, straw wrappers. "Here."

She sat next to him on the bench and together they listened to the music. She bobbed her chin in perfect time. Mr. Kimmelbrod wondered at her sense of rhythm, a hunch quickening in his mind.

"You hear the rhythm," he informed her. He tapped his fingers on the table.

She nodded.

"Can you tap it out as I do?"

She nodded again. Delicately, her long thin fingers nearly soundless on the rough wood of the table, she began tapping in unison with him.

"Do you hear the violin?"

She nodded and tapped out the rapid triplet accompaniment with her right hand, her left continuing with the melody. Mr. Kimmelbrod raised his eyebrow. He was not easily impressed, but the untrained girl's ability to maintain two beats, essentially in opposition to each other, was at least worthy of note.

"Do you play an instrument?" he asked.

Longingly, the girl said, "No."

"What are you talking about?" Jane said. To Mr. Kimmelbrod, "She plays the piano."

"Only it's not a real piano. It's just an electronic keyboard," Samantha said.

Jane shrugged and said, "Real or not, it's the piano you have." She turned back to Mr. Kimmelbrod. "She has a knack. She hears something once, she can play it right back for you."

Mr. Kimmelbrod nodded. To Samantha he said, "Do you take music lessons?"

Jane said, "There's no money for that kind of thing."

The music ended, but Samantha kept up her tapping. Mr. Kimmelbrod watched the girl for a moment, remembering a game he had played with Becca when she was very small. Matching his voice to the rhythm Samantha was still tapping out on the table, he sang, "*Can you hear the trouts a-swimming?*"

She startled, stared at him for a moment, and then smiled. Returning his rhythm, she sang, "*Yes, they swim and swim and swim.*"

He modulated to a minor key. "*Are the trouts now still a-swimming?*"

Samantha frowned, but quickly picked up the modulation, this time humming her response.

Mr. Kimmelbrod looked at Jane. "She has a very good ear. That's rare, especially in a child with no musical education."

"She's a smart little girl," Jane said, in a voice that implied this was not necessarily a recommendation.

"Oh, I think perhaps it's more than that," he said.

"Are you a musician?" Samantha asked him, shyly.

She was very slight, her legs long and bony, her hands large, he thought, for her age. A musician's hands. "Yes. I play the violin. Do you like the violin?"

The girl treated Mr. Kimmelbrod to another of her grand-piano smiles. "It's my favorite instrument."

Jane said, "All right now, Samantha. If you want your ice cream, go on and get it." She pulled a crumpled dollar bill out of her pocket and held it out to the girl.

Reluctantly, Samantha took the dollar. As she turned to abandon Mr. Kimmelbrod and Schubert for the less rarefied pleasure of a chocolate-vanilla swirl, she said, "I *love* the violin."

"So do I," Mr. Kimmelbrod said. He watched her as she took her dollar bill and went to stand on line. "She's your niece?"

"My niece's girl. She's just with me for a few weeks or so, while her mother takes a little rest."

"Ah, yes," he said, recalling now what Iris had told him about the girl's mother's frequent hospital stays. Manic depression, as he recalled. "Is the girl's mother musical?"

"Not particularly. I mean, she doesn't play piano or anything."

"But Samantha is adopted," he said.

"From Cambodia."

"Perhaps she inherited this gift from her Cambodian parents."

"No way to tell," Jane said. "They're a mystery."

"She should have instruction," Mr. Kimmelbrod said.

Jane smiled thinly. "I'll pass that on to my niece."

For the briefest of moments he considered insisting, but what good would it do? Were it of importance to the woman, or to anyone in the child's family, someone would already have noticed the gift and taken steps to nurture it. In Mr. Kimmelbrod's experience, the children whose musical sensitivities were translated into accomplishment were those with aggressive parents, most often mothers, whose ambition propelled them through the exhaustion and tedium that the acquisition of technical skill demanded. The truly musical child possessed innate gifts, but just as important were early and frequent exposure to music and the value placed on musical accomplishment by the parents. Whatever gifts this girl had, ten years of neglect, no matter how benign, had most likely atrophied them, perhaps beyond redemption.

"She's very talented," Mr. Kimmelbrod said.

"She's a smart girl," Jane said again, turning away.

Mr. Kimmelbrod began clearing the table, gathering their crumpled napkins and empty cups. Ruthie took the garbage from him. The trash can was directly in front of Jane's car, and when she approached it she saw Matt sitting in the passenger seat. Had he been hiding from her?

"Hey, Ruthie," he said.

Still clutching the trash in her hands, she said, "Hi." She could not look at him without thinking of his arms around her waist, of the fireworks bursting in the sky.

"Did you just come up from New York?"

"A couple of days ago."

He nodded. "I thought I saw your mom's car yesterday over by Hannaford's."

"Probably, yeah. She went grocery shopping. You know, first big shop of the summer." Ruthie looked down at the leaking milkshake cup in her hands and then dumped it in the trash. As she wiped her sticky hands on her jeans she said, "How've you been?" at the same moment that Matt said, "How was your year?"

After a moment of awkward silence, Ruthie said, "Okay, I guess. Considering. Yours?"

"Same."

After another clumsy silence, Ruthie said, "We were at the cemetery today."

Matt looked startled. "Oh, yeah?"

"Yeah. I liked the picture on John's headstone. He looks really happy."

"Yeah, it's a nice picture."

"Do you ever go out there?"

"I've gone a couple of times," Matt said. "With my mom. Do you mind if I ask you a question?"

"No."

"How come your parents didn't put a headstone on Becca's grave?"

"Oh, we did. We did it today. I mean, I guess they must have put it in yesterday or something. But we unveiled it today."

"Unveiled it?"

"We had to wait a year to put up the marker. It's a Jewish law. Or tradition, whatever. You have a service when you unveil it for the first time."

"Like a memorial."

"It wasn't much of one." Her voice thickened in the back of her throat. "It wasn't really any kind of memorial at all."

"Oh," Matt said. And then after a moment, "I'm sorry." Neither of them was quite sure what he was apologizing for—for the failure of the unveiling ceremony to adequately memorialize Becca's death, for raising the subject of the headstone in the first place, or for making Ruthie cry.

She shook the tears out of her eyes and, with a glance at her grandfather, said, "You know, we're thinking, I was thinking, of having, like, a real memorial for Becca and John." Mr. Kimmelbrod shook his head, but she continued, quickly, "Not a service, but, you know, a celebration. Remember how my parents have that party, every year on the Fourth? And, well, last year it was the rehearsal dinner. Which was kind of like the last time we all were happy together, you know? I mean, we were happy at the wedding, but that was different. The Fourth is a *good* anniversary. It's the anniversary of a happy day. Do you think you'd be interested in coming? I mean, all of you?"

Matt looked over at his mother. Jane crossed her arms over her chest.

"Sure," he said to Ruthie. "Sure we'd come."

"Really? That would be great. We could have fireworks, like last year."

Mr. Kimmelbrod noticed that for some reason his granddaughter blushed when she mentioned the fireworks.

"Do you have fireworks?" Matt said.

"No. But we can get some."

"I could go to New Hampshire for you. I go that way all the time."

In fact he had not been to New Hampshire since the trip with John last summer, but she would have no way of knowing that.

"Really?" Ruthie said. "That would be great."

"We're busy on the Fourth," Jane said.

Ruthie's face fell. "Oh."

"We are?" Matt said. "Doing what?"

"We have plans," Jane said, sharply.

"What plans?"

"Fourth of July plans." She called out to Samantha, "Come on now, girl. We've got to get going."

Samantha stepped away from the cashier's window, walking carefully so as not to topple her towering swirl.

"Well, if you change your mind, or your plans get canceled . . ." Ruthie began.

"Don't you spill that," Jane said to Samantha. Then she slammed the car door shut.

"I just thought it might be nice," Ruthie said to Matt. "To have a way to remember Becca and John that would be celebratory."

Jane leaned her head out of the car and said, "That's not the way we do things. Parties for the dead."

"Oh," Ruthie said.

"Jesus Christ, Mum," Matt muttered. "What the hell? Don't mind her," he said to Ruthie. "I'll get the fireworks."

"Really?" Ruthie smiled. "That'll be really great."

"*Matt*," Jane said, turning on the engine.

"Okay," Ruthie said, lifting her hand in a reflexive wave. "And I'm so sorry, Jane. I mean, for your loss. For all our losses."

Jane pursed her lips. "Well, the Lord doesn't give us more trouble and sorrow than we can bear." Then she jammed the car into reverse and backed out of the parking space. Mr. Kimmelbrod could not make out what Matt said to her, but he could tell the boy was angry.

Ruthie turned to her grandfather. "Why do people say that? Do you think God only gives you as much trouble and sorrow as you can bear?" Ruthie asked.

"I do not believe in God," Mr. Kimmelbrod said.

"Well if not God, then life. Fate, whatever. Do you believe that it only gives you as much as you can bear?"

He clicked his tongue against the roof of his mouth. It was so American, he thought, this notion that there was a supernatural force carefully calculating each individual's capacity for suffering.

"You don't think that's true?" Ruthie said.

"Are you bearing it?"

Chewing her lip, Ruthie said, "I guess I am. I'm still alive. I mean, I'm miserable, and a lot of mornings I feel like I just can't get up and face the idea that Becca died. But I do, don't I? I do get up. I wrote my thesis, I graduated from college. I even got it together to apply for the Fulbright."

Mr. Kimmelbrod had been worried for a time that Ruthie would not even graduate. She had been so very depressed. During the fall semester she had spent more of her time at home in New York than at university, much of it on the living room sofa in his apartment, curled under one of Alice's afghans, holding an unread book in her hand and trying to hide her tears. And then Iris had stepped in, and escorted—perhaps the right word would have been *dragged*—Ruthie back to Cambridge. After that, when Ruthie called, she told him that she was spending all of her time in the library, reading and rereading her assigned texts, revising draft after draft of every seminar paper, creating elaborate study outlines for exams that she could have aced without even bothering to review her notes. She told Mr. Kimmelbrod that the hours she spent studying were the only ones in which she could think of something other than Becca. Ruthie had graduated magna cum laude. Her senior thesis on the construction of girlhood in the works of Christina Rossetti and Elizabeth Barrett Browning had won the English Department's Helen Choate Bell American literature prize. At the end of the year she was awarded a Fulbright to study English literature at Oxford, the very same fellowship her mother had won thirty years before. But he had a terrible sense that these accomplishments meant little to her. She seemed to him to be utterly lost.

"And your mother?" Mr. Kimmelbrod said. "Is she 'bearing' the death of her child?"

"I guess in the same way I am. She went to work. She taught all her classes. She's different than before. She's more withdrawn, I guess. Depressed. But she's alive, right? She's working. So I suppose you could say that she's bearing it."

"So, then, by the logic of the irrepressible Jane, if God—or life—only gives you what you can bear, then had you or your parents simply been weaker people, then Becca would still be alive? If we all weren't so strong, then the driver of the limousine would have driven more slowly?"

"I don't know," Ruthie said. Her nose was growing red and her eyes were damp.

As if one's capacity for pain had anything to do with life's apportionment of agonies, Mr. Kimmelbrod thought. Such idiocy. Such sanctimonious pabulum. What did Jane Tetherly know of what God gives or doesn't give, she who could not even recognize the astonishing gift that fate, God, or genetic chance had given to a child growing up right under her nose?

God only gave you as much as you could bear? He thought of his beloved younger sister, Felice. Felice did not die in Terezin, like their parents and brother, like her husband and her small daughter. With the assistance of the Red Cross, he had retraced his sister's steps. In 1944 Felice was transported first to Auschwitz and then, by some fluke of the genocidal bureaucracy, back to Terezin. She was still alive when the Russians liberated the camp. After liberation she was evacuated to Zeilsheim, a displaced persons' camp near Frankfurt. From Zeilsheim she did not write to her brother in the United States, despite the fact that any musician, any orchestra, would have known how to contact him. She could even have sent a letter care of Carnegie Hall and it would eventually have reached him. But she had never written. Felice, liberated from the camps, no longer forced to battle for every mouthful of food, for every step, every breath, had a moment to consider what it was that she had lost, and it was more, in the end, than she could bear. On May 15, 1946, she sliced open her wrists with a shard of glass and bled to death in a stall in the women's latrine.

If he told his granddaughter about her great aunt she would understand the folly of Jane's words. But he had confided this story to no one, not even to his wife or to his daughter, who had made a career out of scrutinizing and analyzing such stories. He had borne the horror of Felice's death alone, would take it alone to his own grave.

Mr. Kimmelbrod reached across the table and took Ruthie's bony fingers in his gnarled hands. Beneath her soft skin he felt the hard ridge of bone.

"Ruthie, there is no logic to loss. There is no guiding hand allotting tragedy in bearable increments. Good things happen and terrible things happen and we must all just continue." Becca was dead, he thought. Alice was dead, Felice was dead, his family was dead. And then he thought of Samantha, and the gift he thought might be struggling for expression, a tiny shoot of green in an arid landscape. It needed only watering. What was Samantha, then, but proof of the wondrous and terrible randomness of life?

With a sob Ruthie pulled Mr. Kimmelbrod's hand to her face and covered her eyes with it. "When am I going to feel better?" she said. "I need to *do* something."

"So have your Fourth of July. Your celebration. Why not?" Really, why not? he thought. What harm could it do?

She lifted her tear-streaked face. "Will that make me feel better?"

"I don't think it will make you feel worse."

She grabbed his hand. "Will you help me convince Mom?"

"Of course, granddaughter. Of course I will."

III

As Iris was putting the orange juice carton back into the fridge she heard her father's cane thumping down the hall from the guest room where he had spent the night. Last night his knees had locked painfully as he tried to get up from the table after dinner, and he had been unable to face the ride back to his house.

"Good morning, Dad," she said as he made his slow way into the kitchen. "Did you sleep well?"

"I haven't slept well since 1957," Mr. Kimmelbrod said. When he was a young insomniac he would get up and go outside, into the yard in Maine, or onto their small terrace in New York, and play without regard to the sensibilities of his neighbors. He would return to the comforting repertoire of his youth. Seitz, Veracini, pieces he'd learned as a young boy taking weekly violin lessons from Mr. Haim Teplitz, an outlandish and gifted Eastern European Jew who claimed to have outplayed Paganini.

Mr. Kimmelbrod would stand in the dark and play his violin with his eyes closed until he registered the gray light of dawn on the insides of his eyelids. Now at night he lay in his bed and imagined the concertos and sonatas. He performed them in his head, every double stop, every bow stroke, running off arpeggios and cadenzas with his eyes closed and his fingers trembling on top of the blanket. He would never allow himself the indulgence of playing in his mind any better than he had in his life.

"Was the bed comfortable?" Iris asked now.

"Almost as comfortable as my own."

She hesitated, knowing well how much this cost him. "Dad," she said gently, "you've got to be realistic. What would happen to you if you fell? You'd lie on the ground for two days until I came looking for you."

"It would take you two days?"

"Dad!"

"I'm managing fine."

"Now you are, but you won't always be able to."

"So? Neither will you."

She filled a mug only halfway with coffee to spare him the embarrassment of spilling it. Of all the evidence of her father's senescence, it was his tremor that was hardest for her to bear. His mottled, shaking hands broke her heart. She hadn't felt this way about his need for a cane and then a walker, as tragic as that infirmity was. But the sight of soup dripping from his trembling spoon or his shaky signature on a check caught Iris like a hand at her throat. In his youth her father had beautiful hands: long, tapered fingers; slim knuckles; pale skin covered with fine golden hairs. In the 1936 affidavit that convinced the United States State Department to grant Mr. Kimmelbrod a visa, Robert E. Simon of New York's Carnegie Hall had said that Mr. Kimmelbrod's hands possessed a divine magic. Those magic hands had saved his life. Now, trembling and unsteady, they were surrendering it.

"Do you want me to drive you home after breakfast?"

"I have arranged for one of the office assistants to pick me up and take me to Usherman Center."

"Are you teaching today?"

Mr. Kimmelbrod shook his head. "Today I will watch Spiegelman's master class, to make sure he isn't imposing any of his bad habits on my students."

"Lucky Spiegelman," Iris said. "How are your students this year? Anyone worth saving from him?"

"Not particularly," Mr. Kimmelbrod said, taking a sip of his coffee. "It is a disappointing group this summer."

"That's too bad." Iris always sympathized with the students when they were so brutally and impersonally assessed. And never so deeply as on the day he had issued such a withering judgment of Becca. After years of directing her musical education, ensuring she had the best teachers, evaluating her progress, choosing her repertoire, he remained impassive in the face of Becca's decision to quit the Conservatory. Iris had begged him to intervene, had demanded that he dissuade Becca from her disastrous course of action.

"You're the only one she'll listen to," Iris had said.

"I *have* spoken to her," he had said.

"And? Did you tell her she was making a terrible mistake?"

"No, I did not."

"No? What do you mean no?"

"Becca is not suited to the Conservatory."

"Of course she is. This is what she's been planning for her whole life."

"A violinist must be driven by an insatiable need to improve. To set unattainable standards of precision and musicianship and then achieve them."

"Becca does that. She's been practicing four hours a day since she was ten years old."

"Four. Four, my dear, four is a lot, but it is not so much. Becca is a sensible girl. But this drive I am speaking of is not sensible; it is a kind of self-punishment."

"She's always been wholly committed to her music."

"Committed, yes. Wholly committed? I'm not sure."

Mr. Kimmelbrod was a notoriously demanding teacher. His students were in awe of him, both of the depth of his musical talent and of his firm views on the importance of precision. They could not bear to disappoint him. A terse shake of his head could send them spiraling into despair. The granting of a single word of praise made them flush deeply with pleasure. Becca, although never formally a student of her grandfather's, had shared his students' fear of disappointing him, and Iris would always believe that it was because Becca feared she could not meet Mr. Kimmelbrod's expectations that she had determined to escape them entirely by giving up the violin. This, however, was more than Iris had been willing to say.

"She's just reacting to the competitive atmosphere of the Conservatory. As soon as she gets used to the stress she'll start to do well. She's a brilliant violinist."

"Becca is talented, yes," Mr. Kimmelbrod had said. "She has occasional moments of brilliance. With sufficient education she would make a fine orchestra musician. But she is not a soloist, and she has never quite been able to find her footing in chamber ensembles."

"What's that supposed to mean?"

"Becca has confronted the limits of her talent and has made her decision."

"But it's the wrong decision! She's just insecure in the face of competition. She needs to be reassured that she's as good as the other students."

"She knows she is as good as some. Better, perhaps. But not as good as others."

"Not as good as *you*, is that what you mean?"

As stubborn as Becca had been, Iris thought now, years after that conversation, when it came to music she had always deferred to her grandfather. If Mr. Kimmelbrod had scoffed at her insecurities and demanded that she continue, Becca would undoubtedly have graduated. She would have made her debut. And then—? And then, perhaps her father was right; she would not have had a solo career. But there were hundreds of professional orchestras in the United States. If Mr. Kimmelbrod had only been willing to encourage her, to give her the merest push, Becca might today be a principal second violinist in Albany, or Tucson, or even Cincinnati. She might be appearing nightly in the pit of the Shubert Theater on West Forty-fourth Street. She would not, Iris thought with a painful clenching in her belly, be lying under a plain granite stone in the Red Hook cemetery.

To stifle such irrational and dangerous thoughts, Iris began emptying the dishwasher, banging pots and pans into the cupboards and sending silverware ringing into the drawer. Then, when there were no more dishes to put away, she said, "What can I make you for breakfast, Dad?"

"Nothing, thank you," Mr. Kimmelbrod said. "Iris, there is something I'd like to talk to you about."

"Oh?"

"It's Ruthie."

Iris's hands stilled.

"I believe she is struggling."

This was really too much. When she had wanted her father to help her with one of her daughters, to take an interest, to interfere, he had refused. When it had been appropriate for him to be involved, he had opted out. And now? When it had nothing to do with him at all?

Iris said, "Ruthie is grieving, we all are, but she's bearing up remarkably well, considering. Do you know how hard it is to get a Fulbright in *literature*? She beat out hundreds of other applicants."

"I don't mean her schoolwork. I think she is struggling to find a way to deal with her grief."

Iris began shaking her head even before he finished his sentence. "Is this about the unveiling? I'm sorry, Dad. I'm sorry we didn't have some kind of big service or lavish reception. But frankly, I wasn't up to it."

Mr. Kimmelbrod took a trembling sip of his coffee before answering, as if trying by example to show Iris the value of calm. "As much as you or I prefer such things to be private," he said when he put his cup down, "it seems that Ruthie desires some larger, more communal experience."

"What does that mean, 'larger, more communal experience'? You mean this Fourth of July party she's been talking about? I already told her that wasn't going to happen."

"I think perhaps you should reconsider."

"And do *you* really think that's appropriate, Dad? Are you really interested in participating in some public display of mourning, complete with lobster and fireworks?"

Mr. Kimmelbrod smiled thinly. "It would be difficult for me to conceive of a less appealing way to pass my time," he said. "But Ruthie feels differently."

"I know what Ruthie feels," Iris said. "But she's a child. She's got no idea."

Mr. Kimmelbrod lifted his cup to his lips, but his hand was trembling so badly that the china chimed against his teeth, spilling coffee over his hand. He put the cup down on the table and pressed his other hand over the shaking one, stilling it against the tabletop.

The sight caused Iris's anger to melt away. He was so shrunken. He had gray triangular hollows beneath his cheekbones, his teeth had become too large for his face, and his beautiful hands were crazed with ropy blue veins. His attempts in the face of all that to maintain his dignity filled her with a sorrow almost like homesickness.

"I'm sorry," Iris said, rushing to his side. "I'm so sorry, Dad."

He shook his head. "No. No need. You are right, I was intruding in your business. Please accept my apologies."

Iris pulled a chair out and sat down at the table. When Ruthie had suggested the celebration to her, Iris had dismissed it out of hand. Iris was afraid she could not endure the forced graciousness it would require of her. She had explained this to Ruthie, and pretended not to notice Ruthie's disappointment.

"Ruthie's been talking to you," Iris said.

"Please, Iris. I have no right." Mr. Kimmelbrod pressed his lips together.

"No, Dad. It's all right. It's just." She grimaced. "It feels so strange. To throw the same party we throw every year, but have it be a memorial? How could that be anything but tragic? The Fourth of July is a day for parades and fireworks, for celebration. Not for memorials."

"Ruthie imagines a celebration of their lives, I think," he said. "Rather than a memorial."

Iris sighed. The truth was she had had a certain ambivalence about canceling the picnic. They had been doing it for so long. To cancel it seemed like an acceptance of the derailment of the path of their lives. But, then, how could they continue to throw a party the day before the anniversary of Becca's death? That was impossible, no matter what they had always done. But perhaps this celebration of Ruthie's was a way to continue the tradition of the yearly picnic that had always before been so important to Iris, and to honor Becca and John. If this was what Ruthie thought she needed, if this was what she had decided would make her feel better, how could Iris deny it to her? If even Mr. Kimmelbrod was willing to tolerate the mawkishness of a memorial picnic, couldn't Iris stomach it, too? Perhaps Ruthie was right. Perhaps it would be good for them.

"Do you really think a celebration will make Ruthie feel better?" Iris asked.

"No," Mr. Kimmelbrod said.

Iris smiled ruefully, reached over to the sideboard, and picked up a pen and a piece of paper. "I'd better make a shopping list."

IV

Serious measures were required: Iris baked a lime pound cake. It was her most impressive cake; she used a Bundt pan embossed with a complicated pattern of grape clusters and vines. The cake baked up tall and golden brown, and the lime sugar glaze crackled tangy and sweet when you bit into it. She did not make the cake very often, in part because she invariably scraped her knuckles while zesting the limes, and also because Becca used to do most of the baking in the house. But today Iris was aiming to please. She was once again off to negotiate with her *machetaynista*, the woman with whom her native language did not even require her to have a relationship. If she got out of the experience with no injury worse than a few skinned knuckles, she would consider herself to have been fortunate.

Once Iris had agreed to the Fourth of July memorial, she had thrown herself, as always, foursquare into the operation. She planned the menu, she ordered the lobster, she borrowed the extra chairs and tables, she made the calls to let friends know that the Fourth of July picnic was happening this year, albeit with a different focus. And after Ruthie informed her mother (somewhat improbably, in Iris's opinion) that without John's family there, without John's *mother* there, the celebration would be incomplete, Iris found herself sitting, uninvited, in Jane Tetherly's dark little kitchen, bearing unsolicited baked goods.

"It's pretty yummy," Iris said.

"I'm on Weight Watchers," Jane said. "But I guess Matt and Samantha might like it."

"There's a pound of butter in this cake; it's about six points just to sit next to it. Eight if you inhale."

First Jane drew her brows together over her nose and frowned. Then a slow smile crept across her face.

"Maybe I'd better give it to Maureen, then," Jane said. "It's her turn to bring the refreshments to her Overeaters Anonymous meeting."

Now it was Iris's turn to smile.

"You do that Weight Watchers?" Jane said. "Not that you need to. But you know about the points."

"I go on Weight Watchers every January," Iris said. "For about three weeks. I lose one pound the first week, stay even in the second, and gain two in the third. Then I quit."

"That's how it always went for me. Especially during the change. I packed it on when I was going through the change. For ten years I gained at least five pounds a year. But this time I'm sticking to my points. I've lost sixteen pounds so far."

Five pounds a year? For ten years? Iris could not imagine gaining that kind of weight.

"It shows," Iris said. "You look great. So, well, I guess this probably isn't the best time to ask you to bring your famous banana pudding to the memorial we're planning for the Fourth."

The ease of the moment drained away and Jane's face stiffened. Her frown returned and she gazed over Iris's shoulder, as if there were something fascinating, something incredible, happening in the far corner of her kitchen, by the toaster. Iris held her breath. When Jane failed to respond, Iris continued, "Ruthie's calling it a celebration of Becca and John. I think she might have mentioned it?"

Jane nodded curtly, but made no other reply.

"I know it seems strange," Iris said. "I mean, it's the Fourth, and people usually have picnics to go to. And of course the next day, well. No." She waited for a response from Jane, but none came. "It's just that last year the Fourth was such a good day, such a happy day, for all of us."

Jane drew her mouth into a thin, disapproving line crosshatched with wrinkles. "I'm short-staffed and backed up on houses. And I doubt Matt will be able to get away. He's working all kinds of hours down the yard. They've got two boats they're trying to get into the water before August."

"Surely they won't make him work on the Fourth of July?"

"Depends on how things are moving. If they're running slow they might."

"Ruthie's really got her heart set on this," Iris said. "The fireworks, especially. We won't be lighting them until dark. Matt can come whenever he's done."

"Maureen's always got plans with the girls. You know, going to this one's house or that one's. Can't really count on Maureen."

"But you'll come, won't you? And bring Samantha with you?" To distract from the naked pleading in her voice, Iris took a sip of the iced tea Jane had poured for her. The tea was sweet, the ice cubes cold against her teeth.

"I'm afraid not," Jane said.

Iris pushed aside her glass and leaned toward Jane. "Look, Jane, can I be honest here? I—I really could use your help. See, until Ruthie got this idea into her head about the celebration, she was just, well, she's been sinking. Spending most of her time in her room, lying on her bed and staring at the ceiling, and I think she probably lost ten pounds last year. She is not doing well." For a moment Iris worried that she might be laying it on a little thick, but then she realized she had said nothing that was not true.

Jane knotted her fingers in her lap and stared down at them. As the silence stretched between them, Iris found herself beginning to get angry. Was Jane really so cold-hearted that she could so easily and for so little reason reject Iris's entreaties on behalf of her daughter? Was Iris's company really so intolerable that Jane could not manage a single evening of it?

Just as Iris was about to allow herself to lose her temper, to let Jane know exactly what she thought of her selfishness, Jane said, "So she's pretty bad off."

Ruthie *was* bad off. There was no denying it. She had never been particularly resilient, and although Iris had tried, that was simply something you could not teach a child. You were born with it, or you weren't. Whatever measure of resiliency it was Iris's to bequeath had gone to Becca. What a terrible irony that it was the one who could least cope who was left to do so.

"Yes," Iris said. "She's bad off."

"Same with Matt."

"Matt's not doing well?"

"He dropped out of college."

"Oh, no." Iris had never seen Jane look so obviously worried. In fact, in all the years she'd known the woman, there was only one other time that Iris could remember seeing an expression other than impassivity on Jane's face—when she had broken down at the scene of the accident. Now, if Iris hadn't known her, she might have described her as distraught.

Jane said, "First person in the family to go to college. Either side. And he's a smart boy. He never would have dropped out if this hadn't happened."

The truth was that Jane had always felt a certain amount of ambivalence about her son's pursuit of a college degree, or at least about his pursuing it at Amherst. The University of Maine was a fine institution, and she had been supporting it with her tax dollars since she had first drawn a paycheck. She disapproved of his choice to go farther afield for school, to the kind of place where the children of the summer visitors went. It had seemed like striving to her, like trying to turn himself into something he wasn't. But now that he had dropped out she found that she was disappointed. Worried, too. She could not figure out what was going on in the boy's head.

Iris said, "I'm so sorry, Jane. Maybe he just needs more time."

"Well, he's going to get all the time he wants pretty soon. They won't hold his scholarship forever, and I don't know how he thinks he'll pay his tuition without that."

After a protracted process of dueling insurance companies, the threat of a trial, and an out-of-court settlement, the Copaken and the Tetherly families had each received $100,000 from the limousine driver's automobile insurance policy. Iris and Daniel had donated their portion of the money to a variety of Red Hook charities, including Usherman Center's scholarship fund, the library, and the food pantry, which fed a surprising number of local families at the end of every winter. Jane, who could not afford the luxury of philanthropy, divided the sum between Matt, Maureen, Frank, and herself. It gave her a nest egg for the first time in her life, but even if she gave Matt her own portion, what was left of the two combined would not be enough for more than a single year of college.

"I'm sure they understand what he's going through. I know the financial aid process can be confusing, but the decisions are made by compassionate people."

"I suppose," Jane said dubiously. "I don't really talk to them much. Matt takes care of all that himself."

"It's so hard when kids won't do what you know is best for them."

Jane sighed. "Now, isn't that the truth."

"And you can't even tell them that they're making a mistake, because then they'll act just to spite you." As she said this Iris was thinking not about Ruthie, who, despite the evidence of this celebration, generally avoided at all costs making her parents unhappy, but about Becca. Becca, who had always cheerfully brushed off her mother's advice and done exactly what she wanted, up to and including marrying this woman's son.

"Yes, they will," Jane said. She blew air out of her mouth with a noisy huff. "Will your father be there? At this 'celebration'?"

"My father? Yes. Yes, of course."

"Samantha, my niece? She kind of took to him. I guess you know they met up at the Bag."

"No," Iris said. "I didn't know. At the Bait Bag?"

"He had his classical music playing on the radio, and I guess she likes that kind of thing."

"She likes classical music?"

"She's been playing that trout song ever since she heard it."

"The trout song? You mean the Trout Quintet?"

"She picks it out on her electric piano."

"My goodness. Well, I'm sure my father would be happy to play her some music. I mean, play it on the stereo. He can't really play the violin anymore, because of the Parkinson's."

"Samantha checked one of his records out of the library. She's been listening to it pretty much nonstop."

"Did she? That's so sweet. If I'd known I would have brought a few CDs over for her. If you come to the celebration I can have him sign them to her."

"Samantha would like that," Jane said.

Conscious that this chink in Jane's armor might not last, Iris said, "Will you come, Jane?"

Jane sighed. "What time did you say it was?"

"Six," Iris said.

Jane frowned. Then she reached out a finger and swiped it around the edge of Iris's cake plate, scooping up a little lime glaze. She licked her finger and nodded. "That is yummy," she said.

"It's my best recipe," Iris said.

"Maybe we should have just a small slice," Jane said. She bustled around the kitchen, taking plates out of a cupboard, and a knife and two forks out of a drawer. She cut two hefty pieces of cake and slid one across the table to Iris.

"I can't promise anything," Jane said. "But if we're not working, I guess we can make it."

Iris's shoulders sagged with relief. "Thank you so much, Jane. This means a tremendous amount to Ruthie." Then she took a big forkful of cake. The bottom was a tad soggy, and the lime might have been grated a bit more finely. But it was good. It would do.

V

Other than the widow's walk on top of the turret, Iris and Daniel's airy bedroom had the best view in the house of the small East Red Hook cove and the sea beyond. Iris kept the windows bare of curtains so that on clear mornings they were awakened by the sun reflecting off the water. The large room had once been two, but they had taken out the dividing wall and put in a bathroom at one end. Iris had refinished her grandmother's bedroom suite—the tall highboy and the matching double-wide chiffonier. Two bright rag rugs on either side of the bed protected their bare feet from the cold floor in the mornings.

On the bedroom walls hung photographs of the girls and of Iris's various and sundry Maine ancestors, and one of Iris and Daniel, taken on their wedding day down on the beach below the Red Hook Unitarian Church. The only photograph from Daniel's side of the family was of his parents, a stiff, posed black-and-white shot of them wearing evening clothes and smiling uncomfortably into the camera. On the bottom of the picture, in flourishing script, was inscribed "Cunard *RMS Galicia*." The photograph commemorated the single vacation Saul and Irene Copaken had ever taken, a cruise from Miami through the Caribbean, the highlight of which had been a stop in Havana during which Daniel's mother, not normally a gambler, had won seventy-two dollars at baccarat.

Iris stood in front of the closet, discarding one outfit after the other. She yanked a white linen skirt off its hanger, examined its frayed waistband, and tossed it aside. She rejected a flowered cotton skirt because it pulled across the top of her thighs. The confetti-colored sundress made her arms look big. She found a white blouse draped crookedly over a hanger. She held the shirt out in front of her with a lump in her throat.

She'd last worn this to the rehearsal dinner the night before the wedding. A year ago today. There was a yellowish grease mark on the placket and now she remembered having spilled butter down her chin while she was eating her lobster. She should have blotted the stain with cornmeal then soaked the blouse in shampoo, one of the household hints her grandmother had collected in a small scrapbook that hung from a nail in the laundry room. Iris relied on this book, had even updated it with hints of her own—hair spray gets out acrylic paint, vinegar and egg whites loosen chewing gum—but last year she'd failed to follow its prescription for a butter stain. She hadn't, in fact, done any laundry after the accident. Within a few days, a neighbor they didn't know well, one who hadn't even been invited to the wedding, showed up and went quickly through the house emptying hampers, stripping beds, and taking the towels from the bathrooms. That same afternoon a fragrant and folded pile of laundry appeared in a basket just inside the back door. The neighbor had returned a few more times over the summer, ignoring both Iris's perfunctory objections and her grateful tears. Later on Iris found out that the woman had lost her husband in the battle of Khe San, in Vietnam. She knew all too well what the bereaved were likely to forget to do for themselves.

Iris crumpled the blouse in her hands and tossed it in the trash. Then she thought better of it and took it out. She'd tear the blouse up and use it for rags. The soft cotton would be perfect for polishing silver.

Why was she worrying about her clothes, of all things? She knew very well that there was nothing in her closet that didn't make her look like a fifty-one-year-old, menopausal proto-crone. She and Daniel had reached that awful age where a man looks youthful and distinguished and a woman like his elderly aunt. She flicked rapidly through the shirts hanging in the closet. She found a white tank top and went through the closet again, looking for the silvery-blue tunic that she usually wore over it, trying to remember the last time she had it on. Last year, on Memorial Day, to a party at the yacht club. And then Becca had found the tunic hanging on the clothesline and pilfered it; she'd worn it out a few times, and the last time Iris had seen it, the girl was wearing it on the beach as a cover-up. She'd given Becca a piece of her mind, but now couldn't remember if she'd ever gotten the tunic back.

Iris considered going upstairs to look for the tunic in Becca's room, but so far this summer she had managed to avoid even climbing the stairs to the third floor. Anyway, she knew the tunic wasn't there. It hadn't been there last August when she and Daniel had packed up Becca's things.

They'd put off the chore until the last minute. If she'd let him, Daniel would never have done it at all. But he had caved in to her logic that this was not something they'd want hanging over their heads next summer.

"Best just to get it over with," Iris had said, piling his arms with empty cardboard boxes and leading him upstairs.

They'd hesitated in the open doorway. Iris tried but could not remember the first night Becca had slept in this room. When they'd taken possession of the house, the third floor hadn't been used in decades. Iris supposed that when her grandmother was a child there must have been a domestic or two living in the rooms under the eaves. But no one had inhabited those rooms since then. They'd turned one third-floor room into Daniel's office and left the other vacant.

The summer Becca was eleven years old she'd petitioned her parents to be allowed her own room, and over Ruthie's near-hysterical objections, they'd agreed that she could move up to the bedroom next to Daniel's office. Becca had at first made do with a folding cot and a few milk crates, but over the course of the summer, she and Iris had furnished the room, going to yard sales and junk stores as far away as Bangor. Iris recalled the day they'd found the little iron bedstead. It hadn't fit in the Volvo, so they'd left it hanging out the back and driven it home with the hatch open. Becca had to lean over the front seat and clutch the top rail to keep the bed from flying out of the car, Iris's free hand clamped to her ankle, as if that would have kept her from sailing out through the rear door right after the bed. At the time they had found it all terribly funny, and by the time they arrived home they were laughing so hard they were crying and they both needed to pee. But now, after the accident, Iris couldn't bear to think of the careless abandon with which she had driven her children along the winding back roads of Maine.

Nothing in Becca's third-story room matched—the bed was iron, the little desk was walnut, the dresser was painted lemon yellow and decorated with pinkish strawberries. During Becca's childhood the room had been almost spartan, decorated with nothing more than her summertime memorabilia—sailing trophies, pretty shells, shards of beach glass. But when she had left the Conservatory she had brought with her to Maine the contents not just of her dorm room but of her Riverside Drive bedroom as well. The room was packed with clothes, books, jewelry boxes, photographs. And because the kids had been living here the year before they died—during the winter they lived in and took care of the house, and they had decided not to move out until after the wedding—it was full of all of John's things, too. His hockey stick, his jumble of boat-sized sneakers and hiking boots, his clothes, his ball caps, and his dop kit, crowded with a hopeless abandon among Becca's things.

Standing in the doorway of Becca's room that August afternoon a month or so after her death, Daniel had said, "I don't think I can face this." He'd dropped the boxes in the doorway and turned to leave.

Iris grabbed the sleeve of his shirt. "I can't do it by myself."

"Let's just leave it."

But Iris was determined that they take care of it then, before they left. "It's never going to get any easier," she said, and stepped across the threshold, giving him little choice but to follow.

Daniel looked about him with what had seemed to Iris to be a kind of murderous rage. She was sure that if she had not stopped him he would have punched a hole in the wall, or worse. She gave in, told him to leave, and did it herself. She first packed up everything of John's, a task complicated by the fact that she kept breaking down in tears. The poignancy of John's white briefs with their stretched-out leg holes and frayed elastic, of his jeans hanging over the back of a chair, the shape of his body still visible in the creases behind the knees and the white line worn into the brown leather belt looped around the waist. It was almost too much to bear.

But by the time she finished with John's things she had exhausted all her tears. Dry-eyed, she packed up Becca's belongings, packed them all up, except for a few things—Becca's sheet music, a sailing trophy, some old letters, Baby Flame, the little red beanbag horse that had been Becca's lovey when she was a baby. Some of the clothes Iris set aside for Ruthie, figuring that even if she could not bring herself to wear them now, so soon after Becca's death, someday she would be glad to have something of

Becca's to wear. Everything else Iris put in boxes and garbage bags. The next day she went to the Salvation Army, where she donated what was usable. On the way home she stopped at the county dump and threw away what the thrift store would not deign to accept.

In any case, her silvery-blue tunic had not been in Becca's bedroom last summer, Iris was sure of that. So where was it? She went downstairs and ransacked the laundry room, going through the cupboards and pulling out the hamper bins. When it was clear that the tunic was not there, she stood with her arms akimbo, considering the various rooms of her house for a place a shirt might hide. On her way to search the hall closets, Iris passed through the mudroom. She looked at the dozens of L.L. Bean totes in various sizes hanging from hooks on the wall. There were the oversized ones she took to the farmers' market, the beach bags, the ones they used in lieu of picnic baskets. There were the little totes she used as summer purses, and the ones she'd picked up at the factory outlet, monogrammed with other people's initials. Hanging amid all the others, like it was expecting at any minute to be thrown over a shoulder and taken out for a sail, was Becca's old, pink-strapped canvas tote.

Iris pulled the bag down from the hook. The cloth was worn, covered in what appeared to be grease stains. When she opened it up the first thing she saw was a pale-green towel with a pattern of seashells and sea horses, one of a set of beach towels she had picked up a few years back for next to nothing at Reny's. The towel was damp and stank. When she unrolled it she found the red racer-back one-piece bathing suit Becca liked to wear sailing, when she knew she would be working hard and not just sunning herself on deck. The bathing suit was stained with mildew; grayish spots fanned from the crotch all the way up the front. The fabric of the seat was pilled, and the leg holes furred with tiny elastic threads. The suit smelled as wretched as the towel, but still Iris placed it against her cheek and closed her eyes.

Iris had imparted to Becca, through example or nature, a love of the water, of swimming out in the cold and open sea. She'd been a remarkable child. How many seven-year-olds could practice violin for two hours and then jump into a rowboat and take first prize in the harbor pea pod race? How many girls managed to look at home and at ease both on a concert hall stage and up to their knees in bilge water? How many young women looked as beautiful in a stretched-out old bathing suit as they did in performance formal wear? Over the course of her life Iris had met hundreds of musical children, but none had ever been as cheerfully normal as Becca. She had certainly not been an intellectual, but then she hadn't had to be. Becca had embodied the best of all of them: her grandfather's musicality, her father's athleticism, her mother's bustling competence.

Clutching the bathing suit to her heart, Iris turned the tote bag upside down, sending a hail of sand skittering across the tile floor along with a tube of Iris's own French sunscreen, a wide-toothed tortoiseshell comb, a hair band, and a small clamshell case for CDs. And there, balled up in the bottom of the bag, crumpled and smelly but miraculously unstained, was Iris's silvery-blue tunic.

Iris shook the tears from her eyes and put the tunic in the washing machine. She hesitated for a moment, looking at the towel on the ground and at the bathing suit in her hand. With a snap of her wrist she slammed closed the lid of the washer and gathered the contents of Becca's beach bag. She threw away almost everything but the box of CDs, even the bathing suit, taking care to push it all down into the bin so that it wouldn't catch Daniel by surprise when he went to take the trash to the dump. The bag itself she couldn't bring herself to throw away. Instead, she hung it back on its hook, buried behind all the others.

While she waited for the washer's cycle to end, Iris took the box of CDs into the kitchen and flipped through it. *Who's Greatest Hits*, *Nevermind* by Nirvana, *Sparkle and Fade* by Everclear, and *Walk On* by U2. John's music. Rattling loose in the box, missing its plastic case, was a cassette tape labeled in black marker: "Becca, New England Conservatory of Music Audition."

Iris held it in her hand for a few moments. Then she took it into the living room and tucked it behind a random stack of CDs that had teetered on a side table, untouched, for years.

There are only so many ways to set a picnic table, and in spite of Iris's best efforts the backyard looked almost exactly as it had on the night of the rehearsal dinner and on the dozen or so Fourth of July picnics before that. They were using the same tin plates, which Iris had bought at various yard sales and secondhand stores and always used for the picnic. Ruthie had strung fairy lights in the apple tree, although Iris had managed to prevail upon her to refrain from lining the driveway with paper bag luminaria. They'd only ever done that once—last year—and it felt wrong, ghoulish even, to try it again. Just as he did every year, Daniel picked up three dozen steamed lobsters from the pound at the end of Swainsbury Neck. Iris made coleslaw. Tumbling the eight cabbage heads out onto the kitchen counter she tried to remind herself that she'd sliced this many cabbages before, for the picnics, for village gatherings, for library fund-raisers. The rehearsal dinner was not the only time she had ever made coleslaw.

Daniel, too, seemed uncomfortable with how reminiscent the scene was of last year's happy occasion. He stood on the porch holding a massive platter heaped with bright red lobsters, and stared through the screens out to the yard. Ruthie was busily setting up the twenty folding chairs she borrowed from all their neighbors. The same chairs, he thought, that they'd borrowed last year.

"Jesus Christ," he said, when Iris joined him on the porch.

"I know," she said.

"But it doesn't seem to be bothering her."

"It's what she *wanted*," Iris said. "She's doing everything she can to make it look the same."

"And then what?" Daniel said. "What happens when she realizes that she can't turn back the clock?"

Out in the yard Ruthie cast a critical eye over the seating arrangements and then shifted a few chairs around.

"This was a bad idea," Daniel said.

At that moment Ruthie noticed them and called, "Dad, I've cleared a space for the lobsters. You can put them at the end of the table. And Mom, do you want to start melting the butter?"

"It's on the stove," Iris called back.

"Don't forget to skim it," Ruthie said.

"I won't," Iris called. To Daniel she said softly, "Suddenly she's Martha Stewart?"

"Jesus Christ," Daniel repeated, shaking his head.

"It'll be all right," she said. "In a few hours it'll all be over."

"No," Daniel said. "It won't."

Iris watched him slide sideways through the screen door, propping it open with his foot and carefully balancing the platter in his hands. By the time she reached the door to help, he had banged it shut behind him. He put the platter down on the table, and Ruthie adjusted its position once, and then again, before she was satisfied. Daniel suddenly grabbed Ruthie, clasped her close to his chest, and kissed the top of her head. Iris wished at that moment that their embrace could open and include her, just as it had when the girls were little and they would have what they called "four-way hugs." But a three-way hug would seem too poignant, wouldn't it? And at any rate, she could barely remember the last time she and Daniel had embraced.

The guests began arriving, neighbors and people from the village and from Red Hook, friends from the yacht club and from Iris's various boards and committees, the members of the lawn bowling club whose matches Daniel had, for the first time in a dozen years, stopped attending. They were the same people who came every year to the Copakens' Fourth of July picnic, although this year they stood around awkwardly, unsure what behavior was called for under these odd circumstances. Was this a memorial, akin to a funeral? Or was it just the same old party the Copakens threw every year? Were they meant to talk about Becca and John, or to avoid bringing up their names? Was it okay to make chitchat about inconsequential things, or should they keep their voices low and somber?

Iris, no surer of what the occasion demanded than her guests were, avoided conversation beyond the most bland and simple of greetings; she kept herself busy handing out drinks. After a while the gin and beer had their effect, and people began to loosen up, choosing, in the end, to behave as if this were a Fourth of July picnic like any other, which Iris supposed was for the best, and the handy thing about gin and beer.

The Tetherlys were the last to arrive, and by the time they rounded the corner of the Copakens' house, Iris had begun to despair of them coming. Ruthie rushed up to them.

"You came!" Ruthie said. "And look at everything you brought!" Matt was hiding behind two cases of beer piled high in his arms. She tried to wrest one of the cases from him, but he resisted. Finally, laughing, she pointed out the galvanized ice chest. "Did you bring the fireworks?" she called after him.

"They're in the car," he said over his shoulder.

"I was worried you wouldn't have a chance to drive all the way to New Hampshire."

"I was happy to go," he said. "It was a nice ride."

Jane was holding a huge foil baking pan, big enough to roast a tom turkey. She looked over the spread, at the row of glistening pies. She recognized the heavy ceramic pie plates; she had scrubbed them herself. She looked down at her rectangular foil pan and said, "You don't need this."

"No!" Ruthie said. "We *do*. I loved it last year; it's always been one of my favorites. That's why we asked you to bring it. Let me." She moved the pies aside, took the pan from Jane, and set it down with a flourish.

"Mom!" Ruthie called. "The Tetherlys are here."

Iris greeted Jane and Samantha. "Welcome," she said. "I'm so glad you made it."

Jane nodded, looking around the yard. "Big party," she said.

Samantha spied Mr. Kimmelbrod sitting on the other side of the yard. She tugged on her great-aunt's sleeve. "Can I go over there and say hi to him?"

"To who?" Jane said.

"The old man."

"Samantha!" Jane said. "Watch yourself!"

Iris laughed. "Oh, Mr. Kimmelbrod knows he's old. Go on, honey. He could probably use some company."

"I'll take her over," Jane said, and she followed Samantha across the grass. They found Mr. Kimmelbrod struggling out of his webbed patio chair.

Without asking, Jane helped him to his feet.

"I understand the young lady would like to see my violin," he said. "May I take her inside?"

"I don't want her to trouble you," Jane said.

"It's no trouble," Mr. Kimmelbrod said. "On the contrary. I brought it only because Iris told me she was coming. And if you would care to, Samantha, I would very much like to hear you play the piano."

"Please, Aunt Jane," Samantha said.

Jane shrugged her assent and followed the two of them into the house, to the piano that she had arranged to have tuned two months back. This past winter Jane had resumed the caretaking responsibilities for the house that she'd deferred to Becca and John the year before. She'd gotten the oil furnace and the propane tank filled, turned on the water, taken down the storm windows and put up the screens, mowed the meadow and lawn, replaced the water filter, had the piano tuned, and replenished staples like flour, sugar, and the fancy teas Iris liked. Jane had been taking care of this house since long before Iris had inherited it, just as her mother had done before that.

Caretaking for the summer residents was Jane's primary source of winter income. It was what kept her from having to resort to making Christmas wreaths or going south to work at one of the canneries, like other people did. It never used to bother Jane to perform any of the various caretaking tasks, menial or otherwise. But this year she had resented every hour she had spent in the Copaken house, every curtain she had taken down and laundered, every pipe she had drained, every lightbulb she had changed. She had wished she could afford to keep her summer girls on, so that she could foist the job off on one of them. But money was money, and she was not so rich that she could turn her nose up at one hundred dollars a month.

Mr. Kimmelbrod sat down at the piano and directed Samantha to a stool next to him. He said, "I will play for you a little song and I would like for you to hum it. Can you do that?"

"Yes," Samantha said.

He launched into the same piece of music Samantha had been plonking away at for the last ten days.

"This is the Trout Quintet," he said. "What we heard on the radio."

Samantha had already started humming the music. He stopped playing but she continued humming.

"You *remember*?" he said.

Jane said, "She's been playing it on her electric piano. Night and day. I told you, she hears something once and then she can play it."

"Fascinating," he said. "Samantha, can you tell me anything about these two notes?" He played one, and then another an octave higher.

"They're the same," she said. "Just, one's higher."

"Very good. Now I'm going to play two sets of notes. You tell me if the second set is the same as the first."

He played three notes, moved up the keyboard, and then played another three.

"Same," she said.

"And this?"

"Same."

"And this?"

Before he'd even played the third note she waved her hand as if dismissing something unpleasant. "Different."

"Manners," Jane said, warningly.

Mr. Kimmelbrod waved a hand at Jane, dismissing her just as Samantha had dismissed the incorrect notes.

He played another phrase, this one five notes. He paused and played it again.

"Same," Samantha said.

"And again?"

"Different."

"Very good. Now I will play a slightly longer melody. The second time I play it I will change one note. You tell me which note I changed. The first, third, like that."

He played a short tune.

"Fifth," she said.

The next time, she stopped him after the first note. The next time, only at the very end, on the last note.

"That's easy," she said.

"Was the note I changed higher or lower?"

"Higher."

"Correct."

Jane was incredulous. It was not merely that what Samantha was hearing was beyond Jane's ken—she could tell that the bits of music were different from one another, but she could never have articulated why—it was Samantha's authority. She was normally so quiet and polite, all too conscious of her status as guest in Jane's house. If asked to express a preference, she deferred until absolutely forced to make up her mind. How many times had Jane stood over her at dinnertime holding two bottles of soda in her hands and saying, "It doesn't make a damn bit of difference to me whether you drink Pepsi or Diet Pepsi, girl. Just pick one!"? And yet here she was, answering every question correctly. Jane felt a surge of something suspiciously like pride.

Now Mr. Kimmelbrod said, "The notes have names. For example, this note"—he played one in the middle of the keyboard—"is a C."

"Like doe," Samantha said.

He raised his eyebrows in surprise. "You have been taught solfège?"

"Solfège?" Samantha repeated.

"The names for the notes? Someone has taught you this? You have studied sight-singing?"

"She hasn't studied anything," Jane said. "Like I said, she doesn't take lessons. Unless maybe they taught her at school."

"*The Sound of Music*," Samantha said. "You know, the movie. 'Doe a deer, a female deer.' " She sang a clear and perfectly pitched C.

Mr. Kimmelbrod laughed. "*The Sound of Music*, God help us. Well, then, what note is this?"

"Re."

"And this?"

"Fa."

Mr. Kimmelbrod pressed a number of keys together. "This is a chord. What notes do you hear?"

"Re, fa, la. But two re's."

"Turn your back to me."

Samantha scooted around on her stool so that she was looking at Jane instead of at Mr. Kimmelbrod.

"Now what do you hear?" he said, playing another.

"Re and la. And the third is the note right between fa and so. I don't know the name of it."

"F sharp," Mr. Kimmelbrod said. "And now? Do you recognize the chord?"

"Yes," she said. "Like in the Trout."

He turned to Jane. "Your grand-niece appears to possess absolute pitch. Perfect pitch."

"What does that mean?"

"It means, essentially, that if she hears a note she can name it. And vice versa. She can reproduce a note without a reference. Like she did just now. Especially interesting is her ability to recognize the various notes within a chord. I find it curious, because most children who do not receive early musical training lose their capacity for absolute pitch."

"She's been playing that piano of hers for a long time."

"But without a teacher, correct?"

"Yes."

"Just the little electric piano?" he asked.

"Right."

"Marvelous," he said. "Although I am quite frankly even more impressed with her feel for rhythm and melody. Absolute pitch is interesting, but not necessarily a sign of musical talent. It is something like being able instinctively to identify the parts of speech. Just because a person knows a word is a noun does not mean he will be a great writer. Samantha? Shall we keep playing?"

"Yes!" she said.

"Yes, *sir*," Jane said.

Mr. Kimmelbrod played the opening melody from the fourth movement. His hands, far too stiff to play the violin with any competence, could still make music on the piano. "I'd like you to hum it in a different key. Do you know what I mean by that? The different notes are the building blocks of the melody. So instead of this key"—he played the same chord he'd played before—"you'd center the melody on this." He played something else. Samantha closed her eyes for a moment, and then began humming again.

"Perfect," he said. "Can you tell me what note you started with?"

"La."

"Very good. Now start the melody on re."

"Should I make it happy or sad?"

Mr. Kimmelbrod smiled. "Make it sad first, and then happy."

Samantha intoned a perfectly pitched D, and then proceeded to hum a flawless melody. After a few moments she modulated to the major key and hummed it through.

"Now try to make it fit with what I'm playing. It's from the third variation." He began to play a darting accompaniment. Samantha joined him, in perfect sync, both rhythmically and tonally. After a few moments he stopped and clasped his fingers. "Wonderful," he said.

"Mr. Kimmelbrod?" Samantha said shyly.

"Yes?" he said.

"You said I could see your violin?"

"Yes, I did," he said. He reached behind the piano and took out a violin in a battered case.

His tremor made it difficult to unclasp the buckles on the case, but finally he got it open and took the violin from the velvet lining. "It's very old," he said.

She stared at it, her hands twitching by her side.

"Go ahead," he said, holding it out to her. The violin jumped in his hands and he lowered it to his lap so as not to drop it.

Holding her breath, the girl wiped her palms on her shorts and took the violin. She held it as though with the slightest touch it would shatter into a million pieces.

"Will you play it for me?" she said.

He showed her his trembling hands. "You see, my hands no longer work very well."

"Please?"

"Samantha!" Jane said.

"No," he said. "It's all right. I will try." He took the instrument back and lifted it to his chin. Then he hesitated and looked at Jane. "Might I ask you . . ." He paused. "I no longer play in public."

Jane said, "She doesn't need to hear you. She got your record out from the library, that's enough."

"No," he said. "I don't mind playing for the child."

Jane hesitated, but then realized what he meant. She rose hurriedly to her feet. "I'll be outside," she said.

Iris opened the door of the bathroom in time to see Jane leave the living room. Iris had retreated to the bathroom because she hadn't been able to tolerate another moment of standing around making small talk, gossiping about real estate prices and divorces, being updated on the doings of other people's children, pretending that there was anything normal about this picnic. Yet neither could she bring herself to talk about Becca. Whenever anyone placed a condoling hand on her arm, peered into her eyes, and dropped their voice to ask how she *really* was, Iris could answer only, "Fine." As if that one word would satisfy them. As if that one word had anything to do with the roiling confusion of emotions Ruthie's celebration had stirred up.

Readying her false hostess's smile, Iris said, "Is everything okay in there?"

"They seem all right," Jane said.

For a moment they stood awkwardly, then Iris said, "Dinner's ready and waiting outside."

Jane nodded briskly and strode off down the hall.

Before Iris could bring herself to follow, she heard someone, it could only be her father, playing the violin, a G major scale. On the wall opposite the living room door hung a large mirror with a gilt frame. Iris looked into the mirror and saw in it the reflection of an image at once shocking and familiar. Strange and yet somehow perfect. Her father sitting on a stool, his violin tucked beneath his chin, playing for a rapt little girl who could not take her eyes off him. A little girl who seemed to be feeling rather than hearing each and every note as it sailed off the string.

After dinner, as they waited for it to be dark enough to set off the fireworks, a few of the young people began desultorily throwing a football back and forth. Ruthie and Becca's friend Jasmine leaned up against the wall between the yard and the sea, watching them. Matt drew his arm back and Ruthie could see the sharp triangle of his shoulder blade beneath his shirt, like a bird's wing. With a snap of his wrist he let the ball go, and then looked away, as if he didn't care where it landed. He turned toward them and squinted into the light, the three neat lines between his eyebrows so deep and distinct that Ruthie could see them from where she was sitting.

Jasmine jutted her chin in Matt's direction. "I fucked him."

"You did *not*," Ruthie said.

"I did. In our boathouse. On a pile of seat cushions."

"You did *not*," Ruthie said.

"I did indeed."

"When?"

"Last summer."

"Last summer? After . . . after everything?"

"No! God no. Before. Remember that night a few days before when we all went out drinking at the Neptune?"

"Yeah."

"Lauren gave a bunch of us a ride home because she was the only one who wasn't totally wasted, but she was afraid to drive up the hill to his house in the dark, so I said he could crash at our place. We ended up in the boathouse."

"But he's, like, eight years younger than you! He was what, nineteen?"

"He told me he was twenty-one. And they were serving him drinks."

"Oh please, the bartender at the Neptune will serve anyone. I had my first beer there when I was sixteen."

"Well, he said he was twenty-one."

"He's going into his junior year. He's maybe twenty. Did Becca know?"

"God no," Jasmine said. "She would have killed me. She treated him like a little brother, even though it was obvious to everyone that he had a crush on her."

That, Ruthie thought, was Becca to a T. In a way she'd been everybody's big sister, the person who teased you about your clothes or the way your hair stood on end in the morning, and also the person who made sure you learned how to swim, who stuck up for you when you were being picked on, who warned you when you had something green between your teeth. There had always been other people who felt some version of Ruthie's own adoration for Becca, and while that had on occasion made Ruthie jealous, she'd always tried to reassure herself that Becca's generalized goodwill had a very particular focus when it came to her own sister.

"Do you really think Matt had a crush on her?" Ruthie said.

"Totally. Hey, Matt!" Jasmine called. "Come sit with us."

"Jasmine!" Ruthie said, swatting Jasmine on her bare, bony leg. "Don't."

"Come on, Matt," Jasmine called. Matt caught a pass and then pulled his arm back and spun the ball in a neat arc. Again Ruthie watched the lean muscles of his back and shoulders contract. The other player caught the pass, tucked the ball under his arm, and jogged away, waving Matt in the direction of the girls.

Matt walked over, his head down, a few strands of dark hair falling over his eyes. "Hey," he said.

"Have a seat, stay awhile," Jasmine said, patting a patch of grass next to her.

He sat down, missing by a few feet the spot he'd been instructed to take. He sat with his elbows resting on his bent knees and began absently pulling blades of grass, every once in a while putting the white end of a particularly tender blade between his teeth. His face was shiny with sweat and he was giving off a shimmer of heat.

"Having fun?" Jasmine said.

"Sure."

"Talkative guy, aren't you?" Jasmine said.

Matt's neck and ears grew pink.

Ruthie said quickly, "Thanks for buying the fireworks. I really appreciate it."

"No problem. It was good to get away for a day."

Jasmine, said, "Okay, children. I'm going leave you two and see if Iris needs any help clearing up." She sprang lightly to her feet. Ruthie began to scramble up, too, but Jasmine stopped her. "I got it. You two stay here and talk."

She took off across the lawn at a jog. Watching her go Ruthie said, "She's got a lot of energy for someone who hasn't eaten since 1989."

When Matt smiled, his protruding cheekbones lifted, balling up under his eyes.

"I can't believe I said that," she said. "I'm so mean."

"You aren't mean."

"I probably should go help my mom," Ruthie said.

"No, don't," Matt said. "I mean, I think Jasmine and your mom have probably got it under control. And my mom will help. She can't stand to look at a mess."

Ruthie didn't want to be talking to Matt about cleaning or about Jasmine. She wanted to talk to him about *real* things, about pain and sorrow, emptiness, guilt. Of all the people here today, he was the only one with any hope of understanding what she had been going through, how it felt to lose your older sibling, to be suddenly bereft of the presence, of the soul, that was your fixed star, the index of all your ideas and experiences.

"My mom told me that you left school," she said.

"Yeah."

"I can understand that. I thought about doing it, too."

"You did?"

"Definitely. I mean, in the end instead of leaving I did sort of the opposite. I worked *all* the time. If I could have slept in the library I would have."

"That's because you go to *Harvard*," he said, gently mocking her.

Even after all these years Ruthie had never managed to master the Harvard student's pose of studied nonchalance. She felt vaguely embarrassed, as if there were something ostentatious about attending the college, as if her intelligence were something she had to apologize for. "It's just as hard to get into Amherst," she said.

"Not quite."

They were silent for a moment. Then Matt said, "I can see why you'd spend your time in the library. You were trying to get away from everybody."

"Exactly."

"Me, too. It was, like, no one at Amherst knew John, so they just expected me to be the same person as I was before, you know? And I wasn't. I'm not."

"*Exactly*. That's exactly how I felt."

"Maybe I should have thought of hiding in the library," he said ruefully. "I'd probably be better off."

"What are you doing now?"

"I'm working at the boatyard."

"I didn't know you were into boats."

"I wasn't. But I guess I am now. I'm going to try to finish John's old Alden." He looked almost defiant, as if daring her to disapprove of his plan.

"So are you working at the yard to kind of, like, learn how to do it? Or do you already know?"

"John taught me some. But I'm learning down at the yard. You know. Slowly."

"That's great," Ruthie said, doubtfully. "I'm sure John would have wanted the boat to get built." What she was not sure of was whether John would have wanted his younger brother to build it. He'd been so proud of Matt's being the first Tetherly to go to college, of how different he was from the rest of the family. John used to say, in a tone at once proud and wondering, that Matt loved books the way he, John, loved boats. Still, she found something touching in the idea of Matt building the boat that had been John's dream. She felt a sudden wish that she could do something like that for her sister, finish some job Becca had left undone.

While they waited for the sky to grow dark enough for the fireworks, Matt described the boat to her. It had a well-steeved-up bowsprit, a clipper bow with a carved billethead and trailboards, and the cabin was made of exotic South American mahogany. He sounded, Ruthie thought, like he knew what he was talking about, although she had not the slightest idea what half the terms he used meant.

Matt looked nothing like his brother—he was dark where John was fair, slender where John was broad, his eyes aquamarine shot through with flecks of green where John's had been a paler, clearer sky blue—but now when he moved his hands as he talked, describing arcs in the air, there was some deep kinship visible. She was lulled by the sound of his voice, low but emphatic, and by his simple, masculine grace. She felt a sense of gentle melancholy, not an unpleasant sensation, just different. Softer, more diffuse than the gut-wrenching sadness she had felt so many times over the past year.

Although Matt had always deferred to his jovial older brother, it had always been clear, at least to Ruthie, that he was the smarter of the two. Once, a few years ago, on one of the few occasions she could remember hanging out with Matt, the two of them got into an argument about David Foster Wallace's *Infinite Jest*, which she had had to read for a Freshman English class. Ruthie remembered thinking it was funny that this kid had such strong opinions about a book he was probably too young to read. He was two years younger than she was, and back then that had seemed like a lot.

Ruthie wondered if Matt had indeed had a crush on Becca. Perhaps, but it seemed to Ruthie more that he had idolized her like a younger brother would. After all, Becca had been John's girlfriend since Matt was nine years old. She was almost as much a fact of Matt's life as she had been of Ruthie's.

Daniel looked up at the sky, trying to assess whether it was dark enough to light the fireworks. The guests were sprinkled around the yard, sitting on the grass like he was, or in the chairs Ruthie had collected for them. The first mosquitoes had descended and the sharp chemical tang of repellent filled the air. Iris distributed citronella candles in fat glass jars.

So far, Daniel thought, as little as he wanted to be here, as lonely as he felt surrounded by all these people, he had adequately executed his duty for this celebration. No one had sensed his dislocation, his tamped down need to escape, the unforgivable itch in his hands as they ached to ball themselves into fists and strike out at something, anything. He had made no public spectacle of himself.

This celebration was the first some people had seen of one another this summer, and although it had been uncomfortable at first, soon enough the guests seemed to forget that they were there to do anything other than celebrate the independence of the United States from Great Britain and eat lobster and pie. To them it was just another Fourth of July picnic at the Copakens'. Now, though, as it grew dark, conversation ebbed. The twenty or so people who had remained to see the fireworks quietly sipped their drinks and scraped the last traces of Nilla wafer banana pudding from their dessert plates with the tines of their forks.

"It's like waiting for Havdalah," Mary Lou Curran said. She was sitting on a kitchen chair balanced somewhat precariously in the grass.

"Hmm?" Daniel said, looking up at her.

"*You* know, dear. Waiting for the stars."

"The stars?"

"When you can see three stars in the sky, then Shabbat is over."

"Mary Lou Curran," Daniel said, laughing. "You never cease to amaze me. How in the world do you know about Shabbat and Havdalah?"

"My second husband was Jewish, didn't you know? We weren't married long—we met at a bicentennial picnic and he was dead before 1980. But that was long enough for me to learn all about Shabbat and the Havdalah service, my personal favorite, with the lovely braided candle and the spice box. For a while there I collected those little boxes. I even know how to bake a challah. Or at least I used to."

"I'll bet you still can," Daniel said. "So today would have been your anniversary, in a way."

"I suppose it would have been," she said. "Though I think now the day's come to mean something else for all of us."

"I suppose," he said. "But tomorrow would be . . . more accurate."

"Perhaps," Mary Lou said. "But Jewish holidays start the night before." She raised a gnarled finger to the sky. "One—I think we can count Venus, don't you? Two. And there, just barely visible. Three."

Daniel's view of the stars was suddenly obscured by the dark planet of his wife.

"Should we start?" Iris said.

"Where's Ruthie?" he said.

"Down by the water, I think. Do you have the fireworks?"

"Matt put them out at the end of the dock."

"Okay, then." Iris raised her voice. "Everyone! Can I have everyone's attention?"

All remaining conversation stopped and the guests looked expectantly at Iris.

"If you'll all come down to the beach, we'll say a few words and then set off the fireworks."

The guests silently rose and followed her down to the water. It was a ghostly, mute procession. No one knew what to say, so they said nothing at all. When they reached the beach they huddled together, waiting.

"Ruthie," Iris called. "Ruthie? Do you want to start?"

Daniel peered through the dark at the crowd, looking for his daughter. She was standing on the beach. We waved but she shook her head.

"Ruthie?" Iris called again.

Daniel put his hand on his wife's arm and, leaning down to her ear, whispered. "You do it."

Iris seemed about to object, but then she sighed. She lifted her glass in the air and said, "Do you all still have your drinks?" Those who did followed her lead and held their wineglasses, tumblers, and bottles of beer in the air.

"To Becca and John," Iris said.

At that moment, before her toast could be echoed by the other guests, there was a sharp cry. Everyone turned in the direction of the sound and, nearly in unison, gasped as they watched Mr. Kimmelbrod tumble to the ground. His cane had skidded across a slippery boulder and he had lost his footing on the rocky beach.

"Dad!" Iris shouted and ran to his side, pushing people out of her way.

Ruthie was there before her, and fell to her knees, pulling Mr. Kimmelbrod's head into her lap.

"Don't move him!" someone shouted.

The guests pressed closer, straining to see. Across the minds of those who had in the first place disapproved of the idea of a celebration to commemorate the dead couple flitted the thought that this wasn't unexpected. Not that the old man would fall, certainly, but that something bad would happen. Others simply shuddered at the terrible symmetry of this second accident. Had he broken his hip? Hurt his head?

"Please," Iris said, "someone call an ambulance."

"No," Mr. Kimmelbrod said. "I don't need an ambulance. I'm fine."

He was trying to sit, frantically jabbing his cane at the ground to try to push himself up.

"Don't," Iris said. "Just wait until the ambulance gets here."

Ignoring her mother, Ruthie slipped her arm beneath Mr. Kimmelbrod's shoulders and pulled him up to sitting.

"Please," Mr. Kimmelbrod said. "I am fine. Just a clumsy old man."

"Do you want to try to stand up, Grandpa?" Ruthie said.

Iris said, "Dad, don't. Something could be broken. Your hip, your leg."

"Nothing is broken," he said.

Ruthie squatted down next to him and was about to hoist him up when Daniel stepped forward. "Let me," he said, and lifted Mr. Kimmelbrod up to his feet as though he weighed no more than a child.

With sighs and sounds of encouragement, people made room for Mr. Kimmelbrod, supported by Daniel on one side and Ruthie on the other, to walk up to the opening in the low wall that separated the lawn from the rocky beach. After the three of them had passed through, the crowd of guests followed, until everyone was standing on the lawn.

"Up to the house?" Daniel asked.

"No. Here, I think," Mr. Kimmelbrod said.

Matt appeared holding a white wooden folding chair in his hand. He unfolded it and set it on the grass, pushing on first one leg, then the others, to make sure it was steady.

With a wince he tried to suppress, Mr. Kimmelbrod lowered himself into the chair.

Iris said, "Are you sure you're okay, Dad? Do you need an ice pack?"

"Only a drink," he said.

A small hand appeared, holding a tumbler. "It's ginger ale," Samantha said. "I only took two sips."

Mr. Kimmelbrod accepted the glass, patting the girl on the head.

"Thank you. Ginger ale was exactly what I had in mind." He turned to Iris and said, "Please, continue. Light the fireworks."

"I'll sit with you," Ruthie said.

"No, you go down to the water where you can see." He glanced at Samantha, who was hovering anxiously. "This young lady will keep me company, won't she?"

Samantha leaped forward and positioned herself next to his chair like a sentry.

Mr. Kimmelbrod raised his glass in the direction of the guests. "To Becca and John," he said.

People hesitated, looking at one another.

"To Becca and John," he repeated.

"To Becca and John," they replied.

After the last of the fireworks had been lit, after the last of the guests had collected their things and left, Iris sat alone at the end of the dock, her bare feet in the water. She moved her feet in slow circles, trailing twin spirals of green phosphorescence. When Becca was a toddler Iris used to take her out in a little old dory at night. She would strap Becca into a life jacket, throw a few more on the bottom of the boat for padding, and prop the little girl, not much more than a baby, really, on top. Then she would row out to the middle of the harbor, ship the oars, and they would drift. In the too-big life jacket Becca looked like a tortoise flipped on its back, her chubby legs and arms waving uselessly. Periodically she would try to lean over the side of the boat, straining to reach the water. Iris would grab the back strap of the life jacket and lower Becca far enough so she could plunge a fat little hand into the water, waggle it around, and squeal at the sight of its sparkly green wake. She had rejected Iris's explanation of how plankton emitted energy in the form of light when disturbed, and instead insisted that phosphorescence was another word for fairy dust.

The only thing little Becca had loved as much as the sea was music, especially hearing her grandfather play. They would sit together in the living room, the child on the little willow rocking chair that had belonged to generations of tiny Godwins and Hewinses, the old man seated on the piano bench. She would stare at him, rapt, her eyes wide and her mouth hanging partly open, whether he was playing a Bach fugue or a series of scales. Becca had been entranced by Mr. Kimmelbrod and his music, just as Samantha had been entranced by him tonight.

Iris stared at her feet, long and white in the moonlight, like pale salmon swimming in place against a seaward-flowing tide.

"Iris," Daniel called. "Are you coming in?" She winced at the loud insistence of his voice. At night sound traveled well over the water, a fact that, as a teenager, Becca had never seemed to realize. When she was late for curfew, Becca used to have John bring her home in one of the boats from the yacht club, figuring that her parents would be listening for the sound of a car on the road. Iris, from her bedroom overlooking the backyard and the sea, would hear the slap of the oars as the boat approached the dock. She would hear the kids' hushed voices. She would even hear an occasional moan that she did her best not to interpret. She would listen to the slow scrape of the screen door against the frame, and she would know that Becca had caught it before it could make its trademark gunshot slam.

"Iris!" Daniel called again.

Iris wished she could sleep out here, on the water. She didn't think she could bear another night on her side of their wide mattress, another night when she never once touched Daniel's body because she could not bring herself to reach across the divide.

"Iris!"

"I'm coming," she said softly, wondering if her voice would carry like his did, like Becca's had. She padded up the dock in bare feet, then stopped to slip on her tennis shoes before picking her way across the rocky beach. She'd been wearing the same pair of torn Keds for more than a decade. Becca had hated them, had said they looked like an old woman's shoes, with lumps on the side from the corns on her pinkie toes.

She took the long way back to the house, going around to the opening in the wall at the far end of the property instead of using the one near the dock. If she hadn't made the detour she would never have seen the couple sitting on the steps of the Grange Hall's side door. If there hadn't been a moon or if she and Daniel hadn't pulled down the dying white pine between their yard and the Grange Hall's, she wouldn't have noticed the two bodies pressed against the door, less two distinct forms than one dark mass. They didn't see her; she was at least thirty yards away and they were busy with each other. As she watched, one of the forms partly detached itself from the other. At that moment, the cloud that had been obscuring the moon shifted and a ray of clean white moonlight shone on the couple, placed perfectly to illuminate the pale globe of the girl's bare breast. Matt bent his head and the breast disappeared. Iris heard Ruthie moan softly, her voice carrying just like Becca's had, all those years ago.

THE THIRD SUMMER

I

Saul Copaken always claimed that no heavyweight, not Joe Frazier, not George Foreman, not even Ali, could hold a candle to Archie Moore, who fought for twenty-seven years and knocked out his last opponent at the age of fifty. While Daniel had always loved Moore, he had never truly appreciated the majesty of the accomplishment that had so impressed his father until this moment, when he found himself trying to convince the young manager of the Maine Event to let into the ring a fifty-five-year-old man with an amateur's license that had expired before the kid was born.

Daniel had started training the morning after they buried Becca. He found that the harder he pushed his body, the easier it was to empty his mind of grief. At first he had limited himself to running and jumping rope—a modified version of his college boxing coach Tommy Rawson's roadwork regime—and for almost two years that had been enough. This spring, however, he found himself requiring ever more prolonged and more rigorous exertion to achieve that desired hollow space in his head. One Saturday afternoon in early May, still crackling with energy after a ten-mile run through Central Park, he decided to clear out his and Iris's storage locker in the basement of their building on Riverside Drive. Each tenant was entitled to an eight-by-six-foot cage, and theirs was packed full of boxes and odds and ends of furniture. He could not bring himself to open any of the boxes for fear of finding something like Becca's elementary school report cards, or one of the sweaters his mother had knit for her when she was a baby, and in the end he did little more than shift the contents of the cage from one side to the other. The job was taxing, but still, he didn't work up the sweat he had been hoping for.

In the back of the cage he came upon a box salvaged from the attic of his parents' house after his father's death. This box posed little risk of upending his heart, and he opened it. On top, in a cracked wooden frame with a loose nail poking through the paper backing, lay a faded black-and-white photograph of Daniel in boxing trunks and gloves, his lean body slick with sweat. He found he could remember neither the match nor the moment the photograph was taken, but he was sure he had won. You could tell by his grin. In the dim, dank storage locker, Daniel crouched down onto his heels, holding the photograph in his hands. He remembered with heartbreaking clarity what it was like to be so young and powerful. So unencumbered, so free. He remembered in his hands and shoulders how good it felt to fight, how a few minutes in the ring could wipe out a day's worth of frustration, of self-doubt, of everything beyond the instantaneous question of where the next punch would land.

This summer, as soon as they arrived in Red Hook, Daniel had driven up to Newmarket. On that first morning, as he pushed opened the heavy steel door of the Maine Event and walked into the stinking fug of sweat, foot, mildew, leather, and chalk, he felt like he was shedding years and responsibilities and, especially, any pain that could not be treated with a handful of aspirin and an ice pack.

He had been training hard since that first day. Thirty minutes jumping rope, and then another thirty working the heavy bag and the speed bag, shadow boxing in front of the mirror. Then an hour stretching out and soaking in the overchlorinated hot tub. It was a long workout, longer than anyone else's at the gym, even though the other guys were much younger. Every once in a while a couple of guys would take a desultory turn in the ring, but mostly they appeared to spend their time wrapping and unwrapping their hands, and talking shit about their amateur rankings. Sometimes one or another of them would glance Daniel's way, say something to his buddies in an undertone that broke them up, as though there were something funny or even pathetic about the sight of an old man working out so hard. Daniel tried not to give them the satisfaction of hearing him suck wind, but every so often he had to bend down, rest his elbows on his knees, and wait for his heart rate to slow so that he didn't feel like it was going to burst out of his chest and go flapping around the room.

He'd told no one about his workouts, especially not Iris. She'd hated his boxing, had insisted that he quit almost as soon as they met. If she knew where he was, she'd throw a fit. Over the past few weeks he'd found himself concocting ever more Baroque explanations for his three-hour daily absences from home.

At first the exertion and the familiar colors, furnishings, and sounds of the gym—the smells of armpit and feet, the give of the mats beneath his shoes, the weight of the gloves in his hand, the ticking rattle of the speed ball—had been enough. But now, he wanted to fight. When Daniel was in his prime, none of the young fatheads who hung out at the Maine Event would have lasted more than three rounds with him. He knew he could take a couple of them even now, if the little bastard who managed the place would just let him spar.

"How old are you?" the kid asked, smirking. This was the same kid Daniel remembered from two years ago, turtle-shaped, his bullet head jutted out almost horizontally from the Gargantuan hump that was his back and shoulders.

"Four years older than Larry Holmes. How old are you?"

"Twenty-two."

"How many fights have you had?"

"Four," the kid said, with some embarrassment.

"By the time I was twenty-two, I'd beaten half the middleweights on the New England Golden Gloves circuit," Daniel said, in an uncharacteristic show of braggadocio.

A gravelly voice from behind him rasped, "And the other half?"

Daniel turned in the direction of the voice and found himself staring down at the freckled bald pate of an elderly giant in an electric wheelchair. Daniel had seen him around the gym before—he clearly owned the place. Daniel took a step back in order to look more closely into the man's face. He had the mashed nose of a fighter, and one corner of his upper lip was bisected by the twisted thread of a scar. The man's large gnarled hands with their lumpy knuckles rested uselessly on the arms of the wheelchair. The tips of his fingers were bent at sharp right angles, as though they'd been broken and poorly reset.

"The other half kicked my ass," Daniel said.

The man in the wheelchair extended his crippled hand to Daniel. "Jimmy Tunney," he said.

"Any relation to Gene?"

"My father's cousin."

Daniel nodded and took the man's hand. "Daniel Copaken." Tunney's palm was soft and powdery, a surprising contrast to his knotted and calloused fingers.

"How long since your last fight?"

"A while," Daniel said. As he had worked his body back into fighting shape, he had begun to feel that the young man who had danced in the ring, weighed down by nothing but two ten-ounce gloves, was his finest, truest self. His other self—the man who went every day to a job he hated, who held up his end of a marriage that had grown difficult and disconnected, who had lost one child and feared the growing distance between him and the other—that Daniel Copaken felt weighed down by time and failure.

"Back in the late sixties?" Tunney said.

"Thereabouts."

"You ever fight down Lowell way? We're talking late '67, '68?"

"Sure."

"Yeah, I saw you once. I had a boxer on the same card, Damone Pettiford. It was his last amateur bout. And the last decent fight he had."

Daniel remembered the card and the fighter. He could remember every single one of his fights: every punch, every count, every ring of the bell. Over the past weeks, his memories of those long-ago bouts had gradually returned to him, as though his sweat and effort were bringing them to the surface of his mind.

"Pettiford?" Daniel said. "Kind of a showboat. Threw a wicked seven."

Tunney laughed. "That's the one. You fought some kid from the islands. Can't remember his name."

Daniel winced at the memory. "Angel Franqui." He pictured Franqui in his mind. A small man, with muscles bunched like tennis balls under his skin and a birthmark the size and color of a plum across his solar plexus. Daniel remembered taking aim at that birthmark, trying to use it as a target. He had not, he remembered bitterly now, ever managed to connect.

"That's right. Franqui. You lost."

"Only on points," Daniel said, his cheeks reddening beneath the whiskers he had not bothered to shave this morning. One good power punch would have brought pitty-patting Angel Franqui down for the count, but Daniel had had an off night.

"You took a lot of hits."

"Could always take a punch. Still can."

"We'll see," Tunney said. "What do you walk around at, 'bout 190?"

"Closer to 185."

"That's a far cry from 165. Hey, Wiley," Tunney called. "Come on over here."

A thick-legged man with a graying scraggly ponytail stilled the speed ball he'd been hammering and ambled over to them. Despite having worked out in the same gym since Daniel first walked through the door, this was the first time they'd been part of the same conversation. "Yeah, Jimmy?"

"You want to take a round or two in the ring with this guy?"

"With you?" Wiley said to Daniel.

"Sure."

"What are you, like, fifty?"

"I used to be."

"Man, I been the oldest dude in this dump—except for Jimmy—for a long time. But shit, compared to you I'm a fucking ankle biter."

"Archie Moore won his last fight by a knockout, in three, when he was fifty years old," Daniel said.

"Ali kicked Archie Moore's ass," the kid behind the desk said.

"*Cassius Clay* kicked Archie Moore's ass," Daniel said. "And this guy doesn't look like any Cassius Clay to me."

Tunney laughed. "Okay, we get it. You've got, what, fifteen, twenty pounds on Wiley? And he's got fifteen, twenty years on you. I figure that makes it a fair enough fight."

It took only a few minutes for the men to get suited up. Daniel bounced on his toes and shoved the brand new, unmolded mouth guard around with his tongue, trying to keep it from cutting up his gums. The cracked leather of the old headgear rubbed his skin and the borrowed sparring gloves were soggy and stank. He tried not to think of the wide circle of their acquaintance among the damp palms of greater Newmarket. But even without his own equipment, he felt good. The blood rushed to the surface of his skin, waking every cell to the impending relief of battle. He was going to kick Wiley's ass.

Wiley, his ponytail poking out of the back of his headgear, climbed into the ring and did a few ostentatious squat stretches. "All right, old man," he said, turning from the ropes. "I'm gonna lay you out real gentle."

"Just a round or two," Tunney said. "See what happens." He flicked a mangled hand at the kid who worked the front desk. "Jason, you ref. And keep your goddamn eyes open. We don't want either of these old farts getting hurt."

Jason hopped into the ring and motioned the two fighters to the center. They banged their gloves together. Daniel tried to stare into Wiley's eyes, but the man wouldn't look at him. Normally boxers locked eyes at the beginning of every round, dropping their gaze only when the bell rang them into their corners. That kind of singular, steady eye contact, occurring for entire minutes at a time, never happened anywhere outside of a boxing ring. Not even in bed with a woman did a man look so intently, with such unflinching focus. But Wiley's eyes traveled around the ring, up and down, over at Tunney, anywhere but at Daniel. It was disconcerting, Daniel thought, to fight a man who wouldn't look you in the eye.

Tunney rang the ringside bell and Wiley charged forward, swinging a wild, looping hook. Daniel sidestepped and caught Wiley with a quick one-two. The familiar give of flesh beneath his fist filled Daniel with a flush of emotion so warm, so satisfying, that he could call it nothing other than joy. This was what he had been waiting for. He spun around on his left foot and landed a solid straight right. He felt the blow from his fist all the way up to his shoulder. The most satisfying sensation in the world. A blow perfectly landed. An opponent staggered beneath its force. The world narrowed down to only this box.

Wiley couldn't put together a combination; he seemed able to throw only one punch at a time, and those so slowly that each fist seemed to float by itself through the air. But his blows were hard enough that when they did land they hurt, and Daniel liked it. He had been waiting for this pain, simple pain, pain of the body, a tingling electric ache on the top layer of tissue followed by a sharp stab deep inside. During a fight, with his adrenaline pumping, it was not even pain, but an awareness of the promise of pain. During a fight it was possible to forget that the next morning when he woke—head banging, a mouse puffed up under his eye, oozing red patches spread out across his face and body—the promise would be redeemed.

Power was all Wiley had. Daniel danced nimbly out of his path, dodging most of his punches. With every swing Wiley left himself wide open for Daniel to throw to the body. Wiley's right arm kept floating away, allowing Daniel to land jab after jab on his forehead and nose. Daniel's mind cleared, emptied of anything other than this perfect moment, the sound of his fist against Wiley's body. A crashing that sounded less like leather on flesh than metal on metal, harsh and grinding.

Daniel hungered for that knockout blow. It would be so easy—all he needed to do was pack the weight of his entire body onto the few square inches at the front of his fist. Then all other sensation would disappear, and he would feel only the sweet, terrible give of skin and bone under his hands. One punch and then he'd just stand back and admire his work as his opponent crumpled. Daniel ached to throw that punch. He wanted that peace in the pain and the punch and the long slow folding of an opponent onto the canvas.

Just as Daniel felt himself ready to let go, just as he gave himself permission to hit as hard as he was longing to, Jason separated the fighters. Daniel stepped back into his corner, blowing a few ragged breaths, trying to get hold of himself and his knockout rage.

"You want to call it quits?" Tunney said.

"Are you fucking kidding me?" Daniel said.

"Wasn't talking to you. Wiley? You done?"

"Fuck no," Wiley said.

They met in the middle of the ring again. Tunney rang the bell. Daniel took a step back, and then lunged forward. Wiley didn't move with anything resembling the same eagerness. Daniel began practicing combinations, passing on the easy punches for more challenging ones, trying to hold himself in check. Time stretched in the ring, minutes passing so slowly Daniel felt he could hold the seconds in his hand, palpate them for a while, and then send them on their way. It was probably no more than a minute, ninety seconds at the most, before Wiley lifted his gloves in front of his face. Daniel stepped back, again searching for Wiley's eyes but finding only the Everlast label on the front of the headgear on Wiley's bent head. Daniel felt the hunger rising again. It would be so easy now. With a single blow he could send the man to the mat. The headgear provided some protection against soft tissue damage, but it would be like cellophane against Daniel's fist. He could see and hear it so clearly: the thunk of glove against skull, the jerk of the man's head on his spine, the spray of sweat and spit, the shiver under his feet as the man's body smashed to the canvas. Once again everything around him faded—the sounds of the few people crowded around the ring, the smells of sweat and leather, the mats and the ropes—it was all gone. All that was left were his fist and the pain it would cause. He hauled back his fist and narrowed his eyes, ready to propel it through his opponent. Ready to see Wiley crumple and fall. Ready to see Wiley's head bounce on the mat. Ready to hurt him as much as he possibly could. Ready to cause pain, because that was the surest way to forget about feeling it.

Just as he sent his fist sailing through the air he heard from behind an all-too-familiar voice.

"Daniel! What are you doing?"

He turned in the direction of the voice, and thus he did not see his glove graze Wiley's cheek, did not see Wiley spin and bounce against the ropes, did not see Wiley stagger upright, shake his head, and lunge toward him.

The only time Iris ever saw Daniel box she had come prepared to be outraged, prepared even to walk out in disgust. In fact she was there in the stands of the smelly gym in Rahway, New Jersey, only to refute Daniel's argument that there was a beauty in boxing, that it served to civilize rather than enhance or exploit man's essentially violent nature. But as she watched the first bouts on the card, she found herself fascinated by the sound of the fighters' leather gloves pounding against muscle, by the play of force across the muscles of their backs as they flung their fists, by the sprays of sweat lit up by the bright spotlights.

She tried to resist these feelings, to dismiss them as internalized vestiges of oppression. It was a simple physical reflex, she told herself, one that could and ought to be conquered. But watching Daniel walk up the aisle to the ring for his bout she felt awash in a strange sense of pride. The pride of *ownership*. That body—those long legs striated with muscle, the bulging band of deltoids connecting his shoulders and neck, the ropy veins crossing the muscles, the flat hard belly disappearing beneath the wide elastic of his shorts—was hers. All that strength and grace had been bestowed upon her, laid at her feet. He belonged to her.

As he climbed into the ring, Daniel caught her eye, and a flush crept across her face, down her belly, and settled like an itch between her legs. He winked at her and she jumped as though he'd touched her. When he turned to duck under the ropes, she shifted in her seat, clenching her thighs together.

When the bell rang Iris leaned forward in her seat, gripping her knees so tightly that her fingers turned white. There was something about Daniel's expression, something she had not noticed in the faces of the fighters in the prior bouts because she had been so much more interested in their bodies. Daniel and his opponent looked *hungry* as they leaped toward each other. They sized each other up the way you would gaze at a hamburger immediately before sinking your teeth into it. It seemed so obvious, but it had not occurred to her until that moment that to be a boxer a man must enjoy hitting people. He must in some way enjoy the sensation of causing pain. Iris knew that this introduction of violence into her life should repel her. And it did. It horrified her, she told herself. Yet she felt faint, and not with repulsion, at the thought of being fucked by the man who was so competently demolishing his opponent.

By the third round there was not a person in the gym who would not have agreed that Daniel was winning the match. The other boxer had a few pounds on him, but Daniel was outfighting him. He moved faster, his jabs and hooks had more power behind them. He followed up every well-placed punch. And then, as Daniel was watching the guy's right hand, looking for the opening he knew was about to come, he was suddenly on the ground. Later he told Iris that he never saw the blow, didn't even feel himself fall. One minute he was about to strike, the next he was listening to the count. Iris watched Daniel struggle to his knees, his heavy head like a sunflower drooping on the stem of his neck. He reached for the ropes, but couldn't haul himself up. He was momentarily saved from the humiliation of failure by the shrill peal of the bell.

She was on her feet as Daniel dragged himself back to his corner, and by the time he had collapsed onto the stool his coach had slung into the ring, she was reaching for him through the ropes. His eyes were closed, and the coach twisted a paper cylinder under his nose, releasing an acrid, chemical smell. He barely flinched. The ref called the fight.

That night, Iris sat in bed next to Daniel, doing her best to follow the orders given by the physician who had diagnosed his concussion. She was to wake him up every hour to ask him a few questions and make sure he was still responsive. At the beginning her task was made easier by the fact that Daniel kept waking to heave the contents of his empty stomach into the bowl she held for him. But after a while his nausea abated. Through the long hours of the night, she sat curled on the bed, her hands in fists, her fingernails digging into her palms to make sure that she would not fall asleep herself. Every hour on the hour precisely, she would hold his face in her hands, talk to him, beg him to stay awake just for a moment, kiss him urgently when his eyes drifted closed. He was conscious, even tried to talk to her, but he was exhausted from the fight and from the pain in his head, and he wanted to sleep. The harder it got to wake him up, the more frantic she became. She soaked a washcloth in cold water and put it on his face, and then cried when he batted it away and grumbled.

"Please, please," she said as he became more and more difficult to rouse. "Please don't die. Don't die." She was terrified of losing him, and worse, she felt a sick sense of shame. She knew that her excitement in the fight had nothing to do with his injury, but still could not help but imagine that her pleasure had goaded him on. There was that look they'd shared before he entered the ring, the look that had so effectively communicated the thrill she was feeling. Had that moment of eye contact made him take risks he would not have were she not in the audience? She held his face in her hands, trying to rouse him without jostling his delicate, damaged head, feeling as though it were his life she was holding in the palms of her hands, that if she failed to keep him awake, she would lose him forever.

"Don't die," she chanted like a mantra, soaking and soaking again the washcloth, pressing it to his temples.

"For Christ's sake," Daniel mumbled. "It's just a concussion. I'm not going to die."

Only at dawn did she finally give in and let him sleep. She woke him up a few hours later with a cup of tea and two slices of toast.

"I didn't think your stomach would be able to handle more than this," she said.

"Thanks," he said, relieving her of the cup and plate.

Iris sat down on the bed. The mattress shifted slightly under her weight.

"Daniel," she said, taking his hand. "I love you." Her tone was matter-of-fact, as though this were not the first time either of them had said those words.

"I love you, too."

"But I won't be with you if you keep boxing. I won't go through that again."

Daniel argued with her, but at this point he knew that his career was all but over anyway. And he loved this stern and passionate girl, this generous girl who had murmured to him all night long, who had sung to him and kissed him and whose fear of losing him had been so obvious that it was only for her sake that he bothered to follow the doctor's unnecessarily cautious orders at all.

It was Iris who came up with the idea that he attend law school. She persuaded him that the courtroom, like the ring, was a place of controlled violence, and that he would be perfectly suited to its rigors. Iris had filled out his applications and financial aid forms—she said her typing was better than his. If she could have taken the law boards for him she probably would have done that, too. But in the end she was wrong; not about boxing, perhaps, but about his suitability for a career in the law. As a lawyer Daniel had none of the competitor's instinct that had come so naturally to him in the ring. He once told Iris that the kind of pain his colleagues enjoyed causing was complicated and insidious, and far more agonizing than anything he had experienced or inflicted as a boxer. He could not take pleasure in that kind of fight. Back when Daniel was practicing law—

before he failed to make partner and instead took a position as a clinical instructor in a third-rate law school—Iris would try to encourage him with boxing metaphors. "Just keep hitting him," she'd say about a recalcitrant opposing counsel. "File motion after motion. Eventually you'll wear him down, and then, when he's not paying attention, land your knockout blow." But on the rare occasions when Daniel did manage to channel his fighting nature, it would be at the worst possible moment, in a way that disgusted rather than intimidated his colleagues.

Now, more than thirty years later, Iris stood in the dingy boxing gym in Newmarket, her face pale, shouting at him to stop.

"Iris," Daniel said, dropping his fists. Because he was staring at his wife, he did not notice Wiley pinwheeling forward. With a grunt Wiley landed a wild haymaker in Daniel's kidney, directly on his off button. The air shot out of Daniel's lungs in a single blast, and he gagged. Before he could even take the breath he needed to remain upright, Wiley came in with a ferocious jab, the edge of his glove somehow penetrating the inch of padding on Daniel's headgear and opening up a cut under his eyebrow. A rope of thick, sticky blood flowed from the cut, a blackish-red stream across his field of vision. He shook his head and blood flew across his cheek and head gear. He grunted and bent over, and Wiley threw his fist forward again, weakly but low, and square on Daniel's groin.

Jason leaped into the ring, grabbed Wiley, and said, "Shit, dude. Wicked low."

"No kidding," Daniel managed to say.

"I think we're done," Tunney said.

Wiley lifted his gloves over his head, grinning like a fool.

"You fucking punched me in the balls, you little prick," Daniel said.

"Hey, whatever, Grandpa. Who's bleeding all over the ring?"

"Wiley, you were born a horse's ass and you'll die a horse's ass," Tunney said. He rolled closer to the ring. "You need a hand?" he asked Daniel, motioning to Jason to help him up.

"No," Daniel said, unfolding himself with care, like a man opening a broken umbrella. "I'm fine."

"You did all right," Tunney said. "Are we going to see you tomorrow?"

"No doubt," Daniel said.

"Over my dead body," Iris said. When Daniel stooped through the ropes, she stripped off her sweatshirt and pressed it against his forehead, staunching the flow of blood from his split eyebrow. He allowed her to lead him to a chair, let her unbuckle his headgear, even obediently spat out the mouth guard into her waiting palm.

"What are you doing here?" he asked, wiping the saliva from his lips with the back of his hand.

"What do you think I'm doing here? I've been driving around Newmarket all morning looking for your car. What did you think? That I was just going to ignore the fact that you've been disappearing every day? And anyway, what *I'm* doing here is not the question. The question is what the hell *you're* doing here." Her tone was belied only partly by the gentleness of her touch as she pressed her favorite gray hoodie, now ruined, against his cut, holding his head against her soft belly.

"I can't fucking believe you followed me," he said, pulling away.

Tunney rolled up in his wheelchair, a jar of Vaseline in his hand. Daniel bent down obediently and the old trainer fingered up a thick wad and smeared it over the cut. The bleeding stopped.

"I didn't *follow* you," Iris said. "I was *looking* for you. There's a difference."

"Like hell there is," Daniel said, tossing her the sweatshirt.

That night, as Iris lay stewing in her anger in bed, Daniel stood in front of the mirror, studying the damage. His eye was already swollen shut, and blood crusted the row of inexpert stitches across his eyebrow. Jimmy Tunney might have once been able to close his boxers' wounds with serviceable sutures, but while his kit remained stocked and ready, his hands no longer held the dexterity for the delicate work of stitching a man's face. Had Iris not been so aggressive in her demand that he go to the hospital, Daniel probably wouldn't have let the old man near the cut with his needle. As it was he had regretted his decision the moment Tunney pierced his eyebrow, but by then he'd taken a stand and had a point to prove.

Daniel laid the palm of his hand against the sore spot under his rib. He took a breath and winced at the bloom of fire. Delicately he probed an oozing scrape on his shoulder. He moved his sore neck from side to side until he heard the satisfying pop of his vertebrae cracking. It was all going to hurt worse tomorrow, he thought. In the mirror his skewbald face smiled back at him.

11

Jane was a neophyte insomniac—all her life until now her capacity for sleep had saved her sanity. At ten o'clock she would drop insensible into her bed, and once asleep she would not wake, not even when her drunken husband lurched into the bedroom, banging into the furniture and muttering incomprehensible curses. When the kids were little babies she had warmed their middle-of-the-night bottles without ever really coming to. But after the accident she lost her capacity for sleep and had not to this day regained it. She spent every night wandering the house, rarely managing to fall asleep before dawn. She groped through her days in an exhausted fog.

She drove on autopilot, thanking God that every twist, bend, and pothole was as familiar to her as the faces of her children. Jane knew that on Tuesdays and Fridays, Mehitable Hewins, who lived in the double-wide on the intersection of Route 179 and the Bangor Road, hung out her laundry. She knew that every weekday morning at 8:40 A.M. the day-camp bus picked up the kids from Fletcher's Landing in front of the post office. She knew which barns concealed police cars waiting for out-of-state speeders. The trip to Wal-Mart always took her three-quarters of an hour, give or take a minute or two, depending on how she caught the single stoplight in Red Hook and the three in Newmarket. Today, when she pulled into the vast parking lot, she realized that she had not the slightest recollection of the drive.

She parked the car and laid her head on the steering wheel, closing her eyes for what she intended to be a rejuvenating moment. Ninety minutes later, she was awakened by a rapping on the window.

Flustered and embarrassed at having been discovered sacked out in her car like some kind of homeless woman, she rubbed the sleep from her eyes and wiped at the saliva that had dripped from the corner of her mouth. Sheriff Paige stood there, his arms laden with two big shopping bags and a new red plastic cooler. He was out of uniform, and looked worried.

"You all right, Ms. Tetherly?" the sheriff asked.

"I'm fine," she said.

"You've been here over an hour."

"You've been watching me sleep for an hour?"

"No, ma'am. I saw you when I pulled in. And as you were still here when I came out, I decided it might be a good idea to make sure you were okay."

"I'm fine," she said. "Just tired." She collected her purse and opened the door, bumping it into his thighs.

"Oops," he said, backing away.

"Sorry."

As she closed the door, he said, "You might want to get those keys."

Jane looked into the car. Hanging from the ignition was her key chain, loaded with her house keys, the keys of the Unitarian church, the keys of every family for whom she worked, and of course her car keys.

"Rough night?" Sheriff Paige asked, as she yanked the door open.

"They're all rough," she said before she could stop herself.

"Insomnia?" he asked.

"Yes."

He nodded. "I don't sleep well myself."

In the uncomfortable silence that followed her failure to reply, she remembered the last time she had seen him, at the funeral. His forgiving smile when she had tried to make a stumbling apology for her disgraceful behavior at the scene of the accident had shamed her all over again. Now, nearly two years later, she blushed at the memory of those appalling days.

"You might think about taking something for it," Sheriff Paige said.

"Excuse me?"

"They've got good sleeping pills nowadays. Won't make you groggy like the old ones did."

"Is that a fact?"

"Yuh." He patted his pockets until he came up with a pen and a scrap of paper. He scribbled the name of the drug and of his doctor. "You tell him I sent you," he said. "Tell him what all you been through. He's a good man. He'll take care of you."

Jane made an appointment that very day. Paige's doctor blamed her sleeplessness on the change of life; insomnia was a frequent symptom, he told her. Jane did not bother to point out to him that she had gone through menopause years ago, early, like all the women in her family, with a minimum of fuss. Neither did she tell him about John. Her private grief was none of his business. She didn't need a doctor to tell her why she hadn't been able to sleep in two years.

That night, as she lay in bed waiting for the pill to take effect, Jane's thoughts began to drift, first, and perhaps inevitably, to her son. She tried to remember his face, his shape, but whether it was due to the effects of the medication or of time, she found herself struggling to recall the simplest thing. Had his single dimple been on the right or the left cheek? Was it he or Matt who had the slightly protruding belly button? Disturbed by her failure to remember, she turned her thoughts to Matt. The expression on his face every morning when he left for work, dumb resignation, as though someone had forced him into this job and he wasn't permitted to quit. As though he hadn't brought it on himself. But these thoughts, too, were distressing, and so, almost against her will, she found herself thinking about the sheriff. He was a decent man. Steady, polite, even courtly; not like her ex-husband. And nice-looking, too. Then, with a gentle suddenness, as if a great black balloon had been inflated inside her head, she was taken by a deep and dreamless sleep. When she awoke seven and a half hours later she did not even remember that her final conscious thought before going under had been of the way Bill Paige's strong jaw contrasted with the almost feminine cupid's bow of his upper lip.

III

The house where Matt lived with his mother was on the far side of Red Hook Hill, off the Newmarket road, an area that shared nothing with the pretty little town of Red Hook but a zip code. The house stood far inland, with a view not of blue water but of austere hills from which the timber had been logged, and of blueberry bogs that were prettiest in early summer, when the mat-like shrubs bloomed pink and white. The road to the house was paved as far as the two abandoned chicken farms—massive, windowless structures from which periodic blasts of ammonia stench still emanated nearly a decade after the chickens and their manure were gone—but after that it turned to dirt, mud in the spring, and plowed only intermittently in the winter. Like the impeccably restored houses in town, their house was white clapboard (or the front and sides were; the back, unpainted for as long as Matt or anyone else could remember, was driftwood gray), but the clapboard was vinyl, an improvement his mother was still hoping to extend to the rest of the house.

Matt's late great-uncle, a determined if not particularly talented carpenter from whom Jane had bought the house, had added a two-story extension to one side to accommodate his large family, but had failed to take adequate care in pouring the foundation, and the annex had sunk a foot lower than the rest of the house. The line of windows across the upper story deviated from the horizontal at the seam between house and annex, giving the whole establishment a cockeyed look.

Once Matt had left for college, he'd figured he'd never again take up permanent residence in his mother's house, but after he dropped out he moved back in. Lately, though, he had come to spend most of his time in the barn. When he wasn't at work down at the boatyard, he was working on the *Rebecca*. When the weather got warm enough he had pulled an ancient mattress down from the attic and laid it on the floor in the corner farthest from the door, fashioning himself a little bedroom area with a nightstand made from a plastic milk crate on which he placed a battery-operated lamp. In the crate he kept an ever-rotating stack of library books. The mattress smelled of mildew, and the Hudson Bay blanket he used as a bedcover was worn through in places. When he didn't feel like going all the way back to the house he just pissed out the door. The barn had no power, so he relied on the long series of extension cords John had long ago run from Jane's kitchen window across the long expanse of the yard to the barn. Every so often, whenever Jane decided she couldn't stand the mosquitoes and moths flying into her kitchen, Matt would be plunged into sudden darkness.

Other than laying claim to the small area immediately surrounding his mattress, Matt had done nothing to change the barn from the way it had looked before the accident. John's tools were still laid out on the shelves he had built above his rough-hewn workbench. John's work clothes still hung on the nails he had hammered into the bare studs of the walls. John's gloves were still in their place on the hook next to his circular saw, their fingers still curled into the shape of his hands.

This evening it was only a few days away from the summer solstice, and although it was dinnertime, the fat sun still hung high in the sky, filling the barn with light. The sun picked up the dust motes in the air and they glowed yellowish gold, like tiny bits of floating confetti. The wood floors were warm, especially near the windows and the open barn door. A shaft of light from one of the skylights that John had cut into the ceiling fell across Ruthie's bare legs. She lay on Matt's bed, naked but for the stretched and faded Rolling Stones T-shirt that Matt had been wearing a few minutes before.

Last summer, when Matt and Ruthie had begun seeing each other, they had taken refuge in the barn to keep away from the prying eyes of the town. People in Red Hook talked. They knew which lobsterman had drunk away his profits and stood to lose his boat, which father of three had been accused of fondling his children's young friends, which postmistress was meeting her sister's husband at the motel on Route 3 every Tuesday at lunchtime. The locals knew and talked about the summer folk because they took care of their boats and houses, waited on them in the restaurants, filled their gas tanks, and bagged their groceries. The summer people mostly knew one another, and spent most of their time pondering the personal lives of their fellow yacht club members. The middle strata—the boatbuilders and back-to-earthers, the retirees and professionals, those who liked to think of themselves as locals but whom the locals referred to as "year-round summer visitors"—talked about everyone. As the Copakens and Tetherlys traversed all these groups, Ruthie and Matt did their best to maintain a very low profile. They kept themselves to themselves, as his mother would say. They had not reached an agreement to conceal what was going on between them; rather they understood without discussing it that their relationship would be the stuff of gossip, something they both wanted to avoid. In the immediate aftermath of the accident, every time either of them had walked into the library or the liquor store, Neptune's or the food co-op, there would settle over the crowd a little hush. It was the same for the other members of their families. It made going out in public that much harder. By now, though, the tragedy had faded in others' minds. They could pretend to be no different from anyone else. But if people came to know of their relationship, once again they would find themselves back in the spotlight, something neither Ruthie nor Matt could tolerate. And so from the very beginning they'd kept things quiet.

Ruthie traced their relationship from the August night, the summer of the accident, when together they had set off the last of the wedding fireworks. Although they had not even kissed, that was when she considered it to have begun. Matt dated things from the next Fourth of July, after that second evening of fireworks, when they had made out in the dark on the steps of the Grange Hall. Ruthie had led Matt there after the last bottle rocket had been set off because she needed at that moment to touch him, to feel his hands on her body. Watching those bursts of light exploding in the sky had made them both feel untethered, disembodied, as if they, too, were at risk of disappearing like fading sparks in a dark summer sky. They made love for the first time a week or so later, huddled under a blanket on the deck of the *Rebecca*.

Because of the secrecy they had imposed on the relationship, they could not go to the beach, or to the movies. They could not share a pitcher of beer at the Neptune or even an ice cream cone at the Bait Bag. Sex had given them something to do while each enjoyed the comfort of the other's company. Sex was their primary occupation, and yet, even so, once they were separated by thousands of miles they managed to maintain their connection. This despite the fact that Matt did not have a computer and the lines to use the ones in the library were so long that it had taken tenacity and a real sense of purpose to answer Ruthie's e-mails from England.

The ramshackle barn in the back meadow, into which no one but Matt had any reason or desire to enter, was the perfect place for them to find privacy. Ruthie never drove there, for fear of Jane recognizing the car. They would meet in town, and she would leave her car in the parking lot of the library. When Ruthie was with him in his car, Matt would drive quickly up the driveway and across the meadow, parking his truck on the far side of the barn. He kept the barn's broken side door propped open with a jagged piece of cinder block, so that they could enter and exit without the risk of being seen by Jane or anyone else who happened to be in the house. They lay beneath the shadow of the *Rebecca*, the sailboat like a sentinel guarding their secret.

Now Matt lay propped on one elbow, looking at Ruthie. He wondered how he could have known her for so many years without noticing how lovely she was. Her skin was rosy and ripe, especially now, scraped pink from the scratchy blanket on which they'd been rolling. She shaved only the lower half of her legs, and her thighs were covered with translucent gold down. He reached out and held the palm of his hand hovering just above her thigh; he imagined he could feel the faint buzz of static electricity drawing the hair on her legs to the taut skin of his palm.

Although the two had very different coloring, Ruthie reminded him of Becca. They had the same long legs and narrow waist, the same slightly knobby knees and pneumatic ass. Once he'd even told Ruthie this, or rather a more innocuous version—that when her hair was hidden under a bandana, she looked like Becca. Ruthie had been pleased, he could tell.

From the time Matt had first begun to notice girls, Becca had been there. In the house, on the beach, in John's car all summer long. Matt had spent a not inconsiderable part of his adolescence fantasizing about the faint outline of Becca's goose-pimpled aureole rising beneath the thin fabric of her bikini top, or about the strands of light brown pubic hair that occasionally pulled free of the confines of her bathing suit. Ruthie's pubic hair was darker, and looking at it now he felt his cock stirring again.

Ruthie scooted closer to Matt, and he put his arm around her. She looked up at the *Rebecca.* "She's a beautiful boat, Matt."

The truth was, Ruthie didn't care much for boats. In her own family she was the anomaly; even Daniel enjoyed sailing, although he was hardly as obsessed as Iris and Becca were. While her family had jovially accepted Ruthie's aversion to the sport, John had never stopped believing that he could change her mind. The summer Ruthie was fourteen John had made a gift to her of an old dory that he had restored and painted a jolly turquoise blue. He had added a sail to the skiff and, claiming it was unsinkable, insisted that she enter the yacht club's juniors' race, a monthly spectacle Becca had won at least half a dozen times as a girl. He was so eager and so genuinely confident in Ruthie that she agreed; she even wore the "Team Copaken" T-shirt he'd made for her. She spent the race watching ten-year-olds whiz by her as she tried unsuccessfully to hoist the sail out of the water. Despite John's insistence that during the three minutes before she had capsized he had seen in her a nascent marine gift about to catch fire, she never again took the boat out alone. Whenever she was obliged to go sailing, she tried to ensure that her responsibilities were limited to not getting bonked on the head by the boom.

"I hope she'll be beautiful when she's done," Matt said.

"How much longer do you think you'll be working on her?"

"I don't know. Maybe another six months. Every time I run out of money it kind of sets me back." John had had the money from Becca's violin to pay for the restoration of the Alden, but that was all gone by the time he died. Worse, Matt had made dozens of costly errors since beginning the renovation of the boat. He could not bear to consider the number of hours and dollars he had spent on his first attempt at pouring the lead for the ballast keel. He couldn't afford to pay a foundry to make the keel, and since John had planned on doing his own melting and pouring, Matt had decided to do the same. He'd gotten help with the pattern from one of the yard's designers, and built it from white pine timber. The melting and pouring of the lead had been easier than he had expected, and by the time he was fairing the lead with edge tools, going for the kind of sweet-looking line John would have expected, he was feeling pretty good about it. And then, while smoothing the lead with his power planer, he had found the beginning of a bubble. Sick to his stomach with dread, he had poked his finger into the bubble all the way through the lead. He had had two choices. One, he could drop the keel, undo the keel bolts, and let the whole fucking thing down so he could cut back the lead on top of the bubble and repour. Or he could pay the foundry to make the keel ballast, just like he should have done in the first place. It turned out to be a good thing he had decided to max out yet another credit card and pay for the job he failed at, because it was one of the foundry workers who had pointed out to him that the copper keel bolts he had worked so hard to fabricate and install would, within a year, stretch out so much the keel would probably just drop right off. Out they came, to be replaced with bolts of bronze.

Ruthie said, "What about the money from the accident? Can you use that to finish the boat?"

"I used my share up on it already, and no way my mother will let me have hers. She thinks this is a waste of my time. She hates sailing."

"That's weird. She's a Mainer. She lives on the water. And John was such a big sailor."

Ruthie felt almost relieved to hear that Jane shared her antipathy for the water.

"My grandfather died in a hurricane when my mom was a kid. He was out on a big groundfish rig, down near Rhode Island. They tried to ride the storm out. Nobody knows what happened. Probably just got swamped by the waves. There were a lot of boats lost in that storm."

"Oh, Jesus," Ruthie said. "That's awful."

"Mum always says she doesn't really remember my grandfather, but she was twelve years old when he died. It's not like she was a baby. It made her hate the water. It used to make her crazy back when John and I were kids every time my aunt Mary would send us out with my uncle Don in his lobster boat when he was too drunk to be trusted not to get his foot caught in the warp and drown."

"What's the warp?"

"The line connecting the buoy to the trap. You get that wrapped around your foot when the traps are thrown over the side and you're fish food. My mum hated the idea of us out on the water, but she couldn't say anything. If we didn't pull the traps, then Aunt Mary and Uncle Don wouldn't be able to pay the loan on their boat and the bank would take it. But Uncle Don was a regular dub and it was never all that safe for us to be out with him. When it's a thick fog and you can't see more than a few feet ahead of you, it's easy to lose your way, especially if you're a drunk idiot like my uncle. Or sometimes you think it's going be a fine day, and a storm will roll in all of a sudden. Anything can happen out on the water."

"Did your mom mind that John was planning on becoming a charter captain?"

"Sure she did, but John'd just kind of rib her about it. Say he was going to get a life insurance policy and make her his beneficiary, that way she'd stop pitching him shit. Mum loves money a hell of a lot more than she's afraid of water."

It took a moment for the irony of the comment to sink in, but when it did they both grew suddenly still. After a moment, Ruthie, searching for something to fill the silence, said, "It's so nice here. I wish I didn't have to go back to England."

"You've only got one more year."

"That feels like a really long time." Ruthie had been so unhappy at Oxford, isolated despite the ubiquity of American students, maladroit and dull when compared to her British colleagues. She'd made few friends and developed no real personal relationships with her tutors, spending most of her time alone in the dank and anonymous dorm room that she'd been assigned, nothing like the stone grotto she'd imagined when she first found out she'd be attending Oxford. Her unhappiness had not surprised her. It was just a continuation of the misery of her last year of college. The only true pleasure she had was in Matt's e-mails and text messages.

"Well, what would happen if you didn't go back?"

"Oh, God, I don't know." Naturally the thought of bailing on her Fulbright and leaving all that gray misery and loneliness behind had occurred to Ruthie almost every day over the course of the long year in England. But how could she ever turn her back on all those years of hard work, on the incredible good fortune that a Fulbright represented? How could she step off the long-foreseen path of her life without having the faintest idea of what lay on either side of it? She had been telling people, had been telling herself, since she was fourteen years old that she would follow in her mother's footsteps and become an academic, a scholar of literature. And she loved books and stories, loved studying the strange interplay between the life and work of an author, loved pondering the mysteries of Mr. Darcy's erotic life before he met Elizabeth Bennett or the effect of Joyce's transition to dictation on his later work.

But the formal study of literature, she had discovered, was not about love; it was about theory, and the theory of theory, and how smart you could make yourself sound while saying something very small about somebody else's theory of what sounded smart. And she found England unbearable, not just because it was gray and lonely and her work proceeded at a tedious crawl but because Becca had never existed there. It was as if only in mourning and memory could she understand the world; and in England there were no cues, no traces of her loss. As soon as she got on the plane to come home for the summer, she had felt a slight easing of the anxiety that had tugged at taut strings in her chest all winter. In England, Ruthie had to impose her memories on landscapes that held no record of her sister, but Red Hook was safe. It was permeated with Becca's presence. Every cove and every pebble, every teacup and throw pillow in the house, every library book and ear of summer corn steamed in the husk over charcoal, held at its core some memory of Becca and John.

"Well, what would you do if you decided not to go back to England?" Matt said.

"I don't know. I don't even have the beginning of a plan." She laughed. "No plan at all. That would go over well with my mom. That's like anathema to her, no plan. That's like you have cancer of the life." Iris was the queen of checklists, agendas, strategies, long-term forecasts, reservations made years in advance. Her thinking was always ten steps ahead of her current situation and twelve steps ahead of everybody else. Given her mother's example, to Ruthie the idea of dropping out of school with no idea what she was going to do next held a kind of dangerous and seductive terror.

"I don't want to think about it anymore," Ruthie said. She sat up and straddled Matt's waist. "Let's do this instead."

Twenty minutes later, Ruthie had drifted off to sleep, but Matt was too confused by his reaction to the possibility that she might not go back to England to follow suit. He wanted to be with her, that was clear to him. The idea of another long winter alone was too depressing to contemplate for long. One evening toward the end of the previous winter, Matt had driven down Red Hook Road to Jacob's Cove. It was only a little after six, but the sun had set, and the last of the grayish light was fading from the sky. Early in the day, rain had washed away much of the snow, and what was left was crusty with ice and dirt. It gave way beneath his boots with a muffled crunch. Matt left his car running, the beams of the headlights long and yellow across the beach. Shoving his bare hands into his pockets and tucking his chin into the collar of his coat, already clammy with the moisture from his breath, he walked out along the rocky beach until he was a foot or so from where the waves lapped against the pebbles and mud. He stood there, gazing out at the bleak vista. Interspersed among the mass of evergreens was the occasional bare white of a dead tree, its naked branches iced with moonlight. The beach was devoid of life, the sandy earth clotted with dead brown grasses. The ocean was black. Cold even in his down jacket, his ears itchy beneath the wool of his ski hat, Matt stared at the grim, unwelcoming sea and thought how dead it seemed. On that freezing, rainy evening in March, all of Maine seemed dead.

He could not go through another winter alone like that. He wanted to ask Ruthie to stay here and help him bear it. But was he ready to announce their relationship to the world? Even more frightening, was he ready to tell his mother?

There was no point to lying there and worrying. He had a lot he wanted to accomplish this evening, and before too long there wouldn't be enough light to keep working. He pulled on his shorts, a pair of thick socks, and John's old work boots, a size and a half too big. He left Ruthie dozing on the bed.

Because the finishes in the stateroom and the main cabin of the sailboat demanded such craftsmanship, Matt had waited until now to do the finishing work on the cabinetry, honing his skills over the past two years first on the deckhouse, crew quarters, and galley. The Alden's large and elegant stateroom was in an unusual location—at the bow, in what would ordinarily be the fo'c'sle. In most boats of this size, the stateroom was amidships, or at the stern. Matt remembered that when John first bought her, his friends from the boatyard had expressed reservations about the location. "You'll be hurling all night long," had been the general consensus. But John had argued that the deep, heavy hull was sea-kindly; it would sail so easily, even in rough seas, that not even the most tentative or weak-stomached of passengers would be disturbed. In fact, he had always claimed that the spacious stateroom, its private head complete with a bathtub, was perfect for luxury-loving charter customers, and was one of the main reasons he had bought the *Rebecca*. The stateroom and, of course, her name.

Matt was finishing the *Rebecca* precisely to John's specifications, even though he could not imagine sailing her—or any boat, for that matter—to the Caribbean. He wasn't sure what was involved in one's becoming the captain of a charter vessel, but he was fairly confident that whatever it required was something he didn't possess. Indeed, Matt had no idea what he was going to do with the boat once he finished restoring her. Beyond that, in Ruthie's phrase, he had cancer of the life: no plan at all. He did not let himself think about it, ever. He just worked.

Following John's specifications, Matt had replaced the twin berths in the stateroom with a queen-sized bed, comfortable for couples. He'd refinished the clothes cabinet and the drawers, polished the knobs and handles and replaced those that were missing. The one piece of cabinetry that had proved a challenge was the side table. It was an odd design; the edged tabletop was fairly straightforward, but at two corners it had posts capped with elaborately ornamented finials, similar to half of a four-poster bed. One of the finials was in good shape, but a decapitated post with a splintered top was all that remained of the other. Matt had scoured catalogs and Web sites searching for a matching finial, had even posted pleading messages on the Alden Internet discussion groups, but no one had ever seen anything quite like the little table. For a while Matt debated just shearing off the posts at the base. They were so exceptional that no one would notice their absence; the table would seem like any other. But finally Matt couldn't bring himself to lop them off. John, he knew, would have carved a new finial, and he owed it to his brother at least to try.

There were men at the yard who specialized in this kind of fine, finished cabinetry, but Matt was not one of them. His area of expertise, if you could call it that, was sanding, the job they still had him working down at King's, long after other guys who had started with him had moved on. It was a mindless job, requiring only a minimum of arm strength and a reasonably steady hand. You could have trained a smart monkey to do it. Whenever he got discouraged about his inadequate skills and correspondingly low status at the yard, he reminded himself that sanding beat scraping and painting the bottoms of hulls. But despite his inadequacy and lack of experience, after many months and dozens of false starts, he had managed at last to carve something that, if you didn't look too close, strongly resembled the original finial.

Flush with this success, today he had set himself the infinitely easier task of replacing a six-inch strip of ornate molding on the side of the table. Matt plugged his router into the extension cord and, holding the heavy tool in one hand and the bit case in the other, climbed up onto the deck. Before he stepped down into the cabin he glanced down at Ruthie. It was so odd how much she reminded him of Becca, and yet how utterly different they were. Was it only her shape that was like her sister? That, and some undercurrent of sweetness. For all her sass, Becca had been sweet. Kind. Like John. And like Ruthie.

The contoured grip handles on the router's plunge base had begun to wear through, and as he climbed down Matt reminded himself that he should drive into Newmarket and see if the Ace Hardware sold replacements. Yanking the extension cord behind him as he went, he walked through the unfinished main cabin and down the hallway between the galley and the stateroom's private head. There was a single step from the hallway down into the stateroom and he stumbled, catching himself right before he hit the ground. He'd taken that step a thousand times, maybe more, and still it tripped him up nearly every time, especially when he wore John's boots.

"Shit," Matt said, dropping the bit case and getting a firmer grip on the router. "Spaz."

"Spaz" had been one of John's favorite nicknames for Matt. As big as he was, John had been as agile as a gymnast, sure-footed even when shinnying up a sixty-foot spar in the middle of a storm. Matt possessed none of his brother's fluid grace.

Setting the router down on the finished side table, Matt knelt down and dug around in his bit case until he found a three-inch pattern-making bit. He fitted the bit into the router, turned the machine on, and locked the trigger. The grinding, metallic whine of the router's small motor reverberated off the mahogany walls and ceiling. Gripping the router handles, Matt began carefully to carve the bit of molding. He stepped back to get a better look at what he was doing, and caught the toe of his oversized boot on the extension cord. When he tried to kick loose the cord, it wrapped itself around his ankles, like a lasso thrown to hobble an escaping bull. Matt stumbled, caught himself for an instant, and then started to go down. He flung out one hand to break his fall and tried to keep hold of the router with the other, but the foam padding on the handle chose that moment to tear. The machine bolted out of his grip, ricocheted off the top of the side table, and swirled through the air like a furious wasp, crashing into the deck beam and gouging out a splintered chunk of the polished wood. Matt lunged for the router, but it bounced off the face of the cabinet, managing to crack both doors. He hurled his entire body at it, knocked his chin against the side of the table, and missed. The router, like a thing possessed, smashed through a sole board and plunged down into the bilge.

"Fuck!"

He grabbed the cord, trying to drag the router back through the splintered hole. He could hear it crashing around in the bilge, ricocheting off the sides, grinding through thousands of dollars' worth of wood. "Fuck! Fuck!" He hauled on the cord, but it raced through his hands like the warp of a lobster trap, burning his palms. The router dropped back down into the bilge. He could hear the wailing shriek of the steel bit tearing through wood.

Grabbing hold of the electrical cord, he started pulling it, hand over hand, in the other direction, hoping he could jerk the plug loose from the socket, but there was too much slack. He tore out of the stateroom and tripped again over the step, landing on his face and leaping up without even noticing the blood streaming from his swelling nose. As he ran he could hear the router rolling and crashing around the bilge like a lotto ball in a rotating drum.

And then silence.

He scrambled up the ladder to the deck. Jane stood below him in the shadow of the boat, holding the unplugged end of the extension cord. She stared at him with narrowed eyes and a set, grim mouth. Ruthie stood beside her, hair tousled around her head, face still soft with sleep. The old T-shirt reached barely to Ruthie's naked thighs and she stood barefoot, her toes leaving little circular prints on the dusty floor. Behind her the blankets were pushed halfway off the mattress.

Jane's chest heaved with the exertion of her run across the yard. She dropped the end of the cord to the ground. Matt rubbed his nose and looked down at the blood smeared across his hand.

Jane turned to Ruthie. She looked the girl up and down, Ruthie blushing beneath her gaze.

"That's John's shirt," Jane said.

IV

Ruthie and Matt sat in the cab of his truck in the parking lot of the Bait Bag, Ruthie eating her fried clams and Matt his lobster roll, a stained paper bag of onion rings on the armrest between them. They'd thrown on their clothes and raced from the scene of their humiliation, and then, once they were in town, had ended up here. Matt had suggested getting something to eat.

"Do you think we should?" Ruthie had said.

"There's no point in hiding now," Matt said.

"Your mom won't tell anyone, will she?"

Matt laughed grimly. "Hardly. But *she* knows, so what's the point of skulking around?"

"Well, my parents don't know."

"Are you embarrassed? Do you think they'll be pissed off at you if they find out you're seeing me?"

"No," Ruthie said. She didn't really know if she was lying. She wasn't embarrassed. Not of Matt. She liked Matt. More than liked him. But Iris *would* be upset. Or, if not upset, then certainly disappointed. Especially once she knew that Ruthie didn't want to go back to Oxford.

"You're right," Ruthie said. "I'm sick of sneaking around. Let's just get something to eat, like normal people." She reached across and grabbed his hand, pulled it to her lips, and kissed his knuckles, bloody from his mortal combat with the router. "You're my boyfriend, right? There's no reason people shouldn't know."

Were Matt not so distracted by his internal calculations of what his calamitous accident with the router was likely to cost him both in cash and in labor, he might have allowed himself to react to the word. He had never, after all, been anybody's boyfriend before. He'd hooked up with plenty of girls. Well, four. And he'd gone out with more. But he'd never thought of himself as anyone's boyfriend.

Despite their calculated flagrancy, when they arrived at the Bag they saw no one they knew other than Doreen Darling, who worked the pickup window and was famously taciturn. She was not likely to gossip. The only other diners were a group of Finnish backpackers who had, Ruthie supposed, taken a wrong turn on their way to Otter Cliff in Acadia National Park or to the vertical expanses of granite that so attracted climbers to Clifton. Certainly the 940-foot Red Hook Hill could not have been the destination of these ruddy-cheeked men and women, with their heavy-treaded leather-and-mesh hiking boots and tall backpacks festooned with carabiners, lengths of webbing and rope, and patches of their blue-crossed flag. Wherever they were headed, there was no danger of them noting the relationship of two total strangers sharing a greasy meal in a Ford pickup.

Ruthie dipped a clam in tartar sauce but hesitated before putting it in her mouth. "I'm sorry about the boat," she said.

"Yeah." Matt rubbed his forehead. The headache that had started as soon as he saw Jane standing next to Ruthie's nearly naked body was getting worse.

"Will you be able to fix it?"

"Yeah. I mean, I don't have a choice."

"Is there any way I can help?"

"You're sweet, but unless you've been keeping some serious carpentry skills a secret all this time, there's not a whole lot you can do."

Ruthie couldn't muster up a smile. Instead, she ate the fried clam she was holding and licked the grease and tartar sauce from her fingers.

Once they were done Matt said, "Let's go get a beer at the Neptune."

There was no chance of the Neptune being populated solely by reticent acquaintances and disoriented Finns, and while Ruthie might have been able to handle a few familiar faces at the Bait Bag, she was not ready for the stir their entry into the bar would cause. The guys from the boatyard would surely be there, as would the younger summer people, those who would rather drink a two-dollar beer sitting next to a fisherman than a five-dollar G&T in the company of their parents' yacht club friends. There would likely be no one in the Neptune that Ruthie and Matt *didn't* know, and while she understood that their relationship was now going public, she wasn't yet prepared for such a blatant coming-out party.

"I don't think so," she said.

"Are you sure?"

She was sure, but the disappointment in his voice made her wonder if she was being selfish. "Do you need a drink after what happened with your mom?"

"Screw my mom. I need a drink after what happened to *Rebecca.*"

To Ruthie, the calamity had been their discovery. To Matt, that was just icing on the shit cake of John's boat's destruction.

Matt turned the key in the ignition and the Ford coughed once before coming to life. "So, we'll get a beer?"

"I'm sorry, Matt. I really don't feel like it. But you should go."

"That's all right. So what should we do? Just go for a drive? Or do you want me to take you home?"

"No. I don't want to deal with my parents, either."

"So what do you want to do, Ruthie?" His voice betrayed a hint of impatience.

Ruthie looked up the road toward the center of town. Although it was nearly eight o'clock, long after closing, the lights in the library were all on. She felt a sudden longing, random but keen, for the tidiness of the library, its smell of binding glue and furniture wax, for the bright, orderly world it contained and embodied.

"You know what?" Ruthie said. "I think there might be a concert or a lecture at the library tonight."

"A concert," Matt said.

"Or a lecture."

"A lecture," he said. He began backing out of the parking lot.

"You should just drop me off," Ruthie said. "Go to the Neptune. I'm sure I'll be able to get a ride home afterward."

"I don't mind going with you," he said, unconvincingly.

"Seriously, Matt. It's fine. It's actually better if you don't come. It'll probably be full of my parents' friends, and the last thing I want is for my mom to hear about us from one of the library ladies. I want to tell her myself."

By now they'd reached the library. Matt drove past, and then turned into the parking lot of the neighboring Key Bank. He parked on the far side of the lot, where the stream of people entering the library would not be able to see them.

"I can't just leave you in town in the middle of the night," he said.

"It's not the middle of the night. And, seriously, I told you, I won't have any problem getting home. Who knows. My parents might even be here. They come to the library events all the time."

That seemed to convince him. "You're sure?"

"Absolutely." She opened the car door and leaped lightly to the ground. "Go on. It's fine. Call me tomorrow."

"Okay."

Halfway across the parking lot, Ruthie turned and ran back to the car. She tapped on the window and Matt rolled it down. She leaned inside and gave him a soft kiss, gently tugging on his lower lip with her teeth. "Love you," she said lightly, as if the omission of the noun in the sentence made it somehow less startling. Then she turned and walked briskly toward the lit-up library, her hands shoved into the pockets of her jeans.

A novelist held the floor in the event room of the library this evening, a man who had moved to Red Hook to rough it on the proceeds of his trust fund and to complete the novel, entitled *Medicine Hat*, from which he was now reading in an authoritative but not particularly lively way. The event room was crowded, gray metal folding chairs filling every available open space. Many of the audience members were indeed friends or committee colleagues of Iris's, but Ruthie was relieved to see that her parents were not present after all. She took a seat at the back of the room, and for the next hour allowed her mind to wander.

She thought about Matt, about how distraught he'd been, about how she'd assumed that he was upset about his mother and how it had turned out that the Alden was his true concern. She should have known that. After all, she'd been watching him laboriously restore the boat. But Jane's face had been so awful—pinched and furious—it was hard to see how any amount of reconstruction could be worse than facing that.

Finally, the author reached the end of a chapter, placed his finger in the book to mark his place, and said, "Are you sick of me, or should I read just a little more?"

With no choice but to express polite eagerness to have their torment prolonged, the audience put their purses back on the floor, draped their jackets over the backs of their chairs, and settled themselves for another round. Ruthie took this opportunity to slip out the back of the reading room and tiptoed down the hall to the stacks, where she found Mary Lou Curran shelving books and sipping from a plastic wineglass.

"Ruthie!" Mary Lou said. "How delightful to see you. You're welcome to take refuge from the tedium here with me, but I warn you, I'm going to draft you to help me shelve. Do you do Dewey? We're still in the gaslight era here, I'm afraid."

Ruthie said, "My work-study job in college was at the Schlesinger Library."

"A trained professional. Excellent." Mary Lou pointed to a cart. "Start with this one. You strike me as an 823.7 kind of girl. And mind you keep my secret." She lifted her wineglass. "No food or drinks in the stacks, of course."

Ruthie would have known where *Emma* resided even without the labels affixed to the ends of each row of shelves. Periodically Ruthie would go through a voracious Jane Austen period and spend a month rereading everything, even *Mansfield Park*, which she knew some considered the most accomplished of Austen's novels but which she hated because Fanny Price was an insipid little prig. *Emma* was her favorite, and over the years she had checked out this very volume nearly a dozen times.

There was something soothing about shelving books. She took an extra moment with every one, glancing at the card in the back and indulging in idle curiosity about who had checked it out. Many of the books she had read herself, and she greeted them with the warmth due to old friends. The ones she hadn't read seemed suddenly more appealing to her, for having garnered someone's interest. When she'd emptied the cart she wheeled it back to where Mary Lou was working on another.

"What do you think?" Mary Lou asked. "Is it safe to go back?"

"Isn't there usually a question-and-answer period?"

"Indeed. And then after that he'll expect us all to purchase copies and wait patiently in line for the honor of having him scribble something banal on the title page. Let's stay here for a bit longer."

Mary Lou perched on a radiator and patted the spot next to her. Ruthie joined her and the two of them leaned back against the window and prepared to wait it out.

Mary Lou said, "You're back to Oxford at the end of the summer, aren't you? That must be terribly exciting for you."

"Not really," Ruthie said.

"Oh?"

"I mean, yes. Or, rather, it should be. I had a pretty bad year."

Mary Lou patted her hand. "I imagine it might have been lonely, to be so far from home."

"Yes."

The older woman drained the last sip of wine from her glass and said, "I've found in my life that the only kind of unpleasantness worth suffering through is one that is both brief and serves some greater good."

"I guess the trick is figuring out if the greater good is good enough," Ruthie said. "Or great enough."

"Indeed. Hindsight is the only reliable indicator, but that's hardly helpful."

"No." The windowpane was cool against Ruthie's back, and she shivered. She wanted suddenly to tell Mary Lou about Matt. To test her reaction as a barometer, perhaps, of Iris's. But if Iris were to find out that she'd confided first in someone else, she'd be furious.

Mary Lou said, "As long as I'm distributing pearls of ambiguous wisdom, I'll also say that, having lived for a very long time . . ."

"Not that long," Ruthie said.

"You're very kind, dear. But as I was saying, another thing I have learned in my life is that nothing one does in one's twenties, short of having a child, is irrevocable. You could, if you wanted to, simply choose not to return to England, or you could take a year off."

"I'm on a Fulbright," Ruthie said. "I think not going back to Oxford would be fairly irrevocable."

"Yes, I know about your Fulbright. Your mother told me. She's quite proud of you."

Was she? Ruthie wondered. Was Iris really proud of her? She certainly expected things from her, things like doing well in school, earning fellowships. When Ruthie conformed to these expectations her mother didn't seem so much proud as satisfied. For instance, Iris hadn't made a fuss when Ruthie graduated with honors from Harvard. It had been no more, Ruthie supposed, than what her mother had expected.

Mary Lou said, "I'm sure even the administrators of the Fulbright fellowships would understand if you requested a year's hiatus. Or even just one term's. Certainly you should try to find out if that's an option."

"What would I do if I didn't go back to Oxford?"

"Oh for goodness' sake, Ruthie. You're, what? Twenty-five years old? Surely you can come up with a way to fill your time."

"Twenty-three."

"Even better. Travel. Work. You could work here, and *I* could travel. You're already a recognized authority on the Dewey decimal system. You could shelve novels in the day, and read them at night. Which is, come to think of it, more or less how I spend my days. It's quite a nice life. Liven it up with the odd excursion to the movies or an afternoon's sailing and you'll find you pass the time quite easily."

"I don't sail," Ruthie said. "The rest of it sounds kind of not bad."

"You're only twenty-three. God love you." She sighed, and then stood up, grunting a little, as if her knees had stiffened up on her. "We'd best make our way back. I can't imagine the reading is still going on. He's written about Canada, for God's sake. How much can there be to say?"

V

Late that night, Jane sat at her kitchen table in front of a half-eaten blueberry pie, tracing a finger through the grains of sugar she'd spilled when she'd fixed her third cup of tea. She had skipped her pill tonight, to wait up for Matt, though she knew this meant she would be exhausted tomorrow morning. She had to wake up hours earlier than normal if she was to finish work early enough to take Samantha, as promised, down to visit her mother at the state hospital. Jane had already canceled Samantha's visit once this month when two of her crew came down with summer colds (or claimed they had; Maureen swore she saw them in Wal-Mart that very day). Still, while Connie would be upset at not seeing her daughter, Samantha was not likely to be disappointed if they had to postpone the visit again; last time she had not appeared to mind in the least. Samantha barely mentioned her mother these days. She had no time for anything besides her practicing and her lessons. She had started spending most of her days at the Copakens' house, insisting that it was too loud here, what with the girls coming in and out to get their assignments and stock up on supplies, and Matt banging away on that damn Alden every night and all weekend long. But Jane suspected the truth was that the girl just preferred being at the Copakens'.

Jane slivered off another piece of pie and ate it directly out of the tin. Delicately, so as not to cut herself, she licked the berry juice and crumbs of crust off the knife. Then she cut herself another sliver.

At one in the morning, Matt slipped quietly into the house, holding the screen to keep it from banging, and crept on stocking feet past the kitchen. Foolish boy, Jane thought as she watched him slither past the kitchen. So foolish he didn't bother to glance into the room and see her sitting in the dark, waiting to give him a piece of her mind. So foolish he tried to fit himself into his brother's shoes, take his brother's job, fix up his brother's boat, and now, worst of all, come as close as he could to having his brother's girl. Another child in thrall to the goddamn Copakens.

She watched him try to make his way silently through the house, taking slow, measured steps, freezing every time the floor creaked beneath his feet. She recalled how when he first learned to walk he would do it on tiptoe, his skinny little body balanced on the balls of his feet and on his tiny toes. He had looked so unstable, like even a breeze could topple him from his perch. She would hover over him, afraid he would fall. Then, when she was unable to stand it any longer, she would scoop him up and carry him around on her hip. She could almost feel his weight there now.

She called out, "You look like a gawmy idiot, tiptoeing around like that."

Matt gasped and clutched his chest. "Jesus Christ, you scared me." He stood in the hallway, as if he were afraid to come into the room.

"Sit down," Jane said, motioning to an empty chair.

After a longing glance up the dark hallway to the stairs and the safety of his bedroom, Matt joined her at the table.

"You're not planning on sleeping in the barn tonight?" she said.

He shook his head.

"Why not?"

"I don't know."

"You embarrassed about the mess you made out there?"

"I'm not *embarrassed*."

"Don't you go biting my head off. Here." She pushed the pie tin across the table. "There's pie."

"You made a pie?"

"Couldn't sleep. Waiting up for you."

"Oh."

She could tell he was bracing himself for the dressing down they both knew was coming. Matt had always been the more tractable of her two boys. John had never sought approval or permission from anyone. He did what he wanted, trusting the knowledge that his instincts were generally right. He had that kind of confidence. As soon as he was big enough, John defended himself both from his mother's criticism and from his father's brutish attacks, but with restraint, with no more force than was necessary. Matt never had that kind of fortitude. Reproach, criticism, or a whupping left him in tears, but in general such techniques were never even needed. The first time that Jane could honestly remember Matt refusing to do what he was told was last year, when he dropped out of college.

"Won't you have a little pie?"

"Oh, no thanks, Mum, I'm not really—"

"Have some goddamn pie."

Matt jumped, startled, as if he hadn't been waiting for her to explode from the moment she walked into the barn and found the boat in ruins and Ruthie half-naked, wearing only John's shirt. Jane sniffed. He smelled like beer.

Matt reached behind him and took a fork from the drain board. He pulled the pie tin toward him.

"Use a plate."

He got himself a plate and started to slice a narrow slice of pie. She took the knife out of his hand, cut a hefty piece, and served it to him brusquely. She had not cut all the way through, so part of the crust remained behind in the tin. With her fingers she pried it loose and dumped it on top of the misshapen lump of filling and crust on his plate.

"Dig in," she said.

Dutifully, he forked up a large bite and put it in his mouth. He chewed.

"Good?"

He nodded, looking so miserable she felt a sudden pity for him.

"The Citgo had berries today," she said, keeping her tone matter-of-fact. As though they were having any old conversation. As though it were not the middle of the night, and she had not been waiting for him for hours. "I bought enough to put up some jam, too," she continued.

"You planning on staying up all night?" He gave a nervous smile, revealing purple-stained teeth.

"Close your mouth. No, no, I'm hoping to sleep tonight. But considering the way things are going, I might get to the jam and still have a few hours to put up the first of the tomatoes. Where've you been?"

Matt slid his plate away and leaned back, hand on his belly, in a show that he was too stuffed to eat any more.

"Finish your food," Jane said.

There was a pause, and for one instant defiance flared in his eyes. Then he took up his fork again. As he shoveled up the rest of the pie she repeated, "Where have you been?"

"Driving around," he said, with his mouth full.

She licked her finger and dabbed at some sugar that had spilled on the table. Then she put her finger in her mouth, wincing slightly at the sweetness. "Driving by the Neptune, by the stink of it. What is it you think you're doing, son?"

He sighed, and pushed away his plate. "Nothing."

"Nothing?"

"Uh-huh."

Surely the boy knew her well enough to know that she was not the kind of mother to be satisfied with that kind of answer. "You're sleeping with that girl, I don't call that nothing. And let's not even talk about what you've gone and done to John's boat."

Matt pushed his chair back and got to his feet. "I'm tired. I'm going to bed."

"You'll sit your narrow behind down. We're going to talk about this. You don't want to be seeing Ruthie, Matt. You know you don't."

Matt braced his hands on the back of the kitchen chair, digging the pads of his fingers into the vinyl-covered upholstery. He rocked the chair back and forth a few times. "Why not?"

"Why not?" Surely he didn't need her to explain to him what was wrong with what he was doing. Jane's head started to hurt, a dull throb that began at the base of her skull and crept over the top of her head.

"Yeah, why not? I like her. I like being with her. She gets me, you know? She feels the same kinds of things I do. We're alike."

If he'd finished college, if he had gotten his degree, gone on to study marine biology like he had always said he was going to, then he might have had something in common with that girl. But now he was nothing more than a dropout working down at the boatyard. He wasn't even a designer, like his brother had been. "She's nothing like you, boy."

"You're just saying that because you have a chip on your shoulder about her parents. But you need to get over that, Mum. Look what they're doing for Samantha. Ruthie's mom gave her a fucking *violin*! The old man is giving her free lessons. Do you even *get* who he is? He was one of the most famous violinists of his time. He played for, like, JFK. He even played for the fucking queen of *England*! Do you know how much he would charge for lessons, if he even gives them anymore? Like, I don't know, a hundred bucks an hour!"

Jane slapped her hands down on the table, making the pie tin and forks jump. "Watch your language! I've known Mr. Kimmelbrod for forty years. You don't need to tell me who he is. Samantha doesn't have anything to do with this. What's going on between Samantha and Mr. Kimmelbrod is a whole nother problem. This is about you and that girl."

"Why is what's going on with Samantha a problem? She's *lucky*. If it weren't for Iris and Mr. Kimmelbrod, we never would have even known Samantha *had* talent."

"I knew."

"Oh, yeah, right. You knew. Before the Copakens came along, the kid was playing on some little toy Barbie piano. Now she's studying violin with a world-famous virtuoso."

Jane didn't need Matt to tell her that Mr. Kimmelbrod was giving Samantha a tremendous gift, that if not for him, Samantha's talent would have been little more than a party trick. Jane was, in fact, keenly aware of how much she owed the old man and his daughter, of the depth of the emotional and financial hock she was in to the Copaken family. The lessons, and before that the burial plot, and before that the wedding. She could never repay them, even if they would allow her the dignity of trying.

Jane said, "We're not talking about that now. The problem we're dealing with right here and now is you and that girl. I want it to stop."

Matt raised his voice. "Why?"

"Because I said so."

"That's not a good enough reason." Saliva sprayed from his mouth, and with a rough swipe he passed the back of his hand over his lips.

"While you live under my roof that is the best reason there is."

Matt pushed the chair into the table with a bang. "I'm going to bed."

Jane stood up, braced her hands on the edge of the table, and leaned forward until her face was close to Matt's. "We're not done," she said. Her scowl operated on him as it always had. It froze him in place.

For a long minute they faced each other across the expanse of the pockmarked old table, neither one of them moving. The room was silent but for the airplane drone of the cicadas, the occasional booming of a toad, and the hum of the electric clock above the stove.

Finally, Matt said softly, "I'm not sixteen anymore. You can't tell me who I can and can't date. I'm a man." Matt's eyes were wet and Jane was afraid that he was going to cry. Instead, he turned away and walked out of the room. In the doorway he stopped. Without turning to look at her, he said, "I'm sorry, Mum."

"Don't be sorry. Do the right thing."

"I'm sorry," he repeated, and left her alone in the dark kitchen.

As she listened to his heavy tread on the stairs, Jane sat down, put her head in her hands, and rubbed her eyes with her fingertips. She missed John. If he were here she could have thrown up her hands and said, *"I have no idea how to get through to that boy. You deal with him,"* just as she used to whenever Matt would sink into one of his adolescent sulks. Then John would have smiled, given her shoulder a squeeze, and teased her for getting so upset. "Take it easy, Mum," he would have said. "You're going to give yourself a stroke." Then he would have gone to Matt's room, shut the door, and within minutes the two of them would be listening to their music and laughing like fools.

In a life that had of late been composed of vast swaths of solitude, Jane had never felt so completely alone. She pulled the pie over to her, picked up the fork, and took a large bite. She ate the whole thing, and if there had been a second pie, she would have eaten that one, too.

VI

If Iris had not woken up so early, in all likelihood she would have assumed that he had gone into town to wait in the café at the co-op for the *New York Times* to arrive. That was, after all, what he had done nearly every summer morning for more than twenty years. But she had slept fitfully, and he woke her when he got out of bed. She tried for a few minutes to fall back asleep, but when she could not, she went down to the kitchen. She found him standing at the sink drinking a cup of coffee. He was wearing sweatpants and a torn T-shirt, and his gym bag hung from his shoulder. She looked at the gym bag and crossed her arms over her chest.

"It's a stress reliever, Iris," Daniel said. "It makes me feel good. I need it."

"You need your stress relieved? You can run," Iris said. "Lift weights. I don't know. But you can't go getting yourself beaten up. It's ridiculous for a man of your age to think he can box. It's *embarrassing*."

"It was just a little sparring," he muttered, like a recalcitrant child. "And if you hadn't come in and distracted me I never would have gone down."

"Give me a break, Daniel. It's been days and your face still looks like a side of beef. I won't have you boxing anymore."

"You're not my mother, Iris. You're my wife," Daniel said. "You don't get to tell me what you'll have and what you won't have. I'm going to do what I want to do. For once."

Determined not to lose her cool, Iris crossed the kitchen, took a coffee mug from the drain board, and went to fill it, passing next to Daniel on her way to the coffeepot. When her arm brushed against his, he flinched. She was seized by an urge to press herself up against him, to force him to feel her body, her skin, her flesh. She wanted to slap him across the face, to hurt him for making her feel that her touch repulsed him. He never stroked her hair, or kissed her cheek, or held her hand anymore. And they had not made love since the week after Becca and John died.

Before the accident, while not frequent, their lovemaking was regular. If not passionate, it was certainly comfortable, and occurred at least a couple of times a month.

In the immediate aftermath of the accident, for reasons neither of them understood, they had made furious love nearly every night. It began the night after the funeral. First to bed, Iris lay curled on her side between the chilled sheets, shaking. When Daniel slipped into the bed, he spooned himself around her and they lay like that for a while, warming each other. Suddenly Iris was conscious of his penis shifting against her, growing hard. She pressed herself against him, and Daniel groaned.

"Oh, Jesus," he said. "I'm so sorry. I can't help it."

"It's okay," Iris said, turning around so they faced each other. She wrapped her arm around his neck, knotting her fingers in his hair and pulling it, harder than she had intended. They drove their tongues into each other's mouths, biting and sucking as if they were trying to consume each other. With his mouth still pressed to hers, he thrust inside her. He ground his hips against her and she arched her back. It was as if they were trying, at fifty years old, to pound another child into existence to replace the one they had lost. Or as if they were taking out on each other's bodies the rage that had no other obvious target. Soon they were bathed in sweat, their bodies slipping on the sheets. For traction, Daniel grabbed the headboard with one hand. The other he clamped over her mouth to muffle her screams.

They never spoke about it, they never planned it, but for nearly a week they fucked every night, always with the same intensity. When he came Daniel cried, his tears and sweat raining down on Iris's face. Then, suddenly, as inexplicably as it had begun, it stopped. Nearly two years had passed since then, and they had not made love once.

Remembering those nights, Iris could not deny that the violence of their lovemaking had not been an accident. The brutality had been the *point*. Tenderness could follow only because of the aggression, even the pain, that preceded it. She had accepted it then. Even, if she was honest with herself, took a kind of grim pleasure in it. But now, two years later, when he no longer touched her, she could not bear the idea of him finding satisfaction in the ring.

"Please. Daniel," she said. "Please promise me you won't do it anymore. You'll get hurt, and I don't honestly think I can handle that. Not now."

Before he could answer, they heard the tapping of Mr. Kimmelbrod's walker as he made his way down the long hall from the guest bedroom where he was living this summer, having finally conceded that he could no longer manage in the Peter's Point Road cottage on his own. As they waited for him to arrive in the kitchen, they exchanged a long, fraught glance, at the end of which Daniel shrugged the gym bag off his shoulder and tossed it into a corner of the room.

Iris set about preparing the single slice of toast and soft-boiled egg on which Mr. Kimmelbrod breakfasted every morning. After she served it, she called up to Ruthie. By the time the girl was sitting at the table wiping the sleep from her bleary eyes, Iris was sliding a neatly pleated tomato-and-cheese omelet as snug as a love letter onto her plate. She put a pot of Earl Grey tea and two cups on the table and sat next to her daughter. She poured herself a cup of tea and offered one to Ruthie, who shook her head. Daniel presented Ruthie with a cup of coffee. She poured in a splash of milk and drank.

"I'm surprised Oxford didn't turn you into a tea drinker," Iris said. "It certainly did me. I used to drink dozens of cups a day, just to keep warm."

"There are Starbucks all over Oxford now. And, like, twenty other cafés."

"That's a shame," Iris said.

"Why?" Ruthie said, poking at her omelet. "Oxford's no different than anywhere else."

"I don't know," Iris said. "I thought it was pretty special. Although I suppose it's true that the world has experienced a creeping homogeneity since I was a student. Don't you like your omelet?"

Ruthie sighed and pushed away her plate. "Mom, Dad. And Grandpa, too. I have something to tell you."

Iris wrapped her hands around her mug, steeling herself for what could, with that introduction, only be bad news.

"I think I want to take a break from school."

"A break?" Iris said.

"A year off. I'm not quitting the program."

"Of course you're not," Daniel said.

"Just a hiatus. It's very common for people to do that."

"Is it?" Iris said.

"Yes. At least, at Oxford it is. It's called a gap year. People do it to sort of clear their heads. So they can make sure they're certain about their courses of study."

Iris said, "I was under the impression that a gap year was something young people did before they even began university, not something graduate students did in the middle of their degree programs. I can't imagine it's something Fulbright Fellows do."

"All right, not a gap year exactly. Call it a break. As in, 'Give me a goddamn break.' Sorry, Grandpa."

Mr. Kimmelbrod shook his head. "No need to apologize. In fact, I must excuse myself for a moment."

"Dad, don't you want to finish your breakfast?" Iris said.

"A moment," he said. They watched him make his laborious way back up the hall.

When the door to his room clicked shut, Ruthie said, "I've been in school for nineteen years. I don't think it's unreasonable for me to take a year off."

Daniel said, "I don't see why she couldn't take a short break."

"Oh, really, you don't?" Iris said. "Let me explain it, then. She can't take a year off because it'll take her off track. Ruthie, right now you're well positioned to get into a first-rate doctoral program. You could even continue on at Oxford. You don't want to do anything to threaten that. You don't want to end up teaching composition at some crappy college in North Dakota." Iris regretted the words as soon as she said them. The law school at CUNY, where Daniel taught, fell into the category of the kind of institution she was dismissing so harshly.

"Not everybody has to teach at Columbia," Ruthie said.

"Everyone in North Dakota wishes they were teaching at Columbia," Iris said. "But fine. A break. Great. Terrific. So what do you plan to do with your break?"

"I don't know," Ruthie said, all defiance now sapped from her tone.

"What do you mean, you don't know? You can't just quit. You have to have a plan."

"I don't know. I'll get a job or something."

"What kind of job?"

"I don't *know*, Mom. A job. Any job. I can wait tables or work retail. It's not that important."

"Really? What you do isn't important?"

"Come on, Iris," Daniel said. "Leave her alone."

Ruthie said, "I guess it depends on what you mean by 'important.' Clearly, in this case you mean 'important to you.' "

All at once Iris saw, panicking, the life she had imagined for Ruthie slipping away. She had never approved of Ruthie's field; the English departments of America were lousy with scholars of the women novelists and poets Ruthie loved. But despite her poor choice of concentration, Iris knew that Ruthie was perfectly suited to the life of the mind. She, like her mother, took her greatest pleasure from reading. She always had. It didn't make sense for Ruthie to do anything else. She was an ideal scholar, devoted to her subject, patient and thorough, easily immersed. Iris had counseled Ruthie to turn her attention to a lesser-traveled area of study but Ruthie had remained true to her passion, in the end Iris had admired her for it. Ruthie could not give up on her ambitions now, when she was well on her way to seeing them come to fruition. She couldn't follow Becca's pointless path.

"You could work as a paralegal," Daniel said, keeping his eyes firmly averted from his wife, as if her objections were no longer at issue. As if Ruthie's decision had already been made. "Law firms hire kids to work for a year before applying to law school."

"She isn't applying to law school," Iris said. "Or are you, Ruthie? Have you suddenly decided to become a lawyer?"

"No, I'm not going to law school," Ruthie said.

And with that—Ruthie's vagueness, layered on top of Daniel's obtuse acquiescence to her foolishness, an acquiescence Iris knew to be based as much on hostility to her as on concern for Ruthie's welfare—Iris snapped.

"You'd better figure out what you want, Ruthie," she said. "Before you make a complete hash out of your life."

"Will you please give her a break," Daniel said. "She's not making a hash out of her life. She's taking a year off from school, for Christ's sake. You're acting like she's decided to become a crackhead."

Iris said, "I just don't want her to make a mistake that she'll regret." This conversation was far too reminiscent of the argument they'd had in the wake of Becca's decision to quit the Conservatory. Then, too, Daniel had taken Becca's side. At least this time her father had not added his voice to the chorus.

"You can't order her around," Daniel said. "She's not a child."

"Okay, who are we talking about now?" Iris said. "Are we talking about Ruthie and her future, or do you have something you want to say to me?"

"Jesus Christ," Daniel said. "You really are a piece of work." He leaped to his feet and strode across the room, scooped up his gym bag, and stormed out of the house, banging the screen door behind him.

For a moment Iris sat at the table trembling, wanting to leap up and follow him, to take back everything she had said. She took a deep breath and cupped her hands around her warm mug. Then she rose unsteadily and walked out to the screen porch, where her armchair sat waiting for her to settle into its familiar embrace.

She left Ruthie sitting alone at the kitchen table, her head resting in her hands.

VII

"Samantha!" Iris called.

The girl spun around and waved. Then she raced across the yard toward Iris, her brown legs pumping up and down, her hair swinging wildly behind her. Samantha flung her arms up in the air and hurled herself forward in an ungainly cartwheel, her legs bent, her feet splayed every which way. She'd been practicing her violin for the last two hours while Mr. Kimmelbrod napped, and would still be hard at it had Iris not insisted that she take a break. Iris practically had to push Samantha out the door to get some fresh air, but now she was cavorting around like the little girl she was.

"Gather some flowers for the table, why don't you," Iris shouted. "There's a patch of lupines on the other side of the Grange Hall."

A few minutes later, Samantha returned bearing a lavish armload of purple, pink, and white flowers. Iris looked up from the dish of egg salad she had been preparing and saw Samantha holding the bouquet in her arms. Iris grew lupines because it was Becca's favorite flower. Each June since the accident she had kept the house full to bursting with masses of lupines, refreshing the vases as soon as the petals showed the first sign of wilting. She would pick them until there were no more lupines to be had in the garden, or even by the sides of the most remote roads. She liked to be reminded of her daughter this way, and yet something about seeing the young girl with the enormous armload of purple flowers brought the wedding day back too forcefully.

Samantha's smile faded, her eyebrows knotting with concern. "Did I take too many?"

"No," Iris said. "You took the perfect amount. There's an enameled pitcher on the table. You can put them in there."

Samantha buried her face in the flowers, inhaled deeply, then sneezed. Iris burst out laughing. Samantha started to join her, then sneezed again.

"Here," Iris laughed, offering her a tissue.

It was good to have a little girl in the house again. The giggles, the squeak of the bicycle brakes when Samantha pulled up to the house, the small feet running up the porch steps. The sound of the violin. Samantha tuned her A string in a manner very similar to Becca's drawn-out, rising wail that grew louder as the bow traveled across the string. And just as when Becca was a child, the pitch of the string as she tuned it matched precisely the whistle of the old tea kettle that had been Iris's grandmother's. This morning, as on so many mornings long ago, Iris had rushed into the kitchen to pull the kettle off the burner, only to find it sitting unemployed, mocking her with its cold copper sides.

They had lunch on the screen porch and waited for Mr. Kimmelbrod to wake up from his nap. He had seemed tired this morning, and in the middle of the lesson he had excused himself, instructing Samantha to practice the first movement of the Bach Sonata no. 1 in G Minor, which they had been studying for the last few weeks. The piece was challenging for Samantha, more difficult, perhaps, than she could handle, and the effort of teaching her had exhausted him. He had gone to his bedroom, promising to return within the hour. Nearly two and a half hours had passed, and Iris now was starting to worry.

As if attuned to Iris's thoughts, Samantha asked, "Do you think Mr. Kimmelbrod is okay?"

"I'm sure he's fine," Iris said. She would give him another few minutes before going to check on him. Her father was so private that she loathed intruding on him. It had been a very difficult transition for him, getting used to living in her house rather than alone in his. She had tried to make things easier for him by never entering his room uninvited.

"I hope he's not sick," Samantha said.

"Sometimes he just needs to recharge his batteries. He's ninety years old, you know."

Samantha, who had been about to take a large bite of her egg salad sandwich, stopped it midway between the plate and her mouth. "Should I go home and let him rest?"

"Of course not. We'll enjoy our lunch, and by the time we're done he'll be awake. Unless you have somewhere you need to be?"

"This is the only place," Samantha said.

"Are your lessons going well? Is Mr. Kimmelbrod being very hard on you?"

"Oh, no!" Samantha said. "I mean, yes, but I like it."

"My daughter used to say that when he listened to her play he looked like a man in a dentist's chair anticipating a root canal."

Samantha laughed. "Sometimes he does. But sometimes, when he hears something he likes, he kind of nods, like this." She executed a slow, solemn nod of her head. It was a surprisingly faithful reproduction of Mr. Kimmelbrod's grave, slightly stiff Mitteleuropean demeanor, given its presence on the face of a young Asian girl.

"And does he nod often during your lessons?"

"It depends on how well I'm playing."

"I wonder if he nodded for Becca like that," Iris said.

"It must have been so nice for . . ." Samantha hesitated. "For your daughter to have her grandfather to play for."

Iris smiled, touched and saddened as always that it was so hard for Samantha to say Becca's name. So many people, young and old, seemed to be under the impression that the mention of the dead by name was a social transgression, something done in bad taste. No one understood how much Iris craved to hear Becca's name spoken aloud, how important it was to have the fact that Becca had once existed acknowledged by more than just their family. When she made explicit mention of Becca in public, it was as though the name were a heavy stone dropped into the pool of conversation. It disturbed the tranquil surface, sending ripples across the room.

Iris said, "When she wasn't giving him a root canal, Becca loved playing for her grandfather. Your family must enjoy hearing you play."

"Not really. My mom likes rock and roll okay. Like Bon Jovi and stuff."

"Not classical music?"

"Not really." Samantha peeled the bread off the top of her sandwich and poked at the egg salad as though she were looking for something she had lost. "Sometimes I kind of, like, pretend . . ." Her voice trailed away.

"What?" Iris said. "Pretend what?"

"It's stupid."

"I'm sure it isn't. Tell me."

Shyly, Samantha said, "There are these Cambodian stringed instruments that you play with a bow, like a violin. I read about them on the Web. Sometimes I, like, imagine that my birth parents were musicians. That they played the *tro khmer*. If they did, that would explain why I, you know, can play."

"That doesn't seem silly to me at all," Iris said.

"And it would explain why they gave me up, too." Quickening to her topic now, no longer embarrassed or shy, Samantha said, "I was almost three when I was adopted, but I'd been living in the orphanage my whole life. The year I was born there was a drought, and a lot of babies were given up because their families couldn't feed them. During a famine the first thing people would give up would be entertainment, don't you think? If they were musicians my parents wouldn't have been able to earn a living. They'd have been the first people to starve. So they had to give me up, to try to save me."

Iris said, "It sounds like you've really thought this through."

Samantha flushed and returned her gaze to her disassembled sandwich.

Iris hurried to add, "It's a very plausible theory. And of course, musical gifts as profound as yours often run in families."

"Like Becca and Mr. Kimmelbrod."

Iris took Samantha's hand and squeezed it gratefully. "Exactly," Iris said. "And Mr. Kimmelbrod wasn't the first in his family by any stretch. His mother's family was very musical. She was a pianist, but back then a Jewish woman would never have been allowed to have a concert career. I often wonder what my grandmother's life might have been like had she been born in another place and time."

"Like me. Who knows what my life would have been like?"

"True. You might never have seen a violin."

"Or I might have been playing music all my life instead of starting so late. I might have played the *tro khmer* with my mother."

Or, Iris thought, you might have been adopted by a couple of Jewish psychiatrists and been enrolled in Suzuki when you were three years old.

She was touched by the naked yearning for connection, for a coherent explanation of the wonder of herself, that she heard in Samantha's voice. Iris thought of Becca's life, how replete with music it had been. Although neither Iris nor Daniel was particularly musical—she had inherited none of her father's gifts—their house had been filled with music. There was always something playing on the stereo or the radio. Not just classical music, but rock and roll, jazz, blues. Daniel loved Brazilian jazz and bossa nova, and he worshipped Miles Davis. Her daughters' infancies had been bathed in music.

It had been no surprise when Becca proved so receptive to, and fascinated by, music. When she was three, Mr. Kimmelbrod presented her with her first violin, eager to nurture her talent. What might Samantha's life have been like if she had had the same kind of early encouragement? If she had heard Mozart in her cradle, if she had sung before she could speak, if she had studied from toddlerhood with the finest teachers? Although Samantha's musical education was proceeding now with a breakneck speed, and working with a violinist of Mr. Kimmelbrod's stature was an opportunity even the most gifted and affluent prodigies rarely received, Iris could not help but wonder how the girl's life and career might have flourished if she had been adopted by someone else. Someone, for example, like Iris.

It had taken so little to effect dramatic change in Samantha. She was like a desert flower that needed only a smattering of rain to bloom. Just last summer she had known nothing about music, and yet she had learned to sight-read in a few lessons, almost without being taught. Mr. Kimmelbrod had simply explained to her the rules, which she had then instinctively grasped.

Samantha was clearly desperate for the kind of musical life Iris and Mr. Kimmelbrod could give her. The girl had borrowed dozens of recordings from Mr. Kimmelbrod: Mozart, Beethoven, Bach, Mendelssohn, Grieg, even Webern and Schoenberg. Early this summer she had even borrowed a CD of the Kronos Quartet playing George Crumb's surrealistic *Black Angels*, returning the next day and begging Mr. Kimmelbrod to get her a copy of the score from the Usherman Center library.

So obvious was her talent that Mr. Kimmelbrod had arranged for her to study over the winter with the only violinist in the area he trusted not to ruin her with bad habits: Arturo Weinstein, the concert master of the Bangor Symphony Orchestra. Iris had paid for the lessons, never letting her father know that she had given Jane the impression they were free.

Iris had even made Samantha a gift of the three-quarter-sized Gliga that had been Becca's when she was young, so that she would have a respectable instrument to play.

Samantha had made marvelous progress in Bangor over the winter, but not as much as she could have. Weinstein abandoned the state for nearly all of February and March in favor of the warm sun of Florida. Moreover, Jane had resisted Iris's offer to pay for Samantha's travel expenses to and from Bangor, and so Iris was sure that there were times when the lack of transportation had kept Samantha from her lessons. There had been long periods when Samantha had received no instruction at all. This summer Iris was trying without success to find a more reliable instructor for the coming winter.

"It must be very difficult," Iris said now. "Not to know where your talents come from, or even the details of where you come from. Do you know other Cambodian people?"

"I know a bunch of girls adopted from China, but they're mostly younger than me. In the church we used to go to there was another Cambodian adoptee. And two boys from Korea. The pastor was really into international adoption. They were all his kids."

"You don't go to that church anymore?"

"No. It was in Belfast, and when my mom . . . got sick, we moved up here to be closer to her family."

"Do you miss the church? The other children?"

"Yeah. I guess. The Cambodian girl was older than me, and the boys, you know. They're boys. But there was a really good choir at the church. I liked that. And it was nice not to feel quite so different all the time."

"Up here you must feel pretty different."

With uncharacteristic vehemence Samantha said, "Everybody talks about how great it is to be different. Like diversity is so important? But they don't know what it's like to be different all the time. Nobody talks about *that*." She hesitated for a moment, and then in a rush, as though she had been waiting for years to find someone to confide in, said, "When I was little sometimes I used to *forget*; like, I'd be walking along feeling totally normal, and then I'd look in the mirror, and I'd be like, oh yeah, *that's* what I look like."

"You know, Sam," Iris said, laying her hand gently on Samantha's cheek, "I know it's not the same, but I sometimes feel something a little like that about Becca. Every once in a rare while, I almost forget that she's gone. If I get very wrapped up in something, like my work, suddenly I'm not Becca's mom, grieving for her. I feel like . . . well . . . like the old me. Like I always felt, before. And then, usually after just a minute or two, something snaps me back. I'll see something, not even as obvious as her picture, just maybe a cup of coffee on my desk, or a pen with the cap off, and I'll remember how when she was a little girl she liked to drink coffee that was mostly milk, with four teaspoons of sugar, or how she used to leave the tops off the markers so that they were always drying out. And just like you, I'll think, Oh, right. That's who I am. I'm the mom whose daughter died."

Samantha listened intently, nodded in vigorous agreement.

"You know," Iris said. "I have Becca's audition tape for the New England Conservatory of Music. Would you like to hear it?"

"Yes!" Samantha said. "Oh yes."

Although Iris had always meant to listen to the tape, she had never until this moment had the courage. She could not explain why she was suddenly willing to play it for Samantha, who after all had barely known Becca, nor why she hadn't shared it with the people who were most entitled to hear it: Daniel, Ruthie, and Mr. Kimmelbrod.

Iris led Samantha into the living room, knelt down in front of the stereo, and put the cassette into the player. There was a hiss of static, a click, and then Becca's throaty voice. Iris sat down. She closed her eyes and clutched her knees to her chest.

"Rebecca Felice Copaken." That was all; no more than three seconds of sound. It was the first time Iris had heard her daughter's voice since saying good-bye to her on the steps of the church.

The first piece was Paganini's Caprice no. 7 in A Minor. Iris remembered that Becca had originally planned to begin with Mendelssohn's Concerto in A Minor, but Mr. Kimmelbrod had told her that he had heard the first movement of the concerto, over and over, on hundreds of audition tapes submitted with Juilliard and Usherman Center applications. He had urged Caprice no. 24 on her, but she had demurred, claiming that it was too challenging. She chose no. 7, and played it nearly perfectly.

Becca had subsequently played a number of the caprices for her senior recital, and it was this performance that Iris remembered as she listened. Iris recognized her daughter's light touch swiftly skipping from note to note. She remembered how Becca used to toss her head as she played. When the tone turned somber, she would close her eyes and furrow her brow. Becca would frown, and jerk her chin, she would lift her eyebrows and sway when she drew out a note with a long bow stroke. She would rock back and forth, almost dancing. Such a dramatic contrast to her grandfather's mask of performance. When he played, Mr. Kimmelbrod was a model of physical restraint. Most violinists played with their whole bodies. They swooped and dived, the music not only in their fingers and hands but in their arms, their torsos, their legs and feet, even in the mops of hair that flapped and flew around their skulls. Mr. Kimmelbrod was like the trunk of an oak tree, a reviewer had once said, with deep roots anchoring him to the ground.

At Becca's senior recital, Iris had been conscious the whole time that Mr. Kimmelbrod, sitting next to her, kept wincing ever so slightly. Later, he offered a brisk criticism of what he considered Becca's flaws in fluidity and tone.

Iris pushed this memory of her father's displeasure away and let the music wash over her, imagining Becca's long sun-tanned fingers flitting across the strings, her ponytail dancing as her body bobbed and dipped. She glanced at Samantha, who was immobile, straining to hear every note.

Becca played the final notes, ending on a dramatic flourish, and both Iris and Samantha, who had been taut with attention, sagged back, drained.

When they heard the introductory notes of the next piece of music on the tape, the Chaconne, the final movement of Bach's Violin Partita no. 2 in D Minor, Samantha whispered, "Oh I *love* this Bach! I wish I could play it."

"You will," Iris said. "Someday you will."

Mr. Kimmelbrod had disapproved, too, of the lush, soulful quality Becca worked so hard to bring to the Chaconne. "Too much Heifetz," he had said. "Not enough Bach." He made this pronouncement after she completed the audition tape, when she was playing it for them before sending it off. Iris remembered the expression on Becca's face at his words. She went pale, but then she laughed. Iris had tried to reassure her that the piece was fine, better than fine. She had played it beautifully. But Becca had not needed her mother's reassurance. "It's the best I can do," she said. "If they like it, they'll let me in. If not, I'll go to NYU and study anthropology. Or else I'm thinking clown college." Becca had a gift for shining it on, for getting over things, for letting go. Unlike her mother. Right now, for instance, recalling Mr. Kimmelbrod's dry, epigrammatic dismissal of the audition tape, Iris found herself suddenly furious. Becca had played the Chaconne for *him*, in homage to *him*. She played it because he had performed it in his first American solo recital, at Town Hall on June 11, 1936.

"That was so beautiful," Samantha said. "Thank you."

Smiling at her, Iris realized that Samantha's eyes were full of tears. Awash in emotion, grateful beyond measure to this young girl for appreciating the beauty of what they had just heard, Iris said, "Perhaps you'd like to come visit us in New York this year? You could have some lessons with Mr. Kimmelbrod. We could go to a few concerts. We might even be able to find a concert of Cambodian music."

Samantha said, "I've never been to New York. And I've never seen Cambodian music played anywhere except on the Internet."

"We'll definitely go to a concert, then. And you know what? There are lots of Cambodian adoptees in New York. I'm sure I could track down an organization or a support group. Maybe you could attend a meeting. At the very least we could go eat at a Cambodian restaurant."

"I've never eaten Cambodian food," Samantha said. "That would be wicked awesome."

It *would* be wicked awesome, Iris thought. She imagined taking the girl to concerts, sitting in a recital hall and hearing her perform for the first time. She imagined introducing her to Lincoln Center. She imagined sitting in her living room reading a novel while across the room a young girl practiced her scales.

Iris was confident that Samantha had the potential to be a world-class violinist. But most musicians of her caliber began serious study when they were barely out of diapers. By her age they'd already spent five, six, or even seven years learning the repertoire and perfecting their technique. As talented as she was, Samantha had tremendous catching up to do. She could not risk even one more winter of missed lessons and family distractions. She needed to study music and theory, and she needed to be protected from the pressures of her mother's illness and the peripatetic life it foisted upon her, back and forth between Jane and her mother, never knowing for sure where she would spend the next week or month.

"I think it would be a very good idea for you to spend some time with us in New York," Iris said. "I'll talk to your aunt Jane."

The excitement drained from Samantha's expression. "She'll never let me go."

"I'm sure that once she realizes what an opportunity this is for you, she'll agree." Of course Iris was sure of no such thing. Jane was certain to resist the idea of Samantha spending time in New York. And she would be particularly averse to the plan that now began to form in Iris's mind: wouldn't it be remarkable if Samantha could spend a whole *winter* in New York? The girl would have access to a musical education unavailable to her in Red Hook. Think how she would blossom! Iris was sure that her father would be willing, even eager, to fully assume the responsibility for Samantha's musical education. He might even be able to arrange for her to attend the Juilliard precollege program. Samantha was young and untutored, yes, but she was marvelously talented. Even if she were not ready for Juilliard now, certainly she would be with a year or so of concentrated education. In New York Samantha could be surrounded by music every waking hour of her day. She should have the kind of life Iris had given to her own daughter. A musician's life.

Iris was sufficiently self-aware to understand even at that moment that the idea of helping Samantha was not purely altruistic, that it might also go a long way in assuaging the sense of emptiness she had felt since Becca's death. It was so odd. Becca had not lived at home, except in the summers, for nearly a decade, and yet Iris felt so bereft of her day-to-day presence. She would love to have a girl in her life again, one whose musical education she could shepherd properly this time. Iris had learned from her experience with Becca what kind of encouragement and support to give. As gifted as Becca was, Iris thought it likely that Samantha might have something more, an extra dose of ambition or talent. Enough to overcome the challenge of having started so late. So, no, her motives were not entirely, or even primarily, charitable. Iris recognized her selfishness. She was thinking, if she was really honest, about Ruthie, too, who seemed as eager to throw away her future as her sister had been. But did it matter? Wasn't the girl what mattered, and how best she could be nurtured? Even Jane, despite the many roadblocks she was sure to throw up against the plan, would surely, in the end, have no choice but to acknowledge what was best for Samantha. But best to start small. With the idea of a visit.

"I bet that together we could convince your aunt to let you come," Iris said.

"I don't know," Samantha said doubtfully.

"What don't you know?" Mr. Kimmelbrod stood in the doorway, leaning on his walker. He wore a freshly ironed white shirt, dark slacks with a knife-sharp crease, and polished black brogues. The only indication that he had been sleeping for the past two hours was the long red furrow across his cheek where his face had rested against the pillow.

"Nothing, Dad," Iris said. "We were just passing the time."

"So you were not practicing the Bach?" he teased Samantha.

"She was, Dad," Iris said. "For nearly two hours! I made lunch. Can I interest you in an egg salad sandwich?"

"No thank you." To Samantha, Mr. Kimmelbrod said, "Come. Let's hear what progress you have made."

"Can I stay and listen?" Iris asked. Always before now she had made sure to excuse herself when it was time for Samantha's lesson, even going so far as to leave the house to give them the privacy she knew her father expected.

"It's up to Samantha," he said.

Samantha smiled shyly. "I don't mind," she said.

For the next hour Iris sat curled on the living room couch and listened while Samantha and Mr. Kimmelbrod worked on the first movement of the Bach, the adagio. Iris had heard the sonata dozens of times. At Becca's childhood recitals there was often at least one young violinist doing his or her best to bring something other than a turgid solemnity to the first movement, or to get through the second as fast as possible. On certain rare occasions, a particularly talented child would do more than simply make it through. Sometimes a child would bring a depth of feeling to the piece, an adult's intensity.

Samantha, although she was still refining the subtler issues of the piece's phrasing, turned out to be one of those students. She was still struggling with it, but in the places where she was comfortable her playing was precise without rounding off the rough edges. She brought emotion to music that Iris had often heard drained of fire and art.

For most of the hour Iris sat with her eyes closed, listening intently. She opened them only when Mr. Kimmelbrod stopped Samantha to push and prod her fingers into place, or to hum for her the music as he wanted her to play it.

When Becca was a child Iris would on occasion take a book or a pile of papers that needed grading and lie down on the couch while her daughter practiced. Iris would work as Becca went through her scales once, twice, even three times, until they were perfectly in tune. Periodically the music would trail off and Iris would raise her head; a frown was usually enough to get Becca back to work. But had she ever just sat and *listened*? Even when Becca was a small child, Iris had never attended the girl's lessons, and while Becca had often entertained them with impromptu concerts over the years, from "Twinkle, Twinkle, Little Star," when she was a toddler, all the way up to her senior-year performance of Bach's Violin Partita no. 2 in D Minor, Iris could not recall ever just sitting like this, her feet up, her eyes closed, listening to her daughter practice.

Had she known how little opportunity life would bring her, in the end, to hear Becca play, Iris might well have become one of those helicopter mothers, the ones who pressed their ears against the doors of rehearsal studios and sat in the back of empty concert halls, hands folded in their laps, eyes fixed on their children. If only she had known how briefly Becca would be with them, how ephemeral childhood was, how quickly it vanished, she would have paid more attention. If she had, perhaps Becca would never have stopped playing. And if she had not stopped playing, then her life would have been different. If she had married John at all it would likely have been on a different day, in a different place. All it would have taken was a single beat of the butterfly's wings, and Becca would not have died.

"Okay, my dear," Mr. Kimmelbrod said to Samantha, after a little more than an hour. "I think we've worked enough for now."

"I can keep going," Samantha said eagerly. "I'm not tired."

Mr. Kimmelbrod rose from his seat and laid his palm on top of her head. "I see that. But I am afraid that *I* am tired."

Succeeding only partly in suppressing the signs of her disappointment, Samantha carefully packed her violin away in its case.

"I'll drive you home, Sam," Iris said.

"I've got my bike."

"Oh, of course."

As they watched the girl ride away, wobbling on the crushed-gravel driveway, the violin strapped on her back like a backpack, Iris said, "She's really good, isn't she?"

"Yes," Mr. Kimmelbrod said. "She's a unique talent."

"Yes," Iris repeated, nodding her head.

"But the practice rooms of Juilliard and Usherman Center are replete with prodigies."

"The prodigies at Juilliard and Usherman Center all have parents who would happily bankrupt themselves on behalf of their children's talent. Samantha has nobody but us."

"She has a mother and a great-aunt."

"Please. She has a mother who spends more time polishing the buckles on her straightjacket than caring for her daughter, and a great-aunt who doesn't know the first thing about music. Without us Samantha's gift will be wasted."

"Iris, the girl is very talented, but she's eleven years old."

"You were her age when you made your debut."

"By the time I was her age I had been playing for six years. Samantha has barely a year of experience. She has a tremendous amount to learn. There are vast parts of the repertoire that she's never *heard*, let alone played. She's very talented, perhaps even extraordinary, but she is still very young. Musically, she's very young."

"That's my point exactly. She's never going to be able to mature musically in Red Hook. Not if she has to rely on teachers who can't give her the attention she needs."

"We are doing what we can. I am teaching her in the summer, Arturo is doing his best in the winter. There is only so much we can do."

"We could bring her to New York."

Mr. Kimmelbrod gave her a puzzled frown. "Are you serious?"

"Why not? She could live with Daniel and me. She could study with you. It would be wonderful for her."

"Iris, you are stepping far ahead of yourself."

"I know that. I know I'm stepping far, *far* ahead of myself. I haven't asked her aunt. I haven't even really asked her. But she's miserable here, Dad. She's doesn't know any other Cambodian children. She feels isolated and different. It's not good for her. She needs to get away from Maine. She needs to come back with us to New York."

"Are you really saying that you want to take on the responsibility of a young child? You want to transform your life in that way?"

Iris hesitated, instructing herself to give the question the consideration it deserved. Exactly how would this work? Samantha would live with them; they had plenty of room. She would go to school during the day, and to her lessons in the afternoon. Iris would likely have to organize her own schedule to be available to shepherd Samantha from school to her lessons, at least until the girl became comfortable doing it on her own. At her age Becca and Ruthie had freely taken the bus and the subway, but Iris supposed times were different now, and, more important, Samantha was not a city girl. New York would be overwhelming and strange. It would require work on Iris's part, but if she found she couldn't manage it she could always hire a Columbia student to hang out with Samantha after school. It would take planning. But that was all right. Planning was what Iris did best.

"I think it will be fine," Iris said.

"You need to consider why you are doing this, Iris. You need to consider your own motivations."

She thought, I'm doing this because my life has been empty of meaning since my daughter died, and I have a feeling this girl could give it some. Because my marriage is in trouble and I want a distraction from that pain, too. Because my remaining daughter has rejected me. Because I am selfish, and bossy. Because I *need* her.

She said, "I'm doing this because we owe it to Samantha."

"And why do we owe it to her? She is not your child. Not your relative. You have not assumed the burden of her care."

"But she *is* a relative. She's the niece of my *machetaynista*. You're the one who taught me the word."

The raised eyebrow, the slightly curled lip, was an expression that Iris knew well. When she was too rambunctious, too noisy, when she pressed her point of view too firmly, he would give her this look. As a child she had withered beneath it. As an adult it made her dig in her heels.

She knew as well as her father did the obstacles to the plan she was hatching. She knew that Jane was sure to object, and that Daniel might, too. She knew that it would not be easy to care for a child again, especially one new to New York, new to cities in general. She knew that Samantha would require her presence in a way that her girls had not for a very long time. But this was, in the end, exactly what she wanted. To protect and care for a child, to nurture her special talents, to encourage her and participate in her life. To be—in a sense that made her a little uncomfortable to consider—a mother again, or something like a mother.

Mr. Kimmelbrod leaned his head back against the headrest of his chair. His bradykinesia had been particularly acute since the morning, his movements slower even than normal.

"Dad," Iris said. "Are you okay?"

"I'm fine," he said. He closed his eyes.

"Dad, if I convince Jane to let Samantha come back to New York with us, will you agree to keep teaching her?" Iris asked.

Mr. Kimmelbrod sighed, but raised his hands in defeat. "I suppose if she were to visit, I could continue her lessons. She is a thoroughly delightful student."

"You see, it's a great idea."

"Great or not, it's moot, because you may be an irresistible force, but Jane Tetherly is an immovable object."

"Well, we'll see about that, won't we? Thank you, Dad."

Iris left her father in the living room and bustled off to her office. There were people she needed to call, arrangements that had to be made if she were to put the plan into place by the end of the summer. Her first order of business was to sit down and make a list of everything that had to be done.

VIII

Iris and Jane sat in Jane's kitchen, cups of tea growing tepid before them as they battled furiously, though politely, over Samantha's future.

"It's fine in the summer, because my father teaches her," Iris said. "But Arturo travels too much. She needs more consistency, and there isn't another teacher of that caliber in the area."

That they were having this conversation at all boggled Jane's mind. If she were not already all too familiar with Iris's seemingly infinite capacity for shoving her nose where it did not belong—from putting the yacht design course into John's head to insisting that the kids be buried side by side to arranging Samantha's violin lessons in Bangor and only after the fact making a halfhearted show of consulting with Jane—Jane would have assumed she had simply misunderstood the woman. What kind of person tries to take away another woman's child, or even her grand-niece?

"Last year you said that her teacher in Bangor was the best," Jane said.

"He's certainly the best in Maine, and she's learned a tremendous amount from him. As she progresses, however, it becomes more important that she not have long breaks in her instruction. But it's not just that. She needs exposure to better music and to a wider variety of musicians."

"We've got plenty of musicians in Maine. I must have driven that girl over to Bangor ten times this winter to hear the orchestra."

Jane could see, to her satisfaction, that this information surprised Iris. The drive was no small thing. An hour and a half long under the best of conditions, the road was clogged with logging trucks heading in and out of the paper mill in Bucksport. In the winter the bridges iced up, and you had to go the long way around because on the side roads the plows weren't as regular as they might be. Iris clearly had so little respect for Jane, she probably could not even believe that Jane had been willing to contend with that long drive back and forth to Bangor just to take Samantha to the symphony, when she was already taking her twice a week for lessons. Jane hadn't suffered as much at the symphony as she'd expected to. Most of the music was dull, true, but there had been a couple of pieces that she recognized from songs she'd heard as a girl. And she'd enjoyed watching Samantha, who'd hardly seemed to breathe from the moment the orchestra started tuning their instruments until the intermission.

Iris's tone softened. "Wow. I—I didn't know that. It was wonderful of you to do that for her."

Jane shrugged off Iris's compliment. It was neither wonderful nor not wonderful. It was what you did for family. Samantha was her family. Jane thought Iris could stand to be reminded of that fact.

Iris continued, "But as good as the Bangor Symphony is, it's not enough. In New York on any night of the week she could hear a dozen different orchestras and chamber groups. She could go to the opera. She'll meet other students. She'll *live* her music. Jane, please, just consider it. Will you do that? Samantha needs to spend time in New York."

Jane crossed her arms over her chest and said, "She's eleven years old. What she *needs* is to be with her family."

"Of course she does. And you've taken such marvelous care of her, under what can't have been the easiest circumstances. But aren't we family in a way, you and I? We're in-laws. And I care very much for Samantha. I would take very good care of her for you."

In-laws? Jane thought, almost shocked by the idea. Hardly. Whatever terrible moments of tragedy and loss they might have shared, she and Iris had been *in-laws* for all of an hour. And anyway, what kind of nonsense was this—she knew Iris didn't respect her, but did the woman think she was an idiot? Whoever handed over their kid to be raised by an *in-law*?

"I don't know what you think you are to me, Iris, but I know that she's not your daughter," Jane said. "And she's not my daughter, either. Samantha's got a mother already."

"Yes. Yes, of course. But you're her legal guardian, aren't you?"

"No," Jane said.

"You aren't?" Iris said.

Jane cursed herself for revealing what it wasn't Iris's business to know. "I'm taking care of her."

"Because her mother isn't in any shape to care for her, is she? The burden is falling on you."

"It's no burden. She's family. And anyway her mother will be out of the hospital soon enough."

"Jane, I absolutely understand that this is a difficult thing to contemplate. But I worry that if you insist on keeping her here you'll cost her, not just her career, and it could be a marvelous career—my father says he's never seen any child more talented. You'll cost her her happiness. Music is Samantha's whole world, Jane. You know that even better than I do. But most musicians with Samantha's gifts have spent years learning the repertoire by the time they're her age. As talented as she is, Samantha has a tremendous amount of catching up to do."

"Last year you said that going to Bangor every week was the only way she'd catch up. Now she's got to go to New York. What's it going to be next year? China?"

Iris leaned forward, earnestly. "I know how hard this is for you, Jane. I'd have the same feelings if the roles were reversed. And of course you would still have ultimate authority over her—you and her mother. We'd follow any family rules that you expect her to follow. If she has a bedtime, for example." Iris reached into her purse and pulled out a sheaf of pages. "And I've printed out the academic calendar for the year. You can see there are long periods of vacation that she could spend here with you. We could even arrange for her to come home one weekend a month. Or even every other weekend, if that feels more comfortable to you."

Jane refused to allow herself to slip into an attitude of negotiation with Iris. Instead she said, "No."

"Please, Jane. Samantha has the potential to be a world-class musician. A musician who, yes, someday might even play in China. China, Japan, Europe. All over the United States. Conceivably she might even make a handsome living. How can you stand in the way of her future?"

Jane pushed her chair back from the table and stood up. Her manifold debts to the Copakens had all been assumed grudgingly, and she was determined never to incur another. There was no way to repay them for the gravesite, nor for the lessons Mr. Kimmelbrod had been giving Samantha. Iris had done a poor job, too, of concealing the fact that she was paying for the lessons from Mr. Weinstein. Jane had permitted the charade to continue because Samantha had been so desperate for them, so full of joy as she progressed, and Jane could not have afforded even a fraction of the cost. But there was only so much pride she was willing to sacrifice.

"I appreciate your and your father's interest in Samantha," Jane said, as politely as her fury would allow. "But the answer's no, and that's final. If you want to find somebody else to clean your house, I understand."

IX

Late in the evening a few days after Iris's fruitless conversation with Jane, Daniel came upon his wife sitting at the kitchen table with a pot of tea, a pen, and a bottle of Wite-Out, working her way through a formidable stack of printed forms.

He'd been avoiding her as much as he could, spending his mornings at the gym and his afternoons in town, reading the newspapers at the library or just wandering around. A few times he'd even ducked into the Neptune for a beer or two. Anything to keep from going home.

Now he said, "What's all this?"

"Some stuff I downloaded from the New York Board of Education Web site. I was looking to see what our school options would be if Samantha came to stay with us. There's a middle school for gifted and talented kids on West Eighty-fourth Street."

"The Anderson School," Daniel said.

"Right. I thought I'd better get the application in now, just in case. We've already missed the deadline, but I'm hoping they'll make an exception in her case, especially if my father asks the head of the Juilliard youth program to write a letter."

Daniel stood behind a chair on the opposite side of the table, gripping the back. "She's not coming to New York," he said. "Jane said no."

It was maddening to Daniel that Jane's refusal to acquiesce to Iris's plan to bring Samantha back to New York had had no effect on his wife. Nor had his own resistance to the idea. She continued to plot and plan. He could not understand his wife's blithe embrace of the idea of taking on a child. It was as though she had forgotten what parenthood demanded, as though she were willfully refusing to consider how much work and expense were involved. Although he knew that work and expense were not what was really troubling him. What bothered him was the idea of bringing into their home another witness to their struggles and disconnection.

Iris said, "I wish this school had been open back when the girls were young. It's a really remarkable place."

"Iris!" Daniel said.

Iris finally set down her pen. "She'll be no trouble," she said. "She'll be in school all day, and she'll be studying with my father. You'll barely see her. And anyway, it will be nice to have a girl around the house again. Don't you think?"

"We'll have a girl around the house again. Or have you forgotten that Ruthie isn't going back to England?"

"No, I have not forgotten. And at any rate, it's likely that Ruthie will change her mind a dozen times before the end of the summer. But this isn't about Ruthie. Even if Ruthie were to come back to live with us in New York, we would still have room for Samantha."

"This isn't about room."

"Please, Daniel. Samantha desperately needs what we can give her. Why shouldn't we do what we can for her?"

"Because her aunt doesn't want us to. Iris, for Christ's sake, Jane told you she wouldn't let her go."

"Jane doesn't understand what's at stake here. She doesn't realize how important this is for Samantha."

"Jane is her legal guardian. It doesn't matter what she understands or doesn't understand. She's made her decision clear."

"In fact, Daniel, Jane is *not* Samantha's legal guardian. As I understand it, the relationship is completely ad hoc. When Connie goes into the hospital, Jane takes Samantha. When Connie comes out, she takes her back. On and on, like the girl is some kind of yo-yo. Samantha's legal guardian is her adoptive mother, Connie Phelps. Jane has no authority in the matter at all."

How much of his marriage had been spent deferring to Iris, allowing her to assume control of every aspect of their lives? Even their infrequent arguments belonged to her. Iris would state her position and then she would state *his*. She would make his points and then rebut them, one by one, often with little input from him, because the angrier Daniel became, the more impenetrable the silence that engulfed him. But not today; today he would make his position known. Today they would do what *he* wanted.

"This is a terrible idea," he said.

"It's not a terrible idea," Iris said.

"You know it is. We aren't in any position to take on the burden of caring for a child."

"She won't be a burden."

"She's *already* a burden. Look, I like Samantha too, she's a sweet kid, and I didn't say anything when you started paying for her classes, or when you gave her Becca's old violin. Not that it even occurred to you for an instant to ask my opinion. But now I'm telling you: enough is enough."

"So this is about money?"

"No, it's not about money. When have I ever given a *shit* about money?"

"Never," Iris said. "That's why it surprises me to hear you say it now. Since money has never been a big priority for you."

Daniel's jaw twitched. However much she protested he knew it galled her that he didn't earn more. For all the feminist folderol Iris espoused, it came down to this. He felt an urge to punch the wall. Or her.

"It's not a matter of the money."

She tried to take his hand, but he shook her off. "Please, Daniel," she said. "This will be good for us."

"Us."

"You and me."

He stared at her, and the thought came into his mind that perhaps his marriage had been dead for years, for decades preceding the death of their daughter, and that for all that time up to the present moment the only force sustaining it was the incredible power of Iris Copaken's capacity for self-delusion.

"Us," he said.

"You and me. I just think that if we had someone, a child—"

With a sudden jerk, Daniel picked up the chair he was holding on to a few inches off the ground and then slammed it down. The legs shivered and there was an ominous crack of wood.

"I want you to listen to me, Iris," he said, with a softness, a control, that struck him as remarkable under the circumstances. "I want you to shut up, and listen, and maybe, just this one fucking time, allow for the possibility that I may be *right* about something."

Iris's mouth dropped open, and she gazed at him, dumbfounded. Daniel continued, "I'm sick of this complicated psychodrama you're playing out with Samantha. You can't possibly believe that insinuating yourself into that kid's life is ever, *ever*, going to replace what you and I lost. You're too smart for that, for one thing. And for another thing—you and I have lost a lot more than our daughter, Iris. And maybe you want to keep kidding yourself about that. But I don't."

Iris's chin was trembling; Daniel was glad to see that he had cracked the carapace of her superiority, her smugness, her certainty that she knew what was best for everyone.

"I'm not insinuating myself into her life," she finally managed to say.

"Samantha already has a mother."

"I know that, Daniel. Thanks for the insight. And, hey, as long as we're going to stand around diagnosing each other? I have a couple of theories about why a fifty-five-year-old man suddenly decides the thing he wants most in the world is to get beaten to a bloody pulp in the boxing ring."

Daniel froze, his dark eyebrows knit above his nose, his lips clamped into a thin line. His face slowly drained of color, his angry flush receding first from his brow, then his cheeks, and then inching down his neck.

Iris said, "Look, Daniel. I'm not stupid. I know that I'm not being entirely altruistic. I know that I need Samantha as much as she needs me. Having her live with us will be good; I know it will. You have to trust me. I know this is the right thing to do."

Daniel's face was now pale, cold, calm. His brow smoothed. His white-knuckled grip on the chair back loosened. Finally, he returned her look blankly, devoid of emotion. Then he said, "You know what? That's fine. Do what you want."

In two steps he crossed the room. He scooped up his gym bag and grabbed his keys. Forty-five minutes later he was in the Maine Event, pummeling the heavy bag so hard that beneath the thick padding of his gloves his fists ached.

X

The Riverview Psychiatric Center was a brand-new facility, opened just this month on the grounds of the forbidding Gothic pile that had been officially called the Augusta Mental Health Institute but was known to most by its original, grimmer name, the Maine Insane Hospital. Unlike its predecessor, Riverview had no iron-spiked gates or high granite walls. It looked more like the headquarters of a software company than a mental hospital, like a failed office park turned over to the purview of lunatics. A row of spindly trees shivered along the broad cement path between the parking lot and the front door.

The common room of the unit in which Samantha's mother lived was more pleasant than Iris had expected it would be, perhaps because the furniture was brand-new, the walls freshly painted, the carpeting unmarked.

"This place is nicer than the old one," Samantha whispered to Iris as they stood hesitantly in the doorway. The room was crowded, even lively. A group of patients sat around the television. Another played cards. A young man wearing a red T-shirt with a line drawing of a bulldozer and the words "Boston, Can You Dig It?" sat on a sofa next to an older woman in a pink velour sweat suit and matching slippers. He held an elastic band in his mouth and was smoothing the older woman's peroxide-blond hair with his fingers. Iris watched, transfixed, as he executed a perfect French braid.

"Look how pretty you are, Mom," he said, after he snapped the band on the end of the braid. Samantha tugged on Iris's sleeve. "That's my mother," she said, pointing across the room. Connie Phelps, Samantha's mother, wore her hair drawn back into a tight ponytail that served only to highlight the thick stripe of gray on either side of her part. It had been a long time since she had colored her hair. She had small, pale eyes that were sunk into nests of deep wrinkles, and the hollows of her cheeks were gray. Her lips, however, were generous and full, and deep red, as though they had been stained with the juice of some wild berry.

Over the last year, since she had taken on the project of Samantha's musical career, Iris had often wondered about Connie: what she looked like, how she related to her daughter, what their relationship was like. Although she was nervous about the request she was about to make, she found herself eagerly crossing the room to join Connie in the corner where she had staked out three upright chairs. Samantha ran to her mother and hurled herself into her arms. Connie laughed and hugged her.

Iris stuck out her hand. "Hello, Connie. I'm Iris Copaken."

"Copaken?" Connie said, gently steering Samantha into the seat next to her. "You're John's girl's mother?"

"Yes," Iris said. "I'm Becca's mother."

Connie nodded. "I'm sorry for your loss."

"Thank you."

"And your father's the one with the violin lessons, right?"

"Yes."

"Well, then I owe you a thank-you." Her voice was low, not much louder than a whisper, and every few moments she pushed her lips forward in an unconscious, exaggerated osculation. "To you and your father."

"I'm the one who should thank *you*," Iris said. "It's a joy to be able to help a musician like Samantha. She's something very special." Iris sat on the edge of the remaining chair and leaned forward, both because Connie spoke so softly and because she was so anxious to present her case.

Connie tucked a lock of Samantha's hair behind her ear. "That she is."

Samantha leaned into her mother's hand.

Connie said, "Honey, what do you think of this place? Isn't it nice?" She turned back to Iris. "We used to be in a whole other building up the road."

"It's very nice here," Iris said.

"Everything is all new," Connie said.

"Really?" Iris said.

"Brand-new," Connie repeated, nodding. Then she turned to Samantha. "Where's your aunt? She under the weather or something?"

Samantha shook her head. "Aunt Jane's okay. She's been working, is all." The more time she spent with Iris and Mr. Kimmelbrod, the fainter Samantha's Maine accent had become. But around her mother she reverted to dropping her *r*'s and flattening her *a*'s.

Connie frowned. "That old beater she's driving still acting up?"

"I don't know," Samantha said. The girl lifted her feet up onto her chair and wrapped her arms tightly around them. She ducked her chin and mouth behind the small, bony hillocks of her knees so that her face below her nose was hidden from view. She seemed nervous, and how could Iris blame her? What had begun as a visit to New York had been transformed into moving in with Iris, going to school in New York, and studying full-time with Mr. Kimmelbrod. Samantha had made it clear to Iris that she wanted to go, that there was not the slightest doubt in her mind that for the sake of her music she should be there, but Iris could tell she was afraid, both of her aunt Jane's anger and of how her mother would manage without her when she once again got out of this place.

Iris said, "Connie, Jane's not here because Samantha and I wanted to talk to *you* about something."

"To me?"

"Yes. I wonder if you know just how gifted your daughter is. How unusually gifted."

Connie smiled and smoothed Samantha's hair again. "I know that. I know she is. She's always been a special little girl."

"Her progress on the violin is truly remarkable. Especially considering how short a time she's been playing."

"She's always been good at music. If I could have afforded it, I'da had her in lessons a long time ago."

"My father and Samantha have a very special relationship."

"She talks about him all the time," Connie said. As she was speaking she worried a crack in the skin of her knuckle. It began to bleed. The sight of the blood flustered Iris for a moment, and she rooted around in her purse for a tissue. She handed it to Connie, but the woman did not seem to know what to do with it.

"Mumma, you're bleeding," Samantha said. "Your finger's bleeding." She took the tissue from her mother and wrapped it tightly around her finger. Then she closed her hand around the bound finger and squeezed gently.

"Oh dear," Connie said.

"Are you all right?" Iris asked.

"Oh, it's nothing," Connie said. "The air in here just dries out your skin."

Iris hesitated, but then continued. "My father and I think it would be a terrible shame for Samantha to have to stop her lessons come autumn," Iris said.

"Stop her lessons?" Connie asked. "Why should she stop her lessons?"

"My father goes back to New York at the end of August. He still teaches at Juilliard and he has to return in time for the new semester."

"Juilliard?"

"It's a music school. One of the best in the country. He's taught there for nearly forty years. He's taught some of the finest violinists in the world. And now he wants to continue teaching Samantha." Iris hesitated for a moment before plunging on. "My father and I would like to invite Samantha to come with us back to New York." Strictly speaking, Iris told herself, she was not lying. Whatever his reservations, Mr. Kimmelbrod said he would continue teaching Samantha if she came to New York.

Connie gently disengaged her finger from Samantha's fist and said, "I don't understand. Why does she need to go to New York? She has that teacher in Bangor."

"Arturo Weinstein," Iris said. "He's a wonderful violinist. And a good teacher. Unfortunately, he's down south for much of the winter, and while Samantha made a lot of progress this past year, we think that in order to continue to improve she should have more consistency."

Iris glanced over at Samantha. The girl had ducked her head and let her hair fall in front of her eyes. When she was a little girl, Ruthie used to do the same thing when she was feeling embarrassed or shy.

"It's not just the lessons," Iris said. "Being involved in the world of music is critical to her development as an artist. Only in New York can she get the kind of exposure she needs." Iris leaned forward intently, her voice rising. "Her career depends on it."

Connie laughed. "Her *career*? She's a little girl. She doesn't have a *career*."

Iris paused, conscious of how she must seem, how her words must sound to someone unfamiliar with the world she was talking about. In a softer, more placating voice, she said, "Musical careers run on different tracks than regular careers. Most very talented musicians start performing when they're very young. Some even when they're Samantha's age. The violinist Anne-Sophie Mutter began performing with great orchestras when she was only a little older than Samantha." As the words left her lips Iris regretted them. This was no time to drop names that would serve only to make the woman feel ignorant.

"I saw her once," Connie said.

"You did?" Iris said, just as Samantha said, "You did not!"

"I most certainly did," Connie said. "There was a TV show about violin players and I watched it. I remember that woman in particular, because they had so many men." Connie unwound the tissue from her finger and resumed picking at the scab on her knuckle. "Is Samantha like her? Is she that good?"

"I'm confident that she is," Iris said, firmly. Beneath the veil of Samantha's hair, Iris could see her tiny smile of pride. "Or she could be. If we nurture her talent."

"Your daughter played the violin, too, didn't she?" Connie said.

Iris had been charging along, but now she was caught off guard. "Yes," she said, simply.

"Samantha talks about her," Connie said.

"She does?" Iris turned to Samantha. "You do?"

Flushing, Samantha said, "I told my mom you gave me the violin Becca used to use when she was my age."

"Is Samantha as talented as your daughter was?" Connie asked.

"More," Iris said. "My daughter was gifted. Samantha . . . well, the sky's the limit for this little one."

Connie nodded. She lifted Samantha's chin with her hand and smoothed her hair away from her face. "Do you *want* to go to New York?"

Samantha blinked, her mouth trembling. She looked like she was about to burst into tears. "Not if you don't want me to go. If you want me to stay here, I can stay. It's okay."

"But do *you* want to go?"

Samantha nodded, as if frightened to say the words aloud.

Connie released her grip on Samantha's chin and sat back heavily in her seat. Gazing at Samantha with an expression Iris could only describe as apologetic, she said, "It's hard to be separated from your child."

"She'd come home to visit at every opportunity. We'd make sure of that. And we'd bring her back in May for the whole summer."

"I was thinking of you," Connie said.

"Of me?" Iris said.

"Of how hard it must be for you to be separated from your daughter. I know what it's like for me sometimes, while I'm staying here. I miss Samantha so much. I feel for you, losing your girl. I feel your broken heart."

Iris sagged back in her chair. She felt her chin trembling and she gritted her teeth, willing herself not to cry. It still shocked her to find herself switching moods so rapidly. One moment elated by someone mentioning Becca's name, the next moment a show of sympathy making her feel like she'd been slapped in the face.

Connie reached across the empty space between them and took Iris's hand in her scaly one. She squeezed gently. "You know why I like it here so much?"

Iris could do no more than shake her head.

"It's an asylum," Connie said.

"It is *not*, Mumma," Samantha said. "It's a mental-health institute. Nobody calls it the asylum anymore."

"No, they don't call it that no more," Connie said. "But that's what it is. An asylum. A place of refuge, like. A sanctuary. It's a good word, *asylum*. I wish people didn't mind using it. Most of us could use an asylum sometimes. A refuge from the world."

"Yes," Iris said. Of all people to sense the pain and need beneath her strength, it was this strange woman, a woman whose face was contorted with tardive dyskinesia, whose medications no doubt filled an entire suitcase.

"Asylums come in all sorts of forms," Connie said. "Music. Music is an asylum. And children. They can be an asylum. Maybe Samantha is your asylum, Iris."

Iris sucked her breath in with a gasp and pulled her hand loose. "No." She had come prepared for many things, but not for this woman's insight.

"I'm asking too much." She reached blindly for her bag. "We should probably give you some time . . ."

"Samantha, hon," Connie said. "Go on over and look at the TV for a little while. I want to talk to Iris."

Samantha glanced from her mother to Iris and back again. Then she shrugged and walked over to the television, perched on the edge of a plastic chair, and shot periodic glances back at the women.

"Jane said no, didn't she?" Connie said.

Iris simply nodded.

"Wouldn't think she'd agree."

Iris opened her mouth, ready to present to Connie the argument that she had prepared—that it was only Connie who had a right to decide what was best for Samantha—but Connie raised a hand to silence her. "I have failed that girl," she said.

"No, you haven't failed her," Iris said, unconvincingly.

"Of course I have," Connie said. "I have failed her mightily. I took her in, I made her mine, and then I started to do her damage almost right away."

"You haven't damaged her. She's not damaged."

"But she will be if I keep her. She's got a gift, and she deserves to be surrounded by people who understand how good she is. I owe it to her to give her to you."

For the first time Iris felt the incredible weight of the burden she had been pushing to take on, the ramifications of the responsibility she had so blithely determined to assume. "You aren't giving her to me," Iris said. "She'll still be yours."

"No," Connie said firmly. "She doesn't belong to me. If she's going to be who she should be, then she can't belong to me. You've got to take her."

Now it was Iris's turn to accept or reject the offer. She looked over at Samantha, who was rocking slowly to music that only she could hear. "I promise she'll visit you," Iris said.

"When she can," Connie said. "She'll come when she can. And don't worry, I'll deal with Jane."

XI

Daniel ran the four and a half miles to the lobster pound dragging an old red Radio Flyer behind him. The wheels, which had not seen the ministrations of a can of WD-40 for at least fifteen years, squeaked ferociously with every step. The grinding of metal axle against ball bearings served as a kind of screeching, metallic metronome of his progress along the strip of sun-baked country road. The pavement along the side of the road had buckled and rutted from the winter's snows, but there were just enough cars whizzing by to prevent Daniel from running down the smoother middle. At one point, he dragged the wagon over a bad break in the asphalt and it tipped over. As he was righting it he noticed a pink scrap of paper stuck in the gummy dirt in the corner of the wagon. Daniel remembered how when his girls were little he would load them into the wagon and wheel them the couple of hundred yards to Witham's Country Store. As a reward for keeping him company during his grocery shopping he'd allow them each to choose a candy bar. Ruthie loved chocolate, had since she was a baby. Becca liked things she could chew. Gum, caramels, and her favorite, Starburst candies. He scratched the pink Starburst wrapper loose with his fingernail, slipped it into the pocket of his pants, and resumed his trek.

The road between East Red Hook and the cove on Peasbury Neck where Scotty Teasdale kept his lobster pound had once been lined by tall elm trees that had cast a gracious canopy of shade. But every one had been felled by Dutch elm disease, and Daniel found little respite from the strong early-afternoon sun. The band of his ball cap was soaked through, as though it had been dunked in a bucket of water, and his drenched T-shirt clung to his back. He smelled rank, like the inside of an old running shoe.

As each arm started to ache he transferred the handle to the other, and by the time he arrived at the pound he felt like he'd been tortured, his arms hauled behind his back and winched up on a high hook.

The cut over his eye throbbed. He had opened it up again earlier today, when he agreed to go a round with Jason, the dumb-ass gym manager. As useless as the guy was in the ring, he had managed to land a jab that Daniel should have been able to easily dodge. The cut had started to bleed again through its rough crosshatch of stitches, but Daniel had not bothered even to slap a Band-Aid on it. It was still oozing blood when he walked into the house, and Iris's tight-lipped frown when she saw it was one of the reasons he had set out on this expedition. He had stood before her almost defiantly, as if daring her to protest, or even to acknowledge noticing that he had reinjured himself. It had been a struggle for her—that was obvious—but in the end she had simply turned away and resumed cutting up cabbage for the coleslaw. Some perverse impulse had made him set out from the house dragging the red wagon instead of riding in his car.

Scotty Teasdale, a wizened creature in a captain's cap, with a mouthful of oversized gray dentures like a row of tombstones stretching his lips into a wide grimace, was skeptical about Daniel's means of transportation.

"You've got thirty bugs here. That's a lot of weight to be hauling in a kiddy car," he said as he pulled the bright red lobsters out of the vat of water he had on permanent boil and wrapped them in newspaper.

"It's downhill," Daniel said.

With a hoot of laughter and a wet smack, Scotty sucked the top row of his dentures loose of his gums and clacked them back into place. It wasn't until Daniel started down the road back to East Red Hook that he realized what had amused the old man. As hard as it had been to run uphill, down was worse. The wagon kept picking up speed behind him and bashing into the backs of his legs. By the halfway mark his ankles and calves were a mass of bruises and he was cursing whatever foolhardy impulse had inspired his ridiculous errand. Why hadn't he considered the toll on his back and shoulders of dragging fifty pounds, or how a child's wagon would be such a considerable part of the burden it was supposed to be bearing?

About a mile from home he became aware of an overwhelming desire not to be dragging this load any farther. He stopped. The handle of the wagon clanged against the blacktop and he stood for a moment, feeling the ache in the bones of his hand. He listened to the shrill whine of the cicadas and looked out across the rolling meadows by the side of the road. The sun was shining, and the golden hay glowed. A winding path had been mowed through the hay, skirting a tumbledown barn and ending at a small dock. A white rowboat bobbed in the water. He looked down at the Radio Flyer with its load of soggy brown paper grocery bags containing $237 worth of lobsters. He turned his back on the wagon and began walking back the way he had come, toward the neck, away from home, his unencumbered gait now weightless and nimble. He felt like he covered ten feet with every step.

He made it only a dozen yards or so into his escape attempt when a dark-green pickup truck pulled up next to him.

"Daddy?" Ruthie said from the open passenger-side window.

He kept walking, the truck rolling slowly alongside him.

"Daddy, where are you going?"

"Quebec," he said.

"What?"

"Nothing. Nowhere. I'm just . . . walking."

Because Ruthie's head was in the way it took a moment for Daniel to realize who was driving the truck. As the driver braked, her head fell back against the headrest, and he had an unimpeded view of Matt Tetherly.

"Hello, Mr. Copaken." Matt squinted at him beneath the bill of a Red Sox cap.

"Hello, Matt," Daniel said. He looked back at Ruthie. She blushed. So, he thought—with a lack of surprise that was itself, perhaps, surprising—she's fucking Matt Tetherly.

Daniel's hair and clothes were so drenched in sweat that it looked like he had just that moment walked out of the sea. His soaked white T-shirt had become translucent, and where it clung to his chest you could see whorls of dark hair, and even the outline of his nipples. His face was red, both from exertion and from sunburn, and a row of angry black sutures crawled across the suppurating gash above his eye. He looked like the kind of person who might shove a crumpled coffee cup in your face and demand a dollar.

“Isn’t that our wagon?” Ruthie said, pointing up the road.

Daniel made a helpless gesture with his hands. “Yep.”

“It looks like you’ve got bags of lobsters in there.”

“Thirty bugs.”

Matt said, “Uh, Mr. Copaken, uh, do you—should we go get it?”

“Okay.” He turned back toward home again, and began trudging up the road to the wagon. Matt pulled ahead and parked on the shoulder of the road. He jumped lightly out of the cab of the truck and, careful to hold them from the bottom so they wouldn’t tear, moved the heavy paper bags from the wagon into the truck bed. Then he lifted up the wagon and laid it upside down next to the bags, so it wouldn’t roll.

“Get in, Daddy,” Ruthie said. “It’s okay.”

She moved to the narrow rear bench and Daniel climbed in. On the way home, neither Ruthie nor Matt asked why he had abandoned a wagon full of lobsters by the side of the road, nor what had possessed him to bring the wagon in the first place. Nobody said anything. They turned onto the East Red Hook village road, and then into the gravel driveway, pulling off onto the front lawn to leave room for other cars. Matt cut the engine.

Daniel said, “Does Iris know?”

Iris was sitting at the kitchen table folding napkins. Her hands stilled when Daniel walked through the door and then through the mudroom to the kitchen.

“Where do you want these?” he said, as he dumped the soggy bags full of lobsters on the other end of the table.

“Just cover them with a towel,” Iris said.

Iris was shocked at his disheveled appearance, but before she could even decide whether to comment on it the screen door banged again. Ruthie walked into the kitchen, Matt at her side.

“Do you need some help getting ready?” Ruthie said.

With a single glance Iris took it all in. After what she had witnessed last summer, Iris was not particularly surprised to see them together, although Ruthie’s failure ever to mention Matt during the course of their arguments had led her to assume that things between them had begun and ended on that single Fourth of July night. "Sure," she said, finally. "Why don't you put the salads outside."

Ruthie went to the refrigerator, opened the door, and began loading Matt's arms with bowls.

"Matt, I haven't heard from your mother," Iris said. "So I guess she's not coming."

Matt looked vaguely embarrassed. "I, uh, no, I don't think so, Mrs. Copaken. I mean, I haven't seen her today, but she wasn't planning on it."

"I figured as much," Iris said, feeling relieved. She had been dreading another confrontation with Jane, whom she knew must be furious with her for having gone directly to Connie with her New York plan for Samantha.

"Daniel," Iris said. "People are going to be here any minute. Are you going to take a shower?"

"Yes, I am. But before that, if you don't mind, I believe I'm going to have a beer."

Iris shrugged and, picking up a basket of rolls, went outside. Ruthie handed her father a Wicked Ale from the fridge and he opened it and took a long slug. The creak of the wagon's wheels still grated in his ears. He closed his eyes and rolled the cool bottle along his forehead. When he opened them, he saw Matt standing uncomfortably in the middle of the kitchen while Ruthie bustled around.

It could be worse, Daniel thought. He's a nice kid. Like his brother had been. Matt didn't have John's charm or irrepressible good cheer, but he was bright and sweet-natured, a solid citizen.

Ruthie balanced a platter on top of the bowls in Matt's arms and tucked a sheaf of napkins under his arm. The load in Matt's arms threatened to topple, and Ruthie giggled, catching the uppermost dish before it fell. Daniel realized how rare that sound had become in the past two years. He couldn't remember the last time he'd heard Ruthie laugh. Whatever its source, whether she was happy or just relieved that her parents had not reacted negatively to what was going on between her and Matt, he was glad to see her laughing. He said, "Matt, can I interest you in a beer?"

"Maybe later, Mr. Copaken," Matt said. "Once Ruthie's done with me."

Half an hour later, showered and dressed in clean if shabby khakis and his favorite faded polo shirt, Daniel took up his role as host, standing next to the cooler in the yard, ready to hand out drinks to the guests as they arrived. Ruthie and Matt sat side by side on the picnic bench in the middle of the yard, leaning back against the table, their hands twined together, as if to announce their relationship to the company.

The first guest to arrive was Mary Lou Curran.

"Thank you, dear," she said, accepting the gin and tonic Daniel poured her from the tall pitcher Iris had prepared. Mary Lou took a sip, leaving a delicate tracing of pale-pink lipstick on the rim of the plastic cup. "My goodness," she said suddenly.

Daniel followed her gaze over to Ruthie and Matt. Ruthie waved. Mary Lou lifted her hand in return.

"How long has that been going on?" Mary Lou said.

"I don't honestly know," Daniel said. "I just found out about it myself."

Mary Lou raised her thin, penciled eyebrows. "Half the relationships I know are really support groups in disguise."

When Daniel and Iris's immediate neighbor to the south, a pediatric surgeon from Bethesda, arrived, he took one look at Daniel and said, "What the hell happened to you?"

Daniel dodged the question with a vague "I cut myself," as if an inch-long wound only partly stitched closed with irregular knots of black thread could be dismissed as a shaving accident.

"You need to have that cut restitched."

"Probably."

"No, I mean it. That's just—" He made a face. "It offends my sensibilities. Come on."

So Daniel followed Dr. Ethan Haber across the road to the small house in which he spent only three weeks out of every summer. The kitchen had been renovated at an unfortunate time; the countertops were speckled Formica, and the tile of the backsplash featured wicker baskets of garish yellow daisies. There was little evidence of Dr. Haber's residence in the house. No piles of newspapers and unread mail, like in their house across the street. No coat hooks piled with jackets and mackinaws, no boots and shoes heaped in the corners of the mudroom. Just a single fleece jacket emblazoned with the yacht club logo hanging on the back of the Holly Hobby kitchen chair to which the doctor directed Daniel. He brought in a brass desk lamp from the other room and aimed the light at Daniel's chin. With a pair of tweezers, he began tugging the stitches loose.

"Who the hell did this to you? A blind ER tech?"

"No, a crippled corner man."

The doctor gave a bark of laughter. Daniel winced as one of the stitches tugged against his open wound.

"Wish I had some lidocaine for you," Ethan said. "But you are shit out of luck."

"No kidding." Daniel closed his eyes and listened to the faint sounds of the party across the street in his backyard. He could hear voices, an occasional shout. Someone had turned on some music. For a moment he fantasized about staying here in this anonymous house, where he could eavesdrop on his family but neither see nor be seen by them. But was that really a satisfying fantasy? As long as he was fantasizing, couldn't he permit himself the luxury of a complete escape?

Ethan said, "You going to be all right if I stitch this closed again?"

"Yeah."

"So how'd you get this?" Ethan said as he peeled open a small suture pack and picked up the needle with his forceps.

"Boxing." Daniel flinched as the doctor poked the hooked needle through his skin. "Man, that hurts."

"Don't be a pussy," the doctor said. "It can't hurt more than getting punched in the face."

"You'd be surprised."

"Just one more. What the hell are you doing boxing, anyway? An *alter kocker* like you."

Daniel shrugged, his shoulder banging against the doctor's hand. "Fuck!" he said.

"Yeah, well, don't move. You know, a few years ago I took up flying."

"Flying?"

"Yuh. Almost bought myself a Cessna. You're all done." He sat back, snapped off his rubber gloves, and shot them into the trash can.

"Almost?" Daniel said.

"Came to my senses and got a divorce instead. Let's go. They'll be missing you at home."

While the guests ate their lobster, Mr. Kimmelbrod went to his bedroom to fetch his violin. In spite of his tenancy, the room appeared no less anonymous than it had when it had been used as a guest room. His clothes barely filled two of the four drawers. His shirts took up no more than a few inches of the hanging bar in the maple chiffonier that had stood between the two windows on the eastern wall of the room since the spring of 1902, when it had been ordered from the Sears, Roebuck and Co. furniture catalog by Iris's grandmother for $8.45 painstakingly saved from her housekeeping allowance. His black leather wash kit lay, zippered closed, on the back of the toilet. The only way a stranger would know this was Mr. Kimmelbrod's room was by the violin case that lay on the white chenille spread.

Since he had lost his ability to play, Mr. Kimmelbrod had not been sufficiently conscientious about making sure the Dembovski was played as often as it needed to be. To keep its suppleness and tone, an instrument must be played. He remembered how Alice used to say that a violin was like a marriage. Untended, it became stiff and brittle, it lost its sound. He wondered how long it had been since Iris and Daniel had tended to their marriage.

Mr. Kimmelbrod unbuckled the violin case. It was, he knew, foolhardy of him to trust a child with such a valuable Guarneri—he could only imagine what his insurers would say, those neurotics in suits whose demands that the violin be stored at all times in a locked safe he so assiduously ignored—but she handled it with due reverence, and played, despite her inexperience and her size, with confidence and aplomb. At first he had been surprised by Samantha's proficiency on the Guarneri, given that her everyday instrument was only three-quarter size. The spaces between the notes on the strings were more elongated on a bigger violin, and normally a student could not switch back and forth without having serious problems of intonation. Samantha, however, had long fingers for a girl her age, and she managed very well.

He traced the pearwood purfling of his violin with a trembling finger. He was never as conscious of the ruin of his body as when he held his eternal violin. He looked at his gnarled, shaking hands, the spiky black hairs sprouting from his knuckles, the cracked, dry, yellow nails, his loose and papery arm, flakes of skin drifting like dandruff from his elbows. He was a wrecked vessel, a walking carcass, but the Guarneri was whole and unchanging; it mocked and measured his decay. Its timelessness was not in the nature of something inorganic, a gem or a statue; the Dembovski was not an inanimate object. It breathed, it had a personality of its own. He was devoted to his violin as to a lover—a moody, complicated lover who demanded that you touch her in a certain way. He had fallen in love with the Dembovski in the Bond Street showroom of the venerated W. E. Hill & Sons violin dealers on a wet and freezing November afternoon in 1958, and had immediately contacted the generous consortium of music lovers who had offered to buy him a worthy instrument.

His Dembovski was the equal, Mr. Kimmelbrod believed, of Menuhin's Lord Wilton and Heifetz's David. Better than any Stradivarius. For Mr. Kimmelbrod, a Strad, no matter how bright or pure in tone, could not compare to the dark, throaty melancholy of the finest Guarneri del Gesù. Indeed, the Dembovski, Mr. Kimmelbrod sometimes worried, was a better violin than he deserved. He was by any estimation a renowned virtuoso who had had an enviable concert career. He had soloed with the finest orchestras in the world, including the London, New York, and Israel Philharmonics and the Chicago Symphony Orchestra. His 1947 recording of the Brahms Violin Concerto with the Boston Symphony Orchestra under the baton of Sergei Koussevitzky was still considered the finest contemporary interpretation of that most challenging of pieces. Before he and André Previn had their final, irrevocable falling out in 1971, he had toured with the London Symphony Orchestra throughout Europe and Asia, never to anything but warm reviews. But he had never achieved the level of international acclaim of some of his contemporaries: Menuhin, Heifetz, Zimbalist, Stern, or even David Oistrakh.

It was often said about Mr. Kimmelbrod, by those who withheld the highest acclaim in their judgment of him, that he resisted his own talent, that he betrayed his musical self. Had he but permitted himself to embrace without reservation his gift for interpreting the violin works of the Romantic masters, there is no knowing—some said—to what heights he might have soared. Mr. Kimmelbrod's concert career had lasted for decades, but if he was celebrated at all now, it was as a teacher of genius, at Juilliard and here at Usherman Center.

"Mr. Kimmelbrod?" Samantha said. She was standing in the doorway dressed in a pretty party frock, visibly nervous. "Iris said it's time for me to play."

Mr. Kimmelbrod lifted his eyes to the girl and smiled. She was so singular in her focus, so eager to exclude everything from her mind and heart but music. Even with so little experience she exhibited a kind of technical and musical courage he had rarely seen in his career as a teacher of the violin. His granddaughter had not had that courage. At her best Becca played cleanly, solidly. But when confronted with the most difficult pieces, she had sometimes faltered, cowed by the complexity of the music, despite knowing that she possessed the technical skill necessary to play it. Samantha, he felt, would never cower even before the trickiest and most demanding piece. He hoped he would be alive long enough to hear her tackle something like the Britten Violin Concerto, or like the Chaconne.

Iris had asked Mr. Kimmelbrod to introduce Samantha to the guests, but he had declined. Although he was not opposed to the idea of Samantha exhibiting her skills to a small, familiar audience—especially an undiscerning one—neither did he want to endow the occasion with too much portent. As great as her promise was, they all needed to remember that she had been playing only a little more than a year. She would make mistakes today, she *should* make mistakes; only then could he be sure that she was reaching far enough. He did not want her to consider this a performance, but rather an exercise.

"Friends!" Iris called, clapping her hands to attract their attention. "We have a lovely treat in store this evening. I'm sure that most of you will remember Samantha Phelps, from Becca and John's wedding." The crowd grew suddenly still. "Well," Iris continued, "Samantha's talents extend far beyond being a flower girl." A few people laughed. "She's also an accomplished violinist. Tonight she'll be treating us to a little Bach. The first two movements of Sonata no. 1 in G Minor."

Samantha stepped forward. She was wearing a white sundress patterned with red cherries and had her hair pulled back with a shiny red plastic headband. Just as Iris began to lead the guests in a round of applause, Jane came around the corner of the house, bearing her Nilla wafer banana pudding before her like an armored shield. Samantha noticed her aunt immediately and grinned. Then, when her aunt did not return her smile, her face fell. She lowered her violin and waited, as if she thought it possible that Jane had come to call off the recital, to drag her back home to her Casio keyboard and her lonely bedroom and her dreams of a family of people who loved music and lived in music and serenaded each other nightly on the *tro khmer*.

Jane placed the pudding on the picnic table with the other desserts.

"Jane!" called Iris. "It's so good to see you."

Jane smiled grimly. She had had no intention of coming to this party. As Iris had anticipated—it was no great feat of prognostication—Jane was furious with Iris for going behind her back to Connie, for intruding herself once more, and in a way and a place that Jane considered to be completely out of line; so furious that she felt there was no guarantee that she would be able to control herself in Iris's presence. But Samantha had begged her to come to her "debut." The old man was going to let Samantha use his million-dollar Italian violin, and Samantha had insisted on Jane coming to hear her play Bach on the ancient instrument. Jane had heard of Stradivarius, even though Mr. Kimmelbrod's wasn't one of those. And so in her desire to support her niece there was also a certain amount of curiosity to see with her own eyes this high and mighty fiddle.

Jane peeled back the plastic wrap from the Nilla wafer pudding. She had actually been looking forward to not being obliged to make the damn pudding this year, but then, when she had decided to come, she seemed to be unable to prevent herself. And so once again she had found herself standing in her kitchen, slicing four dozen bananas while staring at a sampler her mother-in-law had embroidered for her as a first anniversary gift, with its homely saying that had struck Jane, then as now, as an ironic if not overtly hostile comment on Jane's skill in the kitchen. "Bake a little love into every bite," it read, in letters once bright red and now faded to a murky pink. But the subsequent improvement in Jane's cooking had little to do with love. Baking was no different than anything else; there was a right and a wrong way to do it, and no room for forgiveness of one's mistakes. While she had waited for the meringue to brown in the oven, she had wondered if the bile, fury, and scorn she was baking into every bit of this particular Nilla wafer pudding would manage to affect its flavor.

As she made her way to the back of the crowd, Jane passed Matt and Ruthie. Ruthie smiled and put out her hand, as if to touch Jane's shoulder. Jane flinched and Ruthie drew back. At that moment, Jane saw Bill Paige come around the house with an easy, loping step, carrying two cases of Geary's. He set them next to the cooler, tore open one of the boxes, and pulled out two beers before catching up with Jane. Jane accepted the beer he handed her and watched with pleasure as the realization broke across Iris's face. Serves her right, Jane thought. That'll teach her that she doesn't know half as much as she thinks she does. Jane nodded briskly at Samantha, and now once again the girl lifted up her violin.

Samantha launched into the first movement of the Bach as though she were leaping into the ocean. She threw her whole body into the music, her bow dancing across the strings. Her presence when performing was the opposite of Mr. Kimmelbrod's. Where he had been still, she was kinetic, twisting, shivering, whipping her body back and forth.

At first Iris could barely pay attention to the music, so taken aback was she at the sight of Jane Tetherly and the sheriff together. She watched them closely, trying to asses both the extent of their relationship and the effect of Samantha's playing on them. Iris allowed herself to imagine that Samantha's exceptional playing would move Jane so that she would realize that the girl deserved the opportunities only the Copakens could provide her. Then, perhaps, the lingering guilt Iris felt at having gone behind Jane's back might finally be expunged. Jane's expression, however, was unreadable, although Sheriff Paige looked at once astonished and pleased.

Samantha was so caught up in the joy of playing that when she began the second movement, the fugue allegro, she inadvertently picked up the tempo, her fingers flying, her bow arm flapping. By the end she was racing along, and because there were so many running notes, she had a little trouble with the sixteenth notes. But even those few guests who noticed her mistakes were astonished at her skill.

Listening to Samantha's frantic second movement, Iris tried desperately to recall having heard Becca play the same piece. Surely Becca had performed it in one of the hundreds of recitals in which she had participated over the course of her childhood. She could remember other children performing it; there was a tiny Chinese-American boy, no older than six, who had run through the second movement at such a breakneck pace that it was exhausting to watch. By the time he had finished Iris had been out of breath, too tired to focus on Becca's more stately Schumann. She could remember others playing it, too. One teenage girl who'd sucked her lower lip the whole time. Another who had made so many mistakes she'd been led away after the first movement. But Iris could not remember ever having heard her own daughter attempt this piece.

The two movements were short, no more than eight minutes because of how fast Samantha was playing, and when she drew out her final, climactic note, her face was damp with sweat. Iris leaped to her feet and shouted, "Brava! Brava!" The audience joined her, giving Samantha the first but by no means the last standing ovation of her life. Samantha's face flushed as she stood proudly before the assembly, many of whom had last seen her on the wedding day. If on that day she'd been out of her element, today she was entirely in it. She bent forward and, with a flourish, acknowledged their applause with a bow.

Iris continued clapping until Samantha had retreated to the house to return the violin to its place. Only later did she look around for Daniel. She hoped that Samantha's performance would have convinced him of the girl's promise, and of their own responsibility in helping her achieve it. She found him at the cooler, sending Bill Paige's Geary's splashing into the melted ice, one by one.

"Wasn't she amazing?" Iris said.

"She's great," Daniel said. He took a beer for himself, opened it, and tossed the top into the cooler.

"Do you understand now why I'm so eager to help her?" Iris said. "She's exceptional."

"Her talent was never the issue."

"Her talent is the *only* issue."

"You and I both know that isn't true."

Before they could argue any further, Ruthie and Matt interrupted them. Ruthie held Matt's hand like she had always held her father's, gripping his two middle fingers in her fist.

"Samantha totally rocks," Ruthie said.

"Doesn't she?" Iris said, glancing at Daniel.

Daniel drank deeply from his bottle of beer.

Ruthie looked from her mother to her father, and back again. "Is everything okay?" she said.

"Everything's fine," Iris said. "So, you two are dating?"

Ruthie nodded.

"Why didn't you tell us earlier?"

"I don't know," Ruthie said. "I guess we were worried that you'd think it was weird for us to be together."

"I don't think it's weird," Iris said.

Ruthie pressed closer to Matt, who stiffened momentarily and then slipped his arm around her waist. Ruthie said, "Matt and I have something we want to ask you."

Iris caught Daniel's eye, and they were at once united in a familiar moment of parental trepidation.

"I'm going to stay here this coming year, in Red Hook, with Matt," Ruthie said.

"Oh, Ruthie," Iris said.

"What? You said you wanted me to have a plan."

So Ruthie really did intend to mimic the worst of Becca's decisions, Iris thought.

She looked to Daniel for support, but whatever unity they had moments ago experienced seemed to have passed. He wasn't going to back her up. "Staying in Red Hook isn't a plan," Iris said.

"Yes, it is. It might not be the plan you wanted, but it's a plan. Matt and I—were hoping you'd let us live here over the winter. We could take care of the place."

"I'm getting pretty good at carpentry and stuff," Matt said. "I could build you another set of bookshelves for the living room, and fix the spring on the back door. I could lay in a cord of wood for the fire. Whatever you needed done around here."

Iris said, "But what would you do, Ruthie? Where would you work?"

"At the library."

"The library?"

"Yes. Mary Lou Curran convinced the director to hire me."

"How much can you possibly earn at the library?"

"Well, they're not exactly paying me."

"They're not paying you," Iris said flatly. "Well, then how 'exactly' is that a job?"

"They will pay me, when they get their new budget. They just can't pay me now. So for the first little while I'll be volunteering."

"And how will you support yourself?"

"I'll get a part-time job."

"There are no part-time jobs, Ruthie. Not in Red Hook."

"Becca always worked."

"Becca taught sailing. I don't think that's really an option for you. Particularly in February." God, how Iris missed sailing with Becca. Even when they weren't getting along, they would still sail together. Becca used to tease her that the water was the only place where you could trust Iris to mind her own business. They rarely talked on their sailing excursions, exchanging little more than terse warnings about the boom or instructions to come about or trim a sail. They would enjoy an easy, companionable silence, the kind of silence Iris used to have with Ruthie when they were sitting in the same room, each immersed in her own novel.

Since the accident Iris sailed alone.

Ruthie said, "I know I can find something to tide me over until the library comes through. I can work at one of the inns. Or at the market. I'll find something. And we don't need much money. Not if you let us live in the house while you're gone."

"Are you going to pay the bills, Ruthie? Are you going to pay to heat the house? Do you know how much that would cost?"

"She and Matt will be the caretakers," Daniel said. "We'll pay them what we've always paid Jane."

"We can't take away Jane's income. That wouldn't be right," Iris said.

Matt said, "My mom watches a lot of houses in the winter, Mrs. Copaken. One more or less isn't going to be a big deal." His voice was surprisingly firm, and Iris saw Ruthie give him a grateful squeeze.

"Call me Iris, not Mrs. Copaken," Iris said automatically, and then flinched. She had said that precise thing so often to John that it had become almost a mantra.

"I have a job," Matt said. "At the boatyard. I can pay the bills, and I can even pay rent."

Iris gazed at her daughter for a long, wordless moment. Then she said, her voice gentle, almost pleading, "Ruthie, why are you doing this?"

"Dad?" Ruthie said. "You don't think this is a bad idea, do you?"

Daniel shook his head. "I think you'll be fine."

Iris was not surprised that Daniel had agreed. That had always been his job. To agree with the girls, to support them, to indulge them. She was the taskmaster, the planner, the one who determined the rules and meted out punishment when they were broken. While on occasion she had resented their roles, had wanted to be the good guy just once in a while, she knew that it was she who had determined what parts they'd play to begin with.

Though she wasn't surprised by Daniel's reaction, she was shocked by her utter failure of insight into his motivation. Always before she would have known what his true feelings were. And now she hadn't the faintest idea if he really thought it was a good idea for Ruthie to live some pale simulacrum of Becca's life, or if he opposed the idea but could not bring himself to express it, or if he just didn't care.

How had it come to this? That she had so little insight into the mind of the man who she'd always believed she knew better than she knew herself? And Ruthie. How had they reached a point where Ruthie paid so little heed to her mother's point of view? How had she lost them? What had Iris been *doing*? Where had her mind been, when it should have been focused on her family?

Iris felt her energy for discord simply drain from her. "Fine," she said to Ruthie. "You can stay here in Red Hook and volunteer at the library, or knit sweaters, or weave Christmas wreaths. You can do whatever you want."

The intensity of their discussion had not gone unnoticed, and it was only when Iris had turned away from Daniel and Ruthie that she realized that many of their guests had quietly taken their leave. She considered calling out that there were still fireworks to come, but honestly she didn't care anymore.

Within an hour the yard was empty but for the detritus of the celebration. The picnic table was crowded with empty beer bottles and plastic cups. A large green garbage bag propped against the leg of the table overflowed with lobster shells and paper plates. Empty folding chairs were arranged in crooked rows facing the place where Samantha had played. A few other chairs were scattered across the lawn, one down on its side. The white plastic chairs seemed to glow in the dim light.

Daniel, having just helped a trembling Mr. Kimmelbrod to his room, came down the porch steps. He gazed out over the empty yard. Nothing, he thought, looked as bereft as a party after the guests had gone. He took the green garbage bag, tamped down its contents with his foot, and began gathering the rest of the garbage. He collected the trash, tied up the bag, and tossed it into the bin. He gathered up the beer bottles, filling two recycling bins. Then he began to work on the chairs. He snapped them closed and stacked them inside the barn. He crossed the yard, climbed over the seawall, and made his way across the rocks over to the dock. It was almost dark now.

When he looked back toward the house he could just barely see Iris's figure through the screened windows of the porch. She was sitting in her customary chair, her head bowed. There was a light on in Mr. Kimmelbrod's bedroom; the white curtains glowed yellow against the darkened house. Daniel did not know where Ruthie and Matt were.

Daniel turned his back on the house and walked down the length of the dock. He could hear the water splashing gently against the wood. Over the water a loon gave its mournful cry. It was chilly, and the air raised goose bumps along his bare arms. He had piled the fireworks about halfway along the dock, and when he reached them he kneeled down and chose one of the smaller cakes. The black box was covered with pictures of bursting rockets. It was called, for no reason that he could think of, Meet the Neighbors.

Daniel set the box at the end of the dock. He took the lighter from his pocket and rolled his thumb across the wheel a few times before it caught. He lit the fuse and stepped back. For a moment the cake fizzed and popped, and then it went off, shooting up into the now-dark sky.

Daniel watched as one after another the effects went off, blue, red, white. Short staccato bursts and then larger ones, like giant umbrellas opening up beneath the stars. When the last light fizzled and fell toward the bay, Daniel sat down, wrapped his arms around his legs, leaned his forehead against his knees, and thought about where he would be next summer, because he knew now—had known for a long time—that he would not be here, in this broken place, spoiling the darkness of a Maine summer sky with a lot of cheap effects, noise, and smoke.

THE FOURTH SUMMER

1

Though it was filled with people and with nearly 130 years of history and ghosts, the house felt empty without Daniel. It was more than nine months since he had packed up his belongings and moved out of their apartment in New York—long enough to gestate and give birth to a baby—and yet Iris still felt as if she were stuck in the first trimester of her separation from her husband, lonely, lost, unable to grasp the ramifications of her new situation.

Iris made a pot of tea, but instead of drinking it, she held her mug in her hand and drifted from room to room. In the kitchen she opened the cupboards and gazed at the unopened boxes and tins of Daniel's favorite cereal, the Italian coffee he preferred, the cookies he ate in the evenings before bed. On her first shopping trip after arriving in Maine she had automatically loaded his favorite foods into her cart, not realizing the pointlessness of her purchases until she was standing in the checkout line. She hadn't returned the items to the shelves, had brought them home, as if by laying in a stock of shortbread cookies and Wicked Ale she could lure her husband home. Daniel's favorite foods now sat gathering dust in her pantry.

In the mudroom Becca's swim tote had a rival for Iris's attention: Daniel's boots, his coats and jackets on their hooks, his fishing rod. The living room did not interest her—it was Mr. Kimmelbrod's and Samantha's terrain, the piano heaped with scores, the battered music stand in the middle of the room. In the dining room she sifted through the piles of newspapers and magazines Daniel had left. Every summer he would stack his periodicals and newspapers on one end of the dining table. On the morning they returned to New York he would bundle them together, tie the bundles with twine, and drop them off at the dump as they drove out of town. Last summer when he left he had not bothered to throw out his vast repository of reading material, so here it still was, old copies of the *The Atlantic Monthly* and *Harper's*, weeks' worth of the Red Hook *Daily Packet* still stuffed with year-old circulars and tide charts. Every day Iris determined to haul it all to the dump, and every day she left it gathering dust.

In the days after the Fourth of July party, they'd seen almost nothing of each other. In the mornings Daniel woke early and left before Iris came downstairs. He did not return until well after dinner. She knew that he was spending his time at the boxing gym—their laundry hamper was full of stinking T-shirts, sweatpants, and socks. Once or twice, she tried to tell him how upset it made her that he continued to box, but he listened dumbly, shrugged his shoulders, and walked away. There was a quality of finality in his gestures that made her unable to pursue him.

His departure had been precipitated by no argument. He had merely come up to her one morning about ten days after the Fourth of July celebration as she sat in her accustomed chair on the screen porch drinking tea and cutting out the tide chart from the *Daily Packet* and said, "I'm sorry, Iris. But I don't want to do this anymore."

"Do what?"

"Any of it. You, me. Everything."

For a moment Iris had been uncharacteristically silent. She just blinked, her mouth open and gasping, like a goldfish spilled onto the floor. At last she managed to say, "You want to leave?"

"Yes," he said.

Iris reached up and clasped his hand. He flinched. She said, "You want to leave *me*?"

"Yes."

She pulled her hand away. "You want to walk out on thirty-three years of marriage because Samantha's coming to New York?"

Daniel sat down and said, "That's not why. You know that's not why."

Her voice rough with the tears she was swallowing, Iris said, "Well, then, why? Why do you want to leave me?"

"I'm sorry, Iris."

"Don't leave," she said.

He shrugged helplessly.

He had left her crying on the screen porch, gone upstairs, and packed his things. By noon he was climbing into Walt Mather's beat-up old Chevy Suburban, what passed for Red Hook's taxi service. Iris stayed on the back porch, following the sounds of his preparations and ultimate departure. Only once he was gone did it occur to her that Walt was most likely driving him to the airport, which meant he must have booked a flight at least a day ago. He had known he was leaving last night when they'd stripped off their clothing and gone to bed. He had known as they lay reading beneath the matching yellow glows of their bedside lamps. He had known as they breathed in each other's nighttime exhalations. He had known when he walked into the bathroom this morning while she was showering. He had known while he was urinating loudly into the toilet. All this time he had known he was leaving, and she had never guessed.

As the summer wore on, Iris had called Daniel on his cell phone nearly every day, but on the rare occasions when he answered, their conversations were awkward. She found herself unable to rid her voice of a humiliating tone of supplication, and he barely spoke.

When she returned to New York at the end of August, with Samantha and Mr. Kimmelbrod in tow, Daniel was gone, staying in a dismal furnished efficiency apartment on West Forty-fourth Street. He came back once in September for his clothes and a few other odds and ends. She had not seen him since. For months she had kept calling him, but he refused her entreaties to come over for dinner, ignored her invitations to attend Samantha's recitals. He saw her father occasionally, she knew that. Mr. Kimmelbrod was far too circumspect and respectful of his son-in-law's privacy to breach his confidence, but the home-health-care aide Iris had hired upon their return from Maine held no such compunctions. Iris was kind to Edwina, and Edwina, whose own husband had left her with three children and no savings, felt sorry for her. In the interests of sisterhood, she faithfully reported whenever Daniel showed up to take his father-in-law out to lunch.

The one consolation to Iris's loneliness had been Samantha. Every evening Iris would meet Samantha at Mr. Kimmelbrod's house, where

Samantha would go right after school for her lesson. After her lesson, Samantha would sit on the floor in Mr. Kimmelbrod's living room, doing her homework at the coffee table while he sat in his armchair reading the newspaper or dozing. Iris would arrive as early as her classes would permit, with groceries to prepare their dinner. Only after Mr. Kimmelbrod retired to his bedroom for the night would Iris and Samantha return home. Usually they walked the fifteen blocks between his apartment and hers, huddled together against the wind that blew up Riverside Drive. She had never stopped missing Daniel, but her loneliness and shock had been mitigated to a small extent both by the consuming nature of her job and, especially, by Samantha's company.

But here in Maine, without her classes and faculty meetings to distract her, and with Samantha staying at Jane's house with Connie, who had recently been released from Riverview, not even the company of her father and daughter could alleviate Iris's forlorn desolation at being without Daniel, rudderless in an unfamiliar sea. Ruthie and Matt were living with Iris this summer, sleeping in Ruthie's tiny bedroom down the hall, but they were no louder than two field mice, the occasional rustle of their bedsheets or squeak of a closing drawer the only evidence that they were there at all. Matt was, in fact, gone more often than not. He had reserved the first day of July for the launch of his boat and was frantically working to make sure it would be finished in time. In addition to working at the library, Ruthie had a part-time job as the evening receptionist at the Red Hook Inn. She was rarely home before ten.

Nor did Mr. Kimmelbrod provide his daughter with much in the way of company. His health was poor. His stamina had steadily been decreasing, and although he still managed to rise to the occasion of his lessons with Samantha and the other students with whom he was working this summer at Usherman Center, when he wasn't teaching he spent most of his time behind the closed door of his bedroom, recuperating from his exertions. Iris prepared elaborate stews and casseroles to tempt his meager appetite, meals that required no cutting and little chewing but that would not slosh out of his spoon when his hand shook. Yet even when he felt strong enough to join her at the table, he rarely managed more than a few bites.

He had spent most of today in his room, conserving his energy in anticipation of the master class he was to teach tonight. Iris had asked him to consider postponing or even canceling the class, but he had brushed off her concern. It would not be fair to his students, he told her. He gave only one master class every summer, and the students had been practicing since it was announced. It was Samantha's trio that was to perform, the first time she would appear on the Usherman Center stage, and he could not disappoint her. Moreover, the first master class would set the tone for all the master classes that followed, and he wanted to make sure that the other members of the faculty—especially Spiegelman—had a better understanding of what would be required of them this summer. Poor, long-suffering Spiegelman, Iris thought.

When Iris was finished with her solitary cup of tea, she collected her things and waited in the kitchen, looking at her watch. If they didn't leave soon, they would be late.

"Dad?" she called. "Are you about ready to go?"

After a moment she heard his voice but muffled by his closed door, she could not make out what he was saying. "Dad?" she said again, heading down the long hall to his bedroom. "Is everything okay?"

Iris found her father sitting on the edge of his bed, holding one of his small, impeccably polished shoes, a stricken expression on his face. He had lost weight over the last year. His cheeks were hollow, which made his teeth look overlarge in his mouth. His top incisor had broken a few months before and the dentist, worried that he was not strong enough to undergo replacement surgery, had given him a temporary, removable bridge that he found too uncomfortable to wear. He was terribly self-conscious about the gap and had thus taken to curling his upper lip over his front teeth. He had dark brown circles under his eyes, the marks of the chronic exhaustion that plagued him. His insomnia had grown ever more acute, his sleep disturbed by both the rigidity of his body and the occasional jerking of his limbs, symptoms that infuriated him in their contradiction. He looked weak, nearly shattered, and the sight of him thus diminished broke all the unbroken places in his daughter's heart.

"It appears I am unable to put on my shoe," Mr. Kimmelbrod said, attempting a halfhearted, close-mouthed smile.

Iris rushed to his side. "I've got it," she said. She knelt down and tenderly picked up the gnarled foot in its black silk sock.

"I am terribly sorry," he said.

"There's nothing to be sorry about," she said, forcing a cheerful tone. She would not allow him to see the effect his deterioration had on her.

She eased his foot into the shoe. "Do you remember how Daniel packed two left shoes that summer?" she asked as she tied the knot. "And he had to wear sneakers to the wedding?"

"Is *that* why he wore sneakers?" Mr. Kimmelbrod said.

"You mean you didn't know? He has two pairs of oxfords that look almost exactly alike. Why did you think he was wearing sneakers?"

Mr. Kimmelbrod rested a trembling hand on Iris's head. "You are very good," he said. "Very good and very kind."

"No, I'm not," Iris said. She took her father's hand and pressed it to her lips. "I wish I was, but I'm not." Gently, she pulled his socks up his hairless, bony shins. She propped his feet one by one on her bent thigh and laced the shoes tightly, the way she knew he liked it. As she helped him to his feet she said, "Are you sure I can't convince you to postpone tonight's class? Just until you're feeling better?"

"I am as well as I will be, daughter," Mr. Kimmelbrod said, taking her arm.

The Usherman Center's small performance hall was a weather-beaten, shingled structure. Performances took place on a makeshift stage, a simple wooden platform set up in front of the large stone fireplace, beneath the benevolent gaze of a hulking moose head hanging from nails hammered into the mortar between the chimney's stones. The moose was a legacy of the hall's prior owners, a group of Boston bankers who had used the hall as a hunting lodge until Felix Usherman and the other members of his eponymous quartet purchased the building as their summer rehearsal studio in 1928.

This evening's audience was small. Usherman Center students filled the back four rows, but only a few of the hall's diehard local fans had turned out. Iris knew most of the attendees. John and Emma Love, summer visitors who had a few years ago retired to their family camp on Echo Pond, were there, as was the writer Roscoe Lord, author of a series of dishy potboilers set in a thinly fictionalized Red Hook, books whose publication were always the cause of a good deal of delighted outrage among the locals. Ancient Mary Jane Huntoon's wheelchair occupied the same place in the front row since the hall first began presenting public concerts sixty-three years ago. Miss Huntoon was treated as royalty at Usherman Center both because of her longevity and because of the rumors, started no doubt by the old lady herself, that her will made the hall its primary beneficiary, to the tune of more than ten million dollars. Iris was far too worried both about her father and about Samantha's performance to make competent small talk with the woman, however, and managed no more than a smile in response to Miss Huntoon's inquiry after Mr. Kimmelbrod's health.

At twelve years old, Samantha was much too young to be a regular student at Usherman Center, but she was the prodigy of Usherman Center's most revered faculty member, and her family was local. As the relationship between town and gown, or in this case between town and tails, was always in need of shoring up, accommodations had been made for her. She was not officially enrolled in the program, and thus did not live at Usherman Center. Instead of assigning her to two separate chamber groups, like the other students, Mr. Kimmelbrod placed her in only one trio, with a pianist in her fourth summer at the hall and a cellist whom Mr. Kimmelbrod knew from Juilliard. Samantha thus had three lessons with her mentor every week—two on her own and one with the trio. In addition to her own practice regimen, which, with school out, had crept up to five hours a day, she rehearsed every morning with the trio. In the evenings she would often check scores out from Usherman Center's lending library and read them, playing through pieces she heard other students practicing. The girl was, joyfully and to the calloused tips of her fingers, immersed.

A few more people trickled in, and Iris shifted down a few seats to make room. It was not until Connie Phelps sat down that Iris recognized her. Jane was standing in the aisle, unwilling, it seemed, to follow Connie down the row.

"Hello, Iris," Connie said.

"Connie! How are you? And Jane. So good to see you here."

Connie's face had filled out and was almost rosy. Her hair was colored a purplish auburn and looked freshly cut. "I'm good," she said. "I'm doing all right."

"It's wonderful that you could make it tonight," Iris said.

"Oh, we wouldn't have missed it for the world," Connie said.

With an audible sigh, Jane lowered herself into the aisle seat next to Connie.

Jane stared straight ahead of her, her hands resting on the brown leather pocketbook in her lap. She and Iris had seen each other only once this summer, on Iris's very first day in Red Hook, when she had dropped Samantha off at her aunt's house. They had spoken on the phone as little as possible over the winter, only when there was a specific piece of information about Samantha that needed to be transmitted: the date of her vacation, the time her bus was due to arrive at Port Authority or at the Bangor Greyhound station.

However, despite the hostilities between two of the most important women in her life, Samantha had flourished in New York. She did well and made friends at the Anderson School. Her lessons with Mr. Kimmelbrod were matters of joy and profound importance to teacher and student alike. In fact, he had cut by half the number of students in his Juilliard studio in order to focus more of his limited energy and attention on her.

"You're in for something very interesting," Iris said. "Master classes offer a real window into what goes on between teacher and student."

"So Samantha tells us," Connie said.

"My father's can be a little . . . well . . . idiosyncratic."

"How do you mean?"

"Oh, you'll see."

Each member of the faculty led only a single master class, and it had caused some disgruntled rumblings when Mr. Kimmelbrod selected Samantha's trio to play in his. However, his partiality to this young girl who was so new to the violin was a surprise only to those who had not yet heard her play. The world of music ran on favoritism; he had been the beneficiary and the bestower in the long course of his career. Teachers selected their students carefully, as they had themselves been selected, adding to the long pedagogical lineages of which they were so proud. In

Prague Mr. Kimmelbrod had studied with a teacher who had been one of the last of Antonín Dvořák's violin students before Dvořák had turned his attention full-time to composing. When he moved to New York, Mr. Kimmelbrod had studied with Louis Persinger, who was himself a student of the great Eugène Ysaÿe, who studied with Henri Vieuxtemps, who was a student of Charles de Bériot, who studied with Giovanni Battista Viotti, and on and on back through time. It was remarkable, Iris thought, to imagine the chain of connection between this young girl adopted from Cambodia and an eighteenth-century Italian virtuoso.

Connie said to Iris, "It's awfully nice of Mr. Kimmelbrod to lend her his violin. I've never heard her play it before."

In May, Iris had set herself the task of finding a new violin for Samantha. Over the course of the year the girl had blossomed, and the disparity between her burgeoning capabilities and those of the three-quarter-sized Gliga with which she was obliged to make do had become apparent, and painful, to Iris and her father. She was young still for a full-sized violin, but she had periodically been playing Mr. Kimmelbrod's Guarneri, "keeping it warm" for him, as he put it, and with her long arms and fingers she had never seemed to struggle with the full-sized model.

And so, despite the fact that to pay for it she would need to dip into her retirement account, Iris went shopping for a violin. She hoped to find something like the 1885 Gemunder she and Daniel had given to Becca as a Bat Mitzvah present. Every time Iris thought of the Gemunder, the hurt and the anger that she had felt on learning that Becca had sold it, emotions that Becca's death ought to have vitiated or rendered superfluous, returned afresh: had Becca not sold the Gemunder to invest in John's sailboat, it would have been perfect for Samantha. Although if Becca had not sold the violin, had not abandoned her career, then Iris probably would never have found herself in the position of going into debt to buy Samantha Phelps a fiddle.

Iris asked Ernst Denkenbaum, the violin dealer to whom Mr. Kimmelbrod generally referred his students, to bring a selection of violins to Mr. Kimmelbrod's apartment. One evening after supper, he presented them with three instruments, a 1951 Charles Voirey, an 1851 Honore Derazey, and a new Michel Eggimann. He arrayed his instruments on the coffee table, placing them just so. Mr. Kimmelbrod sat in an armchair, his three-legged cane within easy reach. He handed Samantha his own bow, which was worth far more than any of the three fiddles. "Go ahead," he said. "Try them."

Samantha picked up the Derazey and began warming up with a few arpeggios. She turned slightly away from where Denkenbaum and Iris sat on the couch, and faced Mr. Kimmelbrod. She began the allegro from Vivaldi's Violin Concerto in A Minor. Mr. Kimmelbrod lifted his hand and motioned to her to stop.

"The tone is too big and powerful for you," he said.

The dealer interjected, "Powerful, yes, but very vibrant, don't you think? Lively."

Mr. Kimmelbrod dismissed him with a curt shake of the head. "It's not for her."

"The Voirey?" Denkenbaum asked, picking up the second violin. Nearly as old as the violinist, he had known Mr. Kimmelbrod for decades, and while their enmity (born of a dispute over the cost of a 1946 Carl Becker Mr. Kimmelbrod had desired for one of his students) had never waned, their mutual respect was absolute.

"It's very beautiful," Mr. Kimmelbrod said. "I have always been partial to red varnish. That is why you brought it, yes?"

The dealer inclined his head.

Samantha exchanged the Derazey for the Voirey and played the same bit of the Vivaldi, then the triplet variation from the Trout Quintet. Mr. Kimmelbrod smiled. "It's responsive," he said.

"Very," Samantha said.

"But, too dark, I think," said Mr. Kimmelbrod.

"Shall we try the Eggimann?" Iris asked.

This time Samantha played a few measures of the Vivaldi, then some Bach, the adagio from the sonata she had performed the year before at the Fourth of July picnic.

"It's very warm," Mr. Kimmelbrod said, nodding. "Mature."

The dealer said, "I am not surprised at your choice. You recognize the Dembovski in the Eggimann, of course." To Iris he explained, "Eggimann builds on the Guarneri del Gesù model."

"Does it remind you of your violin, Dad?" Iris said.

Mr. Kimmelbrod raised an eyebrow. "Hardly."

The dealer said, "I have never before seen such workmanship and tone in a new instrument."

Samantha stilled her bow. "It doesn't feel right," she said. "It doesn't feel like the one."

"No?" Mr. Kimmelbrod asked. "It sounded good to me."

She shook her head. "It's not right."

"Well, then," Mr. Kimmelbrod said. He turned to Denkenbaum. "What else can you offer us?"

Not bothering to conceal his irritation, Denkenbaum said, "As good as the Eggimann? Only one. An atelier Vuillaume, built to the model of the Paganini Cannon del Gesù. But that is of course beyond your price range. Your daughter told me to show you instruments in the ten-to-twenty-thousand-dollar range."

"Are you sure about the Eggimann?" Iris asked Samantha.

The girl bit her lip. "I'm sorry." She did not bother to claim to be happy with what she was now playing—they all knew she needed a new violin, and any of these would be in an entirely different class. But it was clear that she found none of the three choices compelling. Choosing a violin is like falling in love. While there is always the chance that one's initial commitment will prove to be a mistake, it is impossible to go forward without that first wave of intense infatuation.

"Do you think I could try a few more? I could come to you, and then if I found one we could bring it to Mr. Kimmelbrod?" Samantha said.

"No," Mr. Kimmelbrod said, suddenly. "There's no need."

Samantha looked momentarily crushed, and then nearly as quickly resigned.

He continued, "Why should we buy another instrument when we have one that needs playing? You will use the Dembovski."

Iris was stunned. It had never crossed her mind that her father would allow Samantha to use his violin for more than just a single performance or an afternoon of practice. She never would have thought that he would lend such a valuable instrument to a twelve-year-old who had been playing for only two years, even if she was his own student. He had certainly never offered it to Becca. Iris felt a stab of envy on behalf of her daughter.

And so, ever since Denkenbaum's fiddles had failed to stir her, Mr. Kimmelbrod had flouted the requirements of his insurers and allowed Samantha to play the Dembovski. She would be playing it tonight, in Mr. Kimmelbrod's master class.

The Usherman students were boisterous, goofy, breaking into song and then silencing one another with exaggerated hushes, like children trying, unsuccessfully, to behave for a room full of adults. They cheered wildly when the door behind the stage opened and the trio filed in. The three musicians were attired in the usual black: a young male Asian cellist wearing black Dockers and a black button-down shirt open at the neck; a redheaded pianist wearing a long black skirt, a skimpy black tank top, and a pair of incongruous white strappy sandals that she kicked off when she sat down at the piano; and Samantha. Before they came up to Maine, Iris had taken the girl shopping for concert attire, the first real performance clothes she had ever owned. They had spent a delightful afternoon picking through the bins and racks at Century 21 before heading uptown to Bloomingdale's. Samantha was tall for her age, and slight, and almost everything she tried on looked beautiful on her. The elegant black dress she had finally chosen made her look five years older than her twelve years. It fit snugly at the waist, but had short fluttering sleeves that left her arms free.

"She looks beautiful, doesn't she?" Connie whispered, loudly.

"She does," Iris said.

"Thank you for the dress. It's so pretty."

"Shh!" Jane said, pointing to the stage, where the musicians had begun tuning their instruments.

This evening the trio was working on the first movement of Mozart's Piano Trio in B flat. Mr. Kimmelbrod allowed them to play it through once. The ginger-haired pianist leaned forward, her lips pursed, like a sparrow pecking for seed. The cellist's brow knotted and he winced whenever he had to play a high note. Samantha's face, however, was serene. The only evidence of her exertion was a sheen of sweat on her forehead.

When they finished the movement, the students in the back of the hall roared their appreciation. Mr. Kimmelbrod, however, hushed the crowd with a flick of his wrist.

To the trio he said, "We should hear a little more music than what we just heard."

Samantha lowered her violin to her lap and leaned forward, staring intently at him.

"Do you understand?" he asked her. "This is a late composition with many inflections. What is the meter?"

Samantha said, "Four-four."

"That was not four-four," Mr. Kimmelbrod said. "Play."

They began again, but he stopped them almost immediately. "You see, already. Ta da dee da," he sang. "Again, and this time remember Mozart is looking for a *decrescendo* on the final notes in the passage. You accented them."

They resumed, and this time he allowed them to continue a bit longer before he said to Samantha, "How long was the last note?"

"A quarter note," she said.

"You tied an extra sixteenth note to it. Try again."

He stopped them after an instant. "No! Not ta dee da! Ta dee dada da da da!" he sang. "Mozart was very clear what he wanted to do with this piece. His notes are *separate*. You cheat on him. Again."

Iris looked to make sure Connie was not disturbed by his criticism of her daughter. She looked awed, and perhaps a little confused. Jane, on the other hand, simply looked on impassively.

After a moment Mr. Kimmelbrod smiled at the pianist. "That's very beautiful." The girl flushed happily. He continued, "Very beautiful, yes. But of course it is not what Mozart wrote. Play for me what is written on the score, please." Her face purpled and she bent to the keyboard.

"And you," he said to Samantha. "Again you started loud. It does not need to be so loud."

Iris had seen her father's master classes countless times, and had always been amused by his vehemence. In his calm, cool way Mr. Kimmelbrod was always hard on his students. He never shouted like some teachers, but neither did he try to hide his displeasure. As his Parkinson's had progressed he had grown ever more stern, as if he could compensate for the disappearance of his own abilities by honing those of his students. Iris had expected him to be critical of Samantha, but she found herself feeling protective of the girl. Couldn't he hear how beautiful Samantha's playing was? How precise? Mr. Kimmelbrod seemed to Iris to be unusually cantankerous, as if the students were inexplicably failing to provide him with something he was expecting.

In her seat next to Iris, Connie took a tissue out of her purse and began worrying it to shreds in her lap.

"Stop!" Mr. Kimmelbrod said to the players. "Listen to me. What we want here is a conversation, you understand?" He turned to the cellist. "She says 'ta dee da,' like she is saying 'I like you.'" The audience laughed, and he continued, "Then you answer, 'I like you very much,' and she says, 'I like you more.' You reply, 'I like you still more.' You understand? A conversation. Again."

This time as they played he conducted with one of his palsied hands. Over the music he said to Samantha, "More bow! Yes, yes. So much prettier." Then he waved them to a stop.

"The sixteenths are too fast. Again." They played through almost to the end before he stopped them. "Don't be afraid of the crescendo," he said. "It is as if you are saying, *That* was the story. *That* is what I have tried to say. Again."

He stopped them after a few moments and leaned over and poked Samantha's score. "You died too soon," he said. "You see? Take it from here."

As Mr. Kimmelbrod turned away from Samantha, his left foot seemed to freeze. He hovered in place for a moment, arms clamped to his sides, his face an expressionless mask. Then, with a near audible creaking of his ancient bones, he fell over to one side, his stiff body crashing to the ground like a wooden plank dropped from a great height.

Iris leaped to her feet and pushed through the crowd to her father's side. She tried to kneel down next to him, but bodies pressed in from all sides.

"Give him air!" an authoritative voice ordered. "Move back."

The crowd eased and as Iris bent over her father she saw Jane with one arm outstretched, pushing people back. With the other hand Jane held her cell phone to her ear, and spoke calmly into the phone.

"An ambulance," Iris heard Jane say. "And an escort. Make it fast."

11

Ruthie and Matt were driving swiftly up Red Hook Road on their way back to the hospital. Iris had sent them home early the night before, although she herself had refused to leave. She had not left Mr. Kimmelbrod's side once in the three days since his fall.

Ruthie was behind the wheel and Matt sat in the passenger seat, leafing through a sheaf of papers. "Shit," he said. "Even if I finish the next course by the end of the summer, I won't have enough sea time to get the upgrade."

Ruthie said, "Why do you need the upgrade? When you took the first captain's course you said that the six-pack license was going to be enough."

The course for Matt's captain's license had cost them $665, plus the cost of getting down to Boston and staying there for two long weekends, money neither of them had. It had been a struggle to make ends meet even after the library started paying Ruthie. She had taken holiday shifts at the Haverford's and even, as her mother had predicted, earned a few hundred dollars after the first frost harvesting the tips of evergreen boughs and making Christmas wreaths. In addition to working at the yard and on the *Rebecca*, Matt had also made wreaths, and had managed to get hired at the UPS store over Christmas. But the *Rebecca* drank up their money faster than they could earn it, and they were perennially broke. In the end, Ruthie had let Matt put the money for the course on her credit card. A month later, at the cash register at the food co-op, Ruthie had been obliged to watch as the checkout clerk—a hostile vegan with a sallow face—snipped Ruthie's credit card in half. With less than four dollars in her pocket, Ruthie had spent a humiliating ten minutes pouring bags of rice, black beans, flour, and quinoa back into the bulk bins.

"Yeah, uh, turns out they won't give me the insurance unless I've got a minimum fifty-ton license."

"But the boat doesn't weigh anywhere *near* that."

"It's not about what the boat weighs, it's just a licensing requirement. Anyway, that's the least of our problems. How the hell are we going to afford the insurance?"

"What was the quote?"

"I don't even want to tell you."

"Come on, Matt. What was the quote?"

"Thirteen thousand dollars."

"What?" she said. "That's *insane*."

"It's not really insane. I mean, think about it. We need a million-dollar liability policy. And the Caribbean is, like, prime hurricane zone. Do you know how many boats went down in Hurricane Ivan?"

"No."

"A lot. It's just, you know, that's what insurance costs. You want to be a charter boat captain, you have to pay the insurance."

They were coming up on Jacob's Cove, and Ruthie pressed her foot more firmly on the gas. Once they were safely past, she said, "Matt? Can I ask you something?"

He was reading again, flipping through pages as though a better answer lay somewhere between the lines of what he'd already read.

"Matt?"

"Yeah?"

"Do you really want to be a charter boat captain?"

"What do you mean? Of course I do."

"Nothing. I don't know. It's just . . . you were totally miserable taking that class."

Ruthie had accompanied Matt on one of his Boston weekends, entertaining herself while he was in class by visiting with those of her friends who were enrolled in various Harvard graduate programs. Matt's class let out at six, and on the first evening they met up with a group at the Cantab Lounge to drink beer and listen to Little Joe Cook reprise his 1957 hit "Peanuts." The next evening, however, Matt claimed to be too drained from sitting in class all day to deal with another late night, and sent

Ruthie out on her own. The third night was the same. Ruthie was sure he just hadn't liked her friends and preferred lying around watching ESPN to going out with them again.

He had gone to Boston alone the next time, and had returned gloomy and depressed. When she confronted him he claimed that the lectures were dry and dull and he was unused to sitting in a classroom, but she had been sure there was more to it than that.

"Yes, I'm sure," Matt said now. "I mean, come on. How can you ask that?"

When John had taken on the project of rebuilding the *Rebecca*, the restoration, while foolishly expensive, made sense. With every board foot of mahogany and piece of sandpaper, with every inch of sailcloth and handful of nails, John had been building a future for himself and Becca. There was no way John could have afforded a new boat of the Alden's size and quality, even with the proceeds from the sale of Becca's violin. Restoring the Alden was the only way he and Becca could realize their dream, conceived in the first days of their falling in love and nurtured tenderly throughout their courtship and engagement, of sailing the Caribbean.

Matt had resumed the project three years ago with not even a clear idea of carrying John's plans through to their full, logical conclusion. His only motivation back then had been a vague compulsion to finish what John had started. He had refused to admit defeat despite a multitude of mistakes and setbacks because to do so would have been a betrayal of his brother's memory. Early this past winter, when he realized that he was close to finishing, he had been forced to confront the question of what to do with the *Rebecca*.

The *Rebecca* was a good boat, with solid bones and a decent provenance: John Alden had built her for a New York plastic surgeon who had operated on the nose of Bette Davis, and the blue-eyed star had signed the boat's log not once but twice. Even so, she was worth little more than what Matt and John had put into her. There was not much of a market for restored boats, whatever their history, especially if they were rebuilt in someone's backyard. The men who could afford the indulgence of a wooden boat wanted one with the most advanced and state-of-the-art aerodynamic design, with a tank-tested keel and a carbon fiber rig. They wanted a boat built for them from the ground up, in a prestigious yard like King's, and they were willing to pay a million dollars, sometimes a lot more, to get it.

So even if he could have brought himself to part with the *Rebecca* after all the work and love he and his brother had sunk into her, Matt wouldn't have been able to sell her. But neither could he afford to keep her as a pleasure boat. The only option Matt could see was the one that John had always intended.

Matt said, "What about you, Ruthie? Are you, like, maybe projecting a little, or something?"

"No."

"So you're into it. You want to take her down to the Caribbean and run charters with me."

When Matt had first broached the possibility of following through on John and Becca's plan, with him as captain and Ruthie in Becca's role as chef and hostess, she had been under the influence of the warm and expansive feelings engendered by her very first Christmas in Maine, complete with tree, tinsel, sugar cookies, and carolers singing on the steps of the Red Hook Town Hall. Matt's idea had struck Ruthie then as an attractive, sunny fantasy. She had managed temporarily to overcome her trepidation about sailing by concentrating on the Caribbean part of the plan. She loved the idea of visiting the islands; she imagined herself lying on the deck of a boat (tied up in a snug harbor), reading novels and eating mangoes plucked moments before from the tree.

And if Ruthie didn't have Becca's natural maritime gifts, at least she knew how to cook; she had managed to learn that from her sister. As the winter progressed, she spent hours surfing the Web for recipes for flying fish and cascadura so she would be able to give their imagined clientele an authentic Caribbean culinary experience. It had been a welcome escape from the long, dark days, when it was so cold that her wet hair froze on the walk between the door and her car. She had happily reported to Matt that the temperature of the Caribbean sea was twice that of the Maine coastal waters. But after a while, as Matt doggedly took ever more concrete steps toward getting his captain's license and preparing both himself and the *Rebecca* for this future, a feeling of dread began to overtake Ruthie. Her volunteer job had, as promised, turned into an actual one, with its own line in the town budget, complete with a tiny salary and health insurance. She did not need Jamaica or St. John's; the cozy library, fires blazing in both the massive stone fireplaces at either end of the reading room, was respite enough, even from the most bitter weather. She reveled in the most mundane of tasks: helping elderly patrons log on to the Internet, sending out overdue notices, shelving. One of her favorite jobs was to work the reference desk. The desk lent a real authority to the person sitting behind it, and Ruthie was constantly amazed that people expected her to provide answers to the most complicated and esoteric questions. But there was a reference book on every subject, and if those failed there was the Web, so Ruthie could, with the help of the *Dictionary of Collective Nouns*, tell a patron that a group of dragons was referred to as a dreadful; or, after a glance at the *Encyclopedia of Bad Taste*, provide another with the name of the inventor of the Lava lamp (Edward Craven Walker, born in 1918 in Singapore). Ruthie had managed to make herself so indispensable in such a short time that, rather than close the library when the rest of the staff went to the state librarians' conference in Augusta, the chief librarian had left her in charge.

Those few days in March when she was the queen of the Red Hook Library had been the most pleasurable of her entire life. Matt took the excuse of her absence to work on the *Rebecca*, and thus she had not felt guilty about leaving him. Keys in hand, she had arrived at the library so early that it was still dark outside. She'd started up the computers and the copiers, checked in the books that had been dropped into the return slot the night before, and wandered through the rooms turning on lights. In each section she had carefully reshelved the display books and spent a long time choosing new ones. For the children she laid out *Lyle, Lyle, Crocodile*, one of her favorite books when she was a child, and a few choice selections of the Frances oeuvre, including *Bread and Jam for Frances*, which she considered the most delightful children's book ever written. For the teens she went with a fantasy theme and, avoiding Harry Potter, offered them *Half Magic*, Philip Pullman's *His Dark Materials*, and the *The Wind in the Willows*. Let them find the Gossip Girls books on their own. In the periodical room she fanned the *National Review* with *The Nation* and *Commentary*, with a stray, inexplicable issue of *Heeb* that had somehow ended up in the collection. There was not much she could do with the new releases, other than to place Lorrie Moore prominently in the middle of the display and to put all the cat mysteries spine-forward. The patrons of the Red Hook library had an insatiable appetite for murder mysteries featuring cat sleuths, and Ruthie was not worried about those books finding their readers. It was the other, less popular volumes that she was concerned with. Each of them was a lost child looking for its mother, or a lover searching for a soul mate, and Ruthie was the matchmaker, tasked with the joyous job of introducing them. There was nothing, she thought, that she was better at. Around midmorning she noticed a young woman—in her late teens perhaps—slowly spinning through the rotating rack of paperback romance novels. The girl came in every week or so and left with a pile of these paperbacks, always choosing the ones with covers festooned with heaving bosoms and Regency gowns.

"You like those, don't you?" Ruthie asked her. "The Regency romances?"

"I love them," the girl said, tucking a lank strand of hair behind an ear still pink from the cold.

Ruthie selected a volume from the rack. Like the others, the picture on the cover was of a young woman in an elegant frock, but this one was not so décolleté. "Have you read this one?"

The girl shook her head. "No, I don't think so."

"Why don't you give it a try," Ruthie said. "It's one of my favorites."

The next week, when the young woman came back to the library, she found Ruthie straightening up the computer section (Dewey Decimal Nos. 004 to 006) and said, "That book was really good! It's different from the others. But I liked it. It made me cry, and I loved the ending, but it's really funny, too, isn't it? I mean, at first I didn't really notice—or I guess maybe I didn't get it—but once you're into it, it's funny. Like Mrs. Bennet? She's, like, a complete idiot."

"You're absolutely right. She is a complete idiot. Would you like to try another by the same author?" And thus did Ruthie create a reader in her own image, one of many girls she would direct, without ever allowing a hint of condescension in her voice, from Barbara Cartland to Jane Austen.

Although she never spoke of it to Matt, the more real the charter boat plan became, the more her apprehension grew, and the more the library became her refuge, a place of asylum from the gathering stresses at home. She talked more and more about the library, both because her work there made her so happy and because she wanted him to know how happy she was. As if once he caught on he might say, "Hey, let's forget the whole boat thing and stay on land, where we both clearly belong."

Ruthie had ached to talk about her anxiety with her mother, to ask her for advice, but while Iris had greeted Matt's plan with studied nonchalance, Ruthie knew how intensely she disapproved. Any apprehension Ruthie expressed would be greeted with relief. There would be no opportunity for the unbiased consideration of the options that she actually sought. So instead of turning to her mother, Ruthie had found herself confiding once again in Mary Lou Curran.

Mary Lou had gotten it into her head that the children's room needed reorganizing, and the library director, all too aware of the fruitlessness of opposing one of Mary Lou's ideas, had asked Ruthie to try to mitigate the damage, under the guise of offering assistance. Mary Lou sat perched on a miniature chair and directed Ruthie around the room.

"I think the beanbag chairs should be distributed throughout the room," Mary Lou said, "rather than gathered in a circle."

"That's an idea. Except that the little ones like to sit in the beanbag chairs for story time."

"They can sit on the carpet for story time," Mary Lou said. "Instead of lolling about on beanbag chairs."

Ruthie laughed. "Have you actually ever *seen* story time?"

"Of course I have. And it wouldn't be such a free-for-all if the children sat in a quiet circle. Don't put the blue beanbag chair under the fish tank. They'll climb on it and end up sending the tank flying. Again."

"Mary Lou," Ruthie said, once she'd situated the beanbag chairs to the elderly woman's satisfaction. "Can I ask your advice about what to do next year?"

"Advice? From me? You can certainly *ask*. Whether I have any to give is debatable."

"I think you're a veritable fountain of sensible information," Ruthie said.

"And now you're teasing me."

"Well, yes." Ruthie smiled. "But it's true. You've always given me good advice. You're the one who told me to come work here."

Mary Lou nodded. "That certainly has worked out, hasn't it?"

"It has," Ruthie said fervently. "I love working in the library."

"All right, then, I will give you some advice. And, like all of my very best advice, it's not based on anything you actually asked me or told me at all. It's offered in total ignorance. A shot in the dark."

"Sounds perfect."

"Go back to school, and get a master's in library science and information studies. I believe Simmons College in Boston has a very good program. Or, if you like, you can even do it online. I met a lovely young woman at the conference who got her degree from Rutgers but did the whole thing on the computer."

Library science! She had known that people got degrees in library science, naturally. She had worked with trained archivists and librarians, first at Harvard and now here in Red Hook. But the idea that this job she merely loved could be more than something she did while she waited to figure out what she was supposed to do had never occurred to her. That she could *be* a librarian, rather than simply work at a library. She was inclined to blame her mother for the fact that she had never considered the idea. She knew exactly how Iris would regard such a career path: true intellectuals, true lovers of literature and of books, did not become librarians, they became scholars. But Ruthie wondered if she really could lay the blame at Iris's feet. Wasn't the fault for her failure of imagination, in the end, only her own?

Now, as she drove up Red Hook Road on her way to visit her ailing grandfather in the hospital, she wished she could just tell Matt exactly how little she wanted to sail to the Caribbean.

"We've got to figure this insurance thing out," Matt said. "We're putting the boat in the water in two days."

"I don't know, Matt. Maybe it's just an insoluble problem."

He looked up from his papers. "What's that supposed to mean?"

"It's just too much money."

Matt sighed heavily. He folded the papers in half and dropped them on the floor by his feet. "I'll figure it out. Maybe we can get a loan or something."

"We can't borrow any more money, Matt." They'd already taken money from Daniel, over her objection.

"I know," he said. "The money's my problem. I'll figure it out." He looked at her quizzically. "Or is it something else? Are you trying to tell me that you don't want to go?"

He was giving her the perfect opportunity. All she had to do was agree, to tell him that she was afraid, that she hated sailing and didn't want to be trapped on a boat, not with him, not with anyone. That she had finally, she thought, found something that *she* wanted to do, not what her mother wanted for her, or what he wanted. Not what Becca had been meant to do, but what she, Ruthie, was meant to do. She took her eyes off the road for a moment and looked at him. His eyes were wide. He looked frightened. "No, it's not that," she said. "It's just . . . maybe we're not ready."

"You don't think I can do this."

"I do. Of course I do. It's just . . . I don't even know if you *want* to do this."

"We're not talking about what I want. We're talking about what you want."

"It's not that I don't want to . . ."

"Well, what is it, then? You don't have faith in me. You think I'll just fuck it up."

She had allowed the moment to slip through her fingers, and now she saw no way out. "I do so have faith in you," she said. "I love you." She reached blindly for his hand and squeezed it. "I love you, Matt."

He brought her fingers to his lips and kissed them. "I love you, too." He sighed again, one of the heavy, burdened sighs she had heard him heave so many times. "Ruthie, I have spent three years of my life on the *Rebecca*. I can't just throw her away."

"Of course you can't. Just ignore me. I'm upset about my grandfather. That's all it is."

After a few long, silent minutes, Matt leaned over, snapped on the radio, and turned up the volume so that there was neither the need nor the possibility of them conversing the rest of the way to the hospital in Newmarket.

III

The risk, Iris told Ruthie and Matt as they stood outside Mr. Kimmelbrod's hospital room, was due not so much to the broken hip, nor even to the surgery that had attempted, with a certain amount of success, to repair it. What had the doctors worried was the possibility that Mr. Kimmelbrod might, as a result of the trauma both of the fall and of the surgery, develop a pulmonary infection or congestive heart failure.

Iris looked terrible. She had dark purple circles under her bloodshot eyes and her curls had gone flat. She had pulled her hair back into a ponytail and tied it with a rubber band without benefit of a mirror; her ponytail was off center, sticking up from the back of her head like a broken handle. Her lips looked chapped and bitten.

"I brought you fresh clothes," Ruthie said, holding up the tote bag she had brought along. "And some moisturizer. The air is so dry in here."

"Thank you, honey," Iris said. She took Ruthie's hand. "You've been so helpful. Grandpa and I both appreciate it so much. You too, Matt. Thank you."

Ruthie squeezed her mother's hand. "Do you want to go home? Just for a couple of hours? You can take a shower, and maybe have a little nap? I can stay here with Grandpa."

"I don't think I should leave him," Iris said.

"It's okay, Mom. You're so tired. If you really want to help him, you have to stay strong for him."

Iris shook her head, but she was clearly exhausted. Dying to take a shower, to get some sleep.

They tiptoed into the room. It was a small box crammed full of instruments and monitors, with barely room for a single chair. Both the front and back walls were made of glass. Pale green curtains partially obscured a view of the parking lot and a strip of spindly evergreens at one end of the room, and of the nurses' station at the other. Iris went to the bed and tugged the blanket up higher on Mr. Kimmelbrod's chest. His eyes were partly closed, only the whites visible above the pink rims of his lower lids.

"Is he awake?" Ruthie whispered.

The corners of her grandfather's mouth turned up in a faint, brief approximation of a smile.

"He is," he said, opening his eyes. His voice was at once creaky and soft, as if the effort of expelling sufficient air to speak were almost too much for him.

"How are you feeling, Grandpa?" Ruthie asked.

He raised one of his long, snowy-white eyebrows.

"Worse than I look," he said. "Trust me."

Iris said, "We're waiting for the morphine drip to start up again."

"Is something wrong with it?" Ruthie said. "Should I go tell the nurse?"

Iris shook her head. "They say that he's supposed to be able to control it himself, and that's true up to a point. But it only gives out so much in an hour." She leaned across the bed and picked up the button and pressed it a few times. "See?" She pointed at the drip. "Nothing."

"Are you in pain, Grandpa?" Ruthie said. She stood at the foot of the bed, resting her hands lightly on Mr. Kimmelbrod's splayed toes.

"There appears to be some concern that I will become a drug addict," Mr. Kimmelbrod said. "Elderly violinist junkies being such a scourge on society."

Iris pursed her lips and gave a little puff of frustrated air.

"I've spent the better part of the morning trying to convince someone to up his dose, to no avail."

Mr. Kimmelbrod once again closed his eyes.

"He's been like that this morning," Iris said. "In and out."

"You should go home, Mom," Ruthie said. "Really, I'll stay with Grandpa. It's fine."

"Yes," Mr. Kimmelbrod said, without opening his eyes. "You must go get some rest, Iris. You are worrying me."

Iris sighed.

"Matt's going to be at his mom's all day, loading up the *Rebecca* and taking her down to the yard," Ruthie said. "I can stay here while you're gone, and then when he's finished he can pick me up." Matt had tried to get the yard to move back his launch date, but their calendar was full. It was either now or wait until the end of the summer, and as appealing as the idea of delay was, it didn't make sense to wait any longer.

"It's going to take me at least a few hours," Matt said. "You'll have plenty of time to get to East Red Hook and back. Have a nap. Take a shower."

"You don't mind?" Iris said. "There's nowhere you need to be, Ruthie? Work?"

"They know I'm here," Ruthie said. "And Matt told the yard he wouldn't be in until after lunch."

Iris allowed herself to be convinced.

Mr. Kimmelbrod's blanket had pulled loose, and Ruthie did her best to remake the bed around him while he slept, managing to form serviceably tight hospital corners, as if there were a standard that she was expected to maintain and might possibly be graded on.

"Very good, my dear," Mr. Kimmelbrod said, sleepily. "They'll have you cleaning the bathrooms next."

"Toilets are where I draw the line," she said. "You'll have to get up and clean your own." She emptied out his plastic cup of water and rinsed both it and the matching pitcher in the shallow sink. When she turned back to Mr. Kimmelbrod, she saw that his eyes were open and he was fumbling for the morphine drip.

"Let me do that, Grandpa," she said. She pumped it a few times. "I think it's working again."

His hands twitched on the bedclothes, and Ruthie put hers over them. They were warm and dry, crosshatched with lines and wrinkles.

"It's ridiculous," he said.

"What is?"

He closed his eyes. She waited to see if he had fallen asleep again, but then he said, "A single misstep."

"Yes. I thought of that, too."

"Turn to the left, go on as you are. Turn to the right, finished."

How many times had she thought that over the past few years? That if the photographer had been satisfied with one less picture, or one more. If the limo driver had paused for a moment to adjust his seat. If Becca had stumbled on her way into the car and adjusted the strap of her shoe. Turn to the left, go on as you are. Turn to the right, finished. And what direction was she turning right now? Or was she so afraid of making a wrong turn that she had stopped dead in her tracks?

Ruthie crouched down over the bed, pressing her cheek against her grandfather's. "Nothing's finished, Grandpa. Your hip will heal, and you'll be home soon. It's just a temporary setback."

But by now he was asleep.

When Iris returned to the hospital she looked much better, in spite of her wet hair and the long red crease in her cheek from her pillow. Either the circles under her eyes had faded, or she had covered them up with makeup. She seemed merely tired, rather than flat-out destroyed.

"Thank you, honey," Iris said. "You were right. I did need a little break." She sat in the chair on the other side of the bed. "Listen, Ruthie. I called your dad."

"You did?" Ruthie said. She had not seen her father since April, when he had come up to Maine for a visit. He had stayed with her and Matt in the house, slept in his own bed, worn the clothes that were still in the drawers of his dresser, drank from his favorite coffee cup. Having him there had been at once perfectly normal and strange.

Iris said, "I asked your father to come up, to see Grandpa."

Her parents' separation had hit Ruthie hard. She had tried to tell herself that she was not a child. She no longer lived with her parents, at least not in the winter. She had no right to feel abandoned. She had no right to feel such grief. But still, when her father visited, Ruthie had felt at once sad and guilty, as though she were betraying her mother by accepting her father's presence in his own house. She had not told Iris of his visit.

Because the purpose of Daniel's trip had been to see Ruthie, and by extension Matt, they all felt obliged to spend time together in a way they never had before. It was as though they were traveling together on a vacation, just the three of them, and thus could not abandon one another to separate activities. It poured all weekend long, a disaster because there was nothing much in Red Hook to occupy a rainy day. Ruthie had introduced Daniel to her colleagues at work, all of whom he'd known for years. She gave him a tour of the library that he'd been visiting since before she was born. They had gone to a bad movie in Newmarket and visited Red Hook's galleries of mediocre vacation art, feigning interest in the muddy landscapes and studies of lighthouses. They had shopped at the L.L. Bean outlet and even driven all the way out to Okamok Isle for a scoop of Daniel's favorite ice cream, only to find that the stand's owner had been arrested for dealing drugs along with the Rocky Road and Moose Tracks. "No wonder the milkshakes were so cheap," Daniel said, as they stood in front of the shuttered shack. By Sunday afternoon they had exhausted all activities apart from videos and endless games of Yahtzee, and Daniel leaped at Matt's suggestion that they go see how the Alden was shaping up.

Relieved to have an hour of solitude, Ruthie stayed behind. When they returned home she was in the side yard trying to remember where she had planted her tulip and daffodil bulbs. The men were deep in conversation when they got out of the car, and didn't see her.

Matt said, "Last summer I ended up replacing half the wood in the stateroom. That set me back a lot."

Daniel said, "How much do you think it's going to take you to finish her?"

Matt said, "Well, I still owe nearly a thousand to the farrier who poured the keel ballast, and I got a deal on the sails, but they're still going to run me at least five grand."

"She's a good-looking boat. It would be a shame not to finish her."

"I'll figure it out," Matt said. "It might just take a while."

"I'd like to help you," Daniel said. "I could be an investor."

"She's not much of an investment, sir. You wouldn't see your money back."

"Let that be my problem," Daniel said. "I've got a little tucked away for a rainy day. And it's definitely raining today."

Matt glanced up at the grim sky.

"Should we say six thousand?" Daniel said.

Ruthie stifled a gasp. How would they ever pay that back?

"That's too much, sir," Matt said.

"Okay, then. Let me give you three. And you come up with the rest yourself."

There was a long silence. Then Matt said, "If it's really okay with you. I can't thank you enough."

"All right, then, three thousand it is."

Ruthie was furious. She was angry both at Matt for having taken the money and at her father for having given it. She walked around the corner of the house and confronted a startled Matt. "Can I talk to you? In private."

Daniel put his hand on Matt's shoulder and gave it a sympathetic squeeze. "I'll be inside."

"That was rude, Ruthie," Matt said, after Daniel had closed the door behind him.

"You know I don't want to take money from my parents!"

"You were eavesdropping?"

Her face burned. "That's not the point. The point is that you took money from my father without asking me first."

"He offered!"

"You should have said no!"

"I'm sorry," Matt said. "I just honestly don't know what to do. I'm in a hole here. That fucking router destroyed I don't even know how many thousands of dollars' worth of joinery and planking. What was I going to do? Patch it with plywood? And the sails. Do you know how much sails cost?"

"I do now. Five thousand dollars."

"Yeah, well, that's five thousand dollars I don't have. And I can't exactly finish her without sails."

When Ruthie tried to thank her father for the money, Daniel shook his head and said, "That's between Matt and me, sweetheart. It's nothing you need to worry about."

She felt so uncomfortable about the money that even now it was hard for her to talk to her father on the phone without feeling like the debt somehow cast a shadow over everything she said. But that awkwardness paled in comparison to the idea of seeing her father here, in Maine, in the same room as her mother.

"If Dad comes up, where's he going to stay?" Ruthie asked Iris.

"I was worried about that, too, but it turns out there's no tenant this week at your grandfather's cottage, so he can stay there. I'll need you to go over and make sure Jane's girls have put fresh linens on the bed. And maybe you could pick up some things for him at the market. Some milk and bread. I packed a box with some of his favorite things—his coffee, and those shortbread cookies. I put in some of his clothes, a few books, and his down pillow—he hates those foam ones Grandma always bought. It's on the kitchen table. Do you think you could take it over to the cottage before he gets here?"

Even with all her worries about Mr. Kimmelbrod, Iris had clearly devoted considerable thought to Daniel, reflecting on what would make him comfortable, what he would enjoy and require.

"When is he coming?"

"Tomorrow. Oh, and stop by the co-op and see if they have any fresh eggs. God knows the last time he had a fresh egg."

"Should I arrange for him to get a massage?" Ruthie said, mock-innocently.

But Iris seemed not to understand the remark or its intent. "A massage?" she said blankly. "I—I don't know."

"Forget it," Ruthie said.

"He said he'd been considering coming up for Matt's launch, anyway."

Had he been? Ruthie hadn't known that. "Are you going to see him?" she said.

"Of course. I'll see him when he comes to visit your grandfather." Iris was clearly trying to appear civilized and reasonable, but Ruthie could hear a note of something like expectation in her tone.

"I mean, you know, outside of the hospital. Like, will you guys have dinner together?"

"Are you asking if I plan on dating your father while he's here? No. I doubt it."

"If we had the Fourth of July celebration this year, we could invite him."

"No, Ruthie."

"Why not?"

"Are you serious? Because your grandfather is in the hospital, and I don't have time to plan a lobster bake for thirty people."

"Of course you must have your celebration," Mr. Kimmelbrod said.

They both jumped when he spoke. Iris put her hand to her chest as if to hold her heart in place. Then they both burst out laughing at how startled they had been.

"How are you feeling, Dad?" Iris said. "Is the morphine working?"

"The pain is not terrible. My arms are extremely itchy, however."

Iris said, "The nurse said that could happen. Is it really bad? They can give you an antihistamine. Would you like that?"

"Yes, I think."

Once Iris was gone on her way to track down the nurse, Mr. Kimmelbrod said to Ruthie, "I would like you to have your celebration, Ruthie."

"No, we can't do that, Grandpa. It wouldn't be the same without you."

Even before Mr. Kimmelbrod's fall, neither Iris nor Ruthie had mustered a great deal of eagerness for the party. Iris had drawn up her customary to-do lists, ticking off the tasks one by one as they were completed, but it had not been with much heart. Iris's reluctance mirrored Ruthie's. But as much as she had been dreading the celebration, Ruthie feared even more what that dread said about her, about her mother and her father, about the passage of time, about their memories of Becca, and, most of all, about the hollowness at the heart of her broken family that seemed, in retrospect, to have underlain all their celebrations since the accident, to have given the lie to all their plans and preparations. She had thought, she had always hoped, that the pain and loss of Becca's and John's deaths might be transformed, even to a degree redeemed, by memorials and celebrations, even by her coming together with Matt. Those deaths were terrible and senseless, but at least they might with time become the means by which they all, Tetherlys and Copakens alike, were brought together, and held together, and sustained. Now it seemed that there had been nothing there to hold together in the first place, and the reason nobody wanted to have the party this year was because it would just make that terrible emptiness plain.

"Have the celebration," Mr. Kimmelbrod said.

"But why? Grandpa, you've never enjoyed them."

"True," he said. "But I will be here, or in rehab. I won't have to suffer through it, but you should."

Ruthie laughed.

"What's so funny?" Iris said as she came into the room. "The nurse will be here in just a minute with the antihistamine."

Maybe, Ruthie thought, now more than ever some kind of statement was required, a refusal to submit to loss, to let it work its mischief on them. And maybe it was that kind of stubbornness in the face of grief—about which Mr. Kimmelbrod knew more than anyone, the art of which, even more than music, he was virtuoso—that could, in the end, redeem them all.

"We're having the celebration on the Fourth," Ruthie said, boldly. Then, hedging, she added, "It was Grandpa's idea."

"We can't possibly," Iris said. "How am I going to throw a party when I'm at the hospital ten hours a day? There's no way."

"If it were anyone else, I would agree," Mr. Kimmelbrod said. "But nothing is beyond you."

"Mom, you don't even have to do anything," Ruthie said. "Seriously, I'll take care of everything. And anyway, everything's basically done."

"But, well, I don't want to sound harsh or unfeeling, but—*why bother?*" She gave a laugh that sounded both bitter and self-mocking. "I mean—look at us. Dad, you're in the hospital. I'm separated from my husband. What's to celebrate?"

Mr. Kimmelbrod opened his eyes and looked squarely at Ruthie, as if he lacked the strength that an answer demanded and was trusting Ruthie to do the job. Ruthie tried to think of a way to summarize or explain to her mother the kind of stubbornness that her grandfather embodied, the persistence of love and work and affection in the face of sorrow that was more, somehow, than the mere habit of being alive. She shrugged.

"It's a tradition," she said.

IV

On his way to King's Boatyard for Matt's launch, Daniel wondered at the thought that today would be his first reunion with Iris since September of last year, when he had moved his things out of the Riverside Drive apartment. He'd arrived in Red Hook late last night, missing hospital visiting hours, and had arranged to meet Iris at the launch. After they saw the boat safely in the water, they'd go up to Newmarket together. How odd to have gone so long without seeing the person whose company had for decades defined who he was, both for good and for ill. He had spent more time with Iris than with anyone else in his life, had slept far more nights with her than alone, had known her body and her face better than his own. He had not intended for their separation to be so absolute. Or perhaps it was more accurate to say that he had not imagined either that it would be or that it wouldn't. At first he hadn't wanted to see her at all, had not even wanted to speak to her on the phone. He'd felt at the beginning well shed of her, that without her there reminding him of his failings, he would finally become the person he was supposed to be.

He had found an inexpensive efficiency apartment, adequate for his needs, and set about doing exactly what it was he wanted to do. He ate what he liked, he ignored the heaps and piles of newspapers and magazines that quickly accumulated on every available surface. He trained four, sometimes five times a week, and on the days he wasn't in the gym he ran four times around the reservoir in Central Park. He had no choice but to go to work, but all the while he was supervising student cases and dealing with his colleagues he tried to imagine what job he would choose if he could be anything he wanted to be.

For a while this was enough. The feeling of liberation he'd experienced when he first left Red Hook sustained him through the autumn and into the winter. His only source of frustration during those months was his inability to come up with a satisfactory alternative to the career his wife had chosen for him. He had never considered himself an inspired teacher, had never found the academic environment to be particularly interesting. While many of his colleagues in the clinical department worked diligently on law review articles that they hoped would catapult them into the more legitimate academic side of law teaching, he had no such ambitions.

He'd for so long blamed Iris for his haplessness, for the frustrations of his failed career, and yet when confronted with the opportunity to make a change, he simply couldn't think of anything else to do. There wasn't another legal job that attracted him, and although he tried to come up with something, there was nothing outside of the law that he'd rather be doing. On the contrary, the more he tried to figure out an alternative, the more appealing his job, with its simple and achievable demands, its academic calendar and long vacations, began to seem.

Then, one evening in late February, while walking out of the locker room at the gym, he tripped over his shoelace and cracked his mouth on the edge of a table, knocking out his front tooth. Here he'd been training for months, even on occasion sparring with fighters younger and often in better shape than himself, and he'd gotten hurt because he forgot to double knot his shoe. For the next couple of months he spent far too much time in the company of dental professionals. Two root canals, an implant, and even a little gum work, just for the heck of it. By the time his last Percodan prescription had run out, he agreed with the dentist that it would be foolish to purposely put his teeth in harm's way. He couldn't keep away from tables, but he didn't have to let anyone punch him in the face. Once sparring was no longer an option, his enthusiasm for training at the boxing gym ebbed. Maybe it was simply that he no longer felt much like hurting someone anymore. His fists no longer brought him peace.

Without boxing, it became harder for Daniel to fill his days. He was bored and, for the first time since he'd left home, lonely. It was in this mood that he made the trip up to Red Hook in April. He'd gone in order to spend some time with Ruthie and Matt, and that had indeed been a pleasure. Ruthie had seemed glad to see him, and although he couldn't quite get a handle on her relationship with Matt, at least she was happy with her job. And Daniel liked Matt. The boy reminded him of himself in a way. Like Daniel, Matt was plodding down a path not entirely of his own choosing. Daniel had wanted so much to help the kid, but he wasn't sure if he hadn't picked the worst possible way. Maybe if Daniel hadn't offered to bail him out financially, Matt would have considered abandoning the project that was clearly giving him so little pleasure. But at least this way Daniel had helped him finish the boat. At least it was done now.

What Daniel had not anticipated from his visit was the feeling that overcame him when he walked into the bedroom he had shared with his wife for more than two decades. It smelled like Iris. Or, rather, it smelled like it always had, a scent he associated with his wife. Lavender from the spray she used on the sheets, the citrus tang of her hand lotion, the cedar chips she tucked between their sweaters, and something more difficult to identify, the barest hint of warm musk, the smell of Iris herself. He looked at the photographs on the wall. The one of his parents on their legendary cruise. The old sepia-toned shots of Iris's ancestors. And the photographs of his daughters as babies, as young girls, and as young women. There was one photograph in particular that struck him. It was taken at the base of Red Hook Hill. The girls were about seven and twelve years old and they were sitting on the top rail of the fence that blocked the path from vehicle traffic. Iris stood between them, an arm looped around each of their waists. It was a blustery day and the girls' hair whipped around their heads, hiding much of their faces. Iris's was tied back, revealing her high forehead and her wide, easy grin. He bent closer to the picture. Around her neck Iris wore a glass pendant on a leather thong. It was a mottled purple blob, meant to be shaped, as he recalled, like an iris. Becca had made it for her in camp one summer. Iris wore it fairly often, long after Becca herself had come to be embarrassed by its lumpiness. Iris had always been like that, Daniel thought, loyal to a fault. She was that way with everyone she loved, tenacious in her defense of them, absolute in her allegiance. This was the other side of her bossiness, her pushiness. She always thought she knew what was best for you, always tried to force you to comply, but she did it because she wanted the best for you. Her love was fierce and unequivocal.

Steadily over the next couple of months, Daniel's feelings about his wife began to turn into a kind of pining. He missed her face across the breakfast table. The way she read sentences from books aloud to him, always so terribly disappointed if he didn't understand the point or the joke, or whatever it was that had so moved her. He started to wonder if all along he'd been blaming Iris for his dissatisfaction, for his sense of being lost and disconnected from the person he used to be, when the truth was that everything that was good about his life wasn't in spite of her, it was *because* of her.

He had tried, periodically, especially over the past two months, to bring himself to pick up the phone and call Iris, but between them lay so much, and he was not sure how to bridge the gap.

She would surely have changed over the past nine and a half months. How strange not to have witnessed those changes. How strange, when for decades he had been the cartographer of her face's and her body's myriad transformations. He could map out her contours, every freckle, every mole, the tiny starburst of a broken blood vessel behind her right knee. He could remember the shape of her breasts and nipples at every stage of their lives together. Creamy and firm when she was young; stippled with blue veins when she was pregnant and nursing, the nipples red and swollen; then slowly deflating as she grew older, her nipples turning pale pink. And his own body? Had it changed? He'd continued running even after he stopped training, but he was softer than he had been when last he saw her. His hair, even on his chest, was more gray now than black. Had Iris allowed the constellation of moles and freckles across his back to fade from her memory, extinguishing one by one like stars winking out in the night sky? Had she forced herself to forget? Was she as nervous about seeing him as he was about seeing her? Was she as eager?

Being back in Maine this time made Daniel long for Iris. Here in Red Hook Becca was constantly in his thoughts, in a way she had not been when he was in New York, and he wished he could share his memories with Iris. Only Iris would recall the way Becca used to purse her lips after she nursed, her eyes lolling, as if she were drunk on milk. Only with Iris could he talk about the time when Becca was two and had escaped his arms, running down the length of the dock and flinging herself into the water, then bobbing to the surface and laughing as Daniel, panicked, dived in after her. He wanted to talk to his wife. He missed her. It was as simple as that. He had left her with his fists up, and he was returning with them down and his arms open.

Daniel was the first of the guests to arrive at the yard. He found Ruthie stacking bottles of cheap champagne and plastic wine cups on top of an oil drum. She'd filled a Mason jar with lupines and daisies, and Daniel recalled how she and Becca used to harvest huge armfuls of lupines every June, filling pitchers and jars all over the house. The memory was less wrenching than he might have expected it to be. Along with the expected pang of loss he felt a kind of warm flush, nearly pleasurable; almost the way he used to feel back before the accident when he'd recall a moment from his daughters' childhoods. A wave of longing, knit with pride and sweetness. The pleasure of nostalgia, only slightly marred by grief.

Ruthie's hair was long and frizzy, braided over her shoulder in a single, thick plait like the one Becca had worn. Daniel remembered how Becca used to complain that there wasn't a decent place in the environs of Red Hook to get her hair cut. During her first couple of years in Maine, she would even take care to schedule an appointment whenever she came home to New York for a visit. Ruthie, on the other hand, had not bothered to come to New York to visit, let alone get her hair cut. She looked tired, Daniel thought. Mr. Kimmelbrod's illness was taking its toll on everyone, but Daniel could not help but wonder if there was more to it than that.

When he hugged her, Daniel gave her an extra squeeze. After a moment, she returned it.

When they separated she said, "You should go look at the boat. It's all loaded up on the Travelift and ready to go."

The Travelift boat hoist stood about twenty-five feet tall and was painted a cheery, bright marine blue. It was a steel frame with four legs, each on three-foot tractor wheels. Two narrow docks led out over the water, a gap between them. Each wheel would roll along its dock, the boat hanging in the hoist over the water between them. Attached to one leg of the Travelift was a small driver's cage, no more than a seat and a steering wheel, with levers that worked the winches that raised and lowered the straps. At one end the hoist was open at both the top and the bottom, supported by only the two vertical legs, so that the boat could enter. On the sides, the legs were supported by horizontal beams, one directly above the wheels, one across the top. It was from these top horizontal beams that the Alden hung, slung across two yellow canvas straps attached to steel cables on either side of the Travelift.

The white hull glistened in the sun, reflecting the images of the young men gathered around her, almost mirrorlike in her shine. The metal railings sparkled, too, and the varnished wood on deck glowed a deep, warm orange. Nothing looks so new, so sharp, as a wooden boat hanging in the cradle of a hoist, ready to be launched. In the end she might not even float, but for now she looked as if she could fly, a shining sea bird about to take off into the sky.

Daniel joined Matt and the group of men milling around the boat. It was a fairly typical crowd for a boat launch. The boatbuilders, men with scruffy beards, frayed shirts, and worn-out work boots; the odd back-to-earther who, when he wasn't baking loaves of twelve-grain bread to sell at the farmers' market, earned a few bucks fetching and carrying at the yard; the grizzled marine rats who showed up early every morning to fish off the ends of the yard's docks and who never missed the free drinks on offer at a boat launch; and a few members of the yacht club set, wealthy men who liked to hang out at the boatyard, where they affected a tone of nearly obsequious respect for the craftsmen, careful never to indicate by word or deed what everyone knew—that they could buy the yard and every builder in it a dozen times over without missing a nickel from their pockets.

"She looks great," Daniel said.

Matt reached out his hand and stroked the glossy white bow. "She does, doesn't she?" He sounded amazed, as if he couldn't quite believe what he had accomplished.

When Daniel saw her in the spring she had been so far from completion that it was almost impossible to believe that this was the same boat. Everything was perfectly fitted out, the built-in tables, benches, and shelves were impeccably crafted. Everything fit, everything worked, the drawers smooth on their runners, the cushions well sewn and tight in the bunks. There was a neat little four-burner stove in the galley, and every brass light fixture gleamed with polish. Matt had even bought pale-blue towels that matched the piping on the upholstery, and had them monogrammed with the boat's name. They hung on a brass towel warmer in the head. The boy had done, in the end, a magnificent job. A job his brother would have been proud of. And that was fortunate, considering how much sweat and treasure and time had gone into it, how many years and tens of thousands of dollars it cost. Daniel wondered whether, in the end, a beautiful boat might not be worthy of all that. He supposed it had a lot to do with how you felt about boats.

Daniel slung his arm around Matt's shoulders. "You should be proud," he said.

Matt flushed and ducked his head as if trying to dodge the compliment.

Ruthie called out, "Are you guys almost ready? Everybody's here."

Daniel turned and saw Iris heading right for him, looking as if she hadn't spotted him yet. He stood still, watching her smooth gait, the way she swung her arms as she walked, the long, capable stride that so easily matched his own. There it was, the body about which he had been thinking so much lately, same as it ever was. Lovely, elegant, beautiful. And then she saw him and stopped in her tracks.

She was wearing a white sunhat with a floppy brim that covered much of her face. A pair of oversized tortoiseshell sunglasses hid most of the rest from view. He recognized neither the hat nor the sunglasses. Her blue seersucker skirt he remembered. It had been one of her favorites one summer maybe a decade ago, when she had worn little else. She must have lost weight, because she had not been able to fit into that skirt for a while. He recognized, as well, the white cotton button-down shirt she wore, rolled up at the sleeves and tied in a knot at her waist. It was his. Or had been his, before she'd appropriated it.

And around her neck, on its homely leather thong, hung the lumpy glass pendant that Becca had so labored over all those years ago.

After the briefest hesitation, Iris continued down the ramp until she stood only a few feet from him. The lenses of her glasses hid her expression.

Ruthie glanced from one of her parents to the other. She seemed flummoxed, as if she were struggling to find something to say, some diplomatic bit of dialogue to smooth over the awkwardness. Daniel hoped she was not going to engage in the supremely ridiculous act of introducing him to his own wife. Instead, however, Ruthie turned and took a step closer to Matt, who had his hands shoved deep into the pockets of his khaki shorts as he accepted the congratulations of the dozen or so assembled guests.

"Hello, Iris," Daniel said.

"Hello," Iris said, her voice cracking slightly. She cleared her throat and tried again. "How are you?"

"I'm well," he said. "And you?"

"Fine."

"And your dad? How's he doing today?"

"He had a bad night. His chest was a little congested, but when I left him he seemed to be doing better. He was sleeping."

"Are they worried about his chest?" Daniel asked.

Iris nodded. "If it gets bad enough he might need a ventilator."

"He'll hate that," Daniel said.

She nodded, chewing on her lower lip. "I don't think he'll agree to it."

"Has he said he won't?"

"No, I haven't been able to bring myself to ask him. Maybe because I know what his answer will be."

Matt cleared his throat and the small crowd quieted down. Jane had brought Bill Paige with her, Daniel saw, so that was still going on. Samantha was there and Matt's sister, Maureen, and her daughters. All together he counted about a dozen guys from the yard, most of whom had, at one point or another during the long period of restoration, given Matt the benefit of their advice.

All but a few of the boatbuilders had been John's friends, and as they watched his kid brother fumble for something appropriate to say, they grew strangely solemn, remembering the many launches John had participated in, a number of them sending boats that he had helped design under way. The last boat they'd seen John launch was one of the first he'd designed all on his own, a twenty-six-foot Jet Drive tender, which the yard had built for a couple from Long Island. John had never been at a loss for words, and surely this occasion, most of all, would have found him with plenty to say.

"Um," Matt said. "I guess you all know the story of how my brother found this boat."

"Tell it!" said one of John's friends.

Matt hesitated.

"Go on, Matt," another said.

Matt shoved his balled-up fists deeper into his pockets and rocked back and forth on his feet. He cleared his throat once, and then again, before continuing. "So, he was up in this boatyard in Machias, and she was just, like, rotting in a corner. He took one look at her, and he knew he had to have her. John said he knew right away that the *Rebecca* could be as beautiful and sea-kindly as her namesake. If he'd been able to finish the job, she may well have ended up that way; as it is I think he was wrong. She's beautiful, all right, but she can't hold a candle to Becca. Or to her sister," he added quickly.

"She looks just fine, Matt," one of the builders said.

"Let's get her in the water and see if she floats!" another said. There was laughter at this. Matt hesitated again.

"Go on, son," an old man carrying a fishing pole said.

Matt flushed but continued. "I guess I just want to thank everybody who helped me finish her, especially my mom, who gave over her barn to John to build her in."

"Hear, hear!" one of the builders said.

Jane waved off their cheers, but she could not help but smile. The morning the truck came to take the boat down to the yard, Matt had finally given Jane a tour. She had not quite been able to believe that, in the end, Matt had managed, despite his inexperience and lack of resources, to build something his brother would have been proud of. She had been so pleased and impressed that she had refrained from asking him where he found the money to pay for it all.

Now, however, Matt gave her and everyone else who had gathered for the launch an idea of where the money had come from. "Thanks to Ruthie, for all her support," he said. "And to her dad, Daniel. If it weren't for him the Alden would still be in the barn."

Iris turned to Daniel, her eyebrows raised. He shrugged sheepishly.

Ruthie was moving through the crowd, handing out plastic cups of champagne. When everybody had one, she took an unopened bottle out of a brown paper bag and brought it to Matt.

Matt lifted up the bottle of Veuve Clicquot to show to the crowd. "We don't really need to christen her, because she's sailed under her name since 1938, but we thought she deserved a bottle of the good stuff, anyway."

He tried to hand the bottle to Ruthie, but she refused it.

"Your mom should do it," she said.

"No," Jane said. "You go ahead."

"Come on, Ruthie," Matt said, pushing the bottle into her hands.

Ruthie held the bottle at arm's length for a moment. Once the boat was in the water there would be no turning back. She had no doubt that Matt would find some way to come up with the money for the insurance, and as soon as he did his master captain's course they would be on their way to the Caribbean. She wished desperately that Becca were here to christen the boat, and to sail away on it in her place. She took a deep breath and stepped to the bow of the boat, clutching the bottle gingerly. Matt had scored the bottle with a glass cutter so that it would break without damaging the paint on the hull, and she was afraid it would explode in her hands.

Matt had prepared for her what he wanted her to say, going so far as to write it on a scrap of paper. "May God and King Neptune bless and keep her," Ruthie read aloud. "And may she bring fair winds and good fortune to all those who sail on her." She swung the bottle and cracked it against the bow. The bottle exploded, spraying her with champagne.

Everyone cheered and downed the contents of their plastic cups. Then the builders swung into action. One got up into the Travelift's driver's seat and turned on the motor. The others started walking on the tracks alongside the boat as the hoist rolled out over the water. Only once the Alden had reached the end of the tracks did they allow the rest of the crowd to join them. Four men took hold of each end of the canvas straps, and on Matt's order the driver pushed the lever to lower the boat. With a jerk the steel cables slowly unwound, lowering the boat into the water. When she was about halfway down the man working the winch paused, and Matt grabbed the rail and vaulted aboard. He held out his hand for Ruthie. She hesitated for a moment, and then allowed him to help her up over the rail. With another jerk the boat resumed her descent into the water. There was barely a splash when she was all the way down. Matt unhooked the rear strap and the builders standing on either side of the Travelift eased the boat back along the channel between the tracks. Once the stern was free they loosened the strap at the bow and she moved out into the deep water of the bay. For a moment Matt disappeared, gone below to hook up a pump to deal with the water seeping into her hull. It would take a while for the wood to swell and seal shut the leaks in the planking.

Matt came back up on the deck and began unfurling the sails. One after another they opened, snapping in the breeze. The boat seemed to rise up in the water as the sails climbed up her two masts. Is there anything as beautiful as a wooden sailboat moving away across a sunlit bay, a bright white arrow piercing the blue of the sea?

Afloat, at last. *Rebecca.*

V

Ruthie stood at the kitchen sink, working the meat from thirty-five pounds of shedders with her bare hands. Her hair was flecked with bits of lobster shell, her shirt drenched with the brine that insulated the lobsters' tender new shells from their soft flesh. A jagged shard of pink had sliced open the pad at the base of her thumb and she had to keep rinsing away the blood that seeped to the surface. She had been standing at the sink for two hours, and her back and shoulders ached. A shelf of dark clouds hung low and threatening in the sky over the little East Red Hook harbor, and although it wasn't raining, the air was thick and close, dense with humidity unusual for Maine. With her wrist she wiped a bead of sweat from her nose.

It was coming on five o'clock, the celebration was due to begin at six, and she still had half a dozen lobsters to go and a host of other jobs to finish before the guests arrived. The task would be easier, she thought, if someone, anyone, had offered to help. But that was unfair. She had said she would do it by herself. And there was good reason for everyone's absence. Mr. Kimmelbrod, still in the hospital more than a week after his fall, had last night once again shown signs of minor chest congestion, and Iris did not want to leave him on his own. She had arranged for Samantha to spell her at the hospital and promised to come home as soon as the girl arrived.

Having read the sky and the falling barometer, Matt had decided to sail the *Rebecca* from the open harbor of King's Boatyard to East Red Hook's sheltered cove. The trip should not take too long, and at least he would arrive before the other guests.

When Ruthie had all the meat free of the shells, she mixed in the celery and mayonnaise, and put it into a blue crockery bowl. In two matching bowls she put the coleslaw she had made from cabbages she grew herself in her small garden plot out in the side yard, and the potato salad. Ruthie put the bowls on the picnic table and then hesitated, wondering if it was too early to put out mayonnaise; if it would spoil. But the blue bowls looked so pretty against the red gingham tablecloth. The strong wind blowing in from the water forced Ruthie to weigh down everything on the table with rocks from the garden, and she worried that the Mason jars of flowers would topple. Early in the morning she had gathered the last of the lupines and the first of the tiger lilies from the overgrown meadow beyond the Grange Hall, and now their heads drooped in the unusual humidity.

Ruthie sat down on the screen porch with a pile of forks and began wrapping them in the gingham-printed paper napkins she had ordered on the Web to match the tablecloth. She had no idea how many to roll. The first year there were at least thirty people at the celebration. Last year there were fewer, but still not less than twenty. But how many would come this year? Ten? Five?

Preparing for the celebration had made Ruthie gloomy, irritable, even resentful, and not merely of the fact that she was obliged to do it alone. Fighting against everyone's resistance had exhausted her, and there were times when she had just wanted to throw up her hands and remind people that she hadn't really wanted to do this either, that it had been Mr. Kimmelbrod's idea, and for his sake they should all just stop bellyaching and force themselves to be, if not eager, then at least merely willing.

A reluctance to attend the party this year had not been confined to members of the immediate family. Even the few close friends and neighbors to whom Ruthie had issued invitations seemed less than eager. Some had begged off, claiming other plans, others had murmured something noncommittal before turning away. If she reminded them that the event was meant to be a celebration of John's and Becca's memories, they tended to look sheepish, as if they had forgotten that, and were ashamed of their forgetting. Or maybe they were just thinking that John and Becca had died a long time ago, and that it was long past time to move on. And Ruthie thought that perhaps they were right, it was time to move on, and that was the most terrible thought of all.

As if to drive this cruel wisdom from her mind, she allowed herself to be overcome by obsessiveness. She pulled the most wilted flowers from the bouquets, wiped the plates clean of nonexistent dust, set the napkin rolls out in an artful arc. She scrubbed the downstairs bathroom and put a votive candle on the back of the toilet. She unloaded the dishwasher, washed all the pots, and scrubbed down the counters so that if anyone came inside they would find the kitchen sparkling clean. She cleared the dining room table of its piles of old newspapers and magazines and hid them in the coat closet. She set out the folding chairs in the yard in neat little conversation circles.

Nobody came.

Every time Ruthie heard a car on the road, she ran to windows at the front of the house, but every car drove by without even slowing. Dr. Haber across the road was up for the weekend—his car was in the driveway and she could see his TV flickering in the window. Even Matt was late. She thought of calling Becca's old friend Jasmine, or Mary Lou Curran, to see why they had not arrived, but it would just be too . . . pathetic. That was the word. She wondered if it described everything about her life—her unhappiness at the prospect of Matt's Caribbean plan, her half-assed attempt to somehow take on her sister's life, her role, and even, dare she say it, a simulacrum of her man. The only thing she could honestly say she enjoyed was her job.

Or perhaps she was just being melodramatic. Maybe nobody was coming because they were worried about the weather.

Finally, she saw Matt climb over the stone wall between the yard and the beach. She ran out to the yard to meet him.

"What happened to you? Why didn't you call?"

"No cell service."

"I haven't been able to reach my father, either. He said he was coming, but he's not here."

Matt looked at the picnic table. "It looks nice." Ruthie was grateful for the compliment, especially because she knew it cost him something. After the launch of the *Rebecca* three days ago, he had been more than usually shut down. Every time she had asked him why he was depressed, however, he had insisted that he was fine.

"Thanks," Ruthie said. "I'm getting worried about rain, though. Do you think we should move everything inside?"

Matt frowned at the sky. "It's so weird. Over in Red Hook it's as clear as can be." He pointed toward town. Beyond the mass of threatening clouds over East Red Hook village, there was blue sky.

"Is it all muggy like this?"

"It's hot, but not like this."

"So, then, why did you sail the *Rebecca* up here, if it was clear down there?"

"The guys down the yard said the wind would probably end up blowing the storm down there."

"So did they move their boats?"

"Most everybody sailed farther down the coast, toward Castine. But I figured the *Rebecca* would be safe up here."

Ruthie gazed back over the small bay. By now the clouds had thickened to a dense, black boil, though in the distance the sun shone in the summery blue sky.

Matt said, "It looks like it's going to pour. Maybe we should bring the stuff in."

Ruthie checked her watch. It was nearly seven. In previous years the celebration would already have been in full swing for an hour. "I can't believe this. Where is everyone? Where's your mom? Did you call her?"

"I'm going to go put on some dry clothes."

"You didn't call her, did you?"

"You know my mother, Ruthie."

"But did you *call* her?"

"Yeah, I called her, okay? You told me to call her and I called her. But she's not coming." He started gathering up the buckets of plastic cutlery, the stacks of plates, and the bowls of food. Grudgingly, Ruthie joined him, and by the time the rain started they'd moved everything inside onto the screen porch. The rain, however, followed them. The wind blew it through the screens onto the porch. It was as though someone were standing outside aiming a hose through the screens. The screens themselves were bowing in, straining against the small rusted nails that had held them in place for more than fifteen years.

"Jesus Christ," Matt whispered, staring out over the bay. The boats were straining at the ends of their moorings, blowing in toward shore.

They grabbed the food and the rest of the picnic things off the table and rushed them into the house, the door between the porch and the kitchen blowing shut with a loud bang every time they opened it. The rain was icy, a sudden and strange shock after the humidity of the day. By the time they'd finished clearing the table they were drenched.

The wind began a sudden and intense roaring. It was so loud it was like they were standing directly beneath a jet engine.

"What *is* this?" Ruthie said.

"Oh my God," Matt said, his voice hoarse with fear. "I think it's a microburst."

"A what?"

"One blew through Castine last fall, remember? Winds like 150 miles an hour. Took down I don't know how many trees and houses. I have to get the *Rebecca* out of here. Oh, *fuck*. I'm such a fucking *idiot*." Matt took off down the porch steps and across the yard. As Ruthie hesitated in the doorway the lights in the house flickered and then went out.

"Matt!" she called, but he couldn't hear her. She stared after him, and then at the remains of the picnic as it blew away. The folding chairs careened across the lawn, one of them smashing into the side of the barn. Ruthie felt a sudden and intense urge to get into the car and drive as far and as fast as she could. But even if she were selfish enough to run away, she couldn't. Iris was in Newmarket with the Volvo, and Matt had left his truck down at the boatyard.

Ruthie ran back into the house and into the mudroom. She dug through the coats hanging on the hooks, throwing them aside until she found her old yellow slicker. She put it on, grabbed her father's oilskin, and took off after Matt. As she crossed the lawn, her feet slipped and skidded in the slick grass. The rain fell freezing on her head, and dripped down into the neck of her coat, soaking her shirt. The wind blew so hard against her face that it bared her teeth. It forced the rain into her eyes. She pushed forward until she reached the seawall, vaguely aware that she was sobbing. She ducked down behind the wall, taking cover, trying to catch her breath.

She got to her feet and called for Matt again, but the wind snatched her voice from her throat. She clambered over the wall and stumbled over the rocks along the beach until she reached the dock. Now she could see Matt at the far end of the dock, his arms hugging one of the pilings. Struggling to stay on her feet, she pulled herself from piling to piling, creosote sticking to her hands. When she reached him, she tried to hand him her father's oilskin, but before he could take it, the wind snatched it from her and sent it sailing back the length of the dock and onto the beach, where it stuck, sleeves splayed against a rock.

He was trying to tell her something, but she couldn't hear him. He bent and put his mouth to her ear. "The *Rebecca*," he shouted. "The other boats are going to wreck her." He pointed, and she saw that six or seven of the boats had broken loose of their moorings. As she watched, the water seemed to cup them like a giant hand, then send them skittering across the cove. Iris's old whaler crashed into the side of a lovingly maintained catamaran owned by one of their neighbors. Dinghies torn loose from their sailboats and upended into the waves crashed into the larger craft like pinballs banging from bumper to bumper.

"The tender!" Matt shouted. At first Ruthie didn't understand. Then Matt grabbed hold of the line that kept their neighbor's little motor boat tied up to the dock.

Ruthie grabbed with one hand at his wet shirt, wrapping the jersey around her fingers. The other arm she kept firmly looped around the piling. "No, Matt! No!"

"I'll be fine." He pried her fingers loose and jumped into the tender. Furious needles of rain stung her face and she cried out in frustration. There was no way he could sail the boat alone in this kind of wind, no way he could control her without help. The boat would capsize or be swamped, and Matt would be washed overboard. Ruthie had no choice. She let go of the piling and threw herself over the side of the dock into the tender.

"What are you doing?" he shouted. "Get out of here!"

"No," she screamed back. "I'm coming with you."

He lunged across the boat and tried to manhandle her back up onto the dock. She slapped away his hand. There was no way he could manage this job alone; she had no choice but to help him, and he had no choice but to accept her aid. "Come on!" she shouted, pushing him toward the motor.

Matt gave her a final, desperate look and then started the motor. They took off into the wind, to save the *Rebecca*.

VI

Although the wind was blowing over in East Red Hook village, in Newmarket it was clear. Samantha poked her head around the curtain that blocked the doorway to Mr. Kimmelbrod's hospital room. The lamp over the head of his bed was on, but otherwise the room lay in darkness. He was asleep, his eyes sunk deep in their sockets. The harsh fluorescent bulb shone on the top of his head. His thin hair looked greasy and stuck to his scalp in a way he would never have tolerated had he been able to take charge of his own toilette. His curved nose, even bigger now that the flesh of his face had fallen away, cast a long shadow over his compressed lips. His inhalations were loud and rasping, and Samantha could see his pulse fluttering beneath the flaking skin of his neck.

Iris was also asleep, her feet propped up on the bed's metal rail, her head lolling against the back of the chair, her mouth hanging open.

Samantha crept into the room on her sneakered feet. She set her tote bag and violin case gently on the ground. She was not supposed to take the Guarneri anywhere but to the Usherman Center's rehearsal halls and to the Copakens' house, but Samantha had been preparing something special for him. She had gone to the music library at the Usherman Center and checked out the score of Bach's Partita no. 2 in D Minor. Mr. Kimmelbrod deserved the relief only Bach, and especially this piece, would bring him. And so, in addition to the music she was working on with her trio, she had been practicing the Chaconne.

The sound of the case against the tile floor woke Iris. She rubbed a string of saliva away from her lower lip and said, apologetically, "I must have fallen asleep."

"You're tired," Samantha said. "I brought you an iced coffee." She handed Iris a sweating plastic cup with a straw.

"You're such a peach. Thank you so much, sweetie," Iris said. "How did you get here?"

"The other members of my trio drove me. They're going to the movies. They said they'd pick me up on their way home. So I can be here for at least two hours. More if you need me."

"I won't be that long," Iris said. "Just an hour or so. Do you want to go to the celebration? Should I arrange for a cab for you when I get back?"

"No thank you," Samantha said. "I'd rather spend the evening practicing." She bit her lip. "I mean, is that okay? I'll go if you want me to."

"There's no reason for you to go. I wish I didn't have to, but Ruthie's been cooking all day." Iris got to her feet and gathered up her purse and jacket. "He'll probably sleep. He's been really tired today."

When Iris left, Samantha took the score from her bag and began studying it. The Chaconne was a complex piece, even its theme not immediately obvious. Samantha had had to study it to figure out where the theme was, how long it was, how it was treated in the variations—all questions that she would normally have looked to Mr. Kimmelbrod to answer. While he slept on, she read and reread the 257 measures, determined not to disappoint him with a poorly thought-out interpretation.

VII

As she rounded the corner to Jacob's Cove, Iris drove into a wall of weather. The sky, clear and cloudless over Red Hook, out of nowhere turned a sudden, ominous black. Rain fell across the car like a sheet of steel. Iris had never seen anything like it. A blast of wind buffeted the car as it began to fishtail. Iris tried to turn into the swerve, the way you were supposed to do. For a long moment the car spun sideways, and coming at her was Jacob's Cove—black beach, black arc of pine trees, black water. She held fast to the wheel with a horrified sense of connection to her lost daughter. Then she felt her tires catch hold of the road's surface, and the car straightened out.

She went on slowly, her face inches from the windshield, trying to see beyond the useless flapping of her wipers. By the time she arrived home she was exhausted, her neck and shoulders stiff from clutching the wheel, her jaw aching from having clenched it so hard.

Iris ran into the house, allowing the screen door to slam shut behind her, and in those few seconds outside found herself soaked. Standing in a pool of water in the mudroom, she kicked off her shoes and took a beach towel down from the shelf. She wrapped herself in the towel and called out, "Ruthie?"

She found the Fourth of July picnic piled haphazardly on the kitchen table. "Ruthie?" she called again.

She ran upstairs, hesitating in front of Ruthie's closed door, remembering the way that she and Daniel liked to pass the time during blackouts, when they were young and the power service to this part of Down East Maine was even less reliable than it was now.

"Ruthie?" Iris called softly. Finally, when no answer was forthcoming, she opened the door. The room was empty.

"Where the hell are you?"

She crossed the hall to her own bedroom, looked out the window and saw the boats in the cove reeling and crashing into one another like toy boats in a bathtub. Down by their dock, a little white tender was fighting its way across the choppy waters toward a sailboat that was heaving and rolling against its mooring, two dark figures sitting hunched against the wind.

Iris tore down the stairs, pulled on a pair of rubber boots, and ran out into the yard and the rain and the darkness.

If Jane had arrived at the bridge over the tidal stream on the outskirts of East Red Hook a moment or two earlier than she did, her truck would have been washed away. The combination of high tide and the crashing storm had flooded the stream, sweeping torrents of water over the railing of the bridge. Jane was stuck on the side of the bridge away from the village.

She could not remember a storm ever having come up so suddenly. When she had left her house to drive down to the Copakens', it had not even been raining. The day was calm, with a light breeze coming in from the east. Certainly the weather had been nothing that would have dissuaded her from driving out to East Red Hook village, and she would have been easy to dissuade.

Jane had not at first intended to come to the celebration today. Indeed, she had planned to make a point of not coming, had left it to the girls to clean Iris's house on their own all summer. It was clear to her that Samantha had blossomed in New York, that she had come into her own in a way she never could have in Red Hook, and perhaps that was part of why Jane was so unwilling to forgive Iris. Or perhaps it was merely that she considered it a fair bargain—Iris got Samantha, and Jane got the pleasure of having Iris leave her the hell alone for the rest of her life. She had exchanged no more than a brief greeting with her when Iris dropped Samantha off at the beginning of the summer, but after Mr. Kimmelbrod's fall, Jane's anger had abated, and when the time came for the celebration, she found herself putting on a decent shirt and clean jeans, and getting into the truck. If Jane were the type to spend time analyzing her own motivations, she might have reasoned that to abandon the yearly memorial celebration would be, in some way, an abandonment of the memory of her son, a statement that she no longer cared enough to mark his death. But Jane was not given to unnecessary introspection, and, more important, she had always resented the notion that this Copaken celebration was any kind of fitting memorial. In the end she was willing to acknowledge only a desire to be polite to a family in crisis, and a decision not to leave Matt on his own to represent their family. Especially now, after the launch, when he was inexplicably gloomy. Let down, she supposed.

The rain surprised her outside of Red Hook, on the road near Jacob's Cove. In itself this was not unusual; thundershowers often came on with thrilling suddenness. But there was something wrong about this rain. It hung before her in a solid wall of falling water, so that as she drove into it she felt as if she had entered another place, a world of rain. The wind, too, was stronger than anything she could remember since the night a hurricane had taken her father's life. All those decades ago she'd watched the wind peel the front porch off the house across the road and send it cartwheeling away. Her mother had pulled her away from the window, and they listened huddled in the basement to the freight train noise as it bore down on them. Tonight as she arrived at the bridge, Jane saw an entire swath of pines keel over, their newly exposed roots white and naked. Her two-ton pickup shook as if it were made of aluminum foil and rubber bands.

Jane slammed on the brakes at the bridge as the water overtopped it, and, although she was not a praying woman, she thanked God that they held. She sat in her truck watching the wild flood. One hundred yards away, on the other side of the washed-out bridge, was the Copakens' house. She would have to turn around and go back. She put the truck into reverse and began carefully to turn it around. The wind abated enough for her to feel like she was not in danger of flipping. She had just looked behind her, one arm draped over the car seat, the other gently rolling the wheel, when she caught a glimpse of something bobbing out in the cove. Jane slammed the truck into park and peered closer.

Beyond the shelf of clouds hanging directly over East Red Hook the sky was clear, and so it was light enough for Jane to make out, through the rain blurring her rear window, a small figure on the water, straining at the oars of a rowboat. The waves tossed the rowboat, it bucked and reared, but the figure at the oars rowed steadily on, skirting the tidal stream, then inching closer to the shore. Jane put her truck back in gear and carefully turned it around so that it faced the cove. Her high beams sent two fuzzy shafts of light far across the water. Clutching her jacket at the throat, Jane jumped out of her truck, and was drenched at once. Though the air was muggy, the rain was cold, and it made her gasp. She hopped down the small embankment, and her boots slipped in the mud. She grabbed an exposed tree root and caught herself in time to keep from tumbling all the way down. She landed on one knee and felt a sharp stabbing pain in her kneecap. Swearing, she scrambled the rest of the way down and limped to the water's edge just as the rowboat crossed the beams from the truck. The figure turned toward the light. It was Iris Copaken.

At that moment a large wave washed over the rowboat, but Iris stopped only long enough to shake the water from her eyes before bending once again to the oars. Jane lifted her arms over her head, waving frantically. Was the woman such a fool as to be out in a storm like this, having herself a nice little tour in her rowboat? Didn't she grasp the power of this storm? Had she never seen houses destroyed by a hurricane, cars flipped, branches torn from trees? Didn't she realize that a boat could capsize and be sent plummeting to the bottom of the sea, the bodies of its crew to be torn apart by tides, consumed by fish, never to be found? Didn't Iris Copaken, the woman so confident of her own intellectual superiority, understand that a storm could erase a person as though she had never been?

"Watch out!" Jane screamed as another wave washed over the rowboat. This one, larger than the first, swamped the boat, sinking it beneath its occupant. Iris hesitated for a moment, and then leaped out. She bobbed to the surface almost immediately, about ten yards from Jane standing on the shore.

"Iris!" Jane shouted. "Swim in!"

Iris attempted a crawl stroke, but before she got more than a few feet, another wave wrapped her up and pulled her under. By now Jane was ankle-deep in freezing water, trying to shout Iris into shore. But Iris was tiring. Her trip across the cove in the rowboat had depleted her strength; the waves were too much for her. Jane took another step, but her shoe lodged in the muck as though the land itself were trying to hold her back, to keep her safe. Jane took a deep breath, trying to steel herself against the tide of panic that threatened to overwhelm her whenever she got too close to the sea. Iris's head slipped under. Jane kicked off her heavy shoes and plunged into the water. When it reached her armpits she began to swim.

Despite her loathing for the sea—or perhaps because of it—Jane was a strong swimmer. Her father had taught her, and every time she went to a pool—never the ocean—she had continued to practice as if for this moment or one like it. Jane did not swim for sport or pleasure. She swam only because it was the only decent alternative to drowning. Now she struck out toward Iris with a sure, powerful stroke. She swam against the current, and for every stroke she took, the waves battered her back. She gained a foot and was pushed back two, gained another and was pushed back. She threw her hands forward at the ends of her arms, steady as hammers. Slowly, creeping along, she made her way toward Iris.

When they were within arm's reach of each other, Jane took another deep breath, ducked under, and with a massive kick propelled herself to Iris's side. She looped her arm around Iris's neck and Iris sagged against her. She knew enough, at least, not to fight her rescuer.

Even with the current in their favor it was rough going. Almost immediately a big wave grabbed them up and tumbled them. Blind, sputtering, Jane worked to keep hold of Iris, tangling her hand in the tail of Iris's shirt.

Jane felt herself being dragged under. Her grip on Iris's shirt loosened, and for the length of a single breath she considered letting Iris go. It was too much, she could not save them both. Then she cursed herself, and cursed the sea, and cursed her poor hapless fisherman of a father. She kicked her powerful legs and broke through to the surface, her grip on Iris now surer than before. Iris began to kick, too, and together they wrestled their way through the waves to shore. When Jane's feet touched the rocky bottom she dug her toes in.

"Can you stand?" she shouted, hauling Iris up behind her. She felt the ache in her arm subside as Iris struggled to her feet. Together they splashed out of the water and collapsed on the rocky beach. They sat side by side, their legs splayed out in front of them, the wind driving the rain into their faces and whipping their hair around their heads. This would not do. She took Iris's arm. "Truck!" she shouted, and dragged Iris to her feet.

After they got in and slammed the doors shut, they were enclosed in a sudden silence, the only sound the muted roar of the sea and the rushing of their own breath. Iris's eyes were closed, her head tipped back against the headrest of the truck. Her chest heaved, her lips were blue, and her teeth chattered. Her hair hung in long, dark coils around her neck. She coughed, then gagged, and for a moment Jane feared she might vomit.

"Are you all right?" Jane said.

Iris wiped the water from her face. "I think so," she said. She worked to gain control of her breathing. "Thank you."

Jane pulled a crumpled tissue out of her purse and used it to wipe her face.

"Current was in your favor. You'd have made it in."

"No I wouldn't have," Iris said. "Is this a four-by-four? We've got to get around. To the other side of the cove. The fire trail is probably washed out by now."

"What are you talking about?"

"Matt and Ruthie. They sailed the *Rebecca* over to the far side of the cove."

Aghast, Jane said, "Why? Why would he do something so stupid?"

"He must have thought that he'd be able to take shelter there. But it's too rocky. If the wind picks up again it will smash them right up against the jetty. Or on the cliffs. We've got to get out there and warn him."

"Why the hell didn't he keep the boat in the marina?"

"I don't know."

Jane turned the key in the ignition. The engine coughed and both women held their breaths until it caught. She jammed the truck into reverse and headed back to the road.

"I don't think he understood what was going on," Iris said. "I've never seen anything like this. It was like a tiny tornado, just right here. Look!" She pointed over the bay toward Red Hook. "It's not even raining in town."

"A microburst," Jane said.

"A what?"

"It's like a ministorm. Huge winds. Only lasts ten minutes or so, sometimes less. But it could come right up again."

"Turn here," Iris said, pointing at a small break in the foliage.

Jane veered off the main road. The small East Red Hook village bay was flanked on one side by the houses of the village, and on the other side, toward Red Hook, by a long fire trail through protected woods. The fire trail led from the road along the shore to the far end of the bay, where Matt had sailed the *Rebecca* to try to seek cover. It was no more than two ruts filled with muddy water. Jane thanked God that she had decided to drive her old pickup rather than the minivan, that she hadn't bothered to change her snow tires this year. They bumped along, sloshing through the mud.

Jane bore down, pushing the truck as fast as it could safely go on the rutted track, and then a little faster. She glanced at Iris, who was gripping the handle above her door. Jane took her foot off the gas, but Iris shook her head.

"It's okay," she said urgently. "Go as fast as you can."

Jane hit the gas again and the truck hurtled forward, tree branches slapping against its sides. She drove over a rock and the truck bounced high, and the women were flung forward in their seats. Iris leaned across Jane's body, grabbed her seat belt, hauled it over and buckled Jane in. Then she did the same for herself. They were moving so fast down the rutted trail that when they took a turn the truck leaned precariously to the side.

After a couple of miles Iris pointed Jane down an even narrower path, and Jane had no choice but to slow down. Finally, the trail opened into a small clearing surrounded by thickets of scrub pine. In the middle of the clearing stood a metal storage shed. At the far end of the clearing there was a trail, far too narrow for any vehicle.

"We have to walk," Iris said. Only when they leaped down from the truck did they realize that they were both shoeless, Iris's rubber boots lost in the sea and Jane's shoes on the beach. The rain had eased up a little, and they began hobbling up the path, Jane in her filthy socks, avoiding the worst of the downed branches. A log lay across their path. Jane tried to step over it, and caught her leg on a branch. She came down hard on the other foot.

"Shit!" She sat down and took her foot in her hand. A shard of sharp wood had torn through her sock and was embedded in the arch of her foot.

"Let me see," Iris said, kneeling down in front of her. She took Jane's foot in her hand, peeled away the sock with care so it would not catch on the sliver, and studied the wound, her fingers hovering over the piece of wood.

"Just do it," Jane said, closing her eyes and turning away. She felt a stab of pain and cried out, and when she looked again at her foot the piece of wood was gone, and blood poured from the wound. Iris propped Jane's foot on her bent knee, and pulled her soaking T-shirt over her head. With her teeth she ripped a strip of fabric from the bottom of the shirt and then tied it tight around Jane's foot. She pulled the remnants of the shirt back over her head, and placed Jane's foot gently on the ground.

"Can you walk?" she said.

"Yes," Jane said, grabbing Iris's extended arm and pulling herself to her feet.

They continued on, Jane leaning on Iris's arm, a shambling three-legged creature. The path opened up again on the edge of a low cliff overlooking a small beach strewn with granite boulders that gleamed black and slick in the rain.

"Look!" Iris said, pointing down the beach.

Jane could make out a sailboat tucked in along the high cliff walls. Its white sails dipped and spun as the boat was lifted in the waves. With each wave the boat was driven closer to the looming granite cliff. One of the sails tore loose and went flapping around the head of a small figure that stood on deck. Jane was sure it was Matt. He scrambled across the wave-washed deck, trying to tie the sail down.

"Where's Ruthie?" Jane said.

Iris spun around and started to run back up the path.

"Where are you going?"

"Come on!" Iris shouted, without turning back. With another glance at Matt, Jane took off after Iris, back the way they came, leaping over the log that had tripped her up before. This time neither bothered to watch for debris, and by the time they burst into the meadow Iris's feet were bloody, too. She ran toward the shed and threw the full weight of her body against the door. She bounced off and tumbled backward.

"What the hell are you doing?" Jane yelled.

"Help me!" Iris shouted.

Without pausing even to consider why, Jane leaped after Iris and together they hurled themselves against the door until it buckled and its hinges snapped loose. Jane grabbed the door and peeled it back. Inside the shed, among the fishing tackle, the folded beach chairs, the weather-beaten lobster buoys, was a rubber dinghy, no more than eight feet long, with an outboard motor. Between them they dragged the boat out of the shed.

"We have to carry it," Iris said. "If we drag it we could puncture it."

They maneuvered themselves into position on either side of the boat, bent down, and twisted their bodies to grasp the handles.

"One, two, three!" Iris shouted. They hauled the boat up, staggered for a moment, and then steadied themselves. The boat was surprisingly light, but Jane's wounded foot added substantially to her burden.

"We've got to move," Jane said. "I can't hold this for long."

They took off, the boat too heavy to allow them to run. They staggered back up the path toward the beach. Jane's elbow and wrist ached from the weight of the boat. They had to climb over another downed log in the middle of the road, and afterward stopped for a moment and lowered the boat, shaking the stiffness from their arms.

"Switch sides," Iris said. They each ran to the other side of the boat and grabbed the handles with their less-exhausted hands.

By the time they reached the low cliff over the beach their arms were trembling. For a moment they stared at the beach. It was no more than twenty feet below them, but the path down was steep. Iris grabbed the small rubber loop protruding from the bow of the boat and motioned Jane to the stern. They heaved it up again and began carefully to descend the hill. Iris held the rubber loop in both hands, behind her back, and as she slid and stumbled, the rubber boat bumped her calves. By the last few feet she was running, Jane trying both to keep up and to prevent the boat from knocking Iris over.

Without speaking they ran into the water, battling the waves to take the little boat deep enough, then scrambled in over the sides. Iris attached the outboard motor, which, blessedly, roared to life. They took off, jumping the waves in the rubber tender as they raced across the water toward the sailboat.

As they neared the *Rebecca* they saw her begin to tilt precariously starboard. Matt flung his body port side as if his negligible weight could right her. The waves kept coming, each one pushing the trim craft closer to the jagged granite cliff. Matt leaped about the boat, one moment struggling to reel in the torn sail, the next ducking as the boom swung toward him, his exertions no more effective than a fly buzzing on the back of a bull. Just as they were nearing the boat, Iris saw a gigantic wave heading her way. She spun the tender around, desperately trying to keep from ending up like the *Rebecca* on the rocks. When she turned back she saw the wave lift the *Rebecca* as though it were nothing more than a twig floating in the water. With a splintering crash, it drove her onto the granite cliff. The wave pulled back, carrying the boat with it, but almost immediately a gust of wind flung Matt across the deck. Jane screamed, clutching her hand to her mouth. He grabbed hold of the mast.

There was a lull between the waves and Iris cupped her hands around her mouth and shouted, "Jump!"

Matt ducked his head and, scrambling hand over hand, made his way to the cabin door. For a moment he disappeared from view, but then he reappeared, one arm wrapped around Ruthie's waist.

Iris sobbed, and Jane realized that she must have thought her daughter had been washed overboard.

Ruthie was wearing a bright-orange life vest. Matt pulled her along beside him to the starboard side of the *Rebecca*, where Jane and Iris bobbed in their small boat, fighting the waves and wind. Suddenly, he slipped and began toppling overboard. Ruthie hauled him upright, took his hand, and together they leaped into the water, as close to the rubber tender as they dared. Jane leaned out of the dinghy and grabbed the loop of Ruthie's life vest with both hands. With a grunt she heaved the girl up and over the side of the boat. At the same time, Iris helped Matt scramble aboard.

"Go!" Jane said, and Iris turned them away from the reeling sailboat. The tender rode low in the water, straining to carry their weight.

"Oh my God," Ruthie shouted. They turned back, following her gaze. The waves were tumbling the *Rebecca* into the side of the cliff. They watched her mast splinter and collapse. They saw a huge rock tear open the hull. And then they looked away. None of them could bear it anymore.

When they reached the shallows they jumped out and dragged the rubber boat ashore. Only once it was hauled up on the beach did Ruthie fall into her mother's arms. Matt stood hunched, sobbing out loud, until his mother grabbed him, too, and hugged him hard against her. Despite his size and the scratch of his beard against her cheek, Jane felt as though she were holding the small boy Matt had been, the vulnerable child who had once fit so comfortably in her lap. She pressed her lips against his bristly chin.

With four of them to do the portage, the little rubber boat was no burden at all, and within a few moments they had her back in the shed. Matt did his best to jam the door closed.

Only then did Jane ask Iris, "How did you know there was a rubber ducky in here?"

"I didn't," Iris said. "I just figured, what else would you store in a shed by the beach?"

Jane stared at her, open-mouthed, and then gave a short bark of laughter. "Let's get out of here," she said.

VIII

A few minutes after Iris had left the hospital room and driven off to East Red Hook and the storm, Mr. Kimmelbrod opened his eyes.

"Hello," Samantha said.

He blinked and licked his lips with a grayish, cracked tongue.

"Are you thirsty?"

He nodded.

There was a pink plastic cup and straw on the table next to the bed. Samantha held it to his mouth and he took a sip. A drop of water dribbled from the corner of his mouth and Samantha wiped it away with the tip of her finger. She swallowed hard, trying to keep herself from crying. The first time she had visited Mr. Kimmelbrod she had burst into tears, earning from him a reproving frown. Since then she had not allowed herself to cry. When the seriousness of his fall became apparent, she had felt a tide of panic, fear at being bereft of him. She was unable to imagine herself as a musician except in the context of his teaching her to be one. His faith in her kept her on course, propelled her forward. How would she go on without his wise hand on her tiller? She had come day after day, hoping that her presence would inspire him to rally, as he inspired her.

"Thank you," Mr. Kimmelbrod said. His voice, although little more than a whisper, was unmistakably his own: his faint accent, the precision with which he pronounced each word, the click of his *k* distinct from the pursed-lipped *y*.

"Iris will be back soon," Samantha said. "She just went home for an hour or so."

Mr. Kimmelbrod closed his eyes again. While he slept Samantha continued studying the score of the Chaconne. The next time she looked up Mr. Kimmelbrod was awake. One of his eyelids drifted close, the iris beneath it drifting slightly inward, toward his nose. His other eye, however, peered at her, sharp and focused. He lifted his chin slightly in the direction of the bound score on her lap.

"This?" Samantha said.

His nod was so small, no more than a twitch of his chin.

"It's the Chaconne," Samantha said. "I brought it for you."

Mr. Kimmelbrod whispered something, but she couldn't hear him. She leaned closer, putting her ear to his mouth. He puffed a bit of air into her ear. She could see his whole body involved in the effort of speaking. His neck tensed, his chest rose.

"Play," he croaked.

She took the Dembovski from its case and began softly to tune it, so as not to attract the attention of the nurses. When she was satisfied, she pulled the table that swung on an arm over Mr. Kimmelbrod's bed closer to her, and propped the music up on it.

"I've only been working on this for a few days. I'm warning you, it is not going to sound very good."

The ends of his mouth curled up in a small smile.

Samantha studied the music, rereading the first four measures. "Okay, so we start with this downward stepwise four-note line. You always say that the downward line is the answer in the conversation. So I'm starting with the answer here, right?"

He lifted his chin slightly.

She played the first four notes. Then she paused. "I'm going to take this very slowly," she said. She played the first four measures of the piece and then paused again. This phrase—the subject of the piece—would be transformed every four measures, thirty times and then thirty more. She had to play it perfectly before she felt comfortable moving on. She looked at Mr. Kimmelbrod. His eyes were still open. She thought he was smiling, but it was difficult to tell. She returned to the score, studying it. She lifted the violin to her chin and played the first four measures again. Then a third time. Then she continued. As the subject reappeared she greeted it with increasing confidence. She played slowly, far too slowly, she knew, but she wanted to be sure she understood how each variation treated the subject, and she wanted to miss as few notes as possible.

Mr. Kimmelbrod closed his eyes and listened. Samantha was a smooth player, even with a piece she barely knew. She played now as always with such confidence, a maturity far beyond her years. She gave the Chaconne a familiar melancholy longing. Without ever having heard him play the piece live, she played it as he had always done. No, he realized suddenly, she played it as he *wished* he could have, with none of the brittle contrivance he sometimes used to hear in his own interpretation. Even as she made her halting way through the music, she played it the way he had always heard it in his mind, deep in his body, beyond his ears. With the one eye out of which he could still see, Mr. Kimmelbrod watched Samantha play. She stared at the music, her lips parted. Her long fingers glided over the strings. Her whole body seemed to be vibrating with the strings of her violin. All this passion, all this longing, rising from such a gentle, comforting girl. He felt as though he were listening to the familiar slow triple-meter saraband rhythm with his entire body.

In Samantha's gifted hands Mr. Kimmelbrod became the music. He became the Chaconne's relentless melodic bass line. It teased out of the theme and variations of his own life. Back again and again, every four measures. And the chromatically descending soprano Samantha was playing now? His wife, Alice Marie, the other side of the conversation of his life. The implied counterpoint to his solo violin. He felt Alice now, felt her in his body, felt her in the music. His longing for her was a variation he could feel, even though he was not playing it. Samantha played it for him; she played Alice, and his grief for Alice. He closed his eyes and in the music saw Alice's face, not as it had been when she died, gaunt and agonized, but as it had been before, the soft features blurred by age, the eyes at once bright and warm. In the music he saw Alice smile. In the music he saw her lips purse in a gentle kiss.

Every variation, every one of Bach's thematic transformations, brought someone else to him, more voices in the music. He lay in the bed, his body motionless but filled with the people of his life. This transposition was his mercurial mother, her moods shifting from key to key; that inversion was his father, a man who wrapped himself in a carapace of sobriety, but whose core, whose root, held a surprising lightness and optimism. This diminution was his sister and her tiny daughter, as like her as a fawn is to a doe; that interpolation was his brother, a scholar of Greek who spent his Sundays at the horse races in Velká Chuchle. Samantha played his longing for them, she played his anguish at their disappearance, their erasure from the world. And finally, when he thought he could not hear any more, could not feel any more, she played Becca. Becca, fragmented and displaced, a variation cut short.

Mr. Kimmelbrod's body was too desiccated to produce more than a few tears, but still they were the first and only tears he had shed for his beloved grandchild, who had played for him this same piece of music, this Chaconne, the piece he had himself performed at his very first American recital at Town Hall in 1936, decades before he had even imagined the possibility of either his granddaughter's or Samantha's existence, when Cambodia was a kingdom ruled by France and he had not even heard of a state called Maine. Samantha played Becca, and she played his grief for Becca, and finally he felt it, with him, inside him. The music of her life, the music of her death.

It took Samantha twenty-nine minutes to struggle through the piece, more than twice as long as she would require years later, after she'd graduated from Juilliard, when Bach's Partita no. 2 in D Minor became a staple of her own repertoire, and the basis of her first solo recording. When she finally put down her violin she was sweating and exhausted, her head aching from the strain of reading the music in the dim light. She twisted her neck back and forth and rubbed the sore spot under her chin.

"I have a lot of work to do on that," she said to Mr. Kimmelbrod.

But he was no longer there to differ or agree with this judgment.

IX

By the time they made their way up the fire road and back to the bridge to East Red Hook, the rain had stopped, the wind died down, and the tide turned. The bridge was passable, though one of the steel railings had torn loose and dangled, swaying, like a snapped violin string. The black clouds had dissipated and the darkness was only the fading light of day. In the balmy, heavy air there lingered a trace of the storm's menace. Hundreds of torn-up trees littered the meadows of the village, and crashed and ruined boats bobbed in the small cove.

An unfamiliar car sat in the driveway, an obvious rental, white and shaped like a throat lozenge. When Iris, Ruthie, Jane, and Matt walked into the house they found Daniel on the porch. He wore a grin of nails tucked between his sealed lips, and he was hammering at the frame of a wooden screen that had been torn loose by the wind. He was working by candlelight. As they came out onto the porch, he spat the nails into his hand and stood up.

"Jesus Christ," he said. "What happened?"

The four of them were dripping wet. Iris and Jane were shoeless, and a muddy, blood-streaked bandage clung in tatters to Jane's left foot.

"It's a long story," Iris said.

"Are you all right?" Daniel asked.

The four of them exchanged a glance, and then Matt said, "We're fine. But there's not going to be anything left of the *Rebecca* but matchsticks."

This assessment turned out to be fairly accurate. The next day Bill Paige would borrow a Maine Marine launch and take Jane out to tour the wreckage. They would crisscross the bay, steering among and poking at the shattered bits of the Alden, looking for something that could be saved. After two hours of searching, Bill would fish out one of the blue hand towels embroidered with the boat's name, a memento that, having been rejected by Matt, Jane would tuck into the back of her linen cupboard. Over the years that followed, when she would come upon the towel, she would take it out, and look at it, taking an odd comfort in remembering not the loss of the boat that Matt had worked so hard to restore, but John and Becca, and the hopes and dreams they had invested in the *Rebecca.*

"I'm so sorry," Daniel said, going to him and putting a hand on his shoulder.

"It's only a boat," Matt said.

And here was the crazy thing: he meant it. As he had sat in the little rubber boat watching the larger of the *Rebecca*'s painstakingly restored masts splinter against the rocks, he had felt something so odd that it took him a moment to recognize it. For three years he had been dragging the boat behind him like a bag of rocks, hauling her along, stumbling and sweating and making far slower progress than seemed possible. At her launch, when she hit the water and floated, seaworthy and solid, he had waited in vain for the burden of her to float away, too. But only when the wind tore the boat to shreds did he finally feel it: relief. He was no longer tethered to her. He could go anywhere he wanted.

Iris said, "Ruthie and Matt, you two go upstairs and take a hot shower. You're both still shivering."

Ruthie started up the stairs. She paused on the third step and turned back to her mother. "Mom?" she said.

"What, sweetheart?"

"Thank you."

"Ruthie . . ." There was so much Iris wanted to say. Not more than half an hour ago she had thought Ruthie had drowned, and amid her terror had been a thread of rage, fury with herself, that once again she was going to lose a daughter without ever having said the things she'd meant to. As they'd bobbed through the waves to the sinking schooner she had sworn that if—no, *when*—she and Jane saved their children, she would tell Ruthie everything. She would tell her how much she loved her. That she'd never loved Becca more, just more thoughtlessly. She would apologize for having been careless with the feelings of the people she loved, too wrapped up in her own expectations to see them for who they were. She would say she was sorry for having imposed her will on Ruthie, and proud of Ruthie for refusing, in the end, to bend to her. She would tell Ruthie that she should follow her own heart and be and do what she loved, and not worry, for even a moment, about what anyone else expected from her.

Ruthie stood trembling on the steps, sagging against the wall, exhausted. There would be time, later, for everything Iris wanted to say.

"Nothing. Just . . . I love you."

Ruthie climbed the stairs, Matt following, and Iris directed Jane to Mr. Kimmelbrod's bathroom, giving her one of Daniel's sweatshirts and a pair of sweatpants to change into. When Iris came back out onto the porch, Daniel stood holding one of her grandmother's crocheted afghans. He opened it to her, and she walked into its outspread wings. He enfolded her in it and pulled her close.

"What happened?" he said, his voice at her ear warm and muffled by her hair.

"The kids tried to get the *Rebecca* away from the other boats by taking her across to the other side of the bay. She ended up on the rocks."

"And you went after them?"

"Jane and I did."

Iris leaned against his chest, as she would lean against him again, at the hospital, after the phones finally started working, and the call about Mr. Kimmelbrod came through.

"Oh," she said, wiping her eyes, not sure what was bringing her to tears. "Poor Matt." That was not sufficient to explain the strange mixture of sorrow and gratitude that she felt, sheltering in her husband's strong arms. But it would have to do.

"Poor Matt," Daniel agreed. "But, like he said, it's only a boat."

That was true, Iris would sometimes think, about marriage: it was only a boat, too. A wooden boat, difficult to build, even more difficult to maintain, whose beauty derived at least in part from its unlikelihood. Long ago the pragmatic justifications for both marriage and wooden-boat building had been lost or superseded. Why invest countless hours, years, and dollars in planing and carving, gluing and fastening, caulking and fairing, when a fiberglass boat can be had at a fraction of the cost? Why struggle to maintain love and commitment over decades when there were far easier ways to live, ones that required no effort or attention to prevent corrosion and rot? Why continue to pour your heart into these obsolete arts? Because their beauty, the way they connect you to your history and to the living world, justifies your efforts. A long marriage, like a classic wooden boat, could be a thing of grace, but only if great effort was devoted to its maintenance. At first your notions of your life with another were no more substantial than a pattern laid down in plywood. Then year by year you constructed the frame around the form, and began layering memories, griefs, and small triumphs like strips of veneer planking bent around the hull of everyday routine. You sanded down the rough edges, patched the misunderstandings, faired the petty betrayals. Sometimes you sprung a leak. You fell apart in rough weather or were smashed on devouring rocks. But then, as now, in the teeth of a storm, when it seemed like all was lost, the timber swelled, the leak sealed up, and you found that your craft was, after all, sea-kindly.

"Why don't you get some dry clothes on," Daniel said. "I'll get some food on the table."

When everyone was clean and dry, they sat in the living room around the light of a fire and of two oil lamps with sky-blue glass bases. Here and there sputtered years of accumulated candle stubs in votives and jelly glasses, a pair of beeswax tapers in Iris's mother's Sabbath candlesticks, a fat, squat candle scented with bergamot. Daniel put bowls of coleslaw and potato salad on the coffee table and scooped lobster salad into hotdog buns that he had toasted over the fire.

None of them spoke as they ate. They just worked their way through the coleslaw and the potato salad, took second and third helpings of the lobster rolls in their charred buns. At last Iris, sitting on the floor, leaned back against the couch, her head resting against Ruthie's thigh.

"I don't suppose you had time to make dessert?" she said.

"As a matter of fact . . ." Ruthie said. She shifted Iris's head aside and went to the kitchen. A few moments later she returned with a heavy ceramic baking pan and a handful of forks.

"You didn't," Jane said from her armchair close to the fireplace. She had slipped off her borrowed slippers and sat warming her toes on the fire screen.

"I did," Ruthie said. She set the Nilla wafer banana pudding down on the carpet and distributed the forks.

"No plates?" Jane said.

"No need," Iris said, and dug her fork into the pan. She took a bite and frowned, cocking her head to one side, "You know, this is pretty good, Ruthie."

"It tastes just like yours, Mom," Matt said, admiringly.

"Better," Jane said.

When they had scraped the pan clean, Daniel got up to throw another log on the fire. The wicker basket they used as a wood box lay beside the living room door, and as he grabbed a log, his gaze strayed to the dense thicket of scribbles in pencil and marker and twenty different colors of ink on the back of the door. It had been a long time since he had taken note of them.

"Look how tiny she was," he said.

Iris came over and knelt on the floor by the door, studying the mark she had made to record the height of her eldest child on the day she turned two. She ran her finger over the name, and then moved up the panel of the door, tracing the course of Becca's flourishing. She ended up on her tiptoes, reading the final entry.

"Jane, come see." She pointed to a mark at the very top of the door, six inches or so beneath the lintel.

Jane brought over a candle, and they all peered up to where John had recorded, in his flawless draftsman's print, his own name. Iris had never noticed it before. It bore the date of the rehearsal dinner; he and Becca must have done it before the guests began to arrive.

"Funny," Jane said. "I remember him much taller than that."

CODA

The group photograph finally accomplished to his satisfaction, the photographer dismissed the members of the wedding party. It took a few minutes for them to disperse, for the bridesmaids to kiss the air next to the bride's cheek, for the bride's parents to hug both her and the groom close, as though in a few minutes they were not all going to see one another down the road at the reception, for the bride's grandfather to be helped down the church steps, for the disgraced flower girl to be bundled into the backseat of the car belonging to the mother of the groom.

Once everyone was gone, the photographer led the bride and groom to the far end of the churchyard, to an opening in the hedge of thickly blooming rugosa.

"Mind your dress," the photographer said. He slipped through the opening and down the short steep slope to the beach, hustling a little, eager to catch the money shot: the bride stepping through the hedge, a burst of pink flowers on either side of her.

She was about to leap the few feet from the break in the hedge down to the beach when the photographer called, "Why don't you let him go first and lift you down?" The photographer had shot four weddings at this church this summer alone, and he knew this was not only the best way to avoid damage to the dress but would also make for two more pretty pictures, one of the groom lifting his pretty bride, and the other of him setting her down gently on the beach.

He had underestimated this bride, however, and thus was caught off guard when she did not wait for her groom's hands to gently span her waist, but leaped, laughing, into his arms. They tumbled backward, and the groom landed on the rocks, the bride splayed out in his lap. The photographer managed to press the shutter a few times before rushing to help them to their feet. The bride and groom laughed. They took no notice of the wet stain on the seat of the groom's pants, or of the ribbon of seaweed that trimmed the hem of the bride's dress.

When they were on their feet the photographer pointed a few yards up the beach. "If you stand there," he said, "I can get the church spire in the frame."

The bride and groom obediently went to the indicated spot. They resisted, however, his efforts to position them with the bouquet between them, the bride staring up into the groom's face, her veil trailing over her shoulder. Instead, the groom nuzzled the bride's neck, making her laugh again, and the photographer took the picture, even though he knew that in the end she would not like seeing herself with her mouth open so wide you could see her back teeth.

For the next fifteen minutes or so he had them move this way and that, until he was finally satisfied that he had what he needed. "Okay," he said. "We're all set. Let's head over to the reception."

"Why don't you go on ahead," the groom said. "We'll catch up in a minute."

When he reached the churchyard the photographer snapped on his telephoto lens and, crouching so that he was shooting through the opening in the rugosa hedge, took one last photograph of the bride and groom. This photograph—the couple in the distance on the rocky beach, the bride's dress and veil blowing out in the sudden gust of breeze, the whole picture framed by the blurry pink of the out-of-focus rugosa blossoms—won him first prize and one thousand dollars in the annual photography contest sponsored by *New England Bride* magazine. On his entry form he declined to mention, not wishing to adversely affect his chances, that behind the pretty picture, though you could not see or guess at it, there lay a tragic tale.

The bride and groom took the long way around and back up to the church, both so that they would not have to scramble up the steep slope to the churchyard in their wedding finery and so that they could spend a few more minutes alone before they were thrust into the adoring throng of their friends and family. The bride hitched up her wide skirt with one hand, and with the other clasped her new husband's hand. She held his hand the way she and her sister had always held their father's, grasping his ring and middle fingers and letting his pinkie, index finger, and thumb rest on the outside of her closed fist.

The groom lifted their joined hand to his lips and kissed her knuckle. "I love you," he said.

The bride smiled. "I love you, too."

"I know," the groom said.

They reached the church, where their limousine waited for them, taking up two parking spaces and even so thrusting its rear bumper halfway into the road. The groom helped the bride into the back of the limousine, taking care not to close her voluminous gown in the door. They backed out onto Red Hook Road.

Four minutes later, the bride and groom heard the sound—the explosive boom, the metallic shriek—but what they saw was only a froth of lace and tulle, swirling in the air around them. The wedding dress, its crinolines, the veil, clung to their faces, wrapping them in a soft, white cocoon.

ACKNOWLEDGMENTS

The Corporation of Yaddo, the MacDowell Colony, Mesa Refuge, and Hedgebrook.

Mary Evans and Sylvie Rabineau. Devin McIntyre, Kevin Sparks, Shahrzad Warkentin, and David Ivanick.

Phyllis Grann, Alison Rich, Jackeline Montalvo, Adrienne Sparks.

Dan Smetanka, Julie Orringer, Ryan Harty.

Pam Johann, Nat Stookey, Ellen Werner, Alicia Anstead, Elizabeth Weisser, Cory Lee, Joshua Robison.

Molly and Eric Blake, Brian and Karen Larkin, Maynard Bray, Lucy Benjamin and Clifton Page, Heidi Julavits and Ben Marcus, Michelle and Michael Keyo, Jonathan Lethem and Amy Barrett, Chris Doyle and Tim Houlihan, Posie and Doug Cowan, David Ziff and Alan Bell, the Brooklin Boat Yard.

Robb Forman Dew, Nancy Johnson, Meredith Maran, Peggy Orenstein, Sylvia Brownrigg.

Nancy Kuhl, Rosie Levy Merlin, and the reference libraries of the Berkeley Public Library and the Blue Hill Library.

Sophal Ear, Jaed Coffin.

Cheri Hickman, Teresa Tauchi.